PEMBROKE

"'IT'S BEAUTIFUL,' ROSE SAID"

PEMBROKE

A Novel

MARY E. WILKINS FREEMAN

Introduction by Charles Johanningsmeier

Northeastern University Press
Boston

Advisor to Northeastern University Press
in American Literature and Culture
Marjorie Pryse

Northeastern University Press edition 2002
First published 1894

Library of Congress Cataloging-in-Publication Data

Freeman, Mary Eleanor Wilkins, 1852–1930.
Pembroke : a novel / Mary E. Wilkins Freeman ;
with an introduction by Charles Johanningsmeier.
p. cm.
Includes bibliographical references (p.).
ISBN 1–55553–515–1 (acid-free paper)
1. New England—Fiction   2. Villages—Fiction.   I. Title.

PS1712 .P4   2002
813'.4—dc21   2001059062

Printed and bound by Thomson-Shore, Inc., in Dexter, Michigan.
The paper is Writers Offset, an acid-free sheet.

MANUFACTURED IN THE UNITED STATES OF AMERICA
06   05   04   03   02   5   4   3   2   1

ILLUSTRATIONS

INTRODUCTION

Most readers today who recognize the name of Mary Wilkins Freeman think of her chiefly as a short story writer, largely because her stories "A New England Nun," "The Revolt of 'Mother,'" and "Old Woman Magoun" are regularly reprinted and anthologized. These stories' vivid and finely wrought portrayals of New England women during moments of crisis in their lives have earned them recognition as some of the best ever written by an American author. Receiving much less attention from critics and scholars, however, have been the thirteen novels that Freeman wrote. *Pembroke*, the second of these novels, was published in 1894 and is widely believed to be her finest; nonetheless, it remains much less well known than her short story masterpieces.

Freeman's true subject in *Pembroke* is not any one character or idea but rather the village of Pembroke itself and the often dysfunctional way it operates. Indeed, in an introductory sketch to the novel's 1899 edition, Freeman wrote that "*Pembroke* is intended to portray a typical New England village of some sixty years ago, as many of the characters flourished at that time." Yet she also wanted to make sure that turn-of-the-century readers, most of whom lived in cities, would not dismiss such a subject as irrelevant to modern times; thus she went on in this introduction to state that "villages of a similar description have existed in New England at a much later date, and they exist today in a very considerable degree."

The interactions among the inhabitants of this village are in large part what make *Pembroke* such a gripping novel. At its most basic level, *Pembroke* is a tragic love story about the troubled relationships among a group of unmarried men and women and their families who live in a small New England town of the 1830s and 1840s. The pivotal event of this tragedy occurs in its first chapter, when, on the eve of his marriage to Charlotte Barnard, Barnabas (Barney) Thayer engages in a heated verbal argument with Cephas Barnard, his fiancée's father. Angered at Barney's Democratic political views, Cephas, a Whig, orders him to never come back to his house. Charlotte, weeping hysterically, pleads with Barney to come back to her, but instead he keeps walking down the road to the unfinished house he has been building for himself and his future wife. During the next few days and weeks various family members and fellow villagers try to convince Barney and Charlotte to ignore her father's interdiction, but to no avail.

The devastation that results from this separation ripples through the community, affecting a number of other couples. Charlotte's aunt, Sylvia Crane, for instance, was at Charlotte's house on the night of the argument and as a result missed her regular date with Richard Alger; upset by this unexplained slight, he cuts off all contact with Sylvia. William Berry, the storekeeper's son, is forbidden by his mother from courting Rebecca Thayer, Barney's sister, because of the scandal attached to the Thayer family; in turn, Rebecca is told by her mother to stay away from William Berry. Some of these separations continue for many years, and the reader is kept in suspense throughout the book to see if—and how—all of these couples might be eventually reunited.

With her trademark economical prose, Freeman intermingles with the stories of these three couples a number of characterizations that rank among her most distinctive and memorable. The most fascinating of these are eccentric, laconic, and no-nonsense New Englanders who steadfastly live according to their own beliefs. Often these characters frustrate the modern reader, for they are all aware of how their actions are making themselves and others unhappy but are unwilling to change. At the same time, though, one must admit grudging admiration for such people, who are willing to suffer in order to remain faithful to their principles. Cephas Barnard, for example, declares to his wife that since "it's the spiritual part of us we want to strengthen," the family should henceforth adopt a completely vegetarian diet. In the midst of carrying out his plan—taking over his wife's kitchen and making a sorrel pie without any lard or butter in the crust—Cephas explains his reasoning: "It's better for us to eat [non-animal-derived food] . . . than eat animal food an' make the animal in us stronger than the spiritual, so we won't be any better than wild tigers an' bears, an' lose our rule over the other animals." Silas Berry is another character obsessed with a particular idea; in his case it is monetary profit. The miserly Silas charges people so much to pick cherries from his orchard that they boycott it, leading his wife to tell him, "You've jest put your own eyes out."

"Silas," Freeman writes, "would say nothing in reply; he would simply make an animal sound of defiance like a grunt in his throat, and frown." Undaunted, he tells his son and daughter that they can invite their friends over to pick cherries for free; afterwards, however, he accosts the friends and demands payment, infuriating and embarrassing his children.

Because of the way she tenaciously holds on to her values despite assaults from every side, Deborah Thayer is possibly the most fascinating character in the novel. Deborah never wavers from her adherence to strict Puritan beliefs. When she learns that her daughter Rebecca is pregnant out of wedlock, she casts her out into a raging snowstorm, telling her husband simply, "I wouldn't have her in the house." When Rebecca's baby dies, Deborah's belief in her daughter's sinfulness will not allow her to attend the funeral or comfort her. Later, her sickly son Ephraim rebels against her strict discipline by going sledding at night when everyone is asleep. The modern reader cheers Ephraim on for this rebellion, exulting in his joy at being outside his mother's control, if only for one night. Experiencing stronger religious feelings by looking at the night stars than he ever did reading his catechism, which his mother forced him to do every day, Ephraim "shouted and hallooed as he shot down the hill. His mother could not have recognized his voice had she heard it, for it was the first time that the boy had ever given full cry to the natural voice of youth and his heart." Unfortunately, Deborah finds out about what she regards as a purely self-indulgent act and tells Ephraim that while "Your brother and your sister have both rebelled against the Lord and against me," she will whip him and make him obey. She justifies her actions by stating, "It is better that your body should suffer than your immortal soul." Shortly after she administers corporal punishment to Ephraim, Deborah offers "a strange prayer, full of remorse, of awful agony, of self-defense of her own act, and her own position as the vicar of God upon earth for her child."

Many early readers and reviewers of *Pembroke* applauded Wilkins's second attempt at novel writ-

ing. Calling *Pembroke* a "distinct success," a reviewer for *The Critic* magazine opined that "this record
of the heart tragedies of a dozen men and women of
the village of Pembroke is not surpassed in our literature for its beauty of style, the delicacy of its character delineation and the enthralling interest of its
narration." In her diary entry for 7 June 1894, fellow American author Kate Chopin wrote of "the
subtle genius which created" *Pembroke* and record-
ed her belief that it was "the most profound, the
most powerful piece of fiction of its kind that has
ever come to the American press." British reviewers
were especially enthusiastic. One writer for the Lon-
don *Spectator* judged it "the gem of Miss Wilkins's
many remarkable productions. It has more body,
more continuity, a broader canvas, and a larger social
grasp than any of her shorter New England tales,"
adding that "It has all the vivacity of Miss Wilkins's
shorter tales, with a much greater massiveness of
effect." Sir Arthur Conan Doyle was even quoted
as stating that *Pembroke* was "the greatest piece of
American fiction since *The Scarlet Letter*."[1]

Such high praise is due in large part to the fact
that Freeman knew her subject—the New England
village of the late nineteenth century—extremely
well. Unlike "the sojourner from cities for the
summer months" whom she disparaged in her 1899
introduction as incapable of seeing beneath the surface of village life because of his or her outsider
status, Freeman lived in small New England towns

until 1902, when she was forty-nine years old. Born in 1852 in Randolph, Massachusetts, then a small community approximately fourteen miles south of Boston, Freeman moved in 1867 with her family to Brattleboro, Vermont, where her father, a carpenter and builder by trade, became a partner in a dry goods store. Freeman remained in Brattleboro (except for a brief stint away at college) until 1883, when at the age of thirty-one she returned to Randolph, where she lived with her childhood friend and neighbor Mary John Wales until 1901.

Freeman also was no stranger to Puritanism, poverty, or complex, sometimes tragic, love stories, all of which figure prominently in the fictionalized Pembroke. Her parents, Warren Wilkins and Eleanor Lothrop, could both trace their lineage back to the early Puritan settlers of New England, and they raised their daughter Mary according to a strict, orthodox Congregationalism. Money was always scarce in Mary's home. In Randolph the family owned a house only because Mary's grandfather had given it to her parents. In Brattleboro, on the other hand, they rented various houses and apartments, an indication of their relatively low-class status and economic vulnerability. The Wilkinses did purchase a building lot in Brattleboro, and Warren Wilkins promised his wife that he would eventually build a large house on it. However, after a business recession in 1873 forced him to sell his dry goods business and return to carpentry and odd jobs, any dreams of homeownership were set aside. Eventually, in 1877, just one year after the death of Mary's younger sister Anna, the Wilkinses were forced to move in with the Reverend Mr. Tyler of Brattleboro, who allowed the family to stay with him in return for Eleanor Wilkins serving as his housekeeper. Such a hard life undoubtedly took its toll on Mary's mother, and she died in 1880; Warren Wilkins died shortly thereafter, in 1883. These deaths, added to the earlier death of her brother Edward in 1858 at the age of three, exposed Mary to much tragedy at a relatively early age. Personal tragedies also, of course, had economic ramifications; after her father's death, Mary was left with no visible means of supporting herself. Fortunately, however, she found a way out by moving back to Randolph to live with the Wales family and becoming a professional writer, soon thereafter beginning to regularly sell her poems and stories to magazines.

Freeman was also very familiar with the type of complicated love stories depicted in *Pembroke*. The central relationship of Barnabas Thayer and Charlotte Barnard, in fact, is based on a family story involving Freeman's maternal uncle, Barnabas Lothrop Jr. Years before Freeman was born, her grandfather, Barnabas Lothrop Sr., had built a house in Randolph for his son, Barnabas Jr., and his fiancée, Mary Thayer, to live in after their marriage. It was almost complete, except for its paint, when Barnabas Jr. (a Whig) and Mary Thayer's father (a Democrat) got into a heated political argument, and Mary's father forbade Barnabas from ever entering his house again. This couple never reunited, but after the house had been left abandoned for ten years, Barnabas Lothrop Sr. gave it to Warren and Eleanor Wilkins as a wedding gift.

In her own adult life, Freeman experienced a number of complex relationships with men and ambivalent feelings about marriage. The latter sentiment, Freeman biographer Leah Blatt Glasser has argued, resulted from Freeman's observations of how her own mother's autonomy and happiness had seemed diminished by her union with Warren Wilkins. Mary's relationship with a young navy ensign named Hanson Tyler, whom she had met in Brattleboro in 1873 while he was home on leave, also well illustrates her uncertainties about marriage. For many years Freeman gave the impression to friends that she viewed Tyler, who spent almost all of his time far away from Brattleboro on naval cruises, as her one true love, even though there is no evidence that they were ever seriously involved with each other. Glasser has convincingly theorized that Freeman, far from being distressed by Tyler never asking her to marry him, held on to her fantasized relationship with Tyler chiefly because it "created an effective excuse not to marry." Scholar Deborah Lambert sees parallels between Freeman's experiences and those of Charlotte Barnard, arguing that Charlotte's willingness to wait for Barney Thayer and her dismissal of other suitors is motivated not by her love of Barney so much as by the same desire to avoid marriage as long as she can. Coincidentally or not, Freeman began writing *Pembroke* in 1892, the year she learned that Hanson Tyler had married. This was also the year when, in Randolph, Freeman regularly enjoyed the company of her neighbor Isaac Tolman, who was single but commonly believed to be almost engaged to another woman; he too, would have been a "safe" male companion.[2] The one relationship Freeman had with a man that resulted in marriage was, in a case where life imitated art, full of starts and stops. Freeman met Dr. Charles Manning Freeman in New Jersey in 1892 but did not become engaged until 1897. Quarreling that year, they did not reconcile until the summer of 1898, and then did not actually marry until 1 January 1902.

Thus, when Freeman began work on *Pembroke* in late 1892, she had a great deal on her mind. In some ways, her decision to write a second novel might have been linked to her decision about whether to marry. Marjorie Pryse contends that after the death of her friend and *Harper's Bazar* editor Mary Louise Booth in 1889, Freeman felt she could not afford "to risk literary difference by remaining a writer of short fiction, and to resist the social stigma of spinsterhood." Becoming a novelist was, according to this view, one way in which Freeman could conform to society's expectations yet not give up too much of her autonomy. Another explanation was offered by Charles Miner Thompson, who in an 1899 *Atlantic Monthly* article opined, "Those cogent reasons which publishers urge, reinforced by the ambition which every writer of fiction feels to try his hand in the most important form of his art, made it inevitable that, sooner or later, Miss Wilkins should write novels."[3]

More prosaic considerations might also have influenced Freeman's decision to write another novel. The early Freeman biographer Edward Foster agreed that ambition entered into this decision, but he also correctly noted that "the royalties for serial rights were a lure that caught most of the writers of the time." Even though Freeman's short stories by the early 1890s regularly commanded quite high prices from the magazines and newspaper syndicates, she knew that true financial success for American fiction authors came from selling the serial rights of their novels to magazines (the income from book royalties usually lagged far behind). As it turned out, Freeman profited a great deal financially from *Pembroke*. A good negotiator with publishers, Freeman received $2,500 in serial rights from *Harper's Weekly* and a 15 percent book royalty, which was greater than the 10 percent she had received for her first novel, *Jane Field*. At a time when Freeman was typically receiving approximately $200–$300 for her short story serial rights, the amounts she earned from *Pembroke* were quite large. Given *Pembroke*'s later popularity in Britain, it is ironic that her publisher, Harper and Brothers, had a difficult time selling serial rights to this novel in Britain, receiving only a lowly offer of £100, or about $500; it is unknown whether Freeman accepted this offer or even if the novel was ever published serially in Britain.[4]

In the United States, *Pembroke* ran in *Harper's Weekly* between 6 January 1894 and 14 April 1894, with large illustrations by C. Carleton accompanying almost every installment. Published in book form later that year by Harper and Brothers in the United States, the Osgood, McIlvaine Co. in Great Britain, and Tauchnitz in Germany (an English edition for the European continent), *Pembroke* did not become a runaway hit. Even so, *Pembroke* was popular enough to merit reprinting in book form by Harper's in 1899, 1900, and 1903. Freeman was never disappointed by the fact that her novels were not extremely popular. As she wrote in 1919, "I never wrote a 'best seller', but I am entirely satisfied without that."[5]

As noted earlier, at the time of its publication *Pembroke* was highly commended by a number of reviewers, most of whom focused on its exploration of the "Puritan temperament" among New Englanders. The Maine poet Edwin Arlington Robinson, writing about *Pembroke* to a friend in 1894, observed that "To the careless modern reader the plot—or rather the plots—will seem impossible and contrary to human nature; but to one who knows anything about Puritanism the book will be interesting and impressive. Narrow minded and unsympathetic readers had better keep away from it." Some critics undoubtedly emphasized Freeman's depiction of New England Puritanism because this reinforced the idea that Freeman was a "local color" writer, one who in the post–Civil War period wrote about the distinctive qualities found in far-flung American locales. As such, she could be relegated to "second-tier" status, since an author who could only write about one region clearly could not be a "great" American writer who wrote about universal themes. The reviewer for the *Edinburgh Review*, however, disagreed with this pigeonholing of Freeman, astutely writing that "the essential features of her New England folk are not merely local; one recognizes behind the New England farmer that hard foundation upon which is built up the most composite of all types—the modern American."[6]

Despite such praise, after 1903 the novel went out of print, not to be republished again until 1970. In the early years of the twentieth century, despite a number of scholars remarking that Freeman's subject matter and symbolism were closely akin to Hawthorne's, Freeman's reputation declined dramatically. When in 1926 Freeman was elected to the National Institute of Arts and Letters (one of the first women to enter this previously all-male organization) and received the first Howells Gold Medal for Distinguished Work in Fiction from the American Academy and Institute of Arts and Letters, many people undoubtedly were surprised to learn that she was still alive.

In the decades immediately following Freeman's death, much of the praise her works received from critics often paradoxically diminished her reputation. For instance, many commended her works for their depictions of New England villages during the late nineteenth century, emptied of men who had left for the West and enervated by the loss of manufacturing jobs to larger cities. In 1940, prominent critic Van Wyck Brooks wrote that Freeman was an excellent describer of "the Yankee ebb-tide, a world of empty houses and abandoned farms, of shuttered windows, relics, ghosts, and silence." Such commendations, however, earned Freeman a reputation as more of a sociologist than a fiction author. That most indefatigable early promoter of American literature, Fred Lewis Pattee, also had many positive things to say about Freeman's work, but even he, writing in 1931, followed such praise with the comment, "Had she had the will of Hawthorne, the ability to starve in a garret rather than surrender to the magazines, she now might stand, perhaps, even at his high level."[7] Today one can see the gender bias inherent in such a remark, for it implies that authors whose works were popular—most often women— had "sold out" their artistic integrity to the commercial marketplace and its readers and thus could not be regarded as true artists. Such a critical view, however, would have been apparent to very few people at mid-century. During the 1950s, Freeman's reputation sank even lower. The academic literary community during these years was greatly intent on finding American writers who expressed the spirit of the entire *nation*, and since what were then known as "local color" authors—most of whom, again, were by no coincidence women—appeared to have written about only one purportedly small portion of America, they were not considered worthy contestants for critical elevation. In 1952 scholar Donald Dike reported that "'Local color' has nowadays become a term of critical abuse, a way of designating the presence in fiction of irrelevant description or of the merely quaint." Not even Perry Westbrook, who emerged as a leading advocate of Freeman's works, was willing to contend that Freeman was a great American author. In 1951 he described *Pembroke* as "once ranked among the greatest American novels, but now unjustly neglected"; however, in his introduction to the 1971 edition of *Pembroke*, he could muster only lukewarm enthusiasm, writing that Freeman should be counted among the "many excellent second-rank authors . . . who deserve something better than oblivion."[8]

Such tepid endorsements are not completely surprising, since these male critics saw in *Pembroke* and Freeman's other works only the rebellion against Puritanism. Edward Foster, for example, argued that both male and female descendants of the Puritans unhealthily stifled their emotions and encouraged others to do the same; the reason he believed *Pembroke* deserved recognition, he stated, was because it was "a deeply felt plea for the natural expression of normal feeling." Yet, even though Arthur Miller would show in *The Crucible* how similar Puritan oppression was to McCarthyism, for a nation of readers more intent on conforming than on being independent, *Pembroke*'s criticism of Puritanism did not appear especially relevant. In 1971, Perry Westbrook continued Foster's line of thinking, applauding *Pembroke* because he viewed it as a massive attack on the evil products of the Puritan will, including the stubbornness of those who, believing themselves "divinely elected," unwaveringly held on to their judgements, and the "tyranny of village opinion," which he said was especially important in Puritan villages: "By the very nature of Calvinism, the behavior and spiritual condition of each member of a community are legitimate objects of public scrutiny."[9] Both men based their interpretations on Freeman's own introduction to the 1899 edition, in which she spoke of *Pembroke* "as a study of the human will in several New England characters, in different phases of disease and abnormal development." She argued that New Englanders of the 1890s had inherited their "spiritual disease" from their Puritan ancestors, and that now they justified their "carrying-out of personal and petty aims and quarrels," by saying they were merely remaining true to the concept of the "Puritan will."

In the 1970s, though, Freeman's reputation began to rise dramatically as a new generation of critics began to interpret her works as being highly relevant to contemporary readers. *Pembroke* was republished by Harper's in 1970, and two other editions by relatively small presses, aimed at the academic market, followed. What accounted for the sudden interest in Freeman and *Pembroke* at this particular historical moment? In large part her "rediscovery" can be attributed to the feminist movement that swept not only the country at large but also the academic world. Feminist critics began to show that just as women themselves had been suppressed in many ways by the patriarchal American society for centuries so, too, had a great number of excellent women authors (such as Freeman) been unfairly neglected by a male-dominated academy because their subjects and styles did not meet the gender-biased criteria for literary excellence.

Critics began to posit that there was much more to Freeman's works in general and *Pembroke* in particular than simply a generic criticism of New England Puritanism. Puritanism in Freeman's works, these critics contended, represented patriarchy in general, a stultifying system with which her

female characters constantly had to contend. Freeman in the 1970s was now considered a valiant war-
rior who wrote works criticizing the type of cold
rationality and gender inequality propagated by
adherents to the Puritan patriarchy—works that
could inspire those women now striving for their
freedom from societal restraints. Susan Allen Toth's
"Defiant Light: A Positive View of Mary Wilkins
Freeman" (1973) signaled a new era in Freeman's
critical reputation; Toth argued that "Many of
[Freeman's] characters suffer, but they also fight
their way to significant victories. Living in drab
poverty, they still struggle with courageous spirit
towards self-expression and independence." In
"Mary Wilkins Freeman: Misanthropy as Propaganda" (1977), Alice Glarden Brand contended that
Freeman's stories in general were "an exposé of contempt for men's impotence, incompetence, and ag-
gression and for women's passivity, dependence,
and rage." In 1985, Sandra Gilbert and Susan
Gubar wrote in the *Norton Anthology of Literature
by Women* that "Freeman's heroines recognize their
isolation and defiantly struggle to preserve their
integrity against the demands of the importunate
suitors, husbands, and preachers who represent all
that is left of a dwindling Puritan culture." Given
this understanding of Freeman's works, it is not surprising that Louisa Ellis of "A New England Nun,"
Hetty Fifield of "A Church Mouse," Sarah Penn of
"The Revolt of 'Mother,'" and Old Woman Magoun

were seen as representative of Freeman's writing and accordingly pushed forward for anthologization and critical recognition. Not all of Freeman's female characters, however, were seen as ultimately successful in their struggles against patriarchy. As Josephine Donovan hypothesizes, "it is not God, who is dead or dying in the world of Mary E. Wilkins Freeman; it is the Mother and a woman-centered world"; the "preindustrial values of that world, female-identified and ecologically holistic," she writes, "are going down to defeat before the imperialism of masculine technology and patriarchal institutions."[10]

Recent criticism of *Pembroke* has reflected these views of Freeman's other works. Pamela Glenn Menke believes that "*Pembroke*'s nature exposes the unnaturalness of women's enclosure in rigid (male) customs, but provides no safe ways to express desire or to enjoy the independence such expression signifies." Heather Kirk Thomas believes *Pembroke* has even wider ramifications, theorizing that "the novel is more than a condemnation of isolationism and orthodoxy; it is a manifesto for the New Woman's essential participation in drafting the range and quality of human existence."[11]

Pembroke is also interpreted as having been extremely important to Freeman herself. Marjorie Pryse asserts that for Freeman, *Pembroke* was "an attempt to find a way, in fiction, to repair her loss of family." To Leah Blatt Glasser, *Pembroke* represents "Freeman's way of voicing both the fear of and the need for heterosexual partnership." Virginia Blum, on the other hand, sees *Pembroke* as representing Freeman's ambivalence between remaining faithful to her art and to herself and making artistic sacrifices in order to be commercially successful.[12]

Moving beyond the discussion over what Freeman intended and what *Pembroke* meant to her personally, a number of critics in recent years have debated what messages the works of Freeman and other women regionalists actually conveyed to their readers. Marjorie Pryse and Judith Fetterley contend that women regionalist writers in particular portrayed the places and characters about which they wrote in such a way that readers could not help but empathize with them and see them as needing to be taken seriously. "Regionalist texts," they write, "allow the reader to view the regional speaker as subject and not as object and to include empathic feeling as an aspect of critical response." Others, though, believe that the fictions of Freeman and women regionalists in general, far from being taken by nineteenth-century readers as powerful voices against the patriarchal status quo, ironically helped enforce it by encouraging genteel magazine readers to see the rural subjects of these fictions as "quaint" and worthy only of passing attention. Richard Brodhead contends, for instance, that regionalist fiction was a type of tourist experience that helped upper-class urban readers consolidate and justify their hegemonic dominance over American culture on a number of fronts. In this view, Mary Wilkins Freeman could be seen as having unwittingly provided readers of *Pembroke*, both as it appeared in *Harper's Weekly* and in book form, with a touristic sojourn in rural New England, similar to the actual trips to such places that were becoming popular in the late nineteenth century.[18] Such print vacations, far from creating empathy for people from rural areas, could thus be seen as having solidified the attitude of urban dwellers that these areas were full of backward people who needed to become more like city people in order to "improve" and become full citizens in the new American nation.

All of these interpretations and hypotheses are valuable in helping illuminate the text of *Pembroke*, but they should not in any way prevent readers from coming to their own conclusions. After all, it is clear now that the long-held belief that Freeman's writing was of interest more to sociologists and historians than to literary scholars has been shown to be quite misleading. Yes, sociologists can learn much about how people in these villages lived. However, readers of *Pembroke* will find in its pages no documentary of the abandoned farms, male-depleted villages, and quiet houses that historians might posit were more prevalent in rural New England at this time. In fact, the fictionalized village of *Pembroke* is all too full of active gossips,

meddling church authorities, male-female romantic intrigues, personal tragedies, and houses where
the tension between family members is revealed in
veiled, barbed conversations.

For most readers today, the thrill of reading *Pembroke* comes not necessarily from the academic
debate surrounding it but more from the heart-
wrenching tension between characters' desires and
what others expect and sometimes demand of
them. In some cases these tensions are the result of
the patriarchal oppression of women, but not
always. Some male characters, for instance, also
wish to rebel against authority. Ephraim Thayer
and his father Caleb want nothing more than to
spend some carefree moments together by the fire-
side playing the game of "holly-gull," but Deborah
Thayer will not allow what she views as such "a
sinful waste of time." William Berry, the storekeeper's son, tired of his father's penny-pinching
ways, finally stands up to his father by giving his
beloved Rebecca two and a half pounds of sugar in
trade for her two dozen eggs. The father objects
strenuously, but the reader cheers when he is finally vanquished by "the combination of mental and
superior physical force in his son."

This scene between father and son highlights
another theme neglected thus far by critics of
Pembroke: its intergenerational conflicts. The children in this village generally wish to break free
from the principles that have choked all the joy in

life out of their elders. Ephraim and Rebecca Thayer are prime examples. Ephraim significantly borrows his brother Barney's sled to carry out his rebellious evening, subverting his mother's authority in a way that his brother never would dare to. Rebecca defies her mother, too, to run after William Berry and comfort him in his hour of shame. When she catches up with him, she says, "I ran away in the face and eyes of them all to comfort you. They saw me, and they can see me now, but I don't care." It is less certain, unfortunately, whether Ephraim and Rebecca's brother Barney will escape inheriting the traits of his mother; at one point, "his face hardened like hers," and Freeman writes, "The mother and son confronting each other looked more alike than ever."

One can argue, too, that such an examination of the dynamics of such a small town, especially of the constraints placed upon the actions of its inhabitants, is much more than a nineteenth-century New England local history and applies to communities of all types everywhere. Can people be their true selves? To what extent will "difference" be allowed? Those who fear being different and consequently being gossiped about—or worse—by the Pembroke villagers suffer greatly, even when they conform to village standards. Sylvia Crane hosts a wedding-shower tea for her niece Rose Berry, even though she has no food to eat herself and is down to her last penny, facing imminent removal to the poor house.

She does so, though, because she knows that tradition and the village demand it; she thinks to herself that "Her sisters and nieces must come to tea; and all the food, which was the village fashion and as absolute in its way as court etiquette, must be provided."

A number of questions come to mind that can even further complicate previous theories and serve as useful guides to future interpretations. While *Pembroke* may be an account of how heroic, strong women fight patriarchal, Puritan control, Freeman here seems to be exploring, in an extremely complex way, how one defines "strength" in a woman. Deborah Thayer is seemingly "strong," but only because she fulfills the conventional male definition of strength. Like Sarah Penn of "The Revolt of Mother," she is frequently described in military terms. At one point she beats eggs and makes a cake, her face as "full of stern desperation as a soldier's on the battlefield," and Freeman adds that "she never yielded to any of the vicissitudes of life; she met them in fair fight like enemies and vanquished them, not with trumpet and spear, but with daily duties." An example used to demonstrate her type of strength is the village story about the time Deborah's first child died in the morning and she cleaned all the windows in the house that afternoon. Later, as Deborah ladles toast gravy, she is compared to "one of her female ancestors in the times of the French and Indian wars, casting bullets with the yells of savages in her ears." Unlike Sarah Penn, however, Deborah is not portrayed as the heroine of this work.

Instead, Freeman appears to be trying to redefine the terms "strength" and "heroism" by making the "strongest" woman in this book the least conventionally heroic. Critics have completely overlooked the eerily fascinating character of Mrs. Jim Sloane, who is ostracized by the "good" villagers (both male and female) because of her poverty and because her husband "had been disreputable and drunken." The community clearly does not allow her an identity of her own, forever associating her with her husband by calling her "Mrs. Jim Sloane." Villagers regard her as unclean, the carrier of a disease all the more threatening because of its proximity. Barney Thayer looks at her "with utter disgust and revulsion. He had always felt a loathing for the woman, and her being a distant relative on his father's side intensified it." The minister's wife, Freeman mentions, "had heard about Mrs. Sloane, and felt as if she were confronted by a woman from Revelation and there was a flash of scarlet in the room." Freeman thus portrays the evil power of village gossip, the destructive lack of empathy, and the extreme class prejudice that prevail in Pembroke.

Yet Mrs. Jim Sloane is also the one person in the village who provides refuge to Rebecca Thayer in her time of need, rescuing her from a snowstorm and certain death. She parries the attempts of William

Berry and Barney Thayer to take Rebecca from the house by force. Eventually, she talks Rebecca into allowing these two men and the minister, Mr. Barnes, to come into her room and speak to her, but in a voice "still high-pitched with anger," Mrs. Sloane tells the men who "were deciding where to take Rebecca," to take her to the house of the minister and his wife. Freeman writes that as Mrs. Sloane does so, she "turn[s] to the minister and his wife, regarding them with a mixture of defiance, sarcasm, and appeal." When they hesitate, Mrs. Sloane pointedly comments, "I shouldn't s'pose you'd need any time to think on it, such good folks as you be." Mrs. Sloane thus prevents the "respectable" villagers from treating Rebecca as an object to be manipulated according to their desires and exposes the hypocritical and self-serving "morality" of these men. Freeman points out, however, that the price one must pay for being strong and defiant is quite high. Rebecca, who has been as rebellious as Mrs. Sloane, begins her journey toward village isolation when she leaves the house: "[her] very identity seemed to be lost, for she wore Mrs. Sloane's blue plaid shawl pinned closely over her head and face."

The ending of the novel, too, is quite problematic and deserves close examination for the ways it reflects Freeman's true intentions. Barney marches to Charlotte's house, puts his arm around her, and "look[s] over her head at her father. 'I've come back,' said he." The final line of the novel reads:

"And Barney entered the house with his old sweet-heart and his old self." In this scene Barney completely disregards Charlotte, looking past her to tell Cephas that their feud is over; it is as if Barney is reclaiming a dog who has no say in her fate. This resolution does not appear to promise a "happy ending" or bode well for their future relationship. Freeman also clearly wished to confound any easy conclusions about this ending with the suggestion that, after ten years of separation and aging, both Charlotte and Barney might still be their "old" selves. Have they learned nothing, matured not at all in those ten years? Contrary to what some critics have proposed, Barney here does not appear to be revealing a gentler, more sentimental side of his personality, but rather seems to be returning to his "old" self, the one that once sacrificed love for politics. Many readers will concur with the assessment offered by a reviewer from *The Critic* magazine in 1894: "we wonder whether, after all, miracles of the spirit can be performed any more than those of the body, and whether Charlotte, in marrying Barnabas, has not united herself to a nature as irretrievably warped and diseased in spirit as his body is bent and broken by work and rheumatism."[14] Charlotte's passivity in this particular scene also jars the reader because it contradicts the strength she has shown during the previous ten years. The discerning reader doubts whether Charlotte truly is Barney's "old sweetheart" and secretly hopes that she will reject the marriage proposal implied by Barney's "return."

Why, the reader might ask, would Freeman have written such an ambiguous, unsettling ending? Quite possibly it can be explained by what Virginia Blum identifies as Freeman's ambivalence toward the commercial literary marketplace. Freeman may have wished to please cursory readers with the reuniting of lovers at the end, thereby satisfying them that this was, after all, a conventional romance, which would have helped boost readership and sales. On the other hand, with this ending Freeman might also have been attempting to remain true to her own ambivalent feelings about marriage by casting doubts about whether "happiness" lay ahead for Barney and Charlotte in a marriage founded on such terms.

Whether such nuances resonated among Freeman's readers is of course a matter of pure speculation. But something significant that previous scholars have not inquired about is the difference it made that *Pembroke* was Freeman's first serialization in *Harper's Weekly*. Previously, her work had appeared chiefly either in the flagship *Harper's Monthly* or in *Harper's Bazar*, both of which were directed toward genteel audiences; the latter was a fashion-oriented periodical read almost exclusively by women. *Harper's Weekly*, in contrast, enjoyed a socioeconomically more diverse audience than the other two publications, was read more by men, and was geared toward those interested in current events, as indicated by the abundance of such pieces, printed near the installments of *Pembroke*, as "Objections to Socialism," "The Crisis in Brazil," "Zoological Possibilities," and "The Generosity of the Poor." One could justifiably posit, then, that these readers would have been more likely to understand *Pembroke* as a work of fiction important to understanding current news events, as well as social, economic, and political developments, rather than as "just" a romance.

It is certainly unlikely that *Pembroke*, appearing in such a print environment, would have been dismissed by readers as a touristic experience that provided its readers with a few hours entertainment and nothing more. Dona Brown has shown that in the late nineteenth century, marketing campaigns for vacations in rural Vermont emphasized "home, mother, and childhood"; "Vermonters were presented as sturdy members of the 'Anglo-Saxon race' and as the vigorous guardians of democratic traditions and religious freedoms." Furthermore, she writes, "New England's countryside was imagined as a kind of underground aquifer that fed the nation's springs of political courage, personal independence, and old-fashioned virtue."[15] The text of *Pembroke*, however, completely refutes any of these idyllic images of a rural New England village and challenges the theories of Brodhead and others about regionalist fiction acting as a form of print tourism. Most of this village's inhabitants are enervated, personal independence and difference of any kind is not tolerated, "home" is no haven, mothers sometimes whip with switches and words, childhood is certainly *not* carefree, neither "democracy" nor "political courage" is anywhere to be found, and "old-fashioned virtue" seems only a tool with which the Orthodox Congregationalists in power can measure and punish those who stray from the "straight and narrow" path.

Freeman in the final chapter goes so far as to mock any readers who hope to act as tourists and derive "hospitable entertainment" from this novel. She satirizes one particular townswoman and her visiting cousin, the former who, by pointing out the houses and people involved in the drama of *Pembroke* during a carriage ride around town, appears to act like a tour bus guide in Beverly Hills. After the tour, the guest sits down for her meal "and all these strange tragedies and histories to which she had listened had less of a savor in her memory, than the fine green tea and the sweet cake on her tongue." Readers of *Pembroke*, Freeman clearly hoped, would not in similar fashion regard their experiences lightly or forget her characters so easily. As Edwin Arlington Robinson aptly put it, *Pembroke* "wasn't a summer vacation."[16]

What makes this novel especially compelling for today's readers is that, while it denies any comforting touristic respite from modern life, its tragic elements generate great interest and simultaneously evoke empathy and pity. It is difficult to imagine readers empathizing with many of the sometimes stubborn, bullying, parsimonious, craven, and sanctimonious people who live in this village, yet one paradoxically pities many of them and their neighbors for the ways in which their lives are seemingly being wasted. Possibly this is what Freeman had in mind when she wrote in her 1899 introduction to the novel: "There is often to a mind from the outside world an almost repulsive narrowness and a pitiful sordidness which amounts to tragedy in the lives of such people as those portrayed in *Pembroke*." She adds, though, that unfortunately these people are unaware of how self-destructive their lives actually are, concluding, "It may be that the lack of unhappiness constitutes the real tragedy."

In her 1922 introduction to *Ethan Frome*, originally published in 1911, Edith Wharton stated that part of her motivation for writing the novel was her "uneasy sense that the New England of [previous] fiction bore little . . . resemblance to the harsh and beautiful land as I had seen it," noting that she believed the harsher realities of life in New England—what she called "the outcropping granite"—had "been overlooked." Wharton here hoped to align herself with a more male-coded realism and against the female-coded regionalists of the previous generation.[17] This statement, however, ignores the fact that eighteen years before *Ethan Frome* was published, Mary Wilkins Freeman had, in *Pembroke*, produced an extremely realistic portrayal of rural New England life, free of any romantic illusions about pastoral peace and harmony. Freeman used irony extensively to advocate breaking free of the past and allowing individuals to forge their own paths in life, rather than remaining nostalgic for the nonexistent "good old days" in which such independence was vehemently suppressed. Thus *Pembroke* in many ways was a pioneering work at the forefront of a male-dominated, harder-edged, realistic regionalism that would emerge after the turn of the century in such works as Sherwood Anderson's *Winesburg, Ohio* (1919) and Sinclair Lewis's *Main Street* (1920). Over one hundred years after *Pembroke*'s original publication, its descriptions of the battles waged between the forces of conservatism and modernism, its abundant supply of enigmatic "granite outcroppings," and its bold confrontation of prevailing images of New England village life, still promise to fascinate and intrigue its readers.

NOTES

1. "Pembroke," *The Critic* 25 (n.s. 22)(21 July 1894): 35; Kate Chopin, A Kate Chopin Miscellany, ed. Per Seyersted and Emily Toth (Natchitoches, La.: Northwestern State University Press, 1979), 96; "Miss Wilkins's Pembroke," Spectator 72 (23 June 1894): 858, 859; Sir Arthur Conan Doyle quoted in "Mary E. Wilkins Freeman," Harper's Weekly 47 (21 November 1903): 1880.

2. For Glasser's theory about Freeman's relationship to her mother, see Leah Blatt Glasser, *In a Closet Hidden: The Life and Works of Mary E. Wilkins Freeman* (Amherst:

University of Massachusetts Press, 1996), 28; Glasser, 54; Deborah G. Lambert, "Rereading Mary Wilkins Freeman: Autonomy and Sexuality in *Pembroke*," in *Critical Essays on Mary Wilkins Freeman*, ed. Shirley Marchalonis (Boston: G. K. Hall, 1991), 202; Freeman's relationship with Tolman is described in Edward Foster, *Mary E. Wilkins Freeman* (New York: Hendricks House, 1956), 121.

3. Marjorie Pryse, "Mary E. Wilkins Freeman," in *Modern American Women Writers*, ed. Lea Baechler and A. Walton Litz (New York: Charles Scribner's Sons, 1991), 145; Charles Miner Thompson, "Miss Wilkins: An Idealist in Masquerade," *Atlantic Monthly* 83 (May 1899): 672.

4. Foster, 112; the amounts Freeman received for *Pembroke* are given in *The Infant Sphinx: Collected Letters of Mary E. Wilkins Freeman*, edited, with biographical and critical introductions by Brent L. Kendrick (Metuchen, N.J.: Scarecrow Press, 1985), 118; the British offer is mentioned in Mary E. Wilkins, letter to Harper & Brothers, 2 October 1893 (see Kendrick, 159).

5. Freeman, letter to Fred Lewis Pattee, 5 September 1919 (see Kendrick, 381).

6. For an example of a review noting the "Puritan temperament," see "Pembroke," *The Critic,* 35; Robinson, letter, 28 October 1894, *Untriangulated Stars, Letters of Edwin Arlington Robinson to Harry De Forest Smith, 1890–1905*, ed. Denham Sutcliffe (Cambridge, Mass.: Harvard University Press, 1947), 174; the *Edinburgh Review* assessment appears in *Marchalonis,* 35.

7. Van Wyck Brooks, *New England: Indian Summer 1865–1915* (New York: E. P. Dutton, 1940) 86; Fred Lewis Pattee, *The Development of the American Short Story* (New York: Harper & Brothers, 1931), 322.

8. Donald Dike, "Notes on Local Color and Its Relation to Realism," *College English* 14 (November 1952): 81; Perry Westbrook, *Acres of Flint: Sarah Orne Jewett and Her Contemporaries* (1951; Metuchen, N.J.: Scarecrow Press, 1981), 92; Westbrook, introduction to *Pembroke*, by Mary E. Wilkins Freeman (New Haven, Conn.: College & University Press, 1971), 26.

9. Foster, 126; Westbrook, introduction to *Pembroke* 20, 21.

10. Emily Toth, "Defiant Light: A Positive View of Mary Wilkins Freeman," *New England Quarterly* 46 (1973): 83; Alice Glarden Brand, "Mary Wilkins Freeman: Misanthropy as Propaganda," *New England Quarterly* 50 (1977): 83; Gilbert and Gubar, headnote to *The Norton Anthology of Literature by Women: The Tradition in English*, ed. Sandra M. Gilbert and Susan Gubar (New York: W. W. Norton, 1985), 1103; Josephine Donovan, *New England Local Color Literature, A Women's Tradition* (New York: Frederick Ungar, 1983), 119.

11. Pamela Glenn Menke, "The Catalyst of Color and Women's Regional Writing: *At Fault*, *Pembroke*, and *The Awakening*," *Southern Quarterly* 37 (1999): 15 ; Heather Kirk Thomas, " 'It's your father's way': The Father-Daughter Narrative and Female Development in Mary Wilkins Freeman's *Pembroke*," *Studies in the Novel* 29 (1997): 27.

12. Pryse, 146; Glasser, 97; Virginia Blum, "Mary Wilkins Freeman and the Taste of Necessity," *American Literature* 65 (1993): 72–73.

13. Judith Fetterley and Marjorie Pryse, introduction to *American Women Regionalists 1850–1910*, ed. Judith Fetterley and Marjorie Pryse (New York: W. W. Norton, 1992), xvii; Richard Brodhead, "The Reading of Regions," chapter 4 of *Cultures of Letters, Scenes of Reading and Writing in Nineteenth-Century America* (Chicago: University of Chicago Press, 1993), 107–141.

14. "Pembroke," *The Critic*, 36.

15. Brown, *Inventing New England: Regional Tourism in the Nineteenth Century* (Washington, D.C.: Smithsonian Institution Press, 1995), 141, 146, 153.

16. Sutcliffe, 175.

17. See Edith Wharton's "Introduction to the 1922 Edition" of *Ethan Frome* (New York: W. W. Norton, 1995), x; Donna M. Campbell, *Resisting Regionalism. Gender and Naturalism in American Fiction, 1885–1915* (Athens, Ohio: Ohio University Press, 1997), 173.

INTRODUCTORY SKETCH
1899 Edition

———

Pembroke was originally intended as a study of the human will in several New England characters, in different phases of disease and abnormal development, and to prove, especially in the most marked case, the truth of a theory that its cure depended entirely upon the capacity of the individual for a love which could rise above all considerations of self, as Barnabas Thayer's love for Charlotte Barnard finally did.

While Barnabas Thayer is the most pronounced exemplification of this theory, and while he, being drawn from life, originally suggested the scheme of the study, a number of other characters, notably Deborah Thayer, Richard Alger, and Cephas Barnard, are instances of the same spiritual disease. Barnabas to me was as much the victim of disease as a man with curvature of the spine; he was incapable of straightening himself to his former stature until he had laid hands upon a more purely unselfish love than he had ever known, through his anxiety for Charlotte, and so raised himself to his own level.

When I make use of the term abnormal, I do not mean unusual in any sense. I am far from any intention to speak disrespectfully or disloyally of those stanch old soldiers of the faith who landed upon our inhospitable shores and laid the foundations, as on a very rock of spirit, for the New England of to-day; but I am not sure, in spite of their godliness, and their noble adherence, in the face of obstacles, to the dictates of their consciences, that their wills were not developed past the reasonable limit of nature. What wonder is it their descendants inherit this peculiarity, though they may develop it for much less worthy and more trivial causes than the exiling themselves for a question of faith, even the carrying-out of personal and petty aims and quarrels?

There lived in a New England village, at no very remote time, a man who objected to the painting of the kitchen floor, and who quarrelled furiously with his wife concerning the same. When she persisted, in spite of his wishes to the contrary, and the floor was painted, he refused to cross it to his dying day, and always, to his great inconvenience, but probably to his soul's satisfaction, walked around it.

A character like this, holding to a veriest trifle with such a deathless cramp of the will, might naturally be regarded as a notable exception to a general rule; but his brethren who sit on church steps during services, who are dumb to those whom they should love, and will not enter familiar doors because of quarrels over matters of apparently no

moment, are legion. *Pembroke* is intended to portray a typical New England village of some sixty
years ago, as many of the characters flourished at
that time, but villages of a similar description have
existed in New England at a much later date, and
they exist to-day in a very considerable degree.
There are at the present time many little towns in
New England along whose pleasant elm or maple
shaded streets are scattered characters as pronounced as any in Pembroke. A short time since a
Boston woman recited in my hearing a list of
seventy-five people in the very small Maine village
in which she was born and brought up, and every
one of the characters which she mentioned had
some almost incredibly marked physical or mental
characteristic.

However, this state of things—this survival of
the more prominent traits of the old stiff-necked
ones, albeit their necks were stiffened by their resistance of the adversary—can necessarily be
known only to the initiated. The sojourner from
cities for the summer months cannot often pene-
trate in the least, though he may not be aware of it,
the reserve and dignified aloofness of the dwellers
in the white cottages along the road over which he
drives. He often looks upon them from the superior height of a wise and keen student of character;
he knows what he thinks of them, but he never
knows what they think of him or themselves. Unless he is a man of the broadest and most demo-

cratic tendencies, to whom culture and the polish of society is as nothing beside humanity, and unless he returns, as faithfully as the village birds to their nests, to his summer home year after year, he cannot see very far below the surfaces of villages of which Pembroke is typical. Quite naturally, when the surfaces are broken by some unusual revelation of a strongly serrate individuality, and the tale thereof is told at his dinner-table with an accompaniment of laughter and exclamation-points, he takes that case for an isolated and by no means typical one, when, if the truth were told, the village windows are full of them as he passes by.

However, this state of things must necessarily exist, and has existed, in villages which, like Pembroke, have not been brought much in contact with outside influences, and have not been studied or observed at all by people not of their kind by birth or long familiarity. In towns which have increased largely in population, and have become more or less assimilated with a foreign element, these characters do not exist in such a large measure, are more isolated in reality, and have, consequently, less claim to be considered types. But there have been, and are to-day in New England, hundreds of villages like Pembroke, where nearly every house contains one or more characters so marked as to be incredible, though a writer may be prevented, for obvious reasons, from mentioning names and proving facts.

There is often to a mind from the outside world an

almost repulsive narrowness and a pitiful sordidness which amounts to tragedy in the lives of such people as those portrayed in *Pembroke*, but quite generally the tragedy exists only in the comprehension of the observer and not at all in that of the observed. The pitied would meet pity with resentment; they would be full of wonder and wrath if told that their lives were narrow, since they have never seen the limit of the breadth of their current of daily life. A singing-school is as much to them as a symphony concert and grand opera to their city brethren, and a sewing church sociable as an afternoon tea. Though the standard of taste of the simple villagers, and their complete satisfaction therewith, may reasonably be lamented, as also their restricted way of life, they are not to be pitied, generally speaking, for their un-happiness in consequence. It may be that the lack of unhappiness constitutes the real tragedy.

MARY E. WILKINS

PEMBROKE

CHAPTER I

At half-past six o'clock on Sunday night Barnabas came out of his bedroom. The Thayer house was only one story high, and there were no chambers. A number of little bedrooms were clustered around the three square rooms—the north and south parlors, and the great kitchen.

Barnabas walked out of his bedroom straight into the kitchen where the other members of the family were. They sat before the hearth fire in a semicircle—Caleb Thayer, his wife Deborah, his son Ephraim, and his daughter Rebecca. It was May, but it was quite cold; there had been talk of danger to the apple blossoms; there was a crisp coolness in the back of the great room in spite of the hearth fire.

Caleb Thayer held a great leather-bound Bible on his knees, and was reading aloud in a solemn voice. His wife sat straight in her chair, her large face tilted with a judicial and argumentative air, and Rebecca's red cheeks bloomed out more brilliantly in the heat of the fire. She sat next her mother, and her smooth dark head with its carven comb arose from her Sunday kerchief with a like carriage. She and her mother did not look alike, but their motions were curiously similar, and perhaps gave evidence to a subtler resemblance in character and motive power.

Ephraim, undersized for his age, in his hitching, home-made clothes, twisted himself about when Barnabas entered, and stared at him with slow regard. He eyed the smooth, scented hair, the black satin vest with a pattern of blue flowers on it, the blue coat with brass buttons, and the shining boots, then he whistled softly under his breath.

"Ephraim!" said his mother, sharply. She had a heavy voice and a slight lisp, which seemed to make it more impressive and more distinctively her own. Caleb read on ponderously.

"Where ye goin', Barney?" Ephraim inquired, with a chuckle and a grin, over the back of his chair.

"Ephraim!" repeated his mother. Her blue eyes frowned around his sister at him under their heavy sandy brows.

Ephraim twisted himself back into position. "Jest wanted to know where he was goin'," he muttered.

Barnabas stood by the window brushing his fine bell hat with a white duck's wing. He was a handsome youth; his profile showed clear and fine in the light, between the sharp points of his dicky bound about by his high stock.　His cheeks were as red as his sister's.

When he put on his hat and opened the door, his mother herself interrupted Caleb's reading.

" Don't you stay later than nine o'clock, Barnabas," said she.

The young man murmured something unintelligibly, but his tone was resentful.

" I ain't going to have you out as long as you were last Sabbath night," said his mother, in quick return.　She jerked her chin down heavily as if it were made of iron.

Barnabas went out quickly, and shut the door with a thud.

" If he was a few years younger, I'd make him come back an' shut that door over again," said his mother.

Caleb read on ; he was reading now one of the imprecatory psalms.　Deborah's blue eyes gleamed with warlike energy as she listened : she confused King David's enemies with those people who crossed her own will.

Barnabas went out of the yard, which was wide and deep on the south side of the house.　The bright young grass was all snowed over with cherry blossoms.　Three great cherry-trees stood in a row through the centre of the yard ; they had been white with blossoms, but now they were turning green ; and the apple-trees were in flower.

There were many apple-trees behind the stone-walls that bordered the wood. The soft blooming branches looked strangely incongruous in the keen air. The western sky was clear and yellow, and there were a few reefs of violet cloud along it. Barnabas looked up at the apple blossoms over his head, and wondered if there would be a frost. From their apple orchard came a large share of the Thayer income, and Barnabas was vitally interested in such matters now, for he was to be married the last of June to Charlotte Barnard. He often sat down with a pencil and slate, and calculated, with intricate sums, the amounts of his income and their probable expenses. He had made up his mind that Charlotte should have one new silk gown every year, and two new bonnets — one for summer and one for winter. His mother had often noted, with scorn, that Charlotte Barnard wore her summer bonnet with another ribbon on it winters, and, moreover, had not had a new bonnet for three years.

"She looks handsomer in it than any girl in town, if she hasn't," Barnabas had retorted with quick resentment, but he nevertheless felt sensitive on the subject of Charlotte's bonnet, and resolved that she should have a white one trimmed with gauze ribbons for summer, and one of drawn silk, like Rebecca's, for winter, only the silk should be blue instead of pink, because Charlotte was fair.

Barnabas had even pondered with tender concern, before he bought his fine flowered satin waistcoat, if he might not put the money it would cost into a

"BARNABAS WENT OUT QUICKLY"

bonnet for Charlotte, but he had not dared to propose it. Once he had bought a little blue-figured shawl for her, and her father had bade her return it.

"I ain't goin' to have any young sparks buyin' your clothes while you are under my roof," he had said.

Charlotte had given the shawl back to her lover. "Father don't feel as if I ought to take it, and I guess you'd better keep it now, Barney," she said, with regretful tears in her eyes.

Barnabas had the blue shawl nicely folded in the bottom of his little hair-cloth trunk, which he always kept locked.

After a quarter of a mile the stone-walls and the spray of apple blossoms ended; there was a short stretch of new fence, and a new cottage-house only partly done. The yard was full of lumber, and a ladder slanted to the roof, which gleamed out with the fresh pinky yellow of unpainted pine.

Barnabas stood before the house a few minutes, staring at it. Then he walked around it slowly, his face upturned. Then he went in the front door, swinging himself up over the sill, for there were no steps, and brushing the sawdust carefully from his clothes when he was inside. He went all over the house, climbing a ladder to the second story, and viewing with pride the two chambers under the slant of the new roof. He had repelled with scorn his father's suggestion that he have a one-story instead of a story-and-a-half house. Caleb had an inordinate horror and fear of wind, and his father, who had built the house in which he lived, had it before him. Deborah often descanted indignantly upon the folly of sleeping in little tucked-up bedrooms instead of good chambers, because folks' fathers had been scared to death of wind, and Barnabas agreed with her. If he had inherited any of his father's and grandfather's terror of wind, he made no manifestation of it.

In the lower story of the new cottage were two square front rooms like those in his father's house, and behind them the great kitchen with a bedroom out of it, and a roof of its own.

Barnabas paused at last in the kitchen, and stood quite still, leaning against a window casement. The windows were not in, and the spaces let in the cool air and low light. Outside was a long reach of field sloping gently upward. In the distance, at the top of the hill, sharply outlined against the sky, was a black angle of roof and a great chimney. A thin column of smoke rose out of it, straight and dark. That was where Charlotte Barnard lived.

Barnabas looked out and saw the smoke rising from the chimney of the Barnard house. There was a little hollow in the field that was quite blue with violets, and he noted that absently. A team passed on the road outside; it was as if he saw and heard everything from the innermost recesses of his own life, and everything seemed strange and far off.

He turned to go, but suddenly stood still in the

middle of the kitchen, as if some one had stopped him. He looked at the new fireless hearth, through the open door into the bedroom which he would occupy after he was married to Charlotte, and through others into the front rooms, which would be apartments of simple state, not so closely connected with every-day life. The kitchen windows would be sunny. Charlotte would think it a pleasant room.

"Her rocking-chair can set there," said Barnabas aloud. The tears came into his eyes; he stepped forward, laid his smooth boyish cheek against a partition wall of this new house, and kissed it. It was a fervent demonstration, not towards Charlotte alone, nor the joy to come to him within those walls, but to all life and love and nature, although he did not comprehend it. He half sobbed as he turned away; his thoughts seemed to dazzle his brain, and he could not feel his feet. He passed through the north front room, which would be the little-used parlor, to the door, and suddenly started at a long black shadow on the floor. It vanished as he went on, and might have been due to his excited fancy, which seemed substantial enough to cast shadows.

"I shall marry Charlotte, we shall live here together all our lives, and die here," thought Barnabas, as he went up the hill. "I shall lie in my coffin in the north room, and it will all be over," but his heart leaped with joy. He stepped out proudly like a soldier in a battalion, he threw back his shoulders in his Sunday coat.

The yellow glow was paling in the west, the evening air was like a cold breath in his face. He could see the firelight flickering upon the kitchen wall of the Barnard house as he drew near. He came up into the yard and caught a glimpse of a fair head in the ruddy glow. There was a knocker on the door; he raised it gingerly and let it fall. It made but a slight clatter, but a woman's shadow moved immediately across the yard outside, and Barnabas heard the inner door open. He threw open the outer one himself, and Charlotte stood there smiling, and softly decorous. Neither of them spoke. Barnabas glanced at the inner door to see if it were closed, then he caught Charlotte's hands and kissed her.

"You shouldn't do so, Barnabas," whispered Charlotte, turning her face away. She was as tall as Barnabas, and as handsome.

"Yes, I should," persisted Barnabas, all radiant, and his face pursued hers around her shoulder.

"It's pretty cold out, ain't it ?" said Charlotte, in a chiding voice which she could scarcely control.

"I've been in to see our house. Give me one more kiss. Oh, Charlotte !"

"Charlotte !" cried a deep voice, and the lovers started apart.

"I'm coming, father," Charlotte cried out. She opened the door and went soberly into the kitchen, with Barnabas at her heels. Her father, mother, and Aunt Sylvia Crane sat there in the red gleam of the firelight and gathering twilight. Sylvia sat a little behind the others, and her face in her white cap had the shadowy delicacy of one of the flowering apple sprays outside.

"How d'ye do?" said Barnabas in a brave tone which was slightly aggressive. Charlotte's mother and aunt responded rather nervously.

"How's your mother, Barnabas?" inquired Mrs. Barnard.

"She's pretty well, thank you."

Charlotte pulled forward a chair for her lover; he had just seated himself, when Cephas Barnard spoke in a voice as sudden and gruff as a dog's bark. Barnabas started, and his chair grated on the sanded floor.

"Light the candle, Charlotte," said Cephas, and Charlotte obeyed. She lighted the candle on the high shelf, then she sat down next Barnabas. Cephas glanced around at them. He was a small man, with a thin face in a pale film of white locks and beard, but his black eyes gleamed out of it with sharp fixedness. Barnabas looked back at him unflinchingly, and there was a curious likeness between the two pairs of black eyes. Indeed, there had been years ago a somewhat close relationship between the Thayers and the Barnards, and it was not strange if one common note was repeated generations hence.

Cephas had been afraid lest Barnabas should, all unperceived in the dusk, hold his daughter's hand, or venture upon other loverlike familiarity. That was the reason why he had ordered the candle lighted when it was scarcely dark enough to warrant it.

But Barnabas seemed scarcely to glance at his sweetheart as he sat there beside her, although in some subtle fashion, perhaps by some finer spiritual vision, not a turn of her head, nor a fleeting expression on her face, like a wind of the soul, escaped him. He saw always Charlotte's beloved features high and pure, almost severe, but softened with youthful bloom, her head with fair hair plaited in a smooth circle, with one long curl behind each ear. Charlotte would scarcely have said he had noticed, but he knew well she had on a new gown of delaine in a mottled purple pattern, her worked-muslin collar, and her mother's gold beads which she had given her.

Barnabas kept listening anxiously for the crackle of the hearth fire in the best room; he hoped Charlotte had lighted the fire, and they should soon go in there by themselves. They usually did of a Sunday night, but sometimes Cephas forbade his daughter to light the fire and prohibited any solitary communion between the lovers.

"If Barnabas Thayer can't set here with the rest of us, he can go home," he proclaimed at times, and he had done so to-night. Charlotte had acquiesced forlornly; there was nothing else for her to do. Early in her childhood she had learned along with her primer her father's character, and the obligations it imposed upon her.

"You must be a good girl, and mind; it's your father's way," her mother used to tell her. Mrs.

Barnard herself had spelt out her husband like a hard and seemingly cruel text in the Bible. She marvelled at its darkness in her light, but she believed in it reverently, and even pugnaciously.

The large, loosely built woman, with her heavy, sliding step, waxed fairly decisive, and her soft, meek-lidded eyes gleamed hard and prominent when her elder sister, Hannah, dared inveigh against Cephas.

" I tell you it is his way," said Sarah Barnard. And she said it as if " his way " was the way of the King.

" His way !" Hannah would sniff back. " His way ! Keepin' you all on rye meal one spell, an' not lettin' you eat a mite of Injun, an' then keepin' you on Injun without a mite of rye ! Makin' you eat nothin' but greens an' garden stuff, an' jest turnin' you out to graze an' chew your cuds like horned animals one spell, an' then makin' you live on meat ! Lettin' you go abroad when he takes a notion, an' then keepin' you an' Charlotte in the house a year !"

" It's his way, an' I ain't goin' to have anything said against it," Sarah Barnard would retort stanchly, and her sister would sniff back again. Charlotte was as loyal as her mother; she did not like it if even her lover intimated anything in disfavor of her father.

No matter how miserable she was in consequence of her acquiescence with her father's will, she sternly persisted.

To-night she knew that Barnabas was waiting impatiently for her signal to leave the rest of the company and go with her into the front room; there was also a tender involuntary impatience and longing in every nerve of her body, but nobody would have suspected it; she sat there as calmly as if Barnabas were old Squire Payne, who sometimes came in of a Sabbath evening, and seemed to be listening intently to her mother and her Aunt Sylvia talking about the spring cleaning.

Cephas and Barnabas were grimly silent. The young man suspected that Cephas had prohibited the front room; he was indignant about that, and the way in which Charlotte had been summoned in from the entry, and he had no diplomacy.

Charlotte, under her calm exterior, grew uneasy; she glanced at her mother, who glanced back. It was to both women as if they felt by some subtle sense the brewing of a tempest. Charlotte unobtrusively moved her chair a little nearer her lover's; her purple delaine skirt swept his knee; both of them blushed and trembled with Cephas's black eyes upon them.

Charlotte never knew quite how it began, but her father suddenly flung out a dangerous topic like a long-argued bone of contention, and he and Barnabas were upon it. Barnabas was a Democrat, and Cephas was a Whig, and neither ever forgot it of the other. None of the women fairly understood the point at issue; it was as if they drew back their feminine skirts and listened amazed and trembling to this male hubbub over something outside their province. Charlotte grew paler and paler. She looked piteously at her mother.

"Now, father, don't," Sarah ventured once or twice, but it was like a sparrow piping against the north wind.

Charlotte laid her hand on her lover's arm and kept it there, but he did not seem to heed her. "Don't," she said; "don't, Barnabas. I think there's going to be a frost to-night; don't you?" But nobody heard her. Sylvia Crane, in the background, clutched the arms of her rocking-chair with her thin hands.

Suddenly both men began hurling insulting epithets at each other. Cephas sprang up, waving his right arm fiercely, and Barnabas shook off Charlotte's hand and was on his feet.

"Get out of here!" shouted Cephas, in a hoarse voice—"get out of here! Get out of this house, an' don't you ever darse darken these doors again while the Lord Almighty reigns!" The old man was almost inarticulate; he waved his arms, wagged his head, and stamped; he looked like a white blur with rage.

"I never will, by the Lord Almighty!" returned Barnabas, in an awful voice; then the door slammed after him. Charlotte sprang up.

"Set down!" shouted Cephas. Charlotte rushed forward. "You set down!" her father repeated; her mother caught hold of her dress.

"Charlotte, do set down," she whispered, glancing

at her husband in terror. But Charlotte pulled her dress away.

"Don't you stop me, mother. I am not going to have him turned out this way," she said. Her father advanced threateningly, but she set her young, strong shoulders against him and pushed past out of the door. The door was slammed to after her and the bolt shot, but she did not heed that. She ran across the yard, calling: "Barney! Barney! Barney! Come back!" Barnabas was already out in the road; he never turned his head, and kept on. Charlotte hurried after him. "Barney," she cried, her voice breaking with sobs—"Barney, do come back. You aren't mad at me, are you?" Barney never turned his head; the distance between them widened as Charlotte followed, calling. She stopped suddenly, and stood watching her lover's dim retreating back, straining with his rapid strides.

"Barney Thayer," she called out, in an angry, imperious tone, "if you're ever coming back, you come now!"

But Barney kept on as if he did not hear. Charlotte gasped for breath as she watched him; she could scarcely help her feet running after him, but she would not follow him any farther. She did not call him again; in a minute she turned around and went back to the house, holding her head high in the dim light.

She did not try to open the door; she was sure it was locked, and she was too proud. She sat down on the flat, cool door-stone, and remained there as dusky and motionless against the old gray panel of the door as the shadow of some inanimate object that had never moved.

The wind began to rise, and at the same time the full moon, impelled softly upward by force as unseen as thought. Charlotte's fair head gleamed out abruptly in the moonlight like a pale flower, but the folds of her mottled purple skirt were as vaguely dark as the foliage on the lilac-bush beside her. All at once the flowering branches on a wide-spreading apple-tree cut the gloom like great silvery wings of a brooding bird. The grass in the yard was like a shaggy silver fleece. Charlotte paid no more attention to it all than to her own breath, or a clock tick which she would have to withdraw from herself to hear.

A low voice, which was scarcely more than a whisper, called her, a slender figure twisted itself around the front corner of the house like a vine. "Charlotte, you there?" Charlotte did not hear. Then the whisper came again. "Charlotte!"

Charlotte looked around then.

A slender white hand reached out in the gloom around the corner and beckoned. "Charlotte, come; come quick."

Charlotte did not stir.

"Charlotte, do come. Your mother's dreadful afraid you'll catch cold. The front door is open."

Charlotte sat quite rigid. The slender figure began moving towards her stealthily, keeping close to the house, advancing with frequent pauses like a wary bird. When she got close to Charlotte she reached down and touched her shoulder timidly. "Oh, Charlotte, don't you feel bad? He'd ought to know your father by this time; he'll get over it and come back," she whispered.

"I don't want him to come back," Charlotte whispered fiercely in return.

Sylvia stared at her helplessly. Charlotte's face looked strange and hard in the moonlight. "Your mother's dreadful worried," she whispered again, presently. "She thinks you'll catch cold. I come out of the front door on purpose so you can go in that way. Your father's asleep in his chair. He told your mother not to unbolt this door to-night, and she didn't darse to. But we went past him real still to the front one, an' you can slip in there and get up to your chamber without his seeing you. Oh, Charlotte, do come!"

Charlotte arose, and she and Sylvia went around to the front door. Sylvia crept close to the house as before, but Charlotte walked boldly along in the moonlight. "Charlotte, I'm dreadful afraid he'll see you," Sylvia pleaded, but Charlotte would not change her course.

Just as they reached the front door it was slammed with a quick puff of wind in their faces. They heard Mrs. Barnard's voice calling piteously. "Oh, father, do let her in!" it implored.

"Don't you worry, mother," Charlotte called out. "I'll go home with Aunt Sylvia."

"Oh, Charlotte!" her mother's voice broke in sobs.

"Don't you worry, mother," Charlotte repeated, with an unrelenting tone in the comforting words. "I'll go right home with Aunt Sylvia. Come," she said, imperatively to her aunt, "I am not going to stand here any longer," and she went out into the road, and hastened down it, as Barnabas had done.

"I'll take her right home with me," Sylvia called to her sister in a trembling voice (nobody knew how afraid she was of Cephas); and she followed Charlotte.

Sylvia lived on an old road that led from the main one a short distance beyond the new house, so the way led past it. Charlotte went on at such a pace that Sylvia could scarcely keep up with her. She slid along in her wake, panting softly, and lifting her skirts out of the evening dew. She was trembling with sympathy for Charlotte, and she had also a worry of her own. When they reached the new house she fairly sobbed outright, but Charlotte went past in her stately haste without a murmur.

"Oh, Charlotte, don't feel so bad," mourned her aunt. "I know it will all come right." But Charlotte made no reply. Her dusky skirts swept around the bushes at the corner of the road, and Sylvia hurried tremulously after her.

Neither of them dreamed that Barnabas watched

them, standing in one of the front rooms of his new house. He had gone in there when he fled from Cephas Barnard's, and had not yet been home. He recognized Charlotte's motions as quickly as her face, and knew Sylvia's voice, although he could not distinguish what she said. He watched them turn the corner of the other road, and thought that Charlotte was going to spend the night with her aunt—he did not dream why. He had resolved to stay where he was in his desolate new house, and not go home himself.

A great grief and resentment against the whole world and life itself swelled high within him. It was as if he lost sight of individual antagonists, and burned to dash life itself in the face because he existed. The state of happiness so exalted that it became almost holiness, in which he had been that very night, flung him to lower depths when it was retroverted. He had gone back to first causes in the one and he did the same in the other; his joy had reached out into eternity, and so did his misery. His natural religious bent, inherited from generations of Puritans, and kept in its channel by his training from infancy, made it impossible for him to conceive of sympathy or antagonism in its fullest sense apart from God.

Sitting on a pile of shavings in a corner of the north room, he fairly hugged himself with fierce partisanship. "What have I done to be treated in this way?" he demanded, setting his face ahead in the darkness; and he did not see Cephas Barnard's threatening countenance, but another, gigantic with its vague outlines, which his fancy could not limit, confronting him with terrible negative power like a stone image. He struck out against it, and the blows fell back on his own heart.

"What have I done?" he demanded over and over of this great immovable and silent consciousness which he realized before him. "Have I not kept all thy commandments from childhood? Have I ever failed to praise thee as the giver of my happiness, and ask thy blessing upon it? What have I done that it should be taken away? It was given to me only to be taken away. Why was it given to me, then?—that I might be mocked? Oh, I am mocked, I am mocked!" he cried out, in a great rage, and he struck out in the darkness, and his heart leaped with futile pain. The possibility that his misery might not be final never occurred to him. It never occurred to him that he could enter Cephas Barnard's house again, ask his pardon, and marry Charlotte. It seemed to him settled and inevitable; he could not grasp any choice in the matter.

Barnabas finally threw himself back on the pile of shavings, and lay there sullenly. Great gusts of cold wind came in at the windows at intervals, a loose board somewhere in the house rattled, the trees outside murmured heavily.

"There won't be a frost," Barnabas thought, his mind going apace on its old routine in spite of its turmoil. Then he thought with the force of an oath

that he did not care if there was a frost. All the
trees this spring had blossomed only for him and
Charlotte; now there was no longer any use in that;
let the blossoms blast and fall!

CHAPTER II

Sylvia Crane's house was the one in which her grandmother had been born, and was the oldest house in the village. It was known as the "old Crane place." It had never been painted, it was shedding its flapping gray shingles like gray scales, the roof sagged in a mossy hollow before the chimney, the windows and doors were awry, and the whole house was full of undulations and wavering lines, which gave it a curiously unreal look in broad daylight. In the moonlight it was the shadowy edifice built of a dream.

As Sylvia and Charlotte came to the front door it seemed as if they might fairly walk through it as through a gray shadow; but Sylvia stooped, and her shoulders strained with seemingly incongruous force, as if she were spending it to roll away a shadow. On the flat doorstep lay a large round stone, pushed close against the door. There were no locks and keys in the old Crane place; only bolts. Sylvia could not fasten the doors on the inside when she went away, so she adopted this expedient, which had been regarded with favor by her mother and grandmother before her, and illustrated natures full of gentle fallacies which went far to make existence comfortable.

Always on leaving the house alone the Crane women had bolted the side door, which was the one in common use, gone out the front one, and laboriously rolled this same round stone before it. Sylvia reasoned as her mother and grandmother before her, with the same simplicity: "When the stone's in front of the door, folks must know there ain't anybody to home, because they couldn't put it there if they was."

And when some neighbor had argued that the evil-disposed might roll away the stone and enter at will, Sylvia had replied, with the innocent conservatism with which she settled an argument, "Nobody ever did."

To-night she rolled away the stone to the corner of the door-step, where it had lain through three generations when the Crane women were at home, and sighed with regret that she had defended the door with it. "I wish I hadn't put the stone up," she thought. "If I hadn't, mebbe he'd gone in an' waited." She opened the door, and the gloom of the house, deeper than the gloom of the night, appeared. "You wait here a minute," she said to Charlotte, "an' I'll go in an' light a candle."

Charlotte waited, leaning against the door-post. There was a flicker of fire within. Then Sylvia held the flaring candle towards her. "Come in," she said; "the candle's lit."

There was a bed of coals on the hearth in the best room; Sylvia had made a fire there before going over to her sister's, but it had burned low. The glow of the coals and the smoky flare of the candle lighted the room uncertainly, scattering and not dispelling the shadows. There was a primly festive air in the room. The flag-bottomed chairs stood by twos, finely canted towards each other, against the wall; the one great hair-cloth rocker stood ostentatiously in advance of them, facing the hearth fire; the long level of the hair-cloth sofa gleamed out under stiff sweeps of the white fringed curtains at the window behind it. The books on the glossy card-table were set canting towards each other like the chairs, and with their gilt edges towards the light. And Sylvia had set also on the table a burnished pitcher of a rosy copper-color full of apple blossoms.

She looked at it when she had set the candle on the shelf. It seemed to her that all the light in the room centred on it, and it shone in her eyes like a copper lamp.

Charlotte also glanced at it. "Why, Richard must have come while you were over to our house," she said.

"It don't make any odds if he did," returned Sylvia, with a faint blush and a bridle. Sylvia was much younger than her sister. Standing there in the dim light she did not look so much older than her niece. Her figure had the slim angularity and primness which are sometimes seen in elderly women who are not matrons, and she had donned a little white lace cap at thirty, but her face had still a delicate bloom, and the wistful wonder of expression which belongs to youth.

However, she never thought of Charlotte as anything but a child as compared with herself. Sylvia felt very old, and the more so that she grudged her years painfully. She stirred up the fire a little, holding back her shiny black silk skirt carefully. Charlotte stood leaning against the shelf, looking moodily down at the fire.

"I wouldn't feel bad if I was you, Charlotte," Sylvia ventured, timidly.

"I guess we'd better go to bed pretty soon," returned Charlotte. "It must be late."

"Had you rather sleep with me, Charlotte, or sleep in the spare chamber?"

"I guess I'll go in the spare chamber."

"Well, I'll get you a night-gown."

Both of their faces were sober, but perfectly staid. They bade each other good-night without a quiver; but Charlotte, after she had said her dutiful and unquestioning prayer, and lay folded in Sylvia's ruffled night-gown in the best bed, shook with great sobs. "Poor Barney!" she kept muttering. "Poor Barney! poor Barney!"

The doors were all open, and once she thought she heard a sob from below, then concluded she must be mistaken. But she was not, for Sylvia Crane was lamenting as sorely as the younger maiden up-stairs.

"Poor Richard!" she repeated, piteously. "Poor Richard! There he came, and the stone was up, and he had to go away."

The faces which were so clear to the hearts of both women, as if they were before their eyes, had a certain similarity. Indeed, Richard Alger and Barnabas Thayer were distantly related on the mother's side, and people said they looked enough alike to be brothers. Sylvia saw the same type of face as Charlotte, only Richard's face was older, for he was six years older than she.

"If I hadn't put the stone up," she moaned, "maybe he would have thought I didn't hear him knock, an' he'd come in an' waited. Poor Richard, I dunno what he thought! It's the first time it's happened for eighteen years."

Sylvia, as she lay there, looked backward, and it seemed to her that the eighteen years were all made up of the Sunday nights on which Richard Alger had come to see her, as if they were all that made them immortal and redeemed them from the dead past. She had endured grief, but love alone made the past years stand out for her. Sylvia, in looking back over eighteen years, forgot the father, mother, and sister who had died in that time; their funeral trains passed before her eyes like so many shadows. She forgot all their cares and her own; she forgot how she had nursed her bedridden mother for ten years; she forgot everything but those blessed Sunday nights on which Richard Alger had come. She

called to mind every little circumstance connected
with them—how she had adorned the best room by
slow degrees, saving a few cents at a time from her
sparse income, because he sat in it every Sunday
night; how she had had the bed which her mother
and grandmother kept there removed because the
fashion had changed, and the guilty audacity with
which she had purchased a hair-cloth sofa to take its
place.

That adorning of the best room had come to be a
religion with Sylvia Crane. As faithfully as any
worshipper of the Greek deity she laid her offerings,
her hair-cloth sofa and rocker, her copper-gilt pitcher
of apple blossoms, upon the altar of love.

Sylvia recalled, sobbing more piteously in the
darkness, sundry dreams, which had never been realized, of herself and Richard sitting side by side and
hand in hand, as confessed lovers, on that sofa.
Richard Alger, during all those eighteen years, had
never made love to Sylvia, unless his constant attend-
ance upon Sabbath evenings could be so construed,
as it was in that rural neighborhood, and as Sylvia
was fain to construe it in her innocent heart.

It is doubtful if Sylvia, in her perfect decorum and
long-fostered maiden reserve, fairly knew that Richard Alger had never made love to her. She scarcely
expected her dreams of endearments to be realized;
she regarded them, except in desperate moods, with
shame. If her old admirer had, indeed, attempted
to sit by her side upon that hair-cloth sofa and hold

her hand, she would have arisen as if propelled by stiff springs of modest virtue. She did not fairly *know* that she was not made love to after the most honorable and orthodox fashion without a word of endearment or a caress; for she had been trained to regard love as one of the most secret of the laws of nature, to be concealed, with shamefaced air, even from herself; but she did know that Richard had never asked her to marry him, and for that she was impatient without any self-reserve; she was even confidential with her sister, Charlotte's mother.

" I don't want to say anything outside," she once said, " but I do think it would be a good deal better for him if we was settled down. He ain't half taken care of since his mother died."

" He's got money enough," returned Mrs. Barnard.

" That can't buy everything."

" Well, I don't pity him; I pity you," said Mrs. Barnard.

" I guess I shall get along a while longer, as far as that goes," Sylvia had replied to her sister, with some pride. " I ain't worried on my account."

" Women don't worry much on their own accounts, but they've got accounts," returned Mrs. Barnard, with more contempt for her sister than she had ever shown for herself. " You're gettin' older, Sylvy."

" I know it," Sylvia had replied, with a quick shrinking, as if from a blow.

The passing years, as they passed for her, stung her like swarming bees, with bitter humiliation; but never for herself, only for Richard. Nobody knew how painfully she counted the years, how she would fain have held time back with her thin hands, how futilely and pitifully she set her loving heart against it, and not for herself and her own vanity, but for the sake of her lover. She had come, in the single-ness of her heart, to regard herself in the light of a species of coin to be expended wholly for the happi-ness and interest of one man. Any depreciation in its value was of account only as it affected him.

Sylvia Crane, sitting in the meeting-house of a Sunday, used to watch the young girls coming in, as radiant and flawless as new flowers, in their Sunday bests, with a sort of admiring envy, which could do them no harm, but which tore her own heart.

When she should have been contrasting the wick-edness of her soul with the grace of the Divine Model, she was contrasting her fading face with the youthful bloom of the young girls. " He'd ought to marry one of them," she thought; " he'd ought to, by good rights." It never occurred to Sylvia that Richard also was growing older, and that he was, moreover, a few years older than she. She thought of him as an immortal youth; his face was the same to her as when she had first seen it.

When it came before a subtler vision than her bodily one, there in the darkness and loneliness of this last Sunday night, it wore the beauty and inno-cent freshness of a child. If Richard Alger could have seen his own face as the woman who loved him saw it, he could never have doubted his own immortality.

"There he came, an' the stone was up, an' he had to go away," moaned Sylvia, catching her breath softly. Many a time she had pitied Richard because he had not the little womanly care which men need; she had worried lest his stockings were not darned, and his food not properly cooked; but to-night she had another and strange anxiety. She worried lest she herself had hurt him and sent him home with a heavy heart.

Sylvia had gone about for the last few days with her delicate face as irresponsibly calm as a sweet-pea; nobody had dreamed of the turmoil in her heart. On the Wednesday night before she had nearly reached the climax of her wishes. Richard had come, departing from his usual custom—he had never called except on Sunday before—and remained later. It was ten o'clock before he went home. He had been very silent all the evening, and had sat soberly in the great best rocking-chair, which was, in a way, his throne of state, with Sylvia on the sofa on his right. Many a time she had dreamed that he came over there and sat down beside her, and that night it had come to pass.

Just before ten o'clock he had arisen hesitatingly; she thought it was to take leave, but she sat waiting and trembling. They had sat in the twilight and young moonlight all the evening. Richard had checked her when she attempted to light a candle.

That had somehow made the evening seem strange, and freighted with consequences; and besides the white light of the moon, full of mystic influence, there was something subtler and more magnetic, which could sway more than the tides, even the passions of the human heart, present, and they both felt it.

Neither had said much, and they had been sitting there nearly two hours, when Richard had arisen, and moved curiously, rather as if he was drawn than walked of his own volition, over to the sofa. He sank down upon it with a little cough. Sylvia moved away a little with an involuntary motion, which was pure maidenliness.

"It's getting late," remarked Richard, trying to make his voice careless, but it fell in spite of him into deep cadences.

"It ain't very late, I guess," Sylvia had returned, tremblingly.

"I ought to be going home."

Then there was silence for a while. Sylvia glanced sidewise, timidly and adoringly, at Richard's smoothly shaven face, pale as marble in the moonlight, and waited, her heart throbbing.

"I've been coming here a good many years," Richard observed finally, and his own voice had a solemn tremor.

Sylvia made an almost inarticulate assent.

"I've been thinking lately," said Richard; then he paused. They could hear the great clock out in

"SYLVIA GLANCED TIMIDLY AT RICHARD'S SMOOTHLY-SHAVEN FACE"

the kitchen tick. Sylvia waited, her very soul straining, although shrinking at the same time, to hear.

"I've been thinking lately," said Richard again, "that—maybe—it would be wise for—us both to—make some different arrangement."

Sylvia bent her head low. Richard paused for the second time. "I have always meant—" he began again, but just then the clock in the kitchen struck the first stroke of ten. Richard caught his breath and arose quickly. Never in his long courtship had he remained as late as that at Sylvia Crane's. It was as if a life-long habit struck as well as the clock, and decided his times for him.

"I must be going," said he, speaking against the bell notes. Sylvia arose without a word of dissent, but Richard spoke as if she had remonstrated.

"I'll come again next Sunday night," said he, apologetically.

Sylvia followed him to the door. They bade each other good-night decorously, with never a parting kiss, as they had done for years. Richard went out of sight down the white gleaming road, and she went in and to bed, with her heart in a great tumult of expectation and joyful fear.

She had tried to wait calmly for Sunday night. She had done her neat household tasks as usual, her face and outward demeanor were sweetly unruffled, but her thoughts seemed shivering with rainbows that constantly dazzled her with sweet shocks when her eyes met them. Her feet seemed constantly flying before her into the future, and she could scarcely tell where she might really be, in the present or in her dreams, which had suddenly grown so real.

On Sunday morning she had curled her soft fair hair, and arranged with trepidation one long light curl outside her bonnet on each side of her face. Her bonnet was tied under her chin with a green ribbon, and she had a little feathery green wreath around her face inside the rim. Her wide silk skirt was shot with green and blue, and rustled as she walked up the aisle to her pew. People stared after her without knowing why. There was no tangible change in her appearance. She had worn that same green shot silk many Sabbaths; her bonnet was three summers old; the curls drooping on her cheeks were an innovation, but the people did not recognize the change as due to them. Sylvia herself had looked with pleased wonder at her face in the glass; it was as if all her youthful beauty had suddenly come up, like a withered rose which is dipped in a vase.

" I sha'n't look so terrible old side of him when I go out bride," she reflected, happily, smiling fondly at herself. All the way to meeting that Sunday morning she saw her face as she had seen it in the glass, and it was as if she walked with something finer than herself.

Richard Alger sat with the choir in a pew beside the pulpit, at right angles with the others. He had a fine tenor voice, and had sung in the choir ever since he was a boy. When Sylvia sat down in her

place, which was in full range of his eyes, he glanced
at her without turning his head; he meant to look
away again directly, so as not to be observed, but her
face held him. A color slowly flamed out on his pale
brown cheeks; his eyes became intense and abstract-
ed. A soprano singer nudged the girl at her side;
they both glanced at him and tittered, but he did not
notice it.

Sylvia knew that he was looking at her, but she
never looked at him. She sat soberly waving a little
brown fan before her face; the light curls stirred
softly. She wondered what he thought of them; if
he considered them too young for her, and silly; but
he did not see them at all. He had no eye for details.
And neither did she even hear his fine tenor, still
sweet and powerful, leading all the other male voices
when the choir stood up to sing. She thought only
of Richard himself.

After meeting, when she went down the aisle, several women had spoken to her, inquired concerning
her health, and told her, with wondering eyes, that
she looked well. Richard was far behind her, but
she did not look around. They very seldom accosted
each other, unless it was unavoidable, in any public
place. Still, Sylvia, going out with gentle flounces of
her green shot silk, knew well that Richard's eyes followed her, and his thought was close at her side.

After she got home from meeting that Sunday,
Sylvia Crane did not know how to pass the time until the evening. She could not keep herself calm and

composed as was her wont on the Sabbath day. She changed her silk for a common gown; she tried to sit down and read the Bible quietly and with under-standing, but she could not. She turned to Canticles, and read a page or two. She had always believed loyally and devoutly in the application to Christ and the Church; but suddenly now, as she read, the re-strained decorously chanting New England love-song in her maiden heart had leaped into the fervid meas-ures of the Oriental King. She shut the Bible with a clap. "I ain't giving the right meaning to it," she said, sternly, aloud.

She put away the Bible, went into the pantry, and got out some bread and cheese for her luncheon, but she could eat nothing. She picked the apple blos-soms and arranged them in the copper-gilt pitcher on the best-room table. She even dusted off the hair-cloth sofa and rocker, with many compunctions, be-cause it was Sunday. "I know I hadn't ought to do it to-day," she murmured, apologetically, "but they do get terrible dusty, and need dusting every day, and he is real particular, and he'll have on his best clothes."

Finally, just before twilight, Sylvia, unable to settle herself, had gone over to her sister's for a little call. Richard never came before eight o'clock, except in winter, when it was dark earlier. There was a cer-tain half-shamefaced reserve about his visits. He knew well enough that people looked from their win-dows as he passed, and said, facetiously, "There goes

Richard Alger to court Sylvy Crane." He preferred slipping past in a half-light, in which he did not seem so plain to himself, and could think himself less plain to other people.

Sylvia, detained at her sister's by the quarrel between Cephas and Barnabas, had arisen many a time to take leave, all palpitating with impatience, but her sister had begged her, in a distressed whisper, to remain.

" I guess you can get along without Richard Alger one Sunday evening," she had said finally, quite aloud, and quite harshly. " I guess your own sister has just as much claim on you as he has. I dunno what's going to be done. I don't believe Charlotte's father will let her in the house to-night."

Poor Sylvia had sunk back in her chair. To her sensitive conscience the duty nearest at hand seemed always to bark the loudest, and the precious moments had gone by until she knew that Richard had come, found the stone before the door, and gone away, and all her sweet turmoil of hope and anticipation had gone for naught.

Sylvia, lying there awake that night, her mind carrying her back over all that had gone before, had no doubt that this was the end of everything. Not originally a subtle discerner of character, she had come insensibly to know Richard so well that certain results from certain combinations of circumstances in his life were as plain and inevitable to her as the outcome of a simple sum in mathematics. " He'd got 'most out of his track for once," she groaned out softly, "but now he's pushed back in so hard he can't get out again if he wants to. I dunno how he's going to get along."

Sylvia, with the roof settling over her head, with not so much upon her few sterile acres to feed her as to feed the honey-bees and birds, with her heart in greater agony because its string of joy had been strained so high and sweetly before it snapped, did not lament over herself at all; neither did she over the other woman who lay up-stairs suffering in a similar case. She lamented only over Richard living alone and unministered to until he died.

When daylight came she got up, dressed herself, and prepared breakfast. Charlotte came down before it was ready. "Let me help get breakfast," she said, with an assumption of energy, standing in the kitchen doorway in her pretty mottled purple delaine. The purple was the shade of columbine, and very becoming to Charlotte. In spite of her sleepless night, her fine firm tints had not faded; she was too young and too strong and too full of involuntary resistance. She had done up her fair hair compactly; her chin had its usual proud lift.

Sylvia, shrinking as if before some unseen enemy as she moved about, her face all wan and weary, glanced at her half resentfully. "I guess she 'ain't had any such night as I have," she thought. "Girls don't know much about it."

"No, I don't need any help," she replied, aloud.

"I 'ain't got anything to do but to stir up an Injun cake. You've got your best dress on. You'd better go and sit down."

"It won't hurt my dress any." Charlotte glanced down half scornfully at her purple skirt. It had lost all its glory for her. She was not even sure that Barney had seen it.

"Set down. I've got breakfast 'most ready," Sylvia said, again, more peremptorily than she was wont, and Charlotte sat down in the hollow-backed cherry rocking-chair beside the kitchen window, leaned her head back, and looked out indifferently between the lilac-bushes. The bushes were full of pinkish-purple buds. Sylvia's front yard reached the road in a broad slope, and the ground was hard, and green with dampness under the shade of a great elm-tree. The grass would never grow there over the roots of the elm, which were flung out broadly like great recumbent limbs over the whole yard, and were barely covered by the mould.

Across the street, seen under the green sweep of the elm, was an orchard of old apple-trees which had blossomed out bravely that spring. Charlotte looked at the white and rosy masses of bloom.

"I guess there wasn't any frost last night, after all," she remarked.

"I dunno," responded Sylvia, in a voice which made her niece look around at her. There was a curious impatient ring in it which was utterly foreign to it. There was a frown between Sylvia's gentle eyes, and she moved with nervous jerks, setting down dishes hard, as if they were refractory children, and lashing out with spoons as if they were whips. The long, steady strain upon her patience had not affected her temper, but this last had seemed to bring out a certain vicious and waspish element which nobody had suspected her to possess, and she herself least of all. She felt this morning disposed to go out of her way to sting, and as if some primal and evil instinct had taken possession of her. She felt shocked at herself, but all the more defiant and disposed to keep on.

"Breakfast is ready," she announced, finally; "if you don't set right up an' eat it, it will be gettin' cold. I wouldn't give a cent for cold Injun cake."

Charlotte arose promptly and brought a chair to the table, which Sylvia always set punctiliously in the centre of the kitchen as if for a large family.

"Don't scrape your chair on the floor that way; it wears 'em all out," cried Sylvia, sharply.

Charlotte stared at her again, but she said nothing; she sat down and began to eat absently. Sylvia watched her angrily between her own mouthfuls, which she swallowed down defiantly like medicine.

"It ain't much use cookin' things if folks don't eat 'em," said she.

"I am eating," returned Charlotte.

"Eatin'? Swallowin' down Injun cake as if it was sawdust! I don't call that eatin'. You don't act as if you tasted a mite of it!"

"Aunt Sylvy, what has got into you?" said Charlotte.

"Got into me? I should think you'd talk about anything gettin' into me, when you set there like a stick. I guess you 'ain't got all there is to bear."

"I never thought I had," said Charlotte.

"Well, I guess you 'ain't."

They went on swallowing their food silently; the great clock ticked slowly, and the spring birds called outside; but they heard neither. The shadows of the young elm leaves played over the floor and the white table-cloth. It was much warmer that morning, and the shadows were softer.

Before they had finished breakfast, Charlotte's mother came, advancing ponderously, with soft thuds, across the yard to the side door. She opened it and peered in.

"Here you be," said she, scanning both their faces with anxious and deprecating inquiry.

"Can't you come in, an' not stand there holdin' the door open?" inquired Sylvia. "I feel the wind on my back, and I've got a bad pain enough in it now."

Mrs. Barnard stepped in, and shut the door quickly, in an alarmed way.

"Ain't you feelin' well this mornin', Sylvy?" said she.

"Oh yes, I'm feelin' well enough. It ain't any matter how I feel, but it's a good deal how some other folks do."

Sarah Barnard sank into the rocking-chair, and sat there looking at them hesitatingly, as if she did not dare to open the conversation.

Suddenly Sylvia arose and went out of the kitchen with a rush, carrying a plate of Indian cake to feed the hens. "I can't set here all day; I've got to do something," she announced as she went.

When the door had closed after her, Mrs. Barnard turned to Charlotte.

"What's the matter with her?" she asked, nodding towards the door.

"I don't know."

"She ain't sick, is she? I never see her act so. Sylvy's generally just like a lamb. You don't s'pose she's goin' to have a fever, do you?"

"I don't know."

Suddenly Charlotte, who was still sitting at the table, put up her two hands with a despairing gesture, and bent her head forward upon them.

"Now don't, you poor child," said her mother, her eyes growing suddenly red. "Didn't he even turn round when you called him back last night?"

Charlotte shook her bowed head dumbly.

"Don't you s'pose he'll ever come again?"

Charlotte shook her head.

"Mebbe he will. I know he's terrible set."

"Who's set?" demanded Sylvia, coming in with her empty plate.

"Oh, I was jest sayin' that I thought Barney was kinder set," replied her sister, mildly.

"He ain't no more set than Cephas," returned Sylvia.

"Cephas ain't set. It's jest his way."

Sylvia sniffed. She looked scornfully at Charlotte, who had raised her head when she came in, but whose eyes were red. "Folks had better been created without ways, then," she retorted. "They'd better have been created slaves; they'd been enough sight happier an' better off, an' so would other folks that they have to do with, than to have so many ways, an' not sense enough to manage 'em. I don't believe in free-will, for my part."

"Sylvy Crane, you ain't goin' to deny one of the doctrines of the Church at your time of life?" demanded a new voice. Sylvia's other sister, Hannah Berry, stood in the doorway.

Sylvia ordinarily was meek before her, but now she faced her. "Yes, I be," said she; "I don't approve of free-will, and I ain't afraid to say it."

Sylvia had always been considered very unlike Mrs. Hannah Berry in face and character. Now, as she stood before her, a curious similarity appeared; even her voice sounded like her sister's.

"What on earth ails you, Sylvy?" asked Mrs. Berry, ignoring suddenly the matter in hand.

"Nothin' ails me that I know of. I don't think much of free-will, an' I ain't goin' to say I do when I don't."

"Then all I've got to say is you'd ought to be ashamed of yourself. Why, I should think you was

crazy, Sylvy Crane, settin' up yourself agin' the doctrines of the Word. I'd like to know what you
know about them."

"I know enough to see how they work," returned
Sylvia, undauntedly, "an' I ain't goin' to pretend
I'm blind when I can see."

Sylvia's serene arc of white forehead was shortened by a distressed frown, her mild mouth dropped
sourly at the corners, and the lips were compressed.
Her white cap was awry, and one of yesterday's curls
hung lankly over her left cheek.

"You look an' act like a crazy creature," said
Hannah Berry, eying her with indignant amazement.
She walked across the room to another rocking-chair,
moving with unexpected heaviness. She was in
reality as stout as her sister Sarah Barnard, but she
had a long, thin, and rasped face, which misled
people.

"Now," said she, looking around conclusively, "I
ain't come over here to argue about free-will. I
want to know what all this is about?"

"All what?" returned Mrs. Barnard, feebly. She
was distinctly afraid of her imperious sister, yet she
was conscious of a quiver of resentment.

"All this fuss about Barney Thayer," said Hannah
Berry.

"How did you hear about it?" Mrs. Barnard asked
with a glance at Charlotte, who was sitting erect
with her cheeks very red and her mouth tightly
closed.

"Never mind how I heard," replied Hannah. "I did hear, an' that's enough. Now I want to know if you're really goin' to set down like an old hen an' give up, an' let this match between Charlotte an' a good, smart, likely young man like Barnabas Thayer be broken off on account of Cephas Barnard's crazy freaks?"

Sarah stiffened her neck. "There ain't no call for you to speak that way, Hannah. They got to talkin' over the 'lection."

"The 'lection! I'd like to know what business they had talkin' about it Sabbath night anyway? I ain't blamin' Barnabas so much; he's younger an' easier stirred up; but Cephas Barnard is an old man, an' he has been a church-member for forty year, an' he ought to know enough to set a better example. I'd like to know what difference it makes about the 'lection anyway? What odds does it make which one is President if he rules the country well? An' that they can't tell till they've tried him awhile anyway. I guess they don't think much about the country; it's jest to have their own way about it. I'd like to know what mortal difference it's goin' to make to Barney Thayer or Cephas Barnard which man is President? He won't never hear of them, an' they won't neither of them make him rule any different after he's chose. It's jest like two little boys — one wants to play marbles 'cause the other wants to play puss-in-the-corner, an' that's all the reason either one of 'em's got for standin' out. **Men** ain't got any too much sense anyhow, when you come right down to it. They don't ever get any too much grown up, the best of 'em. I'd like to know what Cephas Barnard has got to say because he's drove a good, likely young man like Barnabas Thayer off an' broke off his daughter's match? It ain't likely she'll ever get anybody now; young men like him, with nice new houses put up to go right to housekeepin' in as soon as they are married, don't grow on every bush. They ain't quite so thick as wild thimbleberries. An' Charlotte ain't got any money herself, an' her father ain't got any to build a house for her. I'd like to know what he's got to say about it?"

Mrs. Barnard put up her apron and began to weep helplessly.

"Don't, mother," said Charlotte, in an undertone. But her mother began talking in a piteous wailing fashion.

"You hadn't ought to talk so about Cephas," she moaned. "He's my husband. I guess you wouldn't like it if anybody talked so about your husband. Cephas ain't any worse than anybody else. It's jest his way. He wa'n't any more to blame than Barney; they both got to talkin'. I know Cephas is terrible upset about it this mornin'; he 'ain't really said so in so many words, but I know by the way he acts. He said this mornin' that he didn't know but we were eatin' the wrong kind of food. Lately he's had an idea that mebbe we'd ought to eat more meat; he's thought it was more strengthenin', an' we'd ought to eat things as near like what we wanted to strengthen as could be. I've made a good deal of bone soup. But now he says he thinks mebbe he's been mistaken, an' animal food kind of quickens the animal nature in us, an' that we'd better eat green things an' garden sass."

" I guess garden sass will strengthen the other kind of sass that Cephas Barnard has got in him full as much as bone soup has," interrupted Hannah Berry, with a sarcastic sniff.

" I dunno but he's right," said Mrs. Barnard. " Cephas thinks a good deal an' looks into things. I kind of wish he'd waited till the garden had got started, though, for there ain't much we can eat now but potatoes an' turnips an' dandelion greens."

" If you want to live on potatoes an' turnips an' dandelion greens, you can," cried Hannah Berry ; " what I want to know is if you're goin' to settle down an' say nothin', an' have Charlotte lose the best chance she'll ever have in her life, if she lives to be a hundred—"

Charlotte spoke up suddenly ; her blue eyes gleamed with steely light. She held her head high as she faced her aunt.

" I don't want any more talk about it, Aunt Hannah," said she.

" Hey ?"

" I don't want any more talk about it."

" Well, I guess you'll have more talk about it ; girls don't get jilted without there is talk generally. I guess you'll have to make up your mind to it, for all you put on such airs with your own aunt, who left her washin' an' come over here to take your part. I guess when you stand out in the road half an hour an' call a young man to come back, an' he don't come, that folks are goin' to talk some. Who's that comin' now?"

"It's Cephas," whispered Mrs. Barnard, with a scared glance at Charlotte.

Cephas Barnard entered abruptly, and stood for a second looking at the company, while they looked back at him. His eyes were stolidly defiant, but he stood well back, and almost shrank against the door. There seemed to be impulses in Hannah's and Sylvia's faces confronting his.

He turned to his wife. "When you comin' home?" said he.

"Oh, Cephas! I jest run over here a minute. I—wanted to see—if—Sylvy had any emptins. Do you want me an' Charlotte to come now?"

Cephas turned on his heel. "I think it's about time for you both to be home," he grunted.

Sarah Barnard arose and looked with piteous appeal at Charlotte.

Charlotte hesitated a second, then she arose without a word, and followed her mother, who followed Cephas. They went in a procession of three, with Cephas marching ahead like a general, across the yard, and Sylvia and Hannah stood at a window watching them.

" Well," said Hannah Berry, " all I've got to say is I'm thankful I 'ain't got a man like that, an' you ought to be mighty thankful you 'ain't got any man at all, Sylvy Crane."

CHAPTER III

When Cephas Barnard and his wife and daughter turned into the main road and came in sight of the new house, not one of them appeared to even glance at it, yet they all saw at once that there were no workmen about, and they also saw Barnabas himself ploughing with a white horse far back in a field at the left of it.

They all kept on silently. Charlotte paled a little when she caught sight of Barney, but her face was quite steady. " Hold your dress up a little higher; the grass is terrible wet," her mother whispered once, and that was all that any of them said until they reached home.

Charlotte went at once up-stairs to her own chamber, took off her purple gown, and hung it up in her closet, and got out a common one. The purple gown was part of her wedding wardrobe, and she had worn it in advance with some misgivings. " I dunno but you might jest as well wear it a few Sundays," her mother had said; " you're goin' to have your silk dress to come out bride in. I dunno as there's any sense in your goin' lookin' like a scarecrow all the spring because you're goin' to get married."

So Charlotte had put on the new purple dress the

"THEY CAME IN SIGHT OF THE HOUSE"

day before; now it looked, as it hung in the closet, like an effigy of her happier self.

When Charlotte went down-stairs she found her mother showing much more spirit than usual in an altercation with her father. Sarah Barnard stood before her husband, her placid face all knitted with perplexed remonstrance. " Why, I can't, Cephas," she said. " Pies can't be made that way."

" I know they can," said Cephas.

" They can't, Cephas. There ain't no use tryin'. It would jest be a waste of the flour."

" Why can't they, I'd like to know ?"

" Folks don't ever make pies without lard, Cephas."

" Why don't they ?"

" Why, they wouldn't be nothin' more than— You couldn't eat them nohow if they was made so, Cephas. I dunno how the sorrel pies would work. I never heard of anybody makin' sorrel pies. Mebbe the Injuns did; but I dunno as they ever made pies, anyway. Mebbe the sorrel, if it had some molasses on it for juice, wouldn't taste very bad; I dunno; but anyway, if the sorrel did work, the other wouldn't. I can't make pies fit to eat without any lard or any butter or anything any way in the world, Cephas."

" I know you can make 'em without," said Cephas, and his black eyes looked like flint. Mrs. Barnard appealed to her daughter.

" Charlotte," said she, " you tell your father that pies can't be made fit to eat without I put somethin' in 'em for short'nin'."

"No, they can't, father," said Charlotte.

"He wants me to make sorrel pies, Charlotte," Mrs. Barnard went on, in an injured and appealing tone which she seldom used against Cephas. "He's been out in the field, an' picked all that sorrel," and she pointed to a pan heaped up with little green leaves on the table, "an' I tell him I dunno how that will work, but he wants me to make the pie-crust without a mite of short'nin', an' I can't do that nohow, can I?"

"I don't see how you can," assented Charlotte, coldly.

Cephas went with a sudden stride towards the pantry. "I'll make 'em myself, then," he cried.

Mrs. Barnard gasped, and looked piteously at her daughter. "What you goin' to do, Cephas?" she asked, feebly.

Cephas was in the pantry rattling the dishes with a fierce din. "I'm a-goin' to make them sorrel pies myself," he shouted out, "if none of you women folks know enough to."

"Oh, Cephas, you can't!"

Cephas came out, carrying the mixing-board and rolling-pin like a shield and a club; he clapped them heavily on to the table.

Mrs. Barnard stood staring aghast at him; Charlotte sat down, took some lace edging from her pocket, and began knitting on it. She looked hard and indifferent.

"Oh, Charlotte, ain't it dreadful?" her mother

whispered, when Cephas went into the pantry again.

"I don't care if he makes pies out of burrs," returned Charlotte, audibly, but her voice was quite even.

"I don't b'lieve but what sorrel would do some better than burrs," said her mother, "but he can't make pies without short'nin' nohow."

Cephas came out of the pantry with a large bowl of flour and a spoon. "He 'ain't sifted it," Mrs. Barnard whispered to Charlotte, as though Cephas were not there; then she turned to him. "You sifted the flour, didn't you, Cephas?" said she.

"You jest let me alone," said Cephas, grimly. "I'm goin' to make these pies, an' I don't need any help. I've picked the sorrel, an' I've got the brick oven all heated, an' I know what I want to do, an' I'm goin to do it!"

"I've got some pumpkin that would make full as good pies as sorrel, Cephas. Mebbe the sorrel will be real good. I ain't sayin' it won't, though I never heard of sorrel pies; but you know pumpkin is good, Cephas."

"I know pumpkin pies have milk in 'em," said Cephas; "an' I tell you I ain't goin' to have anything of an animal nature in 'em. I've been studyin' into it, an' thinkin' of it, an' I've made up my mind that I've made a mistake along back, an' we've ate too much animal food. We've ate a whole pig an' half a beef critter this winter, to say nothin' of eggs an' milk, that are jest as much animal as meat, accordin' to my way of thinkin'. I've reasoned it out all along that as long as we were animals ourselves, an' wanted to strengthen animal, that it was common-sense that we ought to eat animal. It seemed to me that nature had so ordered it. I reasoned it out that other animals besides man lived on animals, except cows, an' they, bein' ruminatin' animals, ain't to be compared to men—"

"I should think we'd be somethin' like 'em if we eat that," said Mrs. Barnard, pointing at the sorrel, with piteous sarcasm.

"It's the principle I'm thinkin' about," said Cephas. He stirred some salt into the flour very carefully, so not a dust fell over the brim of the bowl.

"Horses don't eat meat, neither, an' they don't chew their cuds," Mrs. Barnard argued further. She had never in her life argued with Cephas; but sorrel pies, after the night before, made her wildly reckless.

Cephas got a gourdful of water from the pail in the sink, and carried it carefully over to the table. "Horses are the exception," he returned, with dignified asperity. "There always are exceptions. What I was comin' at was—I'd been kind of wrong in my reasonin'. That is, I 'ain't reasoned far enough. I was right so far as I went."

Cephas poured some water from the gourd into the bowl of flour and began stirring.

Sarah caught her breath. "He's makin'—paste!" she gasped. "He's jest makin' flour paste!"

"Jest so far as I went I was right," Cephas re-

sumed, pouring in a little more water with a judicial
air. "I said Man was animal, an' he is animal; an'
if you don't take anything else into account, he'd
ought to live on animal food, jest the way I reasoned
it out. But you've got to take something else into
account. Man is animal, but he ain't all animal.
He's something else. He's spiritual. Man has command over all the other animals, an' all the beasts of
the field; an' it ain't because he's any better an'
stronger animal, because he ain't. What's a man to
a horse, if the horse only knew it ? but the horse
don't know it, an' there's jest where Man gets the
advantage. It's knowledge an' spirit that gives Man
the rule over all the other animals. Now, what we
want is to eat the kind of things that will strengthen
knowledge an' spirit an' self-control, because the first
two ain't any account without the last; but there
ain't no kind of food that's known that can do that.
If there is, I 'ain't never heard of it."

Cephas dumped the whole mass of paste with a
flop upon the mixing-board, and plunged his fists
into it. Sarah made an involuntary motion forward,
then she stood back with a great sigh.

"But what we can do," Cephas proceeded, "is to
eat the kind of things that won't strengthen the animal nature at the expense of the spiritual. We know
that animal food does that; we can see how it works
in tigers an' bears. Now, it's the spiritual part of us
we want to strengthen, because that is the biggest
strength we can get, an' it's worth more. It's what

gives us the rule over animals. It's better for us to eat some other kind of food, if we get real weak and pindlin' on it, rather than eat animal food an' make the animal in us stronger than the spiritual, so we won't be any better than wild tigers an' bears, an' lose our rule over the other animals."

Cephas took the rolling-pin and brought it heavily down upon the sticky mass on the board. Sarah shuddered and started as if it had hit her. "Now, if we can't eat animal food," said Cephas, "what other kind of food can we eat? There ain't but one other kind that's known to man, an' that's vegetable food, the product of the earth. An' that's of two sorts: one gets ripe an' fit to eat in the fall of the year, an' the other comes earlier in the spring an' summer. Now, in order to carry out the plans of nature, we'd ought to eat these products of the earth jest as near as we can in the season of 'em. Some had ought to be eat in the fall an' winter, an' some in the spring an' summer. Accordin' to my reasonin', if we all lived this way we should be a good deal better off; our spiritual natures would be strengthened, an' we should have more power over other animals, an' better dispositions ourselves."

"I've seen horses terribly ugly, an' they don't eat a mite of meat," said Sarah, with tremulous boldness. Her right hand kept moving forward to clutch the rolling-pin, then she would draw it back.

"'Ain't I told ye once horses were the exceptions?" said Cephas, severely. "There has to be exceptions.

If there wa'n't any exceptions there couldn't be any rule, an' there bein' exceptions shows there is a rule. Women can't ever get hold of things straight. Their minds slant off sideways, the way their arms do when they fling a stone."

Cephas brought the rolling-pin down upon the paste again with fierce impetus. "You'll break it," Sarah murmured, feebly. Cephas brought it down again, his mouth set hard; his face showed a red flush through his white beard, the veins on his high forehead were swollen and his brows scowling. The paste adhered to the rolling-pin; he raised it with an effort; his hands were helplessly sticky. Sarah could restrain herself no longer. She went into the pantry and got a dish of flour, and spooned out some suddenly over the board and Cephas's hands. "You've got to have some more flour," she said, in a desperate tone.

Cephas's black eyes flashed at her. "I wish you would attend to your own work, an' leave me alone," said he. But at last he succeeded in moving the rolling-pin over the dough as he had seen his wife move it.

"He ain't greasin' the pie-plates," said Sarah, as Cephas brought a piece of dough with a dexterous jerk over a plate; "there ain't much animal in the little mite of lard it takes to grease a plate."

Cephas spread handfuls of sorrel leaves over the dough; then he brought the molasses-jug from the pantry, raised it, and poured molasses over the sorrel with an imperturbable air.

Sarah watched him; then she turned to Charlotte. "To think of eatin' it!" she groaned, quite openly; "it looks like p'ison."

Charlotte made no response; she knitted as one of the Fates might have spun. Sarah sank down on a chair, and looked away from Cephas and his cookery, as if she were overcome, and quite done with all remonstrance.

Never before had she shown so much opposition towards one of her husband's hobbies, but this galloped so ruthlessly over her own familiar fields that she had plucked up boldness to try to veer it away.

Somebody passed the window swiftly, the door opened abruptly, and Mrs. Deborah Thayer entered. "*Good*-mornin'," said she, and her voice rang out like a herald's defiance.

Sarah Barnard arose, and went forward quickly. "Good-mornin'," she responded, with nervous eagerness. "Good-mornin', Mis' Thayer. Come in an' set down, won't you?"

"I 'ain't come to set down," responded Deborah's deep voice.

She moved, a stately high-hipped figure, her severe face almost concealed in a scooping green barège hood, to the centre of the floor, and stood there with a pose that might have answered for a statue of Judgment. She turned her green-hooded head slowly towards them all in turn. Sarah watched her and waited, her eyes dilated. Cephas rolled out another pie, calmly. Charlotte knitted fast; her face was very pale.

"I've come over here," said Deborah Thayer, "to find out what my son has done."

There was not a sound, except the thud of Cephas's rolling-pin.

"Mr. Barnard!" said Deborah. Cephas did not seem to hear her.

"Mr. Barnard!" she said, again. There was that tone of command in her voice which only a woman can accomplish. It was full of that maternal supremacy which awakens the first instinct of obedience in man, and has more weight than the voice of a general in battle. Cephas did not turn his head, but he spoke. "What is it ye want?" he said, gruffly.

"I want to know what my son has done, an' I want you to tell me in so many words. I ain't afraid to face it. What has my son done?"

Cephas grunted something inarticulate.

"What?" said Deborah. "I can't hear what you say. I want to know what my son has done. I've heard how you turned him out of your house last night, and I want to know what it was for. I want to know what he has done. You're an old man, and a God-fearing one, if you have got your own ideas about some things. Barnabas is young, and apt to be headstrong. He ain't always been as mindful of obedience as he might be. I've tried to do my best by him, but he don't always carry out my teachin's. I ain't afraid to say this, if he is my son. I want to know what he's done. If it's anything wrong, I shall be jest as hard on him as the Lord for it. I'm his mother, but I can see his faults, and be just. I want to know what he has done."

Charlotte gave one great cry. " Oh, Mrs. Thayer, he hasn't done anything wrong ; Barney hasn't done anything wrong!"

But Deborah quite ignored her. She kept her eyes fixed upon Cephas. " What has my son done?" she demanded again. " If he's done anything wrong I want to know it. I ain't afraid to deal with him. You ordered him out of your house, and he didn't come home at all last night. I don't know where he was. He won't speak a word this mornin' to tell me. I've been out in the field where he's to work ploughin', and I tried to make him tell me, but he wouldn't say a word. I sat up and waited all night, but he didn't come home. Now I want to know where he was, and what he's done, and why you ordered him out of the house. If he's been swearin', or takin' anything that didn't belong to him, or drinkin', I want to know it, so I can deal with him as his mother had ought to deal."

" He hasn't been doing anything wrong!" Charlotte cried out again ; " you ought to be ashamed of yourself talking so about him, when you're his mother!"

Deborah Thayer never glanced at Charlotte. She kept her eyes fixed upon Cephas. " What has he done?" she repeated.

" I guess he didn't do much of anything," Mrs.

Barnard murmured, feebly; but Deborah did not seem to hear her.

Cephas opened his mouth as if perforce. "Well," he said, slowly, "we got to talkin'—"

"Talkin' about what?"

"About the 'lection. I think, accordin' to my reasonin', that what we eat had a good deal to do with it."

"What?"

"I think if you'd kept your family on less meat, and given 'em more garden-stuff to eat Barney wouldn't have been so up an' comin'. It's what he's eat that's made him what he is."

Deborah stared at Cephas in stern amazement. "You're tryin' to make out, as near as I can tell," said she, "that whatever my son has done wrong is due to what he's eat, and not to original sin. I knew you had queer ideas, Cephas Barnard, but I didn't know you wa'n't sound in your faith. What I want to know is, what has he done?"

Suddenly Charlotte sprang up, and pushed herself in between her father and Mrs. Thayer; she confronted Deborah, and compelled her to look at her.

"I'll tell you what he's done," she said, fiercely. "I know what he's done; you listen to me. He has done nothing—nothing that you've got to deal with him for. You needn't feel obliged to deal with him. He and father got into a talk over the 'lection, and they had words about it. He didn't talk any worse than father, not a mite. Father started it, anyway,

and he knew better; he knew just how set Barney
was on his own side, and how set he was on his; he
wanted to pick a quarrel."

" Charlotte !" shouted Cephas.

" You keep still, father," returned Charlotte, with
steady fierceness. " I've never set myself up against
you in my whole life before; but now I'm going to,
because it's just and right. Father wanted to pick
a quarrel," she repeated, turning to Deborah; " he's
been kind of grouty to Barney for some time. I
don't know why; he took a notion to, I suppose.
When they got to having words about the 'lection,
father begun it. I heard him. Barney answered
back, and I didn't blame him; I would, in his place.
Then father ordered him out of the house, and he
went. I don't see what else he could do. And I
don't blame him because he didn't go home if he
didn't feel like it."

" Didn't he go away from here before nine
o'clock?" demanded Deborah, addressing Charlotte
at last.

" Yes, he did, some time before nine; he had
plenty of time to go home if he wanted to."

" Where was he, then, I'd like to know ?"

" I don't know, and I wouldn't lift my finger to
find out. I am not afraid he was anywhere he hadn't
ought to be, nor doin' anything he hadn't ought to."

" Didn't you stand out in the road and call him
back, and he wouldn't come, nor even turn his head
to look at you ?" asked Deborah.

"Yes, I did," returned Charlotte, unflinchingly. "And I don't blame him for not coming back and not turning his head. I wouldn't if I'd been in his place."

"You'll have to uphold him a long time, then; I can tell you that," said Deborah. "He won't never come back if he's said he won't. I know him; he's got some of me in him."

"I'll uphold him as long as I live," said Charlotte.

"I wonder you ain't ashamed to talk so."

"I am not."

Deborah looked at Charlotte as if she would crush her; then she turned away.

"You're a hard woman, Mrs. Thayer, and I pity Barney because he's got you for a mother," Charlotte said, in undaunted response to Deborah's look.

"Well, you'll never have to pity yourself on that account," retorted Deborah, without turning her head.

The door opened softly, and a girl of about Charlotte's age slipped in. Nobody except Mrs. Barnard, who said, absently, "How do you do, Rose?" seemed to notice her. She sat down unobtrusively in a chair near the door and waited. Her blue eyes upon the others were so intense with excitement that they seemed to blot out the rest of her face. She had her blue apron tightly rolled about both hands.

Deborah Thayer, on her way to the door, looked at her as if she had been a part of the wall, but suddenly she stopped and cast a glance at Cephas.

"What be you makin'?" she asked, with a kind of scorn at him, and scorn at her own curiosity.

Cephas did not reply, but he looked ugly as he slapped another piece of dough heavily upon a plate.

Deborah, as if against her will, moved closer to the table and bent over the pan of sorrel. She smelled of it; then she took a leaf and tasted it, cautiously. She made a wry face. "It's sorrel," said she. "You're makin' pies out of sorrel. A man makin' pies out of sorrel!"

She looked at Cephas like a condemning judge. He shot a fiery glance at her, but said nothing. He sprinkled the sorrel leaves in the pie.

"Well," said Deborah, "I've got a sense of justice, and if my son, or any other man, has asked a girl to marry him, and she's got her weddin' clothes ready, I believe in his doin' his duty, if he can be made to; but I must say if it wa'n't for that, I'd rather he'd gone into a family that was more like other folks. I'm goin' to do the best I can, whether you go half way or not. I'm goin' to try to make my son do his duty. I don't expect he will, but I shall do all I can, tempers or no tempers, and sorrel pies or no sorrel pies."

Deborah went out, and shut the door heavily after her.

CHAPTER IV

AFTER Deborah Thayer had shut the door, the young girl sitting beside it arose. " I didn't know she was in here, or I wouldn't have come in," she said, nervously.

"That don't make any odds," replied Mrs. Barnard, who was trembling all over, and had sunk helplessly into a rocking-chair, which she swayed violently and unconsciously.

Cephas opened the door of the brick oven, and put in a batch of his pies, and the click of the iron latch made her start as if it were a pistol-shot.

Charlotte got up and went out of the room with a backward glance and a slight beckoning motion of her head, and the girl slunk after her so secretly that it seemed as if she did not see herself. Cephas looked sharply after them, but said nothing; he was like a philosopher in such a fury of research and experiment that for the time he heeded thoroughly nothing else.

The young girl, who was Rose Berry, Charlotte's cousin, followed her panting up the steep stairs to her chamber. She was a slender little creature, and was now overwrought with nervous excitement. She fairly gasped for breath when she sat down in the little wooden chair in Charlotte's room. Charlotte sat on the bed. The two girls looked at each other —Rose with a certain wary alarm and questioning in her eyes, Charlotte with a dignified confidence of misery.

"I didn't sleep here last night," Charlotte said, at length.

"You went over to Aunt Sylvy's, didn't you?" returned Rose, as if that were all the matter in hand.

Charlotte nodded, then she looked moodily past her cousin's face out of the window.

"You've heard about it, I suppose?" said Charlotte.

"Something," replied Rose, evasively.

"I don't see how it got out, for my part. I don't believe he told anybody."

Rose flushed all over her little eager face and her thin neck. She opened her mouth as if to speak, then shut it with a catch of her breath.

"I can't imagine how it got out," repeated Charlotte.

Rose looked at Charlotte with a painful effort; she clutched her hands tightly into fists as she spoke. "I was coming up here 'cross lots last night, and I heard you out in the road calling Barney," she said, as if she forced out the words.

"Rose Berry, you didn't tell!"

"I went home and told mother, that's all. I didn't think that it would do any harm, Charlotte."

"It 'll be all over town, that's all. It's bad enough, anyway."

"I don't believe it 'll get out; I told mother not to tell."

"Mrs. Thayer knew."

"Maybe Barney told her."

"Rose Berry, you know better. You know Barney wouldn't do such a thing."

"No; I don't s'pose he would."

"Don't suppose! Don't you know?"

"Yes, of course I do. I know Barney just as well as you do, Charlotte. Oh, Charlotte, don't feel bad. I wouldn't have told mother if I'd thought. I didn't mean to do any harm. I was all upset myself by it. Don't cry, Charlotte."

"I ain't going to cry," said Charlotte, with spirit. "I've stopped cryin'." She wiped her eyes forcibly with her apron, and gave her head a proud toss. "I know you didn't mean to do any harm, Rose, and I suppose it would have got out anyway. 'Most everything does get out but good deeds."

"I truly didn't mean to do any harm, Charlotte," Rose repeated.

"I know you didn't. We won't say any more about it."

"I was just running over across lots last night," Rose said. "I supposed you'd be in the front room with Barney, but I thought I'd see Aunt Sarah. I'd got terrible lonesome; mother had gone to sleep in her chair, and father had gone to bed. When I got out by the stone-wall next the wood I heard you; then I ran right back. Don't you — suppose he'll ever come again, Charlotte?"

"No," said Charlotte.

"Oh, Charlotte!" There was a curious quality in the girl's voice, as if some great hidden emotion in her heart tried to leap to the surface and make a sound, although it was totally at variance with the import of her cry. Charlotte started, without knowing why. It was as if Rose's words and her tone had different meanings, and conflicted like the wrong lines with a tune.

"I gave it up last night," said Charlotte. "It's all over. I'm goin' to pack my wedding things away."

"I don't see what makes you so sure."

"I know him."

"But I don't see what you've done, Charlotte; he didn't quarrel with you."

"That don't make any odds. He can't get married to me now without he breaks his will, and he can't. He can't get outside himself enough to break it. I've studied it all out. It's like ciphering. It's all over."

"Charlotte."

"What is it?"

"Why—couldn't you go somewhere else to get married? What's the need of his comin' here, if he's been ordered out, and he's said he wouldn't?"

"That's just the letter of it," returned Charlotte, scornfully. "Do you suppose he could cheat himself that way, or I'd have him if he could? When Barney Thayer went out of this house last night, and said what he did, he meant that it was all over, that he was never going to marry me, nor have anything more to do with us, and he's going to stand by it. I am not finding any fault with him. I've made up my mind that it's all over, and I'm going to pack away my weddin' things."

"Oh, Charlotte, you take it so calm!"

"What do you want me to do?"

"If it was anybody else, I should think they didn't care."

"Maybe I don't."

"I couldn't bear it so, anyhow! I couldn't!" Rose cried out, with sudden passion. "I wouldn't bear it. I'd go down on my knees to him to come back!" Rose flung back her head and looked at Charlotte with a curious defiance; her face grew suddenly intense, and seemed to open out into bloom and color like a flower. The pupils of her blue eyes dilated until they looked black; her thin lips looked full and red; her cheeks were flaming; her slender chest heaved. "I would," said she; "I don't care, I would."

Charlotte looked at her, and a quivering flush like a reflection was left on her fair, steady face.

"I would," said Rose again.

"It wouldn't do any good."

"It would if he cared anything about you."

"It would if he could give up to the care. Barney

Thayer has got a terrible will that won't always let him do what he wants to himself."

"I don't believe he's enough of a fool to put his own eyes out."

"You don't know him."

"I'd try, anyway."

"It wouldn't do any good."

"I don't believe you care anything about him, Charlotte Barnard!" Rose cried out. "If you did, you couldn't give him up so easy for such a silly thing. You sit there just as calm. I don't believe but what you'll have another fellow on the string in a month. I know one that's dying to get you."

"Maybe I shall," replied Charlotte.

"Won't you, now?" Rose tried to speak archly, but her eyes were fiercely eager.

"I can't tell till I get home from the grave," said Charlotte. "You might wait till I did, Rose." She got up and went to dusting her bureau and the little gilt-framed mirror behind it. Her lips were shut tightly, and she never looked at her cousin.

"Now don't get mad, Charlotte," Rose said. "Maybe I ought not to have spoken so, but it did seem to me you couldn't care as *much*— It does seem to me I couldn't settle down and be so calm if I was in your place, and all ready to be married to anybody. I should want to do something."

"I should, if there was anything to do," said Charlotte. She stopped dusting and leaned against the wall, reflecting. "I wish it was a real mountain to move," said she; "I'd do it."

"I'd go right down in the field where he is ploughing, and I'd make him say he'd come to see me to-night."

"I called him back last night—you heard me," said Charlotte, with slow bitterness. Her square delicate chin dipped into the muslin folds of her neckerchief; she looked steadily at the floor and bent her brow.

"I'd call him again."

"You would, would you?" cried Charlotte, straightening herself. "You would stand out in the road and keep on calling a man who wouldn't even turn his head? You'd keep on calling, and let all the town hear?"

"Yes, I would. I would! I wouldn't be ashamed of anything if I was going to marry him. I'd go on my knees before him in the face and eyes of the whole town."

"Well, I wouldn't," said Charlotte.

"I would, if I was sure he thought as much of me as I did of him."

Charlotte looked at her proudly. "I'm sure enough of that," said she.

Rose winced a little. "Then I wouldn't mind what I did," she persisted, stubbornly.

"Well, I would," said Charlotte; "but maybe I don't care. Maybe all this isn't as hard for me as it would be for another girl." Charlotte's voice broke, but she tossed her head back with a proud motion; she took up the dusting-cloth and fell to work again.

"Oh, Charlotte!" said Rose; "I didn't mean that. Of course I know you care. It's awful. It was only because I didn't see how you could seem so calm; it ain't like me. Of course I know you feel bad enough underneath. Your wedding-clothes all done and everything. They are pretty near all done, ain't they, Charlotte?"

"Yes," said Charlotte. "They're—pretty near— done." She tried to speak steadily, but her voice failed. Suddenly she threw herself on the bed and hid her face, and her whole body heaved and twisted with great sobs.

"Oh, poor Charlotte, don't!" Rose cried, wringing her own hands; her face quivered, but she did not weep.

"Maybe I don't care," sobbed Charlotte; "maybe —I don't care."

"Oh, Charlotte!" Rose looked at Charlotte's pite- ous girlish shoulders shaken with sobs, and the fair prostrate girlish head. Charlotte all drawn up in this little heap upon the bed looked very young and help- less. All her womanly stateliness, which made her seem so superior to Rose, had vanished. Rose pulled her chair close to the bed, sat down, and laid her little thin hand on Charlotte's arm, and Charlotte directly felt it hot through her sleeve. "Don't, Char- lotte," Rose said; "I'm sorry I spoke so."

"Maybe I don't care," Charlotte sobbed out again. "Maybe I don't."

"Oh, Charlotte, I'm sorry," Rose said, trembling. "I do know you care; don't you feel so bad because I said that."

Rose tightened her grasp on Charlotte's arm; her voice changed suddenly. "Look here, Charlotte," said she, "I'll do anything in the world I can to help you; I promise you that, and I mean it, honest."

Charlotte reached around a hand, and clasped her cousin's.

"I'm sorry I spoke so," Rose said.

"Never mind," Charlotte responded, chokingly. She sobbed a little longer from pure inertia of grief; then she raised herself, shaking off Rose's hand. "It's all right," said she; "I needn't have minded; I know you didn't mean anything. It was just—the last straw, and — when you said that about my wedding-clothes—"

"Oh, Charlotte, you did speak about them yourself first," Rose said, deprecatingly.

"I did, so nobody else would," returned Charlotte. She wiped her eyes, drooping her stained face away from her cousin with a kind of helpless shame; then she smoothed her hair with the palms of her hands. "I know you didn't mean any harm, Rose," she added, presently. "I got my silk dress done last Wednesday; I wanted to tell you." Charlotte tried to smile at Rose with her poor swollen lips and her reddened eyes.

"I'm sorry I said anything," Rose repeated; "I ought to have known it would make you feel bad, Charlotte."

"No, you hadn't. I was terrible silly. Don't you want to see my dress, Rose?"

"Oh, Charlotte! you don't want to show it to me?"

"Yes, I do. I want you to see it—before I pack it away. It's in the north chamber."

Rose followed Charlotte out of the room across the passageway to the north chamber. Charlotte had had one brother, who had died some ten years before, when he was twenty. The north chamber had been his room, the bureau drawers were packed with his clothes, and the silk hat which had been the pride of his early manhood hung on the nail where he had left it, and also his Sunday coat. His mother would not have them removed, but kept them there, with frequent brushings, to guard against dust and moths.

Always when Charlotte entered this small long room, which was full of wavering lines from its uneven floor and walls and ceiling and the long arabesques on its old blue-and-white paper, whose green paper curtains with fringed white dimity ones drooping over them were always drawn, and in summertime when the windows were open undulated in the wind, she had the sense of a presence, dim, but as positive as the visions she had used to have of faces in the wandering design of the old wall-paper when she had studied it in her childhood. Ever since her brother's death she had had this sense of his presence in his room ; now she thought no more of it than of any familiar figure. All the grief at his death had vanished, but she never entered his old room that the thought of him did not rise up before her and stay with her while she remained.

Now, when she opened the door, and the opposite green and white curtains flew out in the draught towards her, they were no more evident than this presence to which she now gave no thought, and pushed by her brother's memory without a glance.

Rose followed her to the bed. A white linen sheet was laid over the chintz counterpane. Charlotte lifted the sheet.

" I took the last stitch on it Wednesday night," she said, in a hushed voice.

" Didn't he come that night ?"

" I finished it before he came."

" Did he see it ?"

Charlotte nodded. The two girls stood looking solemnly at the silk dress.

" You can't see it here ; it's too dark," said Charlotte, and she rolled up a window curtain.

" Yes, I can see better," said Rose, in a whisper. " It's beautiful, Charlotte."

The dress was spread widely over the bed in crisp folds. It was purple, plaided vaguely with cloudy lines of white and delicate rose-color. Over it lay a silvery lustre that was the very light of the silken fabric.

Rose felt it reverently. "How thick it is!" said she.

"Yes, it's a good piece," Charlotte replied.

"You thought you'd have purple?"

"Yes; he liked it."

"Well, it's pretty, and it's becoming to you."

Charlotte took up the skirt, and slipped it, loud with silken whispers, over her head. It swept out around her in a great circle; she looked like a gorgeous inverted bell-flower.

"It's beautiful," Rose said.

Charlotte's face, gazing downward at the silken breadths, had quite its natural expression. It was as if her mind in spite of herself would stop at old doors.

"Try on the waist," pleaded Rose.

Charlotte slipped off her calico waist, and thrust her firm white arms into the flaring silken sleeves of the wedding-gown. Her neck arose from it with a grand curve. She stood before the glass and strained the buttons together, frowning importantly.

"It fits you like a glove," Rose murmured, admiringly, smoothing Charlotte's glossy back.

"I've got a spencer-cape to wear over my neck to meeting," Charlotte said, and she opened the uppermost drawer in the chest and took out a worked muslin cape, and adjusted it carefully over her shoulders, pinning it across her bosom with a little brooch of her brother's hair in a rim of gold.

"It's elegant," said Rose.

"I'll show you my bonnet," said Charlotte. She went into a closet and emerged with a great green bandbox.

Rose bent over, watching her breathlessly as she opened it. "Oh!" she cried. "Oh, Charlotte!"

Charlotte held up the bonnet of fine Dunstable straw, flaring in front, and trimmed under the brim with a delicate lace ruche and a wreath of feathery white flowers. Bows of white gauze ribbon stood up from it stiffly. Long ribbon strings floated back over her arm as she held it up.

"Try it on," said Rose.

Charlotte stepped before the glass and adjusted the bonnet to her head. She tied the strings carefully under her chin in a great square bow; then she turned towards Rose. The fine white wreath under the brim encircled her face like a nimbus; she looked as she might have done sitting a bride in the meeting-house.

"It's beautiful," Rose said, smiling, with grave eyes. "You look real handsome in it, Charlotte." Charlotte stood motionless a moment, with Rose surveying her.

"Oh, Charlotte," Rose cried out, suddenly, "I don't believe but what you'll have him, after all!" Rose's eyes were sharp upon Charlotte's face. It was as if the bridal robes, which were so evident, became suddenly proofs of something tangible and real, like a garment left by a ghost. Rose felt a sudden conviction that the quarrel was but a temporary thing;

that Charlotte would marry Barney, and that she knew it.

A change came over Charlotte's face. She began untying the bonnet strings.

"Sha'n't you?" repeated Rose, breathlessly.

"No, I sha'n't."

Charlotte took the bonnet off and smoothed the creases carefully out of the strings.

"If I were you," Rose cried out, " I'd feel like tearing that bonnet to pieces !"

Charlotte replaced it in the bandbox, and began unfastening her dress.

"I don't see how you can bear the sight of them. I don't believe I could bear them in the house !" Rose cried out again. "I would put that dress in the rag-bag if it was mine !" Her cheeks burned and her eyes were quite fierce upon the dress as Charlotte slipped it off and it fell to the floor in a rustling heap around her.

"I don't see any sense in losing everything you have ever had because you haven't got anything now," Charlotte returned, in a stern voice. She laid the shining silk gown carefully on the bed, and put on her cotton one again. Her face was quite steady.

Rose watched her with the same sharp question in her eyes. "You know you and Barney will make it up," she said, at length.

"No, I don't," returned Charlotte. "Suppose we go down-stairs now. I've got some work I ought to do."

Charlotte pulled down the green paper shades of the windows, and went out of the room. Rose followed. Charlotte turned to go down-stairs, but Rose caught her arm.

"Wait a minute," said she. "Look here, Charlotte."

"What is it?"

"Charlotte," said Rose again; then she stopped.

Charlotte turned and looked at her. Rose's eyes met hers, and her face had a noble expression.

"You write a note to him, and I'll carry it," said Rose. "I'll go down in the field where he is, on my way home."

Tears sprang into Charlotte's eyes. "You're real good, Rose," she said; "but I can't."

"Hadn't you better?"

"No; I can't. Don't let's talk any more about it."

Charlotte pushed past Rose's detaining hand, and the girls went down-stairs. Mrs. Barnard looked around dejectedly at them as they entered the kitchen. Her eyes were red, and her mouth drooping; she was clearing the débris of the pies from the table; there was a smell of baking, but Cephas had gone out. She tried to smile at Rose. "Are you goin' now?" said she.

"Yes; I've got to. I've got to sew on my muslin dress. When are you coming over, Aunt Sarah? You haven't been over to our house for an age."

"I don't care if I never go anywhere!" cried Sarah Barnard, with sudden desperation. "I'm discouraged." She sank in a chair, and flung her apron over her face.

"Don't, mother," said Charlotte.

"I can't help it," sobbed her mother. "You're young and you've got more strength to bear it, but mine's all gone. I feel worse about you than if it was myself, an' there's so much to put up with besides. I don't feel as if I could put up with things much longer, nohow."

"Uncle Cephas ought to be ashamed of himself!" Rose cried out.

Sarah stood up. "Well, I don't s'pose I have so much to put up with as some folks," she said, catching her breath as if it were her dignity. "Your Uncle Cephas means well. It did seem as if them sorrel pies were the last straw, but I hadn't ought to have minded it."

"You haven't got to eat sorrel pies, have you?" Rose asked, in a bewildered way.

"I don't s'pose they'll be any worse than some other things we eat," Sarah answered, scraping the pie-board again.

"I don't see how you can."

"I guess they won't hurt us any," Sarah said, shortly, and Rose looked abashed.

"Well, I must be going," said she.

As she went out, she looked hesitatingly at Charlotte. "Hadn't you better?" she whispered. Charlotte shook her head, and Rose went out into the spring sunlight. She bent her head as she went down the road before the sweet gusts of south wind; the white apple-trees seemed to sing, for she could not see the birds in them.

Rose's face between the green sides of her bonnet had in it all the quickened bloom of youth in spring; her eyes had all the blue surprise of violets; she panted softly between red swelling lips as she walked; pulses beat in her crimson cheeks. Her slender figure yielded to the wind as to a lover. She passed Barney Thayer's new house; then she came opposite the field where he was at work ploughing, driving a white horse, stooping to his work in his blue frock.

Rose stood still and looked at him; then she walked on a little way; then she paused again. Barney never looked around at her. There was the width of a field between them.

Finally Rose went through the open bars into the first field. She crossed it slowly, holding up her skirts where there was a wet gleam through darker grass, and getting a little nosegay of violets with a busy air, as if that were what she had come for. She passed through the other bars into the second field, and Barney was only a little way from her. He did not glance at her then. He was ploughing with the look that Cadmus might have worn preparing the ground for the dragon's teeth.

Rose held up her skirts, and went along the furrows behind him. " Hullo, Barney," she said, in a trembling voice.

"Hullo," he returned, without looking around, and he kept on, with Rose following.

"Barney," said she, timidly.

"Well?" said Barney, half turning, with a slight show of courtesy.

"Do you know if Rebecca is at home?"

"I don't know whether she is or not."

Barney held stubbornly to his rocking plough, and Rose followed.

"Barney," said she, again.

"Well?"

"Stop a minute, and look round here."

"I can't stop to talk."

"Yes, you can; just a minute. Look round here."

Barney stopped, and turned a stern, miserable face over his shoulder.

"I've been up to Charlotte's," Rose said.

"I don't know what that is to me."

"Barney Thayer, ain't you ashamed of yourself?"

"I can't stop to talk."

"Yes, you can. Look here. Charlotte feels awfully."

Barney stood with his back to Rose; his very shoulders had a dogged look.

"Barney, why don't you make up with her?"

Barney stood still.

"Barney, she feels awfully because you didn't come back when she called you last night."

Barney made no reply. He and the white horse stood like statues.

"Barney, why don't you make up with her? I wish you would." Rose's voice was full of tender inflections; it might have been that of an angel peace-making.

Barney turned around between the handles of the plough, and looked at her steadily. "You don't know anything about it, Rose," he said.

Rose looked up in his face, and her own was full of fine pleading. "Oh, Barney," she said, "poor Charlotte does feel so bad! I know that anyhow."

"You don't know how I am situated. I can't—"

"Do go and see her, Barney."

"Do you think I'm going into Cephas Barnard's house after he's ordered me out?"

"Go up the road a little way, and she'll come and meet you. I'll run ahead and tell her."

Barney shook his head. "I can't; you don't know anything about it, Rose." He looked into Rose's eyes. "You're real good, Rose," he said, as if with a sudden recognition of her presence.

Rose blushed softly, a new look came into her eyes, she smiled up at him, and her face was all pink and sweet and fully set towards him, like a rose for which he was a sun.

"No, I ain't good," she whispered.

"Yes, you are; but I can't. You don't know anything about it." He swung about and grasped his plough-handles again.

"Barney, do stop a minute," Rose pleaded.

"I can't stop any longer; there's no use talking,"

Barney said; and he went on remorselessly through the opening furrow. Just before he turned the corner Rose made a little run forward and caught his arm.

"You don't think I've done anything out of the way speaking to you about it, do you, Barney?" she said, and she was half crying.

"I don't know why I should think you had; I suppose you meant all right," Barney said. He pulled his arm away softly, and jerked the right rein to turn the horse. " G'lang!" he cried out, and strode forward with a conclusive air.

Rose stood looking after him a minute; then she struck off across the field. Her knees trembled as she stepped over the soft plough-ridges.

When she was out on the road again she went along quickly until she came to the Thayer house. She was going past that when she heard some one calling her name, and turned to see who it was.

Rebecca Thayer came hurrying out of the yard with a basket on her arm. " Wait a minute," she called, "and I'll go along with you."

CHAPTER V

Rebecca, walking beside Rose, looked like a woman of another race. She was much taller, and her full, luxuriant young figure looked tropical beside Rose's slender one. Her body undulated as she walked, but Rose moved only with forward flings of delicate limbs.

"I've got to carry these eggs down to the store and get some sugar," said Rebecca.

Rose assented, absently. She was full of the thought of her talk with Barney.

"It's a pleasant day, ain't it?" said Rebecca.

"Yes, it's real pleasant. Say, Rebecca, I'm awful afraid I made Barney mad just now."

"Why, what did you do?"

"I stopped in the field when I was going by. I'd been up to see Charlotte, and I said something about it to him."

"How much do you know about it?" Rebecca asked, abruptly.

"Charlotte told me this mornin', and last night when I was going to her house across lots I saw Barney going, and heard her calling him back. I thought I'd see if I couldn't coax him to make up with her, but I couldn't."

"Oh, he'll come round," said Rebecca.

"Then you think it 'll be made up?" Rose asked, quickly.

"Of course it will. We're having a terrible time about poor Barney. He didn't come home last night, and it's much as ever he's spoken this morning. He wouldn't eat any breakfast. He just went into his room, and put on his other clothes, and then went out in the field to work. He wouldn't tell mother anything about it. I never saw her so worked up. She's terribly afraid he's done something wrong."

"He hasn't done anything wrong," returned Rose. "I think your mother is terrible hard on him. It's Uncle Cephas; he just picked the quarrel. He hasn't never more'n half liked Barney. So you think Barney will make up with Charlotte, and they'll get married, after all?"

"Of course they will," Rebecca replied, promptly. "I guess they won't be such fools as not to for such a silly reason as that, when Barney's got his house 'most done, and Charlotte has got all her wedding-clothes ready."

"Ain't Barney terrible set?"

"He's set enough, but I guess you'll find he won't be this time."

"Well, I'm sure I hope he won't be," Rose said, and she walked along silently, her face sober in the depths of her bonnet.

They came to Richard Alger's house on the right-

hand side of the road, and Rebecca looked reflective-
ly at the white cottage with its steep peak of Gothic
roof set upon a ploughed hill. "It's queer how he's
been going with your aunt Sylvy all these years,"
she said.

"Yes, 'tis," assented Rose, and she too glanced up
at the house. As they looked, a man came around
the corner with a basket. He was about to plant
potatoes in his hilly yard.

"There he is now," said Rose.

They watched Richard Alger coming towards
them, past a great tree whose new leaves were as
red as flowers.

"What do you suppose the reason is?" Rebecca
said, in a low voice.

"I don't know. I suppose he's got used to living
this way."

"I shouldn't think they'd be very happy," Rebecca
said; and she blushed, and her voice had a shame-
faced tone.

"I don't suppose it makes so much difference
when folks get older," Rose returned.

"Maybe it don't. Rose."

"What is it?"

"I wish you'd go into the store with me."

Rose laughed. "What for?"

"Nothing. Only I wish you would."

"You afraid of William?" Rose peered around
into Rebecca's bonnet.

Rebecca blushed until tears came to her eyes.

"I'd like to know what I'd be afraid of William Berry for," she replied.

"Then what do you want me to go into the store with you for?"

"Nothing."

"You're a great ninny, Rebecca Thayer," Rose said, laughing, "but I'll go if you want me to. I know William won't like it. You run away from him the whole time. There isn't another girl in Pembroke treats him as badly as you do."

"I don't treat him badly."

"Yes, you do. And I don't believe but what you like him, Rebecca Thayer; you wouldn't act so silly if you didn't."

Rebecca was silent. Rose peered around in her face again. "I was only joking. I think a sight more of you for not running after him, and so does William. You haven't any idea how some of the girls act chasing to the store. Mother and I have counted 'em some days, and then we plague William about it, but he won't own up they come to see him. He acts more ashamed of it than the girls do."

"That's one thing I never would do — run after any fellow," said Rebecca.

"I wouldn't either."

Then the two girls had reached the tavern and the store. Rose's father, Silas Berry, had kept the tavern, but now it was closed, except to occasional special guests. He had gained a competency, and his wife Hannah had rebelled against further toil. Then, too, the railroad had been built through East Pembroke instead of Pembroke, the old stage line had become a thing of the past, and the tavern was scantily patronized. Still, Silas Berry had given it up with great reluctance; he cherished a grudge against his wife because she had insisted upon it, and would never admit that business policy had aught to do with it.

The store adjoining the tavern, which he had owned for years, he still retained, but his son William had charge of it. Silas Berry was growing old, and the year before had had a slight shock of paralysis, which had made him halt and feeble, although his mind was as clear as ever. However, although he took no active part in the duties of the store, he was still there, and sharply watchful for his interests, the greater part of every day.

The two girls went up the steps to the store piazza. Rose stepped forward and looked in the door. "Father's in there, and Tommy Ray," she whispered. "You needn't be afraid to go in." But she entered as she spoke, and Rebecca followed her.

There was one customer in the great country store, a stout old man, on the grocery side. His broad red face turned towards them a second, then squinted again at some packages on the counter. He was haggling for garden seeds. William Berry, who was waiting upon him, did not apparently look at his sister and Rebecca Thayer, but Rebecca had entered his heart as well as the store, and he saw her face deep in his own consciousness.

Tommy Ray, the great white-headed boy who helped William in the store, shuffled along behind the counter indeterminately, but the girls did not seem to see him. Rose was talking fast to Rebecca. He lounged back against the shelves, stared out the door, and whistled.

Out of the obscurity in the back of the store an old man's narrow bristling face peered, watchful as a cat, his body hunched up in a round-backed arm-chair.

"Mr. Nims will go in a minute," Rose whispered, and presently the old farmer clamped past them out the door, counting his change from one hand to the other, his lips moving.

William Berry replaced the seed packages which the customer had rejected on the shelves as the girls approached him.

"Rebecca's got some eggs to sell," Rose announced.

William Berry's thin, wide-shouldered figure towered up behind the counter; he smiled, and the smile was only a deepening of the pleasant intensity of his beardless face, with its high pale forehead and smooth crest of fair hair. The lines in his face scarcely changed.

"How d'ye do?" said he.

"How d'ye do?" returned Rebecca, with fluttered dignity. Her face bloomed deeply pink in the green tunnel of her sun-bonnet, her black eyes were as soft and wary as a baby's, her full red lips had a grave, innocent expression.

"'REBECCA'S GOT SOME EGGS TO SELL'"

"How many dozen eggs have you got, Rebecca?" Rose inquired, peering into the basket.

"Two; mother couldn't spare any more to-day," Rebecca replied, in a trembling voice.

"How much sugar do you give for two dozen eggs, William?" asked Rose.

William hesitated; he gave a scarcely perceptible glance towards the watchful old man, whose eyes seemed to gleam out of the gloom in the back of the store. "Well, about two pounds and a half," he replied, in a low voice.

Rebecca set her basket of eggs on the counter.

"How many pound did you tell her, William?" called the old man's hoarse voice.

William compressed his lips. "About two and a half, father."

"How many?"

"Two and a half."

"How many dozen of eggs?"

"Two."

"You ain't offerin' of her two pound of sugar for two dozen eggs?"

"I said two pounds and a half of sugar, father," said William. He began counting the eggs.

"Be you gone crazy?"

"Never mind," whispered Rebecca. "That's too much sugar for the eggs. Mother didn't expect so much. Don't say any more about it, William." Her face was quite steady and self-possessed now, as she looked at William, frowning heavily over the eggs.

"Give Rebecca two pounds of sugar for the eggs, father, and call it square," Rose called out.

Silas Berry pulled himself up a joint at a time; then he came forward at a stiff halt, his face pointing out in advance of his body. He entered at the gap in the counter, and pressed close to his son's side. Then he looked sharply across at Rebecca. "Sugar is fourteen cents a pound now," said he, "an' eggs ain't fetchin' more'n ten cents a dozen. You tell your mother."

"Father, I told her I'd give her two and a half pounds for two dozen," said William; he was quite pale. He began counting the eggs over again, and his hands trembled.

"I'll take just what you're willing to give," Rebecca said to Silas.

"Sugar is fourteen cents a pound, an' eggs is fetchin' ten cents a dozen," said the old man; "you can have a pound and a half of sugar for them eggs if you can give me a cent to boot."

Rebecca colored. "I'm afraid I haven't got a cent with me," said she; "I didn't fetch my purse. You'll have to give me a cent's worth less sugar, Mr. Berry."

"It's kinder hard to calkilate so close as that," returned Silas, gravely; "you had better tell your mother about it, an' you come back with the cent by-an'-by."

"Why, father!" cried Rose.

William shouldered his father aside with a sudden motion. "I'm tending to this, father," he said, in a stern whisper; "you leave it alone."

"I ain't goin' to stan' by an' see you givin' twice as much for eggs as they're worth 'cause it's a gal you're tradin' with. That wa'n't never my way of doin' business, an' I ain't goin' to have it done in my store. I shouldn't have laid up a cent if I'd managed any such ways, an' I ain't goin' to see my hard earnin's wasted by you. You give her a pound and a half of sugar for them eggs and a cent to boot."

"You sha'n't lose anything by it, father," said William, fiercely. "You leave me alone."

The sugar-barrel stood quite near. William strode over to it, and plunged in the great scoop with a grating noise. He heaped it recklessly on some paper, and laid it on the steelyards.

"Don't give me more'n a pound and a half," Rebecca said, softly.

"Keep still," Rose whispered in her ear.

Silas pushed forward, and bent over the steelyards. "You've weighed out nigh three," he began. Then his son's face suddenly confronted his, and he stopped talking and stood back.

Almost involuntarily at times Silas Berry yielded to the combination of mental and superior physical force in his son. While his own mind had lost nothing of its vigor, his bodily weakness made him distrustful of it sometimes, when his son towered over him in what seemed the might of his own lost strength and youth, brandishing his own old weapons.

William tied up the sugar neatly; then he took the eggs from Rebecca's basket, and put the parcel in their place. Silas began lifting the eggs from the box in which William had put them, and counted them eagerly.

"There ain't but twenty-three eggs here," he called out, as Rebecca and Rose turned away, and William was edging after them from behind the counter.

"I thought there were two dozen," Rebecca responded, in a distressed voice.

"Of course there are two dozen," said Rose, promptly. "You 'ain't counted 'em right, father. Go along, Rebecca; it's all right."

"I tell ye it ain't," said Silas. "There ain't but twenty-three. It's bad enough to be payin' twice what they're wuth for eggs, without havin' of 'em come short."

"I tell you I counted 'em twice over, and they're all right. You keep still, father," said William's voice at his ear, in a fierce whisper, and Silas subsided into sullen mutterings.

William had meditated following Rebecca to the door; he had even meditated going farther; but now he stood back behind the counter, and began packing up some boxes with a busy air.

"Ain't you going a piece with Rebecca, and carry her basket, William?" Rose called back, when the two girls reached the door.

Rebecca clutched her arm. "Oh, don't," she gasped, and Rose giggled.

"Ain't you, William?" she said again.

Rebecca hurried out the door, but she heard William reply coldly that he couldn't, he was too busy. She was half crying when Rose caught up with her.

"William wanted to go bad enough, but he was too upset by what father said. You mustn't mind father," Rose said, peering around into Rebecca's bonnet. "Why, Rebecca, what is the matter?"

"I didn't go into that store a step to see William Berry. You know I didn't," Rebecca cried out, with sudden passion. Her voice was hoarse with tears; her face was all hot and quivering with shame and anger.

"Why, of course you didn't," Rose returned, in a bewildered way. "Who said you did, Rebecca?"

"You know I didn't. I hated to go to the store this morning. I told mother I didn't want to, but she didn't have a mite of sugar in the house, and there wasn't anybody else to send. Ephraim ain't very well, and Doctor Whiting says he ought not to walk very far. I had to come, but I didn't come to see William Berry, and nobody has any call to think I did."

"I don't know who said you did. I don't know what you mean, Rebecca."

"You acted as if you thought so. I don't want William Berry seeing me home in broad daylight,

when I've been to the store to trade, and you needn't
think that's what I came for, and he needn't."

"Good land, Rebecca Thayer, he didn't, and I was
just in fun. He'd have come with you, but he was
so mad at what father said that he backed out. William's just about as easy upset as you are. I didn't
mean any harm. Say, Rebecca, come into the house
a little while, can't you? I don't believe your mother is in any great hurry for the sugar." Rose took
hold of Rebecca's arm, but Rebecca jerked herself
away with a sob, and went down the road almost on
a run.

"Well, I hope you're touchy enough, Rebecca
Thayer," Rose called out, as she stood looking after
her. "Folks will begin to think you did come to
see William if you make such a fuss when nobody
accuses you of it, if you don't look out."

Rebecca hastened trembling down the road. She
made no reply, but she knew that Rose was quite
right, and that she had attacked her with futile re-
proaches in order to save herself from shame in her
own eyes. Rebecca knew quite well that in spite of
her hesitation and remonstrances, in spite of her
maiden shrinking on the threshold of the store, she
had come to see William Berry. She had been glad,
although she had turned a hypocritical face towards
her own consciousness, that Ephraim was not well
enough and she was obliged to go. Her heart had
leaped with joy when Rose had proposed William's
walking home with her, but when he refused she was

crushed with shame. "He thought I came to see him," she kept saying to herself as she hurried along, and there was no falsehood that she would not have sworn to to shield her modesty from such a thought on his part.

When she got home and entered the kitchen, she kept her face turned away from her mother. "Here's the sugar," she said, and she took it out of the basket and placed it on the table.

"How much did he give you?" asked Deborah Thayer; she was standing beside the window beating eggs. Over in the field she could catch a glimpse of Barnabas now and then between the trees as he passed with his plough.

"About two pounds."

"That was doin' pretty well."

Rebecca said nothing. She turned to go out of the room.

"Where are you going?" her mother asked, sharply. "Take off your bonnet. I want you to beat up the butter and sugar; this cake ought to be in the oven."

Deborah's face, as she beat the eggs and made cake, looked as full of stern desperation as a soldier's on the battle-field. Deborah never yielded to any of the vicissitudes of life; she met them in fair fight like enemies, and vanquished them, not with trumpet and spear, but with daily duties. It was a village story how Deborah Thayer cleaned all the windows in the house one afternoon when her first child had died in the morning. To-day she was in a tumult of wrath and misery over her son; her mouth was so full of the gall of bitterness that no sweet on earth could overcome it; but she made sweet cake.

Rebecca took off her sun-bonnet and hung it on a peg; she got a box from the pantry, and emptied the sugar into it, still keeping her face turned away as best she could from her mother's eyes.

Deborah looked approvingly at the sugar. "It's nigher three pounds than anything else. I guess you were kind of favored, Rebecca. Did William wait on you?"

"Yes, he did."

"I guess you were kind of favored," Deborah repeated, and a half-smile came over her grim face.

Rebecca said nothing. She got some butter, and fell to work with a wooden spoon, creaming the butter and sugar in a brown wooden bowl with swift turns of her strong white wrist. Ephraim watched her sharply; he sat by a window stoning raisins. His mother had forbidden him to eat any, as she thought them injurious to him; but he carefully calculated his chances, and deposited many in his mouth when she watched Barney; but his jaws were always gravely set when she turned his way.

Ephraim's face had a curious bluish cast, as if his blood were the color of the juice of a grape. His chest heaved shortly and heavily. The village doctor had told his mother that he had heart-disease, which might prove fatal, although there was a chance of his outgrowing it, and Deborah had set her face against that.

Ephraim's face, in spite of its sickly hue, had a perfect healthiness and naturalness of expression, which insensibly gave confidence to his friends, although it aroused their irritation. A spirit of boyish rebellion and importance looked out of Ephraim's black eyes; his mouth was demure with mischief, his gawky figure perpetually uneasy and twisting, as if to find entrance into small forbidden places. There was something in Ephraim's face, when she looked suddenly at him, which continually led his mother to infer that he had been transgressing. " What have you been doin', Ephraim ?" she would call out, sharply, many a time, with no just grounds for suspicion, and be utterly routed by Ephraim's innocent, wondering grin in response.

The boy was set about with restrictions which made his life miserable, but the labor of picking over plums for a cake was quite to his taste. He dearly loved plums, although they were especially prohibited. He rolled one quietly under his tongue, and watched Rebecca with sharp eyes. She could scarcely keep her face turned away from him and her mother too.

" Say, mother, Rebecca's been cryin' !" Ephraim announced, suddenly.

Deborah turned and looked at Rebecca's face bending lower over the wooden bowl ; her black lashes rested on red circles, and her lips were swollen.

"I'd like to know what you've been cryin' about," said Deborah. It was odd that she did not think that Rebecca's grief might be due to the worry over Barney; but she did not for a minute. She directly attributed it to some personal and strictly selfish consideration which should arouse her animosity.

"Nothing," said Rebecca, with sulky misery.

"Yes, you've been cryin' about something, too. I want to know what 'tis."

"Nothing. I wish you wouldn't, mother."

"Did you see William Berry over to the store?"

"I told you I did once."

"Well, you needn't bite my head off. Did he say anything to you?"

"He weighed out the sugar. I know one thing: I'll never set my foot inside that store again as long as I live!"

"I'd like to know what you mean, Rebecca Thayer."

"I ain't going to have folks think I'm running after William Berry."

"I'd like to know who thinks you are. If it's Hannah Berry, she needn't talk, after the way her daughter has chased over here. Mebbe it's all you Rose Berry has been to see, but I've had my doubts. What did Hannah Berry say to you?"

"She didn't say anything. I haven't seen her."

"What was it, then?"

But Rebecca would not tell her mother what the trouble had been; she could not bring herself to reveal how William had been urged to walk home with her and how coldly he had refused, and finally Deborah, in spite of baffled interest, turned upon her. "Well, I hope you didn't do anything unbecoming," said she.

"Mother, you know better."

"Well, I hope you didn't."

"Mother, I won't stand being talked to so !"

"I rather think I shall talk to you all I think I ought to for your own good," said Deborah, with fierce persistency. "I ain't goin' to have any daughter of mine doin' anything bold and forward, if I know it."

Rebecca was weeping quite openly now. "Mother, you know you sent me down to the store yourself; there wasn't anybody else to go," she sobbed out.

"Your goin' to the store wa'n't anything. I guess you can go to the store to trade off some eggs for sugar when I'm makin' cake without William Berry thinkin' you're runnin' after him, or Hannah Berry thinkin' so either. But there wa'n't any need of your makin' any special talk with him, or lookin' as if you was tickled to death to see him."

"I didn't. I wouldn't go across the room to see William Berry. You haven't any right to say such things to me, mother."

"I guess I've got a right to talk to my own daughter. I should think things had come to a pretty pass

if I can't speak when I see you doin' out of the way.
I know one thing, you won't go to that store again.
I'll go myself next time. Have you got that butter
an' sugar mixed up?"

"I hope you will go, I'm sure. I don't want to,"
returned Rebecca. She had stopped crying, but her
face was burning; she hit the spoon with dull thuds
against the wooden bowl.

"Don't you be saucy. That's done enough; give
it here."

Deborah finished the cake with a master hand.
When she measured the raisins which Ephraim had
stoned she cast a sharp glance at him, but he was
ready for it with beseechingly upturned sickly face.
"Can't I have just one raisin, mother?" he pleaded.

"Yes, you may, if you 'ain't eat any while you was
pickin' of 'em over," she answered. And he reached
over a thumb and finger and selected a large fat
plum, which he ate with ostentatious relish. Ephraim's stomach oppressed him, his breath came harder,
but he had a sense of triumph in his soul. This de-
priving him of the little creature comforts which he
loved, and of the natural enjoyments of boyhood,
aroused in him a blind spirit of revolution which he
felt virtuous in exercising. Ephraim was absolutely
conscienceless with respect to all his stolen pleasures.

Deborah had a cooking-stove. She had a pro-
gressive spirit, and when stoves were first introduced
had promptly done away with the brick oven, except
on occasions when much baking-room was needed.

After her new stove was set up in her back kitchen, she often alluded to Hannah Berry's conservative principles with scorn. Hannah's sister, Mrs. Barnard, had told her how a stove could be set up in the tavern any minute; but Hannah despised new notions. "Hannah won't have one, nohow," said Mrs. Barnard. "I dunno but I would, if Cephas could afford it, and wa'n't set against it. It seems to me it might save a sight of work."

"Some folks are rooted so deep in old notions that they can't see their own ideas over them," declared Deborah. Often when she cooked in her new stove she inveighed against Hannah Berry's foolishness.

"If Hannah Berry wants to heat up a whole brick oven and work the whole forenoon to bake a loaf of cake, she can," said she, as she put the pan of cake in the oven. "Now, you watch this, Rebecca Thayer, and don't you let it burn, and you get the potatoes ready for dinner."

"Where are you going, mother?" asked Ephraim.

"I'm just goin' to step out a little way."

"Can't I go too?"

"No; you set still. You ain't fit to walk this mornin'. You know what the doctor told you."

"It won't hurt me any," whined Ephraim. There were times when the spirit of rebellion in him made illness and even his final demise flash before his eyes like sweet overhanging fruit, since they were so strenuously forbidden.

"You set still," repeated his mother. She tied on her own green sun-bonnet, stiffened with pasteboard, and went with it rattling against her ears across the fields to the one where her son was ploughing. The grass was not wet, but she held her dress up high, showing her thick shoes and her blue yarn stockings, and took long strides. Barney was guiding the plough past her when she came up.

"You stop a minute," she said, authoritatively. "I want to speak to you."

"Whoa!" said Barney, and pulled up the horse. "Well, what is it?" he said, gruffly, with his eyes upon the plough.

"You go this minute and set the men to work on your house again. You leave the horse here—I'll watch him—and go and tell Sam Plummer to come and get the other men."

"G'lang!" said Barney, and the horse pulled the plough forward with a jerk.

Mrs. Thayer seized Barney's arm. "You stop!" said she. "Whoa, whoa! Now you look here, Barnabas Thayer. I don't know what you did to make Cephas Barnard order you out of the house, but I know it was something. I ain't goin' to believe it was all about the election. There was something back of that. I ain't goin' to shield you because you're my son. I know jest how set you can be in your own ways, and how you can hang on to your temper. I've known you ever since you was a baby; you can't teach me anything new about yourself. I don't know what you did to make Cephas mad, but I know what you've got to do now. You go and set the men to work on that house again, and then you go over to Cephas Barnard's, and you tell him you're sorry for what you've done. I don't care anything about Cephas Barnard, and if I'd had my way in the first place I wouldn't have had anything to do with him or his folks either; but now you've got to do what's right if you've gone as far as this, and Charlotte's all ready to be married. You go right along, Barnabas Thayer!"

Barnabas stood immovable, his face set past his mother, as irresponsively unyielding as a rock.

"Be you goin'?"

Barnabas did not reply. His mother moved, and brought her eyes on a range with his, and the two faces confronted each other in silence, while it was as if two wills clashed swords in advance of them.

Then Mrs. Thayer moved away. "I ain't never goin' to say anything more to you about it," she said; "but there's one thing—you needn't come home to dinner. You sha'n't ever sit down to a meal in your father's and mother's house whilst this goes on."

"G'lang!" said Barnabas. The horse started, and he bent to the plough. His mother stepped homeward over the plough-ridges with stern unyielding steps, as if they were her enemies slain in battle.

Just as she reached her own yard her husband drove in on a rattling farm cart. She beckoned to him, and he pulled the horse up short.

"I've told him he needn't come home to dinner," she said, standing close to the wheel.

Caleb looked down at her with a scared expression. "Well, I s'pose you know what's best, Deborah," he said.

"If he can't do what's right he's got to suffer for it," returned Deborah.

She went into the house, and Caleb drove clanking into the barn.

Before dinner the old man stole off across lots, keeping well out of sight of the kitchen windows lest his wife should see him, and pleaded with Barnabas, but all in vain. The young man was more outspoken with his father, but he was just as firm.

"Your mother's terrible set about it, Barney. You'd better go over to Charlotte's an' make up."

"I can't; it's all over," Barney said, in reply; and Caleb at length plodded soberly and clumsily home.

After dinner he went out behind the barn, and Rebecca, going to feed the hens, found him sitting under the wild-cherry tree, fairly sobbing in his old red handkerchief.

She went near him, and stood looking at him with restrained sympathy.

"Don't feel bad, father," she said, finally. "Barney 'll get over it, and come to supper."

"No, he won't," groaned the old man—"no, he won't. He's jest like your mother."

CHAPTER VI

THE weeks went on, and still Barnabas had not
yielded. The story of his quarrel with Cephas Barnard and his broken engagement with Charlotte had
become an old one in Pembroke, but it had not yet
lost its interest. A genuine excitement was so rare
in the little peaceful village that it had to be made
to last, and rolled charily under the tongue like a
sweet morsel. However, there seemed to be no lack
now, for the one had set others in motion: everybody knew how Barnabas Thayer no longer lived
at home, and did not sit in his father's pew in
church, but in the gallery, and how Richard Alger
had stopped going to see Sylvia Crane.

There was not much walking in the village, except to and from church on a Sabbath day ; but now
on pleasant Sabbath evenings an occasional couple,
or an inquisitive old man with eyes sharp under white
brows, and chin set ahead like a pointer's, strolled
past Sylvia's house and the Thayer house, Barney's
new one and Cephas Barnard's.

They looked sharply and furtively to see if Sylvia
had a light in her best room, and if Richard Alger's
head was visible through the window, if Barney
Thayer had gone home and yielded to his mother's

commands, if any more work had been done on the new house, and if he perchance had gone a-courting Charlotte again.

But they never saw Richard Alger's face in poor Sylvia's best room, although her candle was always lit, they never saw Barney at his old home, the new house advanced not a step beyond its incompleteness, and Barney never was seen at Charlotte Barnard's on a Sabbath night. Once, indeed, there was a rumor to that effect. A man's smooth dark head was visible at one of the front-room windows opposite Charlotte's fair one, and everybody took it for Barney's.

The next morning Barney's mother came to the door of the new house. "I want to know if it's true that you went over there last night," she said; her voice was harsh, but her mouth was yielding.

"No, I didn't," said Barney, shortly, and Deborah went away with a harsh exclamation. Before long she knew and everybody else knew that the man who had been seen at Charlotte's window was not Barney, but Thomas Payne.

Presently Ephraim came slowly across to the garden-patch where Barney was planting. He was breathing heavily, and grinning. When he reached Barney he stood still watching him, and the grin deepened. "Say, Barney," he panted at length.

"Well, what is it?"

"You've lost your girl; did you know it, Barney?"

Barney muttered something unintelligible; it

sounded like the growl of a dog, but Ephraim was not intimidated. He chuckled with delight and spoke again. "Say, Barney, Thomas Payne's got your girl; did you know it, Barney?"

Barney turned threateningly, but he was helpless before his brother's sickly face, and Ephraim knew it. That purple hue and that panting breath had gained an armistice for him on many a battle-field, and he had a certain triumph in it. It was power of a lugubrious sort, certainly, but still it was power, and so to be enjoyed.

"Thomas Payne's got your girl," he repeated; "he was over there a-courtin' of her last night; a-settin' up along of her."

Barney took a step forward, and Ephraim fell back a little, still grinning imperturbably. "You mind your own business," Barney said, between his teeth; and right upon his words followed Ephraim's hoarse chuckle and his "Thomas Payne's got your girl."

Barney turned about and went on with his planting. Ephraim, standing a little aloof, somewhat warily since his brother's threatening advance, kept repeating his one remark, as mocking as the snarl of a mosquito. "Thomas Payne's got your girl, Barney. Say, did you know it? Thomas Payne's got your girl."

Finally Ephraim stepped close to Barney and shouted it into his ear: "Say, Barney, Barney Thayer, be you deaf? Thomas Payne has got—your—*girl!*"

But Barney planted on; his nerves were quivering, the impetus to strike out was so strong in his arms that it seemed as if it must by sheer mental force affect his teasing brother, but he made no sign, and said not another word.

Ephraim, worsted at length by silence, beat a gradual retreat. Half-way across the field his panting voice called back, "Barney, Thomas Payne has got your girl," and ended in a choking giggle. Barney planted, and made no response; but when Ephraim was well out of sight, he flung down his hoe with a groaning sigh, and went stumbling across the soft loam of the garden-patch into a little woody thicket beside it. He penetrated deeply between the trees and underbrush, and at last flung himself down on his face among the soft young flowers and weeds. "Oh, Charlotte!" he groaned out. "Oh, Charlotte, Charlotte!" Barney began sobbing and crying like a child as he lay there; he moved his arms convulsively, and tore up handfuls of young grass and leaves, and flung them away in the unconscious gesturing of grief. "Oh, I can't, I can't!" he groaned. "I—can't—Charlotte! I can't—let any other man have you! No other man shall have you!" he cried out, fiercely, and flung up his head; "you are mine, mine! I'll kill any other man that touches you!" Barney got up, and his face was flaming; he started off with a great stride, and then he stopped short and flung an arm around the slender trunk of a white-birch tree, and pulled it against him and leaned against it as if it were Charlotte, and laid his cheek on the cool white bark and sobbed again like a girl. " Oh, Charlotte, Charlotte !" he moaned, and his voice was drowned out by the manifold rustling of the young birch leaves, as a human grief is overborne and carried out of sight by the soft, resistless progress of nature.

Barney, although his faith in Charlotte had been as strong as any man's should be in his promised wife, had now no doubt but this other man had met with favor in her eyes. But he had no blame for her, nor even any surprise at her want of constancy. He blamed the Lord, for Charlotte as well as for himself. " If this hadn't happened she never would have looked at any one else," he thought, and his thought had the force of a blow against fate.

This Thomas Payne was the best match in the village ; he was the squire's son, good-looking, and college-educated. Barney had always known that he fancied Charlotte, and had felt a certain triumph that he had won her in the face of it. " You might have somebody that's a good deal better off if you didn't have me," he said to her once, and they both knew whom he meant. " I don't want anybody else," Charlotte had replied, with her shy stateliness. Now Barney thought that she had changed her mind ; and why should she not ? A girl ought to marry if she could ; he could not marry her himself, and should not expect her to remain single all her life for his sake. Of course Charlotte wanted to be mar-

ried, like other women. This probable desire of
Charlotte's for love and marriage in itself, apart from
him, thrilled his male fancy with a certain holy awe
and respect, from his love for her and utter ignorance of the attitude of womankind. Then, too, he
reflected that Thomas Payne would probably make
her a good husband. "He can buy her everything
she wants," he thought, with a curious mixture of
gratulation for her and agony on his own account.
He thought of the little bonnets he had meant to
buy for her himself, and these details pierced his
heart like needles. He sobbed, and the birch-tree
quivered in a wind of human grief. He saw Charlotte going to church in her bridal bonnet with
Thomas Payne more plainly than he could ever see
her in life, for a torturing imagination reflects life
like a magnifying-glass, and makes it clearer and
larger than reality. He saw Charlotte with Thomas
Payne, blushing all over her proud, delicate face when
he looked at her; he saw her with Thomas Payne's
children. "O God!" he gasped, and he threw himself down on the ground again, and lay there, face
downward, motionless as if fate had indeed seized
him and shaken the life out of him and left him
there for dead; but it was his own will which was
his fate.

"Barney," his father called, somewhere out in the
field. "Barney, where be you?"

"I'm coming," Barney called back, in a surly voice,
and he pulled himself up and pushed his way out of

the thicket to the ploughed field where his father stood.

"Oh, there you be!" said Caleb. Barney grunted something inarticulate, and took up his hoe again. Caleb stood watching him, his eyes irresolute under anxiously frowning brows. "Barney," he said, at length.

"Well, what do you want?"

"I've jest heard—" the old man began; then he stopped with a jump.

"I don't want to hear what you've heard. Keep it to yourself if you've heard anything!" Barney shouted.

"I didn't know as you knew," Caleb stammered, apologetically. "I didn't know as you'd heard, Barney."

Caleb went to the edge of the field, and sat down on a great stone under a wild-cherry tree. He was not feeling very well; his head was dizzy, and his wife had given him a bowl of thoroughwort and ordered him not to work.

Caleb pushed his hat back and passed his hand across his forehead. It was hot, and his face was flushed. He watched his son following up his work with dogged energy as if it were an enemy, and his mind seemed to turn stupid in the face of speculation, like a boy's over a problem in arithmetic.

There was no human being so strange and mysterious, such an unknown quantity, to Caleb Thayer as his own son. He had not one trait of character in common with him—at least, not one so translated into his own vernacular that he could comprehend it. It was to Caleb as if he looked in a glass expecting to see his own face, and saw therein the face of a stranger.

The wind was quite cool, and blew full on Caleb as he sat there. Barney kept glancing at him. At length he spoke. " You'll get cold if you sit there in that wind, father," he sang out, and there was a rude kindliness in his tone.

Caleb jumped up with alacrity. "I dunno but I shall. I guess you're right. I wa'n't goin' to set here but a minute," he answered, eagerly. Then he went over to Barney again, and stood near watching him. Barney's hoe clinked on a stone, and he stooped and picked it out of the loam, and threw it away. "There's a good many stone in this field," said the old man.

" There's some."

" It was a heap of work clearin' of it in the first place. You wa'n't more'n two year old when I cleared it. My brother Simeon helped me. It was five year before he got the fever an' died." Caleb looked at his son with anxious pleading which was out of proportion to his words, and seemed to apply to something behind them in his own mind.

Barney worked on silently.

" I don't believe but what — if you was — to go over there—you could get her back again now, away from that Payne fellar," Caleb blurted out, suddenly ; then he shrank back as if from an anticipated blow.

Barney threw a hoeful of earth high in air and faced his father.

"Once for all, father," said he, " I don't want to hear another word about this."

" I shouldn't have said nothin', Barney, but I kinder thought—"

" I don't care what you thought. Keep your thoughts to yourself."

" I know she allers thought a good deal of you, an'—"

" I don't want another word out of your mouth about it, father."

" Well, I ain't goin' to say nothin' about it if you don't want me to, Barney ; but you know how mother feels, an'— Well, I ain't goin' to say no more."

Caleb passed his hand across his forehead, and set off across the field. Just before he was out of hearing, Barney hailed him.

" Do you feel better'n you did, father?" said he.

" What say, Barney ?"

" Do you feel better'n you did this morning?"

" Yes, I feel some better, Barney—some considerable better." Caleb started to go back to Barney ; then he paused and stood irresolute, smiling towards him. "I feel considerable better," he called again ; " my head ain't nigh so dizzy as 'twas."

" You'd better go home, father, and lay down, and see if you can't get a nap," called Barney.

" Yes, I guess I will ; I guess 'twould be a good plan," returned the old man, in a pleased voice. And he went on, clambered clumsily over a stone-wall, disappeared behind some trees, reappeared in the open, then disappeared finally over the slope of the hilly field.

It was just five o'clock in the afternoon. Presently a woman came hurrying across the field, with some needle-work gathered up in her arms. She had been spending the afternoon at a neighbor's with her sewing, and was now hastening home to get supper for her husband. She was a pretty woman, and she had not been married long. She nodded to Barney as she hurried past him, holding up her gay-flowered calico skirt tidily. Her smooth fair hair shone like satin in the sun; she wore a little blue kerchief tied over her head, and it slipped back as she ran against the wind. She did not speak to Barney nor smile; he thought her handsome face looked severely at him. She had always known him, although she had not been one of his mates; she was somewhat older.

Barney felt a pang of misery as this fair, severe, and happy face passed him by. He wondered if she had been up to Charlotte's, and if Charlotte or her mother had been talking to her, and if she knew about Thomas Payne. He watched her out of sight in a swirl of gay skirts, her blue and golden head bobbing with her dancing steps; then he glanced over his shoulder at his poor new house, with its fireless chimneys. If all had gone well, he and Charlotte would have been married by this time, and she would have been bestirring herself to get supper for

him—perhaps running home from a neighbor's with
her sewing as this other woman was doing. All the
sweet domestic comfort which he had missed seemed
suddenly to toss above his eyes like the one desired
fruit of his whole life; its wonderful unknown flavor tantalized his soul. All at once he thought how
Charlotte would prepare supper for another man,
and the thought seemed to tear his heart like a pan-
ther. "He sha'n't have her!" he cried out, quite
loudly and fiercely. His own voice seemed to quiet
him, and he fell to work again with his mouth set
hard.

In half an hour he quitted work, and went up to
his house with his hoe over his shoulder like a bayonet. The house was just as the workmen had left
it on the night before his quarrel with Cephas Barnard. He had himself fitted some glass into the
windows of the kitchen and bedroom, and boarded
up the others—that was all. He had purchased a
few simple bits of furniture, and set up his miserable
bachelor house-keeping. Barney was no cook, and
he could purchase no cooked food in Pembroke.
He had subsisted mostly upon milk and eggs and a
poor and lumpy quality of corn-meal mush, which he
had made shift to stir up after many futile efforts.

The first thing which he saw on entering the
room to-night was a generous square of light Indian
cake on the table. It was not in a plate, the edges
were bent and crumbling, and the whole square
looked somewhat flattened. Barney knew at once

that his father had saved it from his own supper, had slipped it slyly into his pocket, and stolen across the field with it. His mother had not given him a mouthful since she had forbidden him to come home to dinner, and his sister had not dared.

Barney sat down and ate the Indian cake, a solitary householder at his solitary table, around which there would never be any faces but those of his dead dreams. Afterwards he pulled a chair up to an open window, and sat there, resting his elbows on the sill, staring out vacantly. The sun set, and the dusk deepened; the air was loud with birds; there were shouts of children in the distance; gradually these died away, and the stars came out. The wind was damp and sweet; over in the field pale shapes of mist wavered and changed like phantoms. A woman came running noiselessly into the yard, and pressed against the door panting, and knocked. Barney saw the swirl of light skirts around the corner; then the knock came.

He got up, trembling, and opened the door, and stood there looking at the woman, who held her hooded head down.

"It's me, Barney," said Charlotte's voice.

"Come in," said Barney, and he moved aside.

But Charlotte stood still. "I can say what I want to here," she whispered, panting. "Barney."

"Well, what is it, Charlotte?"

"Barney."

Barney waited.

"BARNEY SAT STARING AT VACANCY"

"I've come over here to - night, Barney, to see you," said Charlotte, with solemn pauses between her words. "I don't know as I ought to; I don't know but I ought to have more pride. I thought at first I never—could—but afterwards I thought it was my duty. Barney, are you going to let—anything like this—come between us—forever?"

"There's no use talking, Charlotte."

Charlotte's hooded figure stood before him stiff and straight. There was resolution in her carriage, and her pleading tone was grave and solemn.

"Barney," she said again; and Barney waited, his pale face standing aloof in the dark.

"Barney, do you think it is right to let anything like this come between you and me, when we were almost husband and wife?"

"It's no use talking, Charlotte."

"Do you think this is right, Barney?"

Barney was silent.

"If you can't answer me I will go home," said Charlotte, and she turned, but Barney caught her in his arms. He held her close, breathing in great pants. He pulled her hood back with trembling strength, and kissed her over and over, roughly.

"Charlotte," he half sobbed.

Charlotte's voice, full of a great womanly indignation, sounded in his ear. "Barney, you let me go," she said, and Barney obeyed.

"When I came here alone this way I trusted you to treat me like a gentleman," said she. She pulled her hood over her face again and turned to go. "I shall never speak to you about this again," said she. "You have chosen your own way, and you know best whether it's right, or you're happy in it."

"I hope you'll be happy, Charlotte," Barney said, with a great sigh.

"That doesn't make any difference to you," said Charlotte, coldly.

"Yes, it does; it does, Charlotte! When I heard about Thomas Payne, I felt as if—if it would make you happy. I—"

"What about Thomas Payne?" asked Charlotte, sharply.

"I heard—how he was coming to see you—"

"Do you mean that you want me to marry Thomas Payne, Barney Thayer?"

"I want you to be happy, Charlotte."

"Do you want me to marry Thomas Payne?"

Barney was silent.

"Answer me," cried Charlotte.

"Yes, I do," replied Barney, firmly, "if it would make you happy."

"You want me to marry Thomas Payne?" repeated Charlotte. "You want me to be his wife instead of yours, and go to live with him instead of you? You want me to live with another man?"

"It ain't right for you not to get married," Barney said, and his voice was hoarse and strange.

"You want me to get married to another man? Do you know what it means?"

Barney gave a groan that was half a cry.

" Do you ?"

" Oh, Charlotte !" Barney groaned, as if imploring her for pity.

" You want me to marry Thomas Payne, and live with him—"

" He'd—make you a good husband. He's—Charlotte — I can't. You've got to be happy. It isn't right—I can't—"

" Well," said Charlotte, " I will marry him. Goodnight, Barney Thayer." She went swiftly out of the yard.

" Charlotte !" Barney called after her, as if against his will ; but she never turned her head.

CHAPTER VII

On the north side of the old tavern was a great cherry orchard. In years back it had been a source of considerable revenue to Silas Berry, but for some seasons his returns from it had been very small. The cherries had rotted on the branches, or the robins had eaten them, for Silas would not give them away. Rose and her mother would smuggle a few small baskets of cherries to Sylvia Crane and Mrs. Barnard, but Silas's displeasure, had he found them out, would have been great. "I ain't a-goin' to give them cherries away to nobody," he would proclaim. "If folks don't want 'em enough to pay for 'em they can go without."

Many a great cherry picnic had been held in Silas Berry's orchard. Parties had come in great rattling wagons from all the towns about, and picked cherries and ate their fill at a most overreaching and exorbitant price.

There were no cherries like those in Silas Berry's orchard in all the country roundabout. There was no competition, and for many years he had had it all his own way. The young people's appetite for cherries and their zeal for pleasure had overcome their indignation at his usury. But at last Silas's greed got the better of his financial shrewdness; he increased his price for cherries every season, and the year after the tavern closed it became so preposterous that there was a rebellion. It was headed by Thomas Payne, who, as the squire's son and the richest and most freehanded young man in town, could incur no suspicion of parsimony. Going one night to the old tavern to make terms with Silas for the use of his cherry orchard, for a party which included some of his college friends from Boston and his fine young-lady cousin from New York, and hearing the preposterous sum which Silas stated as final, he had turned on his heel with a strong word under his breath. " You can eat your cherries yourself and be damned," said Thomas Payne, and was out of the yard with the gay swagger which he had learned along with his Greek and Latin at college. The next day Silas saw the party in Squire Payne's big wagon, with Thomas driving, and the cousin's pink cheeks and white plumed hat conspicuous in the midst, pass merrily on their way to a cherryless picnic at a neighboring pond, and the young college men shouted out a doggerel couplet which the wit of the party had made and set to a rough tune.

" Who lives here?" the basses demanded in grim melody, and the tenors responded, " Old Silas Berry, who charges sixpence for a cherry."

Silas heard the mocking refrain repeated over and over between shouts of laughter long after they were out of sight.

Rose, who had not been bidden to the picnic, heard it and wept as she peered around her curtain at the gay party. William, who had also not been bidden, stormed at his father, and his mother joined him.

"You're jest a-puttin' your own eyes out, Silas Berry," said she; "you hadn't no business to ask such a price for them cherries; it's more than they are worth; folks won't stand it. You asked too much for 'em last year."

"I know what I'm about," returned Silas, sitting in his arm-chair at the window, with dogged chin on his breast.

"You wait an' see," said Hannah. "You've jest put your own eyes out."

And after - events proved that Hannah was right. Silas Berry's cherry orchard was subjected to a species of ostracism in the village. There were no more picnics held there, people would buy none of his cherries, and he lost all the little income which he had derived from them. Hannah often twitted him with it. "You can see now that what I told you was true," said she; "you put your own eyes out." Silas would say nothing in reply; he would simply make an animal sound of defiance like a grunt in his throat, and frown. If Hannah kept on, he would stump heavily out of the room, and swing the door back with a bang.

This season Hannah had taunted her husband more than usual with his ill-judged parsimony in the matter of the cherries. The trees were quite loaded with the small green fruit, and there promised to be a very large crop. One day Silas turned on her. "You wait," said he; "mebbe I know what I'm about, more'n you think I do."

Hannah scowled with sharp interrogation at her husband's shrewdly leering face. "What be you agoin' to do?" she demanded. But she got no more out of him.

One morning about two weeks before the cherries were ripe Silas went halting in a casual way across the south yard towards his daughter Rose, who was spreading out some linen to bleach. He picked up a few stray sticks on the way, ostentatiously, as if that were his errand.

Rose was spreading out the lengths of linen in a wide sunny space just outside the shade of the cherry-trees. Her father paused, tilted his head back, and eyed the trees with a look of innocent reflection. Rose glanced at him, then she went on with her work.

"Guess there's goin' to be considerable many cherries this year," remarked her father, in an affable and confidential tone.

"I guess so," replied Rose, shortly, and she flapped out an end of the wet linen. The cherries were a sore subject with her.

"I guess there's goin' to be more than common," said Silas, still gazing up at the green boughs full of green fruit clusters.

Rose made no reply; she was down on her knees in the grass stretching the linen straight.

"I've been thinkin', " her father continued, slowly, "that—mebbe you'd like to have a little—party, an' ask some of the young folks, an' eat some of 'em when they get ripe. You could have four trees to pick off of."

"I should think we'd had enough of cherry parties," Rose cried out, bitterly.

"I didn't say nothin' about havin' 'em pay anything," said her father.

Rose straightened herself and looked at him incredulously. "Do you mean it, father?" said she.

"'Ain't I jest said you might, if you wanted to?"

"Do you mean to have them come here and not pay, father?"

"There ain't no use tryin' to sell any of 'em," replied Silas. "You can talk it over with your mother, an' do jest as you're a mind to about it, that's all. If you want to have a few of the young folks over here when them cherries are ripe, you can have four of them trees to pick off of. I ain't got no more to say about it."

Silas turned in a peremptory and conclusive manner. Rose fairly gasped as she watched his stiff one-sided progress across the yard. The vague horror of the unusual stole over her. A new phase of her father's character stood between her and all her old memories like a supernatural presence. She left the rest of the linen in the basket and sought her mother in the house. " Mother !" she called out, in a cautious voice, as soon as she entered the kitchen. Mrs. Berry's face looked inquiringly out of the pantry, and Rose motioned her back, went in herself, and shut the door.

" What be you a-shuttin' the door for ?" asked her mother, wonderingly.

" I don't know what has come over father."

" What do you mean, Rose Berry ? He 'ain't had another shock ?"

" I'm dreadful afraid he's going to ! I'm dreadful afraid something's going to happen to him !"

" I'd like to know what you mean ?" Mrs. Berry was quite pale.

" Father says I can have a cherry party, and they needn't pay anything."

Her mother stared at her. " He didn't !"

" Yes, he did."

They looked in each other's eyes, with silent renewals of doubt and affirmation. Finally Mrs. Berry laughed. " H'm ! Don't you see what your father's up to ?" she said.

" No, I don't. I'm scared."

" You needn't be. You ain't very cute. He's an old head. He thinks if he has this cherry party for nothin' folks will overlook that other affair, an' next year they'll buy the cherries again. Mebbe he thinks they'll buy the other trees this year, after the party. How many trees did he say you could have ?"

" Four. Maybe that is it."

"Of course 'tis. Your father's an old head. Well, you'd better ask 'em. They won't see through it, and it 'll make things pleasanter. I've felt bad enough about it. I guess Mis' Thayer won't look down on us quite so much if we ask a party here and let 'em eat cherries for nothin'. It's more'n she'd do, I'll warrant."

"Maybe they won't any of them come," said Rose.

"H'm! Don't you worry about that. They'll come fast enough. I never see any trouble yet about folks comin' to get anything good that they didn't have to pay for."

Rose and her mother calculated how many to invite to the party. They decided to include all the available young people in Pembroke.

"We might jest as well while we're about it," said Hannah, judiciously. "There are cherries enough, and the Lord only knows when your father 'll have another freak like this. I guess it's like an eclipse of the sun, an' won't come again very soon."

Within a day or two all the young people had been bidden to the cherry party, and, as Mrs. Berry had foretold, accepted. Their indignation was not proof against the prospect of pleasure; and, moreover, they all liked Rose and William, and would not have refused on their account.

The week before the party, when the cherries were beginning to turn red, and the robins had found them out, was an arduous one to little Ezra Ray, a young brother of Tommy Ray, who tended in Silas Berry's store. He was hired for twopence to sit all day in the cherry orchard and ring a cow-bell whenever the robins made excursions into the trees. From earliest dawn when the birds were first astir, until they sought their little nests, did Ezra sit uncomfortably upon a hard peaked rock in the midst of the orchard and jingle his bell.

He was white-headed, and large of his age like his brother. His pale blue eyes were gravely vacant under his thick white thatch; his chin dropped; his mouth gaped with stolid patience. There was no mitigation for his dull task; he was not allowed to keep his vigil on a comfortable branch of a tree with the mossy trunk for a support to his back, lest he might be tempted to eat of the cherries, and turn pal of the robins instead of enemy. He dared not pull down any low bough and have a surreptitious feast, for he understood well that there were likely to be sharp eyes at the rear windows of the house, that it was always probable that old Silas Berry, of whom he was in mortal fear, might be standing at his back, and, moreover, he should be questioned, and had not falsehood for refuge, for he was a good child, and would be constrained to speak the truth.

They would not let him have a gun instead of a bell, although he pleaded hard. Could he have sat there presenting a gun like a sentry on duty, the week, in spite of discomfort and deprivations, would have been full of glory and excitement. As it was, the dulness and monotony of the jingling of the cow-bell made even his stupid childish mind dismal. All the pleasant exhilaration of youth seemed to have deserted the boy, and life to him became as inane and bovine as to the original ringer of that bell grazing all the season in her own shadow over the same pasture-ground.

And more than all, that twopence for which Ezra toiled so miserably was to go towards the weaving of a rag carpet which his mother was making, and for which she was saving every penny. He could not lay it out in red-and-white sugar-sticks at the store. He sat there all the week, and every time there was a whir of little brown wings and the darting flash of a red breast among the cherry branches he rang in frantic haste the old cow-bell. All the solace he obtained was an occasional robin-pecked cherry which he found in the grass, and then Mr. Berry questioned him severely when he saw stains around his mouth and on his fingers.

He was on hand early in the morning on the day of the cherry picnic, trudging half awake, with the taste of breakfast in his mouth, through the acres of white dewy grass. He sat on his rock until the grass was dry, and patiently jingled his cow-bell. It was to young Ezra Ray, although all unwittingly, as if he himself were assisting in the operations of nature. He watched so assiduously that it was as if he dried the dewy grass and ripened the cherries.

When the cherry party began to arrive he still sat

on his rock and jingled his bell; he did not know when to stop. But his eyes were upon the assembling people rather than upon the robins. He watched the brave young men whose ignominy of boyhood was past, bearing ladders and tossing up shining tin pails as they came. He watched the girls swinging their little straw baskets daintily; his stupidly wondering eyes followed especially Rebecca Thayer. Rebecca, in her black muslin, with her sweet throat fairly dazzling above the half-low bodice, and wound about twice with a slender gold chain, with her black silk apron embroidered with red roses, and beautiful face glowing with rich color between the black folds of her hair, held the instinctive attention of the boy. He stared at her as she stood talking to another girl with her back quite turned upon all the young men, until his own sister touched him upon the shoulder with a sharp nudge of a bony little hand.

Amelia Ray's face, blonde like her brother's, but sharp with the sharpness of the thin and dark, was thrust into his. "You must go right home now," declared her high voice. "Mother said so."

"I'm going to stay and help pick 'em," said Ezra, in a voice which was not affirmative.

"No, you ain't."

"I can climb trees."

"You've got to go right straight home. Mother wants you to wind balls for the rag carpet."

And then Ezra Ray, with disconsolate gaping face

over his shoulder, retreated with awkward lopes across the field, the cow-bell accompanying his steps with doleful notes.

There were about forty young people at the party when all were assembled. They came mostly in couples, although now and then a little group of girls advanced across the field, and young men came singly. Barnabas Thayer came alone, and rather late; Rebecca had come some time before with one of her girl mates who had stopped for her. Barnabas, slender and handsome in his best suit, advancing with a stern and almost martial air, tried not to see Charlotte Barnard; but it was as if her face were the natural focus for his eyes, which they could not escape. However, Charlotte was not talking to Thomas Payne; he was not even very near her. He was already in the top of a cherry-tree picking busily. Barney saw his trim dark head and his bright blue waistcoat among the branches, and his heart gave a guilty throb of relief. But soon he noted that Charlotte had not her basket, and the conviction seized him that Thomas had it and was filling it with the very choicest cherries from the topmost branches, as was indeed the case.

Charlotte never looked at Barney, although she knew well when he came. She stood smiling beside another girl, her smooth fair hair gleaming in the sun, her neck showing pink through her embroidered lace kerchief, and her gleaming head and her neck seemed to survey Barney as consciously as her

"CHARLOTTE STOOD BESIDE ANOTHER GIRL"

face. Suddenly the fierceness of the instinct of possession seized him; he said to himself that it was his wife's neck; no one else should see it. He felt like tearing off his own coat and covering her with rude force. It made no difference to him that nearly every other girl there, his sister among the rest, wore her neck uncovered by even a kerchief; he felt that Charlotte should not have done so. The other young men were swarming up the trees with the girls' baskets, but he stood aloof with his forehead knitted; it was as if all his reason had deserted him. All at once there was a rustle at his side, and Rose Berry touched him on the arm; he started, and looked down into her softly glowing little face.

"Oh, here you are!" said she, and her voice had adoring cadences.

Barney nodded.

"I was afraid you weren't coming," said she, and she panted softly through her red parted lips.

Rose's crisp pink muslin gown flared scalloping around her like the pink petals of a hollyhock; her slender white arms showed through the thin sleeves. Barney could not look away from her wide-open, unfaltering blue eyes, which suddenly displayed to him strange depths. Charlotte, during all his courtship, had never looked up in his face like that. He could not himself have told why; but Charlotte had never for one moment lost sight of the individual, and the respect due him, in her lover. Rose, in the heart of New England, bred after the precepts of orthodoxy, was a pagan, and she worshipped Love himself. Barney was simply the statue that represented the divinity ; another might have done as well had the sculpture been as fine.

"I told you I was coming," Barney said, slowly, and his voice sounded odd to himself.

"I know you did, but I was afraid you wouldn't."

Rose still held her basket. Barney reached out for it. "Let me get some cherries for you," he said.

"Oh, I guess you hadn't better," Rose returned, holding the basket firmly.

"Why not ?"

"I'm—afraid Charlotte won't like it," Rose said. Her face, upturned to Barney, was full of pitiful seriousness, like a child's.

"Give me the basket," demanded Barney, and she yielded. She stood watching him as he climbed the nearest tree ; then she turned and met Charlotte's stern eyes full upon her. Rose went under the tree herself, pulled down a low branch, and began to eat; several other girls were doing the same. Thomas Payne passed the tree, bearing carefully Charlotte's little basket heaped with the finest cherries. Rose tossed her head defiantly. "She needn't say anything," she thought.

The morning advanced, the sun stood high, and there was a light wind, which now and then caused the cherry-leaves to smite the faces of the pickers. There were no robins in the trees that morning; there were only swift whirs of little wings in the distance, and sweet flurried calls which were scarcely noted in the merry clamor of the young men and girls.

Silas Berry stood a little aloof, leaning on a stout cane, looking on with an inscrutable expression on his dry old face. He noted everything; he saw Rose talking to Barney; he saw his son William eating cherries with Rebecca Thayer out of one basket; but his expression never changed. The predominant trait in his whole character had seemed to mould his face to itself unchangeably, as the face of a hunting-dog is moulded to his speed and watchfulness.

"Don't Mr. Berry look just like an old miser?" a girl whispered to Rebecca Thayer; then she started and blushed confusedly, for she remembered suddenly that William Berry was said to be waiting upon Rebecca, and she also remembered that Charlotte Barnard, who was within hearing distance, was his niece.

Rebecca blushed, too. "I never thought of it," she said, in a constrained voice.

"Well, I don't know as he does," apologized the girl. "I suppose I thought of it because he's thin. I always had an idea that a miser was thin." Then she slipped away, and presently whispered to another girl what a mistaken speech she had made, and they put their heads together with soft, averted giggles.

The girls had brought packages of luncheon in their baskets, which they had removed to make space for the cherries, and left with Mrs. Berry in the tavern. At noon they sent the young men for them, and prepared to have dinner at a little distance from the trees where they had been picking, where the ground was clean. William and Rose also went up to the tavern, and Rose beckoned to Barney as she passed him. "Don't you want to come?" she whispered, as he followed hesitatingly; "there's something to carry."

When the party returned, Mrs. Berry was with them, and she and Rose bore between them a small tub of freshly-fried hot doughnuts. Mrs. Berry had utterly refused to trust it to the young men. "I know better than to let you have it," she said, laughing. "You'd eat all the way there, and there wouldn't be enough left to go round. Me and Rose will carry it; it ain't very heavy." William and Barney each bore two great jugs of molasses-and-water spiced with ginger.

Silas pulled himself up stiffly when he saw them coming; he had been sitting upon the peaked rock whereon Ezra Ray had kept vigil with the cow-bell. Full of anxiety had he been all day lest they should pick from any except the four trees which he had set apart for them, and his anxiety was greater since he knew that the best cherries were not on those four trees. Silas sidled painfully towards his wife and daughter; he peered over into the tub, but they swung it remorselessly past him, even knocking his shin with its iron-bound side.

" What you got there ?" he demanded, huskily.

" Don't you say one word," returned his wife, with a fierce shake of her head at him.

" What's in them jugs ?"

" It's nothing but sweetened water. Don't, father," pleaded Rose under her breath, her pretty face flaming.

Her mother scowled indomitably at Silas tagging threateningly at her elbow. " Don't you say one word," she whispered again.

" You ain't goin' to—give 'em— "

" Don't you speak," she returned, hissing out the " s."

Silas said no more. He followed on, and watched the doughnuts being distributed to the merry party seated in a great ring like a very garland of youth under his trees ; he saw them drink his sweetened water.

" Don't you want some ?" asked his wife's defiantly pleasant voice in his ear.

" No, I don't want none," he returned.

Finally, long before they had finished eating, he went home to the tavern. There was no one in the house. He stole cautiously into the pantry, and there was a reserve of doughnuts in a large milk-pan sitting before the window. Silas crooked his old arm around the pan, carried it painfully across the great kitchen and the entry into the best room, and pushed it far under the bureau. Then he returned, and concealed the molasses-jug in the brick oven. He stood for a minute in the middle of the kitchen floor, chuckling and nodding as if to the familiar and confidential spirit of his own greed; then he went out, and a short way down the road to the cottage house where old Hiram Baxter lived and kept a little shoemaker's shop in the L. He entered, and sat down in the little leather-reeking place with Hiram, and was safe and removed from inquiry when Mrs. Berry returned to the tavern for the remaining doughnuts and to mix more sweetened water. The doughnuts could not be found, but she carried a pail across to the store, got more molasses from the barrel, and so in one point outwitted her husband.

Mrs. Berry was famous for her rich doughnuts, and the first supply had been quite exhausted. William went up to her at once when she returned to the party. "Where's the rest of the doughnuts?" he whispered.

"Your father's hid 'em," she whispered back. "Hush, don't say anything."

William scowled and made an exclamation. "The old—"

"Hush!" whispered his mother again; "go up to the house and get the sweetened water. I've mixed another jug."

"Where is he?" demanded William.

"I dunno. He ain't to the store."

William strode off across the field, and he searched through the house with an angry stamping and banging of doors, but he could not find his father or the doughnuts. "Father!" he called, in an angry shout, standing in the doorway, "Father!" But there was no reply, and he went back to the others with the jug of sweetened water. Rebecca watched him with furtive, anxious eyes, but he avoided looking at her. When he passed her a tumbler of sweetened water she took it and thanked him fervently, but he did not seem to heed her at all.

After dinner they played romping games under the trees—hunt the slipper, and button, and Copenhagen. Mrs. Barnard and two other women had come over to see the festivity, and they sat at a little distance with Mrs. Berry, awkwardly disposed against the trunks of trees, with their feet tucked under their skirts to keep them from the damp ground.

Copenhagen was the favorite game of the young people, and they played on and on while the afternoon deepened. Clinging to the rope they formed a struggling ring, looping this way and that way as the pursuers neared them. Their laughter and gay cries formed charming discords; their radiant faces had the likeness of one family of flowers, through their one expression. The wind blew harder; the girls' muslin skirts clung to their limbs as they moved against it, and flew out around their heels in fluttering ruffles. The cherry boughs tossed over their heads full of crisp whispers among their dark leaves and red fruit clusters. Over across the field, under the low-swaying boughs, showed the old red wall of the tavern, and against it a great mass of blooming phlox, all vague with distance like purple smoke. Over on the left, fence rails glistened purple in the sun and wind—a bluebird sat on a crumbling post and sang. But the young men and girls playing Copenhagen saw and heard nothing of these things.

They heard only that one note of love which all unwittingly, and whether they would or not, they sang to each other through all the merry game. Charlotte heard it whether she would or not, and so did Barney, and it produced in them as in the others a reckless exhilaration in spite of their sadness. William Berry forgot all his mortification and annoyance as he caught Rebecca's warm fingers on the rope and bent over her red, averted cheek. Barney, when he had grasped Rose's hands, which had fairly swung the rope his way, kissed her with an ardor which had in it a curious, fierce joy, because at that moment he caught a glimpse of Thomas Payne's handsome, audacious face meeting Charlotte's.

Barney had not wished to play, but he played with zeal, only he never seemed to see Charlotte's fingers on the rope, and Charlotte never saw his. The girls' cheeks flushed deeper, their smooth locks became roughened. The laughter waxed louder and longer; the matrons looking on doubled their broad backs with responsive merriment. It became like a little bacchanalian rout in a New England field on a summer afternoon, but they did not know it in their simple hearts.

At six o'clock the mist began to rise, the sunlight streamed through the trees in slanting golden shafts, long drawn out like organ chords. The young people gathered up their pails and baskets and went home, flocking down the road together, calling back farewells to Rose and William and their mother, who stood in front of the tavern watching them out of sight.

They were not quite out of sight when they came to Hiram Baxter's little house, and Silas Berry emerged from the shop door. "Hullo!" he cried out, and they all stopped, smiling at him with a cordiality which had in it a savor of apology. Indeed, Thomas Payne had just remarked, with a hearty chorus of assents, that he guessed the old man wasn't so bad after all.

Silas advanced towards them; he also was smiling. He fumbled in his waistcoat pocket, and drew out a roll of paper which he shook out with trembling fingers. He stepped close to Thomas Payne and extended it.

"What is it?" asked the young man.

Silas smiled up in his face with the ingenuous smile of a child.

"What is it?" Thomas Payne asked again.

The others crowded around.

"It's nothin' but the bill," replied Silas, in a wheedling whisper. His dry old face turned red, his smile deepened.

"The bill for what?" demanded Thomas Payne, and he seized the paper.

"For the cherries you eat," replied Silas. "I've always been in the habit of chargin' more, but I've took off a leetle this time." His voice had a ring of challenge, his eyes were sharp, while his mouth smiled.

Thomas Payne scowled over the bill. The other young men peered at it over his shoulder, and repeated the amount with whistles and half-laughs of scorn and anger. The girls ejaculated to each other in whispers. Silas stood impervious, waiting.

The young men whipped out their purses without a word, but Thomas motioned them back. "I'll pay, and we'll settle afterwards. We can't divide up here," he said, and he crammed some money hard in Silas's eagerly outstretched hand. "Thank you for your hospitality, Mr. Berry," said Thomas Payne, his face all flaming and his eyes flashing, but his voice quite steady. "I hope you'll have as good luck selling your cherries next year."

There was a little exulting titter over the sarcasm among the girls, in which Rebecca did not join; then the party kept on. The indignant clamor waxed loud in a moment; they scarcely waited for the old man's back to be turned on his return to the tavern.

But the young people, crying out all together against this last unparalleled meanness, had not reached the foot of the hill, where some of them separated, when they heard the quick pound of running feet behind them and a hoarse voice calling on Thomas Payne to stop. They all turned, and William came up, pale and breathing hard. "What did you pay him?" he asked of Thomas Payne.

"See here, William, we all know you had nothing to do with it," Thomas cried out.

"What did you pay him?" William repeated, in a stern gasp.

"It's all right."

"You tell me what you paid him."

Thomas Payne blushed all over his handsome boyish face. He half whispered the amount to William, although the others knew it as well as he.

William pulled out his purse, and counted out some money with trembling fingers. "Take it, for God's sake!" said he, and Thomas Payne took it. "We all know that you knew nothing about it," he said again. The others chimed in with eager assent, but William gave his head a shake, as if he shook off water, and broke away from them all, and pelted up the hill with his heart so bitterly sore that it seemed as if he trod on it at every step.

A voice was crying out behind him, but he never heeded. There were light, hurrying steps after him, and a soft flutter of girlish skirts, but he never looked away from his own self until Rebecca touched his arm. Then he looked around with a start and a great blush, and jerked his arm away.

But Rebecca followed him up quite boldly, and caught his arm again, and looked up in his face. "Don't you feel bad," said she; "don't you feel bad. You aren't to blame."

" Isn't he my father ?"

" You aren't to blame for that."

" Disgrace comes without blame," said William, and he moved on.

Rebecca kept close to his side, clinging to his arm. " It's your father's way," said she. " He's honest, anyway. Nobody can say he isn't honest."

" It depends upon what you call honest," William said, bitterly. " You'd better run back, Rebecca. You don't want them to think you're going with me, and they will. I'm disgraced, and so is Rose. You'd better run back."

Rebecca stopped, and he did also. She looked up in his face; her mouth was quivering with a kind of helpless shame, but her eyes were full of womanly courage and steadfastness. " William," said she, " I ran away in the face and eyes of them all to comfort you. They saw me, and they can see me now, but I don't care. And I don't care if you see me; I always have cared, but I don't now. I have always been terribly afraid lest you should think I was running after you, but I ain't afraid now. Don't you feel bad, William. That's all I care about. Don't you feel bad; nobody is going to think any less of you. I don't; I think more."

William looked down at her; there was a hesitating appeal in his face, as in that of a hurt child. Suddenly Rebecca raised both her arms and put them around his neck; he leaned his cheek down against her soft hair. "Poor William," she whispered, as if he had been her child instead of her lover.

A girl in the merry party speeding along at the foot of the hill glanced around just then; she turned again, blushing hotly, and touched a girl near her, who also glanced around. Then their two blushing faces confronted each other with significant half-shamed smiles of innocent young girlhood.

They locked arms, and whispered as they went on. "Did you see?" "Yes." "His head?" "Yes." "Her arms?" "Yes." Neither had ever had a lover.

But the two lovers at the top of the hill paid no heed. The party were all out of sight when they went slowly down in the gathering twilight. William left Rebecca when they came opposite her house.

CHAPTER VIII

When Rebecca entered the house, her mother was standing over the stove, making milk-toast for supper. The boiling milk steamed up fiercely in her face. " What makes you so long behind the others?" she demanded, without turning, stirring the milk as she spoke.

" I guess I ain't much, am I ?" Rebecca said, evasively. She tried to make her voice sound as it usually did, but she could not. It broke and took on faltering cadences, as if she were intoxicated with some subtle wine of the spirit.

Her mother looked around at her. Rebecca's face was full of a strange radiance which she could not subdue before her mother's hard, inquiring gaze. Her cheeks burned with splendid color, her lips trembled into smiles in spite of herself, her eyes were like dark fires, shifting before her mother's, but not paling.

" Ephraim see 'em all go by half an hour ago," said her mother.

Rebecca made no reply.

" If," said her mother, " you stayed behind to see William Berry, I can tell you one thing, once for all: you needn't do it again."

"I had to see him about something," Rebecca faltered.

"Well, you needn't see him again about anything. You might jest as well understand it first as last: if you've got any idea of havin' William Berry, you've got to give it up."

"Mother, I'd like to know what you mean!" Rebecca cried out, blushing.

"Look 'round here at me!" her mother ordered, suddenly.

"Don't, mother."

"Look at me!"

Rebecca lifted her face perforce, and her mother eyed her pitilessly. "You ain't been tellin' of him you'd have him, now?" said she. "Why don't you speak?"

"Not—just."

"Then you needn't."

"Mother!"

"You needn't talk. You can jest make up your mind to it. You ain't goin' to marry William Berry. Your brother has had enough to do with that family."

"Mother, you won't stop my marrying William because Barney won't marry his cousin Charlotte? There ain't any sense in that."

"I've got my reasons, an' that's enough for you," said Deborah. "You ain't goin' to marry William Berry."

"I am, if you haven't got any better reason than

that. I won't stand it, mother; it ain't right!" Rebecca cried out.

"Then," said Deborah, and as she spoke she began spooning out the toast gravy into a bowl with a curious stiff turn of her wrist and a superfluous vigor of muscle, as if it were molten lead instead of milk; and, indeed, she might, from the look in her face, have been one of her female ancestors in the times of the French and Indian wars, casting bullets with the yells of savages in her ears—"then," said she, "I sha'n't have any child but Ephraim left, that's all!"

"Mother, don't!" gasped Rebecca.

"There's another thing: if you marry William Berry against your parents' wishes, you know what you have to expect. You remember your aunt Rebecca."

Rebecca twisted her whole body about with the despairing motion with which she would have wrung her hands, flung open the door, and ran out of the room.

Deborah went on spooning up the toast. Ephraim had come in just as she spoke last to Rebecca, and he stood staring, grinning with gaping mouth.

"What's Rebecca done, mother?" he asked, pleadingly, catching hold of his mother's dress.

"Nothin' for you to know. Go an' wash your face an' hands, an' come in to supper."

"Mother, what's she done?" Ephraim's pleading voice lengthened into a whine. He took more liberties with his mother than any one else dared; he even jerked her dress now by way of enforcing an answer. But she grasped his arm so vigorously that he cried out. "Go out to the pump, an' wash your face an' hands," she repeated, and Ephraim made a little involuntary run to the door.

As he went out he rolled his eyes over his shoulder at his mother with tragic surprise and reproach, but she paid no attention. When he came in she ignored the great painful sigh which he heaved and the podgy hand clapped ostentatiously over his left side. "Draw your chair up," said she.

"I dunno as I want any supper. I've got a pain. Oh dear!" Ephraim writhed, with attentive eyes upon his mother; he was like an executioner turning an emotional thumbscrew on her. But Deborah Thayer's emotions sometimes presented steel surfaces. "You can have a pain, then," said she. "I ain't goin' to let you go to ruin because you ain't well, not if I know it. You've got to mind, sick or well, an' you might jest as well know it. I'll have one child obey me, whether or no. Set up to the table."

Ephraim drew up his chair, whimpering; but he fell to on the milk-toast with ardor, and his hand dropped from his side. He had eaten half a plateful when his father came in. Caleb had been milking; the cows had been refractory as he drove them from pasture, and he was late.

"Supper's been ready half an hour," his wife said, when he entered.

"The heifer run down the old road when I was a-drivin' of her home, an' I had to chase her," Caleb returned, meekly, settling down in his arm-chair at the table.

"I guess that heifer wouldn't cut up so every night if I had the drivin' of her," remarked Deborah. She filled a plate with toast and passed it over to Caleb.

Caleb set it before him, but he did not begin to eat. He looked at Rebecca's empty place, then at his wife's face, long and pale and full of stern rancor, behind the sugar-bowl and the cream-pitcher.

"Rebecca got home?" he ventured, with wary eyes upon her.

"Yes, she's got home."

Caleb winked, meekly. "Ain't she comin' to supper?"

"I dunno whether she is or not."

"Does she know it's ready?" Deborah vouchsafed no reply. She poured out the tea.

Caleb grated his chair suddenly. "I'll jest speak to her," he proclaimed, courageously.

"She knows it's ready. You set still," said Deborah. And Caleb drew his chair close again, and loaded his knife with toast, bringing it around to his mouth with a dexterous sidewise motion.

"She ain't sick, is she?" he said, presently, with a casual air.

"No, I guess she ain't sick."

"I s'pose she eat so many cherries she didn't want

any supper," Caleb said, chuckling anxiously. His wife made no reply. Ephraim reached over slyly for the toast-spoon, and she pushed his hand back.

"You can't have any more," said she.

"Can't I have jest a little more, mother?"

"No, you can't."

"I feel faint at my stomach, mother."

"You can keep on feelin' faint."

"Can't I have a piece of pie, mother?"

"You can't have another mouthful of anything to eat to-night."

Ephraim clapped his hand to his side again and sighed, but his mother took no notice.

"Have you got a pain, sonny?" asked Caleb.

"Yes, dreadful. Oh!"

"Hadn't he ought to have somethin' on it?" Caleb inquired, looking appealingly at Deborah.

"He can have some of his doctor's medicine if he don't feel better," she replied, in a hard voice. "Set your chair back now, Ephraim, and get out your catechism."

"I don't feel fit to, mother," groaned Ephraim.

"You do jest as I tell you," said his mother.

And Ephraim, heaving with sighs, muttering angrily far under his breath lest his mother should hear, pulled his chair back to the window, and got his catechism out of the top drawer of his father's desk, and began droning out in his weak, sulky voice the first question therein: "What is the chief end of man?"

"Now shut the book and answer it," said his mother, and Ephraim obeyed.

Ephraim was quite conversant with the first three questions and their answers, after that his memory began to weaken; either he was a naturally dull scholar, or his native indolence made him appear so. He had been drilled nightly upon the "Assembly's Catechism" for the past five years, and had had many a hard bout with it before that in his very infancy, when his general health admitted—and sometimes, it seemed to Ephraim, when it had not admitted.

Many a time had the boy panted for breath when he rehearsed those grandly decisive, stately replies to those questions of all ages, but his mother had been obdurate. He could not understand why, but in reality Deborah held her youngest son, who was threatened with death in his youth, to the "Assembly's Catechism" as a means of filling his mind with spiritual wisdom, and fitting him for that higher state to which he might soon be called. Ephraim had been strictly forbidden to attend school —beyond reading he had no education; but his mother resolved that spiritual education he should have, whether he would or not, and whether the doctor would or not. So Ephraim laboriously read the Bible through, a chapter at a time, and he went, step by step, through the wisdom of the Divines of Westminster. No matter how much he groaned over it, his mother was pitiless. Sometimes Caleb plucked up courage and interceded. "I don't believe he feels quite ekal to learnin' of his stint to-night," he would say, and then his eyes would fall before the terrible stern pathos in Deborah's, as she would reply in her deep voice: "If he can't learn nothin' about books, he's got to learn about his own soul. He's got to, whether it hurts him or not. I shouldn't think, knowin' what you know, you'd say anything, Caleb Thayer."

And Caleb's old face would quiver suddenly like a child's; he would rub the back of his hand across his eyes, huddle himself into his arm-chair, and say no more; and Deborah would sharply order Ephraim, spying anxiously over his catechism, to go on with the next question.

It was nearly dark to-night when Ephraim finished his stint; he was slower than usual, his progress being somewhat hindered by the surreptitious eating of a hard red apple, which he had stowed away in his jacket-pocket. Hard apples were strictly forbidden to Ephraim as articles of diet, and to eat many during the season required diplomacy.

The boy's jaws worked with furious zeal over the apple during his mother's temporary absences from the room on household tasks, and on her return were mumbling solemnly and innocently the precepts of the catechism, after a spasmodic swallowing. His father was nodding in his chair and saw nothing, and had he seen would not have betrayed him. After a little inefficient remonstrance on his own account,

Caleb always subsided, and watched anxiously lest Deborah should discover the misdemeanor and descend upon Ephraim.

To-night, after the task was finished, Deborah sent Ephraim stumbling out of the room to bed, muttering remonstrances, his eyes as wild and restless as a cat's, his ears full of the nocturnal shouts of his playfellows that came through the open windows.

"Mother, can't I go out an' play ball a little while?" sounded in a long wail from the dusk outside the door.

"You go to bed," answered his mother. Then the slamming of a door shook the house.

"If he wa'n't sick, I'd whip him," said Deborah, between tight lips; the spiritual whip which Ephraim held by right of his illness over her seemed to sing past her ears. She shook Caleb with the force with which she might have shaken Ephraim. "You'd better get up an' go to bed now, instead of sleepin' in your chair," she said, imperatively; and Caleb obeyed, staggering, half-dazed, across the floor into the bedroom. Deborah was only a few years younger than her husband, but she had retained her youthful vigor in much greater degree. She never felt the drowsiness of age stealing over her at nightfall. Indeed, oftentimes her senses seemed to gain in alertness as the day wore on, and many a night she was up and at work long after all the other members of her family were in bed. There came at such times to Deborah Thayer a certain peace and triumphant security, when all the other wills over which her own held contested sway were lulled to sleep, and she could concentrate all her energies upon her work. Many a long task of needle-work had she done in the silence of the night, by her dim oil lamp; in years past she had spun and woven, and there was in a clothes-press up-stairs a wonderful coverlid in an intricate pattern of blue and white, and not a thread of it woven by the light of the sun.

None of the neighbors knew why Deborah Thayer worked so much at night; they attributed it to her tireless industry. "The days wa'n't never long enough for Deborah Thayer," they said—and she did not know why herself.

There was deep in her heart a plan for the final disposition of these nightly achievements, but she confided it to no one, not even to Rebecca. The blue-and-white coverlid, many a daintily stitched linen garment and lace-edged pillow-slip she destined for Rebecca when she should be wed, although she frowned on Rebecca's lover and spoke harshly to her of marriage. To-night, while Rebecca lay sobbing in her little bedroom, the mother knitted assiduously until nearly midnight upon a wide linen lace with which to trim dimity curtains for the daughter's bridal bedstead.

Deborah needed no lamplight for this knitting-work; she was so familiar with it, having knitted yards with her thoughts elsewhere, that she could knit without seeing her needles.

So she sat in the deepening dusk and knitted, and heard the laughter and shouts of the boys at play a little way down the road with a deeper pang than Ephraim had ever felt over his own deprivation.

She was glad when the gay hubbub ceased and the boys were haled into bed. Shortly afterwards she heard out in the road a quick, manly tread and a merry whistle. She did not know the tune, but only one young man in Pembroke could whistle like that. "It's Thomas Payne goin' up to see Charlotte Barnard," she said to herself, with a bitter purse of her lips in the dark. That merry whistler, passing her poor cast-out son in his lonely, half-furnished house, whose dark, shadowy walls she could see across the field, smote her as sorely as he smote him. It seemed to her that she could hear that flute-like melody even as far as Charlotte's door. In spite of her stern resolution to be just, a great gust of wrath shook her. "Lettin' of him come courtin' her when it ain't six weeks since Barney went," she said, quite out loud, and knitted fiercely.

But poor Thomas Payne, striding with his harmless swagger up the hill, whistling as loud as might be one of his college airs, need not, although she knew it not and he knew it not himself, have disturbed her peace of mind.

Charlotte, at the cherry party, had asked him, with a certain dignified shyness, if he could come up to her house that evening, and he had responded with alacrity. "Why, of course I can," he cried, blush-

"MANY A LONG TASK OF NEEDLE-WORK HAD SHE DONE"

ing joyfully all over his handsome face—"of course I can, Charlotte !" And he tried to catch one of her hands hanging in the folds of her purple dress, but she drew it away.

"I want to see you a few minutes about something," she said, soberly; and then she pressed forward to speak to another girl, and he could not get another word with her about it.

Charlotte, after she got home from the party, had changed her pretty new gown for her every-day one of mottled brown calico set with a little green sprig, and had helped her mother get supper.

Cephas, however, was late, and did not come home until just before Thomas Payne arrived. Sarah had begun to worry. "I don't see where your father is," she kept saying to Charlotte. When she heard his shuffling step on the door-stone she started as if he had been her lover. When he came in she scrutinized him anxiously, to see if he looked ill or disturbed. Sarah Barnard, during all absences of her family, dug busily at imaginary pitfalls for them; had they all existed the town would have been honeycombed.

"There ain't nothin' happened, has there, Cephas?" she said.

"I dunno of anythin' that's happened."

"I got kind of worried. I didn't know where you was." Sarah had an air of apologizing for her worry. Cephas made no reply; he did not say where he had been, nor account for his tardiness; he did not look at his wife, standing before him with her pathetically inquiring face. He pulled a chair up to the table and sat down, and Charlotte set his supper before him. It was a plate of greens, cold boiled dock, and some rye-and-Indian bread. Cephas still adhered to his vegetarian diet, although he pined on it, and the longing for the flesh-pots was great in his soul. However, he said no more about sorrel pies, for the hardness and the flavor of those which he had prepared had overcome even his zeal of invention. He ate of them manfully twice; then he ate no more, and he did not inquire how Sarah disposed of them after they had vainly appeared on the table a week. She, with no pig nor hens to eat them, was forced, with many misgivings as to the waste, to deposit them in the fireplace.

"They actually made good kindlin' wood," she told her sister Sylvia. "Poor Cephas, he didn't have no more idea than a baby about makin' pies." All Sarah's ire had died away; to-night she set a large plump apple-pie slyly on the table—an apple-pie with ample allowance of lard in the crust thereof; and she felt not the slightest exultation, only honest pleasure, when she saw, without seeming to, Cephas cut off a goodly wedge, after disposing of his dock greens.

"Poor father, I'm real glad he's tastin' of the pie," she whispered to Charlotte in the pantry; "greens ain't very fillin'."

Charlotte smiled, absently. Presently she slipped into the best room and lighted the candles. "You expectin' of anybody to-night?" her mother asked, when she came out.

"I didn't know but somebody might come," Charlotte replied, evasively. She blushed a little before her mother's significantly smiling face, but there was none of the shamed delight which should have accompanied the blush. She looked very sober—almost stern.

"Hadn't you better put on your other dress again, then?" asked her mother.

"No, I guess this 'll do."

Cephas ate his pie in silence—he had helped himself to another piece—but he heard every word. After he had finished, he fumbled in his pocket for his old leather purse, and counted over a little store of money on his knee.

Charlotte was setting away the dishes in the pantry when her father came up behind her and crammed something into her hand. She started. "What is it?" said she.

"Look and see," said Cephas.

Charlotte opened her hand, and saw a great silver dollar. "I thought mebbe you'd like to buy somethin' with it," said Cephas. He cleared his throat, and went out through the kitchen into the shed. Charlotte was too amazed to thank him; her mother came into the pantry. "What did he give you?" she whispered.

Charlotte held up the money. "Poor father," said Sarah Barnard, "he's doin' of it to make up. He was dreadful sorry about that other, an' he's tickled 'most to death now he thinks you've got somebody else, and are contented. Poor father, he ain't got much money, either."

" I don't want it," Charlotte said, her steady mouth quivering downward at the corners.

" You keep it. He'd feel all upset if you didn't. You'll find it come handy. I know you've got a good many things now, but you had ought to have a new cape come fall; you can't come out bride in a muslin one when snow flies." Sarah cast a half-timid, half-shrewd glance at Charlotte, who put the dollar in her pocket.

" A green satin cape, lined and wadded, would be handsome," pursued her mother.

" I sha'n't ever come out bride," said Charlotte.

" How you talk. There, he's comin' now !"

And, indeed, at that the clang of the knocker sounded through the house. Charlotte took off her apron and started to answer it, but her mother caught her and pinned up a stray lock of hair. " I 'most wish you had put on your other dress again," she whispered.

Sarah listened with her ear close to the crack of the kitchen door when her daughter opened the outside one. She heard Thomas Payne's hearty greeting and Charlotte's decorous reply. The door of the front room shut, then she set the kitchen door ajar softly, but she could hear nothing but a vague hum of voices across the entry ; she could not distinguish a word. However, it was as well that she could not, for her heart would have sunk, as did poor Thomas Payne's. .

Thomas, with his thick hair brushed into a shining roll above his fair high forehead, in his best flowered waistcoat and blue coat with brass buttons, sat opposite Charlotte, his two nicely booted feet toeing out squarely on the floor, his two hands on his knees, and listened to what she had to say, while his boyish face changed and whitened. Thomas was older than Charlotte, but he looked younger. It seemed, too, as if he looked younger when with her than at other times, although he was always anxiously steady and respectful, and lost much of that youthful dash which made him questioningly admired by the young people of Pembroke.

Charlotte began at once after they were seated. Her fair, grave face colored, her voice had in it a solemn embarrassment. "I don't know but you thought I was doing a strange thing to ask you to come here to-night," she said.

"No, I didn't; I didn't think so, Charlotte," Thomas declared, warmly.

"I felt as if I ought to. I felt as if it was my duty to," said she. She cast her eyes down. Thomas waited, looking at her with vague alarm. Somehow some college scrapes of his flashed into his head, and he had a bewildered idea that she had found them out and that her sweet rigid innocence was shocked, and she was about to call him to account.

But Charlotte continued, raising her eyes, and meeting his gravely and fairly :

"You've been coming here three Sabbath evenings running, now," said she.

"Yes, I know I have, Charlotte."

"And you mean to keep on coming, if I don't say anything to hinder it ?"

"You know I do, Charlotte," replied Thomas, with ardent eyes upon her face.

"Then," said Charlotte, "I feel as if it was my duty to say this to you, Thomas. If you come in any other way than as a friend, if you come on any other errand than friendship, you must not come here any more. It isn't right for me to encourage you, and let you come here and get your feelings enlisted. If you come here occasionally as a friend in friendship I shall be happy to have you, but you must not come here with any other hopes or feelings."

Charlotte's solemnly stilted words, and earnest, severe face chilled the young man opposite. His face sobered. "You mean that you can't ever think of me in any other way than as a friend," he said.

Charlotte nodded. "You know it is not because there's one thing against you, Thomas."

"Then it is Barney, after all."

"I was all ready to marry him a few weeks ago," Charlotte said, with a kind of dignified reproach.

Thomas colored. "I know it, Charlotte; I ought not to have expected—I suppose you couldn't get over it so soon. I couldn't if I had been in your place, and been ready to marry anybody. But I didn't know about girls; I didn't know but they were different; I always heard they got over things quicker. I ought not to have thought— But, oh, Charlotte, if I wait, if you have a little more time, don't you think you will feel different about it?"

Charlotte shook her head.

" But he is such a good-for-nothing dog to treat you the way he does, Charlotte!" Thomas cried out, in a great burst of wrath and jealous love.

" I don't want to hear another word like that, Thomas Payne," Charlotte said, sternly, and the young man drooped before her.

" I beg your pardon, Charlotte," said he. " I suppose I ought not to have spoken so, if you— Oh, Charlotte, then you don't think you ever can get over this and think a little bit of me?"

" No," replied Charlotte, in a steady voice, " I don't think I ever can, Thomas."

" I don't mean that I am trying to get you away from any other fellow, Charlotte—I wouldn't do anything like that; but if he won't — Oh, Charlotte, are you sure?"

" I don't think I ever can," repeated Charlotte, monotonously, looking at the wall past Thomas.

" I've always thought so much of you, Charlotte, though I never told you so."

" You'd better not now."

" Yes, I'm going to, now. I've got to. Then I'll

never say another word—I'll go away, and never say
another word." Thomas got up, and brought his
chair close to Charlotte's. "Don't move away," he
pleaded; "let me sit here near you once—I never shall
again. I'm going to tell you, Charlotte. I used to
look across at you sitting in the meeting-house, Sabbath days, when I was a boy, and think you were the
handsomest girl I ever saw. Then I did try to go
with you once before I went to college ; perhaps you
didn't know that I meant anything, but I did. Barney was in the way then a little, but I didn't think
much of it. I didn't know that he really meant to
go with you. You let me go home with you two or
three times—perhaps you remember."

Charlotte nodded.

"I never forgot," said Thomas Payne. "Well,
father found it out, and he had a talk with me. He
made me promise to wait till I got through college-be-
fore I said anything to you; he was doing a good
deal for me, you know. So I waited, and the first
thing I knew, when I came home, they said Barney
Thayer was waiting on you, and I thought it was all
settled and there was nothing more to be done. I
made up my mind to bear it like a man and make the
best of it, and I did. But this spring when I was
through college, and that happened betwixt you and
Barney, when he—didn't come back to you, and you
didn't seem to mind so much, I couldn't help having a
little hope. I waited and kept thinking he'd make up
with you, but he didn't, and I knew how determined

he was. Then finally I began to make a few advances, but—well, it's all over now, Charlotte. There's only one thing I'd like to ask: if I hadn't waited, as I promised father, would it have made any difference? Did you always like Barney Thayer?"

"Yes; it wouldn't have made any difference," Charlotte said. There were tears in her eyes.

Thomas Payne arose. "Then that is all," said he. "I never had any chance, if I had only known. I've got nothing more to say. I want to thank you for asking me to come here to-night and telling me. It was a good deal kinder than to let me keep on coming. That would have been rather hard on a fellow." Thomas Payne fairly laughed, although his handsome face was white. "I hope it will all come right betwixt you and Barney, Charlotte," he said, "and don't you worry about me, I shall get on. I'll own this seems a little harder than it was before, but I shall get on." Thomas brushed his bell hat carefully with his cambric handkerchief, and stowed it under his arm. "Good-bye, Charlotte," said he, in his old gay voice; "when you ask me, I'll come and dance at your wedding."

Charlotte got up, trembling. Thomas reached out his hand and touched her smooth fair head softly. "I never touched you nor kissed you, except in games like that Copenhagen to-day," said he; "but I've thought of it a good many times."

Charlotte drew back. "I can't, Thomas," she faltered. She could not herself have defined her reason for refusing her cast-off lover this one comfort, but it was not so much loyalty as the fear of disloyalty which led her to do so. In spite of herself, she saw Barney for an instant beside Thomas to his disadvantage, and her love could not cover him, extend it as she would. The conviction was strong upon her that Thomas was the better man of the two, although she did not love him.

"All right," said Thomas, "I ought not to have asked it of you, Charlotte. Good-bye."

As soon as Thomas Payne got out in the dark night air, and the door had shut behind him, he set up his merry whistle. Charlotte stood at the front window, and heard it from far down the hill.

CHAPTER IX

ONE Sunday evening, about four months after the cherry party, Barnabas Thayer came out of his house and strolled slowly across the road. Then he paused, and leaned up against some pasture bars and looked around him. There was nobody in sight on the road in either direction, and everything was very still, except for the vibrating calls of the hidden insects that come to their flood-tide of life in early autumn.

Barnabas listened to those calls, which had in them a certain element of mystery, as have all things which reach only one sense. They were in their humble way the voices of the unseen, and as he listened they seemed to take on a rhythmic cadence. Presently the drone of multifold vibrations sounded in his ears with even rise and fall, like the mighty breathing of Nature herself. The sun was low, and the sky was full of violet clouds. Barney could see outlined faintly against them the gray sweep of the roof that covered Charlotte's daily life.

Soon the bell for the evening meeting began to ring, and Barney started. People might soon appear on their way to meeting, and he did not want to see them. Barney avoided everybody now; he had been nowhere since the cherry party, not even

to meeting. He led the life of a hermit, and seldom met his kind at all, except at the store, where
he went to buy the simple materials for his solitary
meals.

Barney turned aside from the main road into the
old untravelled one leading past Sylvia Crane's house.
It appeared scarcely more than a lane ; the old wheel-
ruts were hidden between green weedy ridges, the
bordering stone-walls looked like long green barrows,
being overgrown with poison - ivy vines and rank
shrubs. For a long way there was no house except
Sylvia Crane's. There was one cellar where a house
had stood before Barney could remember. There
were a few old blackened chimney-bricks still there,
the step-stone worn by dead and forgotten feet, and
the old lilac-bushes that had grown against the front
windows. Two poplar-trees, too, stood where the
front yard had met the road, casting long shadows
like men. Sylvia Crane's house was just beyond,
and Barney passed it with a furtive anxious glance,
because Charlotte's aunt lived there. He saw nobody at the windows, but the guardian - stone was
quite rolled away from the door, so Sylvia was at
home.

Barney walked a little way beyond ; then he sat
down on the stone-wall, and remained there, motionless. He heard the meeting-bell farther away, then
it ceased. The wind was quite crisp and cool, and
it smote his back from the northwest. He could
smell wild - grapes and the pungent odor of decay-

" HE REMAINED THERE MOTIONLESS "

ing leaves. The autumn was beginning, and over his thoughts, raised like a ghost from the ashes of the summer, stole a vague vision of the winter. He saw for a second the driving slant of the snow-storm over the old drifting road, he saw the white slant of Sylvia's house-roof through it. And at the same time a curious, pleasant desire, which might be primitive and coeval with the provident passion of the squirrels and honey-bees, thrilled him. Then he dismissed it bitterly. What need of winter-stores and provisions for sweet home-comfort in the hearts of freezing storms was there for him? What did he care whether or not he laid in stores of hearth-wood, of garden produce, of apples, just for himself in his miserable solitude? The inborn desire of Northern races at the approach of the sterile winters, containing, as do all desires to insure their fulfilment, the elements of human pleasure, failed suddenly to move him when he remembered that his human life, in one sense, was over.

Opposite him across the road, in an old orchard, was a tree full of apples. The low sun struck them, and they showed spheres of rosy orange, as brilliant as Atalanta's apples of gold, against the background of dark violet clouds. Barney looked at this tree, which was glorified for the time almost out of its common meaning as a tree, as he might have looked at a gorgeous procession passing before him, while his mind was engrossed with his own misery, seeming to project before his eyes like a veil.

Presently it grew dusky, and the glowing apples faded; the town-clock struck eight. Barney counted the strokes; then he arose and went slowly back. He had not gone far when he saw at a distance down the road a man and woman strolling slowly towards him. They disappeared suddenly, and he thought they had turned into a lane which opened upon the road just there. He thought to himself, and with no concern, that it might have been his sister Rebecca —something about the woman's gait suggested her— and William Berry. He knew that William was not allowed in his mother's house, and that he and Rebecca met outside. He looked up the dusky lane when he came to it, but he saw nobody.

When he reached Sylvia Crane's house he noticed that the front door was open, and a woman stood there in a dim shaft of candle-light which streamed from the room beyond. He started, for he thought it might be Charlotte; then he saw that it was Sylvia Crane leaning out towards him, shading her eyes with her hand.

He said " Good-evening " vaguely, and passed on. Then he heard a cry of indistinct words behind him, and turned. " What is it?" he called. But still he could not understand what she said, her voice was so broken, and he went back.

When he got quite close to the gate he understood. " You ain't goin' past, Richard? You ain't goin' past, Richard?" Sylvia was wailing over and over, clinging to the old gate-post.

Barney stood before her, hesitating. Sylvia reached out a hand towards him, clutching piteously with pale fingers through the gloom. Barney drew back from the poor hand. "I rather think—you've—made a mistake," he faltered out.

"You ain't goin' past, Richard?" Sylvia wailed out again. She flung out her lean arm farther towards him. Then she wavered. Barney thought she was going to fall, and he stepped forward and caught hold of her elbow. "I guess you don't feel well, do you, Miss Crane?" he said. "I guess you had better go into the house, hadn't you?"

"I feel—kind of—bad—I—thought you was goin' —past," gasped Sylvia. Barney supported her awkwardly into the house. At times she leaned her whole trembling weight upon him, and then withdrew herself, all unnerved as she was, with the inborn maiden reticence which so many years had strengthened; once she pushed him from her, then drooped upon his arm again, and all the time she kept moaning, "I thought you was goin' right past, Richard, I thought you was goin' right past."

And Barney kept repeating, "I guess you've made a mistake, Miss Crane"; but she did not heed him.

When they were inside the parlor he shifted her weight gently on to the sofa, and would have drawn off; but she clung to his arm, and it seemed to him that he was forced to sit down beside her or be rough with her. "I thought you was goin' right past, Richard," she said again.

"I ain't Richard," said Barney; but she did not seem to hear him. She looked straight in his face with a strange boldness, her body inclined towards him, her head thrown back. Her thin, faded cheeks were burning, her blue eyes eager, her lips twitching with pitiful smiles. The room was dim with candle-light, but everything in it was distinct, and Sylvia Crane, looking straight at Barney Thayer's face, saw the face of Richard Alger.

Suddenly Barney himself had a curious impression. The features of Richard Alger instead of his own seemed to look back at him from his own thoughts. He dashed his hand across his face with an impatient, bewildered motion, as if he brushed away unseen cobwebs, and stood up. "You have made—" he began again; but Sylvia interrupted him with a weak cry. "Set down here, set down here, jest a minute, if you don't want to kill me!" she wailed out, and she clutched at his sleeve and pulled him down, and before he knew what she was doing had shrunk close to him, and laid her head on his shoulder. She went on talking desperately in her weak voice— strained shrill octaves above her ordinary tone.

"I've had this — sofa ten years," she said—"ten years, Richard—an' you never set with me on it before, an'—you'd been comin'—here a long while before that came betwixt us last spring, Richard. Ain't you forgiven me yet?"

Barney made no reply.

"Can't you put your arm around me jest once,

Richard?" she went on. "You ain't never, an' you've been comin' here a long while. I've had this sofa ten years."

Barney put his arm around her, seemingly with no volition of his own.

"It's six months to-day sence you came last," Sylvia said—"it's six whole months; an' when I see you goin' past to-night, it didn't seem as if I could bear it—it didn't seem as if I could bear it, Richard." Sylvia turned her pale profile closer to Barney's breast and sobbed faintly. "I've watched so long for you," she sighed out; "all these months I've sat there at the window, strainin' my eyes into the dark. Oh, you don't know, Richard, you won't never know!"

Barney trembled with Sylvia's sobs. He sat with a serious shamefacedness, his arm around the poor bony waist, staring over the faded fair head, which had never lain on any lover's breast except in dreams. For the moment he could not stir; he had a feeling of horror, as if he saw his own double. There was a subtle resemblance which lay deeper than the features between him and Richard Alger. Sylvia saw it, and he saw his own self reflected as Richard Alger in that straining mental vision of hers which exceeded the spiritual one.

"Can't you forgive me, an'—come again the way —you used to?" Sylvia panted out. "I couldn't get home before, that night, nohow. I couldn't, Richard —'twas the night Charlotte an' Barney fell out. They had a dreadful time. I had to stay there. It wa'n't my fault. If Barney had come back, I could have got here in season; but poor Charlotte was settin' out there all alone on the doorstep, an' her father wouldn't let her in, an' Sarah took on so I had to stay. I thought I should die when I got back an' found out you'd been here an' gone. Ain't you goin' to forgive me, Richard?"

Barney suddenly removed his arm from Sylvia's waist, pushed her clinging hands away, and stood up again. " Now, Miss Crane," he said, " I've got to tell you. You've got to listen, and take it in. I am not Richard Alger; I am Barney Thayer."

" What?" Sylvia said, feebly, looking up at him. " I don't know what you say, Richard; I wish you'd say it again."

" I ain't Richard Alger; I am Barney Thayer," repeated Barney, in a loud, distinct voice. Sylvia's straining, questioning eyes did not leave his face. " You made a mistake," said Barney.

Sylvia turned her eyes away; she laid her head down on the arm of the hair-cloth sofa, and gasped faintly. Barney bent over her. " Now don't feel bad, Miss Crane," said he; " I sha'n't ever say a word about this to anybody."

Sylvia made no reply; she lay there half gasping for breath, and her face looked deathly to Barney.

" Miss Crane, are you sick?" he cried out in alarm. When she did not answer, he even laid hold of her shoulder, and shook her gently, and repeated the question. He did not know if she were faint or dying; he had never seen anybody faint or die. He wished instinctively that his mother were there; he thought for a second of running for her in spite of everything.

"I'll go and get some water for you, Miss Crane," he said, desperately, and seized the candle, and went with it, flaring and leaving a wake of smoke, out into the kitchen. He presently came back with a dipper of water, and held it dripping over Sylvia. "Hadn't you better drink a little?" he urged. But Sylvia suddenly motioned him away and sat up. "No, I don't want any water; I don't want anything after this," she said, in a quick, desperate tone. "I can never look anybody in the face again. I can never go to meetin' again."

"Don't you feel so about it, Miss Crane," Barney pleaded, his own voice uncertain and embarrassed. "The room ain't very light, and it's dark outside; maybe I do look like him a little. It ain't any wonder you made the mistake."

"It wa'n't that," returned Sylvia. "I dunno what the reason was; it don't make any difference. I can't never go to meetin' again."

"I sha'n't tell anybody," said Barney; "I sha'n't ever speak of it to any human being."

Sylvia turned on him with sudden fierceness. "You had better not," said she, "when you're doin' jest the same as Richard Alger yourself, an' you're makin' Charlotte sit an' watch an' suffer for nothin' at all, jest as he makes me. You had better not tell of it,

Barney Thayer, when it was all due to your awful will that won't let you give in to anybody, in the first place, an' when you are so much like Richard Alger yourself that it's no wonder that anybody that knows him body and soul, as I do, took you for him. You had better not tell."

Again Barney seemed to see before his eyes that image of himself as Richard Alger, and he could no more change it than he could change his own image in the looking-glass. He said not another word, but carried the dipper of water back to the kitchen, returned with the candle, setting it gingerly on the white mantel-shelf between a vase of dried flowers and a mottle-backed shell, and went out of the house. Sylvia did not speak again; but he heard her moan as he closed the door, and it seemed to him that he heard her as he went down the road, although he knew that he could not.

It was quite dark now; all the light came from a pale wild sky. The moon was young, and feebly intermittent with the clouds.

Barney, hastening along, was all trembling and unnerved. He tried to persuade himself that the woman whom he had just left was ill, and laboring under some sudden aberration of mind; yet, in spite of himself, he realized a terrible rationality in it. Little as he had been among the village people of late, and little as he had heard of the village gossip, he knew the story of Richard Alger's desertion of Sylvia Crane. Was he not like Richard Alger in his own desertion of Charlotte Barnard? and had not Sylvia been as little at fault in taking one for the other as if they had been twin brothers? Might there not be a closer likeness between characters than features—perhaps by a repetition of sins and deformities? and might not one now and then be able to see it?

Then the question came, was Charlotte like Sylvia? Was Charlotte even now sitting watching for him with that awful eagerness which comes from a hunger of the heart? He had seen one woman's wounded heart, and, like most men, was disposed to generalize, and think he had seen the wounded hearts of all women.

When he had reached the turn of the road, and had come out on the main one where his house was, and where Charlotte lived, he stood still, looking in her direction. He seemed to see her, a quarter of a mile away in the darkness, sitting in her window watching for him, as Sylvia had watched for Richard.

He set his mouth hard and crossed the road. He had just reached his own yard when there was the pale flutter of a skirt out of the darkness before him, and a little shadowy figure met him with a soft shock. There was a smothered nervous titter from the figure. Barney did not know who it was; he muttered an apology, and was about to pass into his yard when Rose Berry's voice arrested him. It was quite trembling and uncertain; all the laughter had gone out of it.

"Oh, it's you," said she; "you frightened me. I didn't know who it was."

Barney felt suddenly annoyed without knowing why. "Oh, is it you, Rose?" he returned, stiffly. "It's a pleasant evening;" then he turned.

"Barney!" Rose said, and her voice sounded as if she were weeping.

Barney stopped and waited.

"I want to know if—you're mad with me, Barney."

"No, of course I ain't; why?"

"I thought you'd acted kind of queer to me lately."

Barney stood still, frowning in the darkness. "I don't know what you mean," he said at length. "I don't know how I've treated you any different from any of the girls."

"You haven't been to see me, and—you've hardly spoken to me since the cherry party."

"I haven't been to see anybody," said Barney, shortly; and he turned away again, but Rose caught his arm. "Then you are sure you aren't mad with me?" she whispered.

"Of course I'm sure," Barney returned, impatiently.

"It would kill me if you were," Rose whispered. She pressed close to him; he could feel her softly panting against his side, her head sunk on his shoulder. "I've been worrying about it all these months," she said in his ear. Her soft curly hair brushed his cheek, but her little transient influence over him was all gone. He felt angry and ashamed.

"I haven't thought anything about it," he said, brusquely.

Rose sobbed faintly, but she did not move away from him. Suddenly that cruel repulsion which seizes mankind towards reptiles and unsought love seized Barney. He unclasped her clinging hands, and fairly pushed her away from him. "Goodnight, Rose," he said, shortly, and turned, and went up the path to his own door with determined strides.

"Barney!" Rose called after him; but he paid no attention. She even ran up the path after him; but the door shut, and she turned back. She was trembling from head to foot, there was a great rushing in her ears; but she heard a quick light step behind her when she got out on the road, and she hurried on before it with a vague dread.

She almost ran at length; but the footsteps gained on her. A dark skirt brushed her light-colored one, and Charlotte's voice, full of contempt and indignation, said in her ear: "Oh, I thought it was you."

"I—was coming up—to your—house," Rose faltered; she could hardly get her breath to speak.

"Why didn't you come, then?" demanded Charlotte. "What made you go to Barney Thayer's?"

"I didn't," said Rose, in feeble self-defence. "He was out in the road—I—just stopped to—speak to him—"

"You were coming out of his yard," Charlotte said, pitilessly. "You followed him in there—I saw you. Shame on you!"

"Oh, Charlotte, I haven't done anything out of the way," pleaded Rose, weakly.

"You have tried your best to get Barney Thayer all the time you have been pretending to be such a good friend to me. I don't know what you call out of the way."

"Charlotte, don't—I haven't."

"Yes, you have. I am going to tell you, once for all, what I think of you. You've been a false friend to me; and now when Barney don't notice you, you follow him up as no girl that thought anything of herself would. And you don't even care anything for him; you haven't even that for an excuse."

"You don't know but what I do!" Rose cried out, desperately.

"Yes, I do know. If anybody else came along, you'd care for him just the same."

"I shouldn't — Charlotte, I should never have thought of Barney if he—hadn't left you, you know I shouldn't."

"That's no excuse," said Charlotte, sternly.

"You said yourself he would never come back to you," said Rose.

"Would you have liked me to have done so by you, if you had been in my place?"

Rose twitched herself about. "You can't expect him never to marry anybody because he isn't going to marry you," she said, defiantly.

"I don't—I am not quite so selfish as that. But he won't ever marry anybody he don't like because she follows him up, and I don't see how that alters what you've done."

Rose began to walk away. Charlotte stood still, but she raised her voice. " I am not very happy," said she, " and I sha'n't be happy my whole life, but I wouldn't change places with you. You've lowered yourself, and that's worse than any unhappiness."

Rose fled away in the darkness without another word, and Charlotte crossed the road to go to her Aunt Sylvia's.

Rose, as she went on, felt as if all her dreams were dying within her; a dull vision of the next morning when she should awake without them weighed upon her. She had a childish sense of shame and remorse, and a conviction of the truth of Charlotte's words. And yet she had an injured and bewildered feeling, as if somewhere in this terrible nature, at whose mercy she was, there was some excuse for her.

Rose was nearly home when she began to meet the people coming from meeting. She kept close to the wall, and scudded along swiftly that no one might recognize her. All at once a young man whom she had passed turned and walked along by her side, making a shy clutch at her arm.

"Oh, it's you," she said, wearily.

" Yes ; do you care if I walk along with you ?"

" No," said Rose, " not if you want to."

An old pang of gratitude came over her. It was only the honest, overgrown boy, Tommy Ray, of the store. She had known he worshipped her afar off; she had laughed at him and half despised him, but now she felt suddenly humble and grateful for even this devotion. She moved her arm that he might hold it more closely.

"It's too dark for you to be out alone," he said, in his embarrassed, tender voice.

"Yes, it's pretty dark," said Rose. Her voice shook. They had passed the last group of returning people. Suddenly Rose, in spite of herself, began to cry. She sobbed wildly, and the boy, full of alarm and sympathy, walked on by her side.

"There ain't anything — scared you, has there?" he stammered out, awkwardly, at length.

"No," sobbed Rose.

"You ain't sick?"

"No, it isn't anything."

The boy held her arm closer; he trembled and almost sobbed himself with sympathy. Before they reached the old tavern Rose had stopped crying—she even tried to laugh and turn it off with a jest. "I don't know what got into me," she said; "I guess I was nervous."

"I didn't know but something had scared you," said the boy.

They stood on the door-steps; the house was dark. Rose's parents had gone to bed, and William was out. The boy still held Rose's arm. He had adored her secretly ever since he was a child, and he had never dared as much as that before. He had thought of Rose like a queen or a princess, and the thought had ennobled his boyish ignorance and commonness.

"No, I wasn't scared," said Rose, and something in her voice gave sudden boldness to her young lover.

He released her arm, and put both his arms around her. "I'm sorry you feel so bad," he whispered, panting.

"It isn't anything," returned Rose, but she half sobbed again; the boy's round cheek pressed against her wet, burning one. He was several years younger than she. She had half scorned him, but she had one of those natures that crave love for its own sweetness as palates crave sugar.

She wept a little on his shoulder; and the boy, half beside himself with joy and terror, stood holding her fast in his arms.

"Don't feel bad," he kept whispering. Finally Rose raised herself. "I must go in," she whispered; "good-night."

The boy's pleading face, his innocent, passionate lips approached hers, and they kissed each other.

"Don't you—like me a little?" gasped the boy.

"Maybe I will," Rose whispered back. His face came closer, and she kissed him again. Then, with a murmured "good-night," she fled into the house, and the boy went down the hill with sweeter dreams in his heart than those which she had lost.

CHAPTER X

On the Sunday following the one of Barnabas
Thayer's call Sylvia Crane appeared at meeting in a
black lace veil like a Spanish señorita. The heavily
wrought black lace fell over her face, and people
could get only shifting glimpses of her delicate features behind it.

Richard Alger glanced furtively at the pale face
shrinking austerely behind the net-work of black
silk leaves and flowers, and wondered at some change
which he felt but could not fathom. He scarcely
knew that she had never worn the veil before. And
Richard Alger, had he known, could never have fathomed the purely feminine motive compounded of
pride and shame which led his old sweetheart to un-
earth from the depths of a bandbox her mother's
worked-lace veil, and tie its narrow black drawing-
string with trembling fingers over her own bonnet.

"I'd like to know what in creation you've got that
veil on for?" whispered her sister, Hannah Berry, as
they went down the aisle after meeting.

"I thought I would," responded Sylvia's muffled
voice behind the veil.

"You've got the flowers right over your eyes. I
shouldn't think you could see to walk. You ain't

never worn a veil in your life. I can't see what has got into you," persisted Hannah.

Sylvia edged away from her as soon as she could, and glided down the road towards her own house swiftly, although her knees trembled. Sylvia's knees always trembled when she came out of church, after she had sat an hour and a half opposite Richard Alger. To-day they felt weaker than ever, after her encounter with Hannah. Nobody knew the terror Sylvia had of her sister's discovering how she had called in Barnabas Thayer, and in a manner unveiled her maiden heart to him. When Charlotte had come in that night after Barnabas had gone, and discovered her crying on the sofa, she had jumped up and confronted her with a fierce instinct of concealment.

"There ain't nothin' new the matter," she said, in response to Charlotte's question; "I was thinkin' about mother; I'm apt to when it comes dusk." It was the first deliberate lie that Sylvia Crane had ever told in her life. She reflected upon it after Charlotte had gone, and reflected also with fierce hardihood that she would lie again were it necessary. Should she hesitate at a lie if it would cover the maiden reserve that she had cherished so long?

However, Charlotte had suspected more than her aunt knew of the true cause of her agitation. A similar motive for grief made her acute. Sylvia, mourning alone of a Sabbath night upon her haircloth sofa, struck an old chord of her own heart. Charlotte dared not say a word to comfort her directly. She condoled with her for the fifteen-years-old loss of her mother, and did not allude to Richard Alger; but going home she said to herself, with a miserable qualm of pity, that poor Aunt Sylvia was breaking her heart because Richard had stopped coming.

"It's harder for Aunt Sylvia because she's older," thought Charlotte, on her way home that night. But then she thought also, with a sorer qualm of self-pity, that Sylvia had not quite so long a life before her, to live alone. Charlotte had nearly reached her own home that night when two figures suddenly slunk across the road before her. She at once recognized Rebecca Thayer as one of them, and called out "Good-evening, Rebecca!" to her.

Rebecca made only a muttered sound in response, and they both disappeared in the darkness. There was a look of secrecy and flight about it which somehow startled Charlotte, engrossed as she was with her own troubles and her late encounter with Rose.

When she got into the house she spoke of it to her mother. Cephas had gone to bed, and Sarah was sitting up waiting for her.

"I met Rebecca and William out here," said she, untying her hat, "and I thought they acted real queer." Sarah cast a glance at the bedroom door, which was ajar, and motioned Charlotte to close it. Charlotte tiptoed across the room and shut the door softly, lest she should awaken her father; then her mother beckoned her to come close, and whispered something in her ear.

Charlotte started, and a great blush flamed out all over her face and neck. She looked at her mother with angry shame. "I don't believe a word of it," said she; "not a word of it."

"I walked home from meetin' with Mrs. Allen this evenin'," said her mother, "an' she says it's all over town. She says Rebecca's been stealin' out, an' goin' to walk with him unbeknownst to her mother all summer. You know her mother wouldn't let him come to the house."

"I don't believe one word of it," repeated Charlotte.

"Mis' Allen says it's so," said Sarah. "She says Mis' Thayer has had to stay home from evenin' meetin' on account of Ephraim—she don't like to leave him alone, he ain't been quite so well lately—an' Rebecca has made believe go to meetin' when she's been off with William. Mis' Thayer went to meetin' to-night."

"Wasn't Mr. Thayer there?"

"Yes, he was there, but he wouldn't know what was goin' on. 'Tain't very hard to pull the wool over Caleb Thayer's eyes."

"I don't believe one word of it," Charlotte said, again. When she went up-stairs to bed that whisper of her mother's seemed to sound through and above all her own trouble. It was to her like a note of despair and shame, quite outside her own gamut of life. She could not believe that she heard it at all. Rebecca's face as she had always known her came up before her. "I don't believe one word of it," she said again to herself.

But that whisper which had shocked her ear had already begun to be repeated all over the village—by furtive matrons, behind their hands, when the children had been sent out of the room ; by girls, blushing beneath each other's eyes as they whispered; by the lounging men in the village store; it was sent like an evil strain through the consciousness of the village, until everybody except Rebecca's own family had heard it.

Barnabas saw little of other people, and nobody dared repeat the whisper to him, and they had too much mercy or too little courage to repeat it to Caleb or Deborah. Indeed, it is doubtful if any woman in the village, even Hannah Berry, would have ventured to face Deborah Thayer with this rumor concerning her daughter.

Deborah had of late felt anxious about Rebecca, who did not seem like herself. Her face was strangely changed; all the old meaning had gone out of it, and given place to another, which her mother could not interpret. Sometimes Rebecca looked like a stranger to her as she moved about the house. She said to many that Rebecca was miserable, and was incensed that she got so little sympathy in response. Once when Rebecca fainted in meeting, and had to be carried out, she felt in the midst of her alarm a certain triumph. " I guess folks will see now that I ain't been fussin' over her for nothin'," she thought. When Rebecca revived under a sprinkle of water, out in the vestibule, she said impatiently to the other women bending their grave, concerned faces over her, " She's been miserable for some time. I ain't surprised at this at all myself."

Deborah watched over Rebecca with a fierce, pecking tenderness like a bird. She brewed great bowls of domestic medicines from nuts and herbs, and made her drink whether she would or not. She sent her to bed early, and debarred her from the night air. She never had a suspicion of the figure slipping softly as a shadow across the north parlor and out the front door night after night.

She never exchanged a word with Rebecca about William Berry. She tried to persuade herself that Rebecca no longer thought much about him; she drove from her mind the fear lest Rebecca's illness might be due to grief at parting from him. She looked at Thomas Payne with a speculative eye; she thought that he would make a good husband for Rebecca; she dreamed of him, and built bridal castles for him and her daughter, as she knitted those yards of lace at night, when Rebecca had gone to bed in her little room off the north parlor. When Thomas Payne went west a month after Charlotte Barnard had refused him, she transferred her dreams to some fine stranger who should come to the village and at once be smitten with Rebecca. She never thought it possible that Rebecca could be persisting in her engagement to William Berry against her express command. Her own obstinacy was incredible to her in her daughter; she had not the slightest suspicion of it, and Rebecca had less to guard against.

As the fall advanced Rebecca showed less and less inclination to go in the village society. Her mother fairly drove her out at times. Once Rebecca, utterly overcome, sank down in a chair and wept when her mother urged her to go to a husking-party in the neighborhood.

"You've got to spunk up an' go, if you don't feel like it," said her mother. "You'll feel better for it afterwards. There ain't no use in givin' up so. I'm goin' to get you a new crimson woollen dress, an' I'm goin' to have you go out more'n you've done lately."

"I—don't want a new dress," returned Rebecca, with wild sobs.

"Well, I'm goin' to get you one to-morrow," said her mother. "Now go an' wash your face an' do up your hair, an' get ready. You can wear your brown dress, with the cherry ribbon in your hair, to-night."

"I don't—feel fit to, mother," moaned Rebecca, piteously.

But Deborah would not listen to her. She made her get ready for the husking - party, and looked at her with pride when she stood all dressed to go, in the kitchen.

"You look better than you've done for some time," said she, "an' that brown dress don't look bad, either, if you have had it three winters. I'm goin' to get you a nice new crimson woollen this winter. I've had my mind made up to for some time."

After Rebecca had gone and Ephraim had said his catechism and gone to bed, Deborah sat and knitted, and planned to get the crimson dress for Rebecca the next day.

She looked over at Caleb, who sat dozing by the fire. "I'll go to-morrow, if he ain't got to spend all that last interest-money for the parish taxes an' cuttin' that wood," said she. "I dunno how much that wood-cuttin' come to, an' he won't know to-night if I wake him up. I can't get it through his head. But I'll buy it to-morrow if there's money enough left."

But Deborah was forced to wait a few weeks, since it took all the interest - money for the parish taxes and to pay for the wood-cutting. She had to wait until Caleb had sold some of the wood, and that took some time, since seller and purchasers were slow-motioned.

At last, one afternoon, she drove herself over to Bolton in the chaise to buy the dress. She went to Bolton, because she would not go herself to Silas Berry's store and trade with William. She could send Caleb there for household goods, but this dress she would trust no one but herself to purchase.

She had planned that Rebecca should go with her, but the girl looked so utterly wan and despairing that day that she forbore to insist upon it. Caleb would have accompanied her, but she would not let him. " I never did think much of men-folks standin' round in stores gawpin' while women-folks was tradin'," said she. She would not allow Ephraim to go, although he pleaded hard. It was quite a cold day, and she was afraid of the sharp air for his laboring breath.

A little after noon she set forth, all alone in the chaise, slapping the reins energetically over the white horse's back, a thick green veil tied over her bonnet under her chin, and the thin, sharp wedge of face visible between the folds crimsoning in the frosty wind.

While she was gone Rebecca sat beside the window and sewed, Caleb shelled corn in the chimney-corner, and Ephraim made a pretence of helping him. " You set down an' help your father shell corn while I am gone," his mother had sternly ordered.

Occasionally Ephraim addressed whining remon-strances to his father, and begged to be allowed to go out-of-doors, and Caleb would quiet him with one effectual rejoinder : " You know she won't like it if you do, sonny. You know what she said."

Caleb, as he shelled the corn with the pottering patience of old age and constitutional slowness, glanced now and then at his daughter in the window. He thought she looked very badly, and he had all the time lately the bewildered feeling of a child who sees in a familiar face the marks of emotions unknown to it.

" Don't you feel as well as common to-day, Rebecca?" he asked once, and cleared his throat.

" I don't feel sick, as I know of, any day," replied Rebecca, shortly, and her face reddened.

As she sewed she looked out now and then at the wild December day, the trees reeling in the wind, and the sky driving with the leaden clouds. It was too cold and too windy to snow all the afternoon, but towards night it moderated, and the wind died down. When Mrs. Thayer came home it was snowing quite hard, and her green veil was white when she entered the kitchen. She took it off and shook it, sputtering moisture in the fireplace.

" There's goin' to be a hard storm; it's lucky I went to-day," said she. " I kept the dress under the buffalo-robe, an' that ain't hurt any."

Deborah waxed quite angry, when she proudly shook out the soft gleaming crimson lengths of thibet, because Rebecca showed so little interest in it. " You don't deserve to have a new dress; you act like a stick of wood," she said.

Rebecca made no reply. Presently, when she had gone out of the room for something, Caleb said, anxiously, " I guess she don't feel quite so well as common to-night."

" I'm gettin' most out of patience; I dunno what ails her. I'm goin' to have the doctor if this keeps on," returned Deborah.

Ephraim, sucking a stick of candy brought to him from Bolton, cast a strange glance at his mother—a glance compounded of shrewdness and terror; but she did not see it.

It snowed hard all night; in the morning the snow was quite deep, and there was no appearance of clearing. As soon as the breakfast dishes were put away, Deborah got out the crimson thibet. She had learned the tailoring and dressmaking trade in her youth, and she always cut and fitted the garments for the family.

She worked assiduously; by the middle of the forenoon the dress was ready to be tried on. Ephraim and his father were out in the barn, she and Rebecca were alone in the house.

She made Rebecca stand up in the middle of the kitchen floor, and she began fitting the crimson gown to her. Rebecca stood drooping heavily, her eyes cast down. Suddenly her mother gave a great start, pushed the girl violently from her, and stood aloof. She did not speak for a few minutes; the clock ticked in the dreadful silence. Rebecca cast one glance at her mother, whose eyes seemed to light the innermost recesses of her being to her own vision; then she would have looked away, but her mother's voice arrested her.

"Look at me," said Deborah. And Rebecca looked; it was like uncovering a disfigurement or a sore.

"What—ails you?" said her mother, in a terrible voice.

Then Rebecca turned her head; her mother's eyes

could not hold her any longer. It was as if her very soul shrank.

"Go out of this house," said her mother, after a minute.

Rebecca did not make a sound. She went, bending as if there were a wind at her back impelling her, across the kitchen in her quilted petticoat and her crimson thibet waist, her white arms hanging bare. She opened the door that led towards her own bedroom, and passed out.

Presently Deborah, still standing where Rebecca had left her, heard the front door of the house shut. After a few minutes she took the broom from its peg in the corner, went through the icy north parlor, past Rebecca's room, to the front door. The snow heaped on the outer threshold had fallen in when Rebecca opened it, and there was a quantity on the entry floor.

Deborah opened the door again, and swept out the snow carefully; she even swept the snow off the steps outside, but she never cast a glance up or down the road. Then she beat the snow off the broom, and went in and locked the door behind her.

On her way back to the kitchen she paused at Rebecca's little bedroom. The waist of the new gown lay on the bed. She took it out into the kitchen, and folded it carefully with the skirt and the pieces; then she carried it up to the garret and laid it away in a chest.

When Caleb and Ephraim came in from the barn

they found Deborah sitting at the window knitting a stocking. She did not look up when they entered.

The corn was not yet shelled, and Caleb arranged his baskets in the chimney-corner, and fell to again. Ephraim began teasing his mother to let him crack some nuts, but she silenced him peremptorily. "Set down an' help your father shell that corn," said she. And Ephraim pulled a grating chair up to his father, muttering cautiously.

Caleb kept looking at Deborah anxiously. He glanced at the door frequently.

"Where's Rebecca?" he asked at last.

"I dunno," replied Deborah.

"Has she laid down?"

"No, she ain't."

"She ain't gone out in the snow, has she?" Caleb said, with deploring anxiety.

Deborah answered not a word. She pursed her lips and knitted.

"She ain't, has she, mother?"

"Keep on with your corn," said Deborah; and that was all she would say.

Presently she arose and prepared dinner in the same dogged silence. Caleb, and even Ephraim, watched her furtively, with alarmed eyes.

When Rebecca did not appear at the dinner-table Caleb did not say anything about it, but his old face was quite pale. He ate his dinner from the force of habit of over seventy years, during which time he had always eaten his dinner, but he did not taste it consciously.

He made up his mind that as soon as he got up from the table he would go over to Barney's and consult him. After he pushed his chair away he was slipping out shyly, but Deborah stopped him.

"Set down an' finish that corn. I don't want it clutterin' up the kitchen any longer," said she.

"I thought I'd jest slip out a minute, mother."

Deborah motioned him towards the chimney-corner and the baskets of corn with a stern gesture, and Caleb obeyed. Ephraim, too, settled down beside his father, and fell to shelling corn without being told. He was quite cowed and intimidated by this strange mood of his mother's, and involuntarily shrank closer to his father when she passed near him.

Caleb and Ephraim both watched Deborah with furtive terror, as she moved about, washing and putting away the dinner-dishes and sweeping the kitchen.

They looked at each other, when, after the after-dinner housework was all done, she took her shawl and hood from the peg, and drew some old wool socks of Caleb's over her shoes. She went out without saying a word. Ephraim waited a few minutes after the door shut behind her; then he ran to the window.

"She's gone to Barney's," he announced, rolling

great eyes over his shoulder at his father; and the old man also went over to the window and watched Deborah plodding through the snow up the street.

It was not snowing so hard now, and the clouds were breaking, but a bitter wind was blowing from the northwest. It drove Deborah along before it, lashing her skirts around her gaunt limbs; but she leaned back upon it, and did not bend.

The road was not broken out, and the snow was quite deep, but she went along with no break in her gait. She went into Barney's yard and knocked at his door. She set her mouth harder when she heard him coming.

Barney opened the door and started when he saw who was there. " Is it you, mother?" he said, involuntarily; then his face hardened like hers, and he waited. The mother and son confronting each other looked more alike than ever.

Deborah opened her mouth to speak twice before she made a sound. She stood upright and unyielding, but her face was ghastly, and she drew her breath in long, husky gasps. Finally she spoke, and Barney started again at her voice.

" I want you to go after William Berry and make him marry Rebecca," she said.

" Mother, what do you mean?"

" I want you to go after William Berry and make him marry Rebecca."

" Mother!"

" Rebecca is gone. I turned her out of the house

this mornin'. I don't know where she is. Go and find her, and make William Berry marry her."

"Mother, before the Lord, I don't know what you mean!" Barney cried out. "You didn't turn Rebecca out of the house in all this storm! What did you turn her out for? Where is she?"

"I don't know where she is. I turned her out because I wouldn't have her in the house. You brought it all on us; if you hadn't acted so I shouldn't have felt as I did about her marryin'. Now you can go an' find her, and get William Berry an' make him marry her. I ain't got anything more to do with it."

Deborah turned, and went out of the yard.

"Mother!" Barney called after her, but she kept on. He stood for a second looking after her retreating figure, struggling sternly with the snow - drifts, meeting the buffets of the wind with her head up; then he went in, and put on his boots and his overcoat.

Barney had heard not one word of the village gossip, and the revelation in his mother's words had come to him with a great shock. As he went up the hill to the old tavern he could hardly believe that he had understood her rightly. Once he paused and turned, and was half inclined to go back. He was as pure - minded as a girl, and almost as ignorant; he could not believe that he knew what she meant.

Barney hesitated again before the store; then he opened the great clanging door and went in. A farmer, in a blue frock stiff with snow, had just completed his purchases and was going out. William, who had been waiting upon him, was quite near the door behind the counter. At the farther end of the store could be seen the red glow of a stove and Tommy Ray's glistening fair head. Some one else, who had shrunk out of sight when Barney entered, was also there.

Barney saw no one but William. He looked at him, and all his bewilderment gathered itself into a point. He felt a sudden fierce impulse to spring at him.

William looked at Barney, and his face changed in a minute. He took up his hat, and came around the counter. "Did you want to see me?" he said, hoarsely.

"Come outside," said Barney. And the two men went out, and stood in the snow before the store.

"Where is Rebecca?" said Barney. He looked at William, and again the savage impulse seized him. William did not shrink before it.

"What do you mean?" he returned. His lips were quite stiff and white, but he looked back at Barney.

"Don't you know where she is?"

"Before God I don't, Barney. What do you mean?"

"She left home this morning. Mother turned her out."

"Turned her out!" repeated William.

"Come with me and find her and marry her, or

"'WHERE IS REBECCA?' SAID BARNEY"

I'll kill you," said Barney, and he lashed out suddenly with his fist in William's face.

"You won't need to, for I'll kill myself if I don't," William gasped out. Then he turned and ran.

"Where are you going?" Barney shouted, rushing after him, in a fury.

"To put the horse in the cutter," William called back. And, indeed, he was headed towards the barn. Barney followed him, and the two men put the horse between the shafts. Once William asked, hoarsely, "Any idea which way?" and Barney shook his head.

"What time did she go?"

"Some time this forenoon."

William groaned.

The horse was nearly harnessed when Tommy Ray came running out from the store, and beckoned to Barney. "Rose says she see her going up the turnpike this morning," he said, in a low voice. "She was up in her chamber that looks over the turnpike, and she see somebody goin' up the turnpike. She thought it looked like Rebecca, but she supposed it must be Mis' Jim Sloane. It must have been Rebecca."

"What time was it?" William asked, thrusting his white face between them. The boy turned aside with a gesture of contempt and dislike. "About half-past ten," he answered, shortly. Then he turned on his heel and went back to the store. Rose was peering around the half-open door with a white, shocked face. Somehow she had fathomed the cause of the excitement.

"We'll go up the turnpike, then," said Barney. William nodded. The two men sprang into the cutter, and the snow flew in their faces from the horse's hoofs as they went out the barn door.

The old tavern stood facing the old turnpike road to Boston, but the store and barn faced on the new road at its back, and people generally approached the tavern by that way.

William and Barney had to drive down the hill; then turn the corner, and up the hill again on the old turnpike.

There was not a house on that road for a full mile. William urged the horse as fast as he could through the fresh snow. Both men kept a sharp lookout at the sides of the road. The sun was out now, and the snow was blinding white; the north wind drove a glittering spray as sharp and stinging as diamond-dust in their faces.

Once William cried out, with a dry sob, "My God, she'll freeze in this wind, if she's out in it!"

And Barney answered, "Maybe it would be better for her if she did."

William looked at him for the first time since they started. "See here, Barney," he said, "God knows it's not to shield myself—I'm past that; but I've begged her all summer to be married. I've been down on my knees to her to be married before it came to this."

"Why wouldn't she?"

"I don't know, oh, I don't know! The poor girl

was near distracted. Her mother forbade her to marry me, and held up her Aunt Rebecca, who married against her parents' wishes and hung herself, before her, all the time. Your trouble with Charlotte Barnard brought it all about. Her mother never opposed it before. I begged her to marry me, but she was afraid, or something, I don't know what."

"Can't you drive faster?" said Barney.

William had been urging the horse while he spoke, but now he shook the whip over him again.

Mrs. Jim Sloane's house was a long, unpainted cottage quite near the road. The woman who lived alone there was under a kind of indefinite ban in the village. Her husband, who had died several years before, had been disreputable and drunken, and the mantle of his disgrace had seemed to fall upon his wife, if indeed she was not already provided with such a mantle of her own. Everybody spoke slightingly of Mrs. Jim Sloane. The men laughed meaningly when they saw her pass, wrapped in an old plaid shawl, which she wore summer and winter, and which seemed almost like a uniform. Stories were told of her dirt and shiftlessness, of the hens which roosted in her kitchen. Poor Mrs. Jim Sloane, in her blue plaid shawl, tramping frequently from her solitary house through the village, was a byword and a mocking to all the people.

When William and Barney came abreast of her house they saw the blue flutter of Mrs. Jim Sloane's shawl out before, above the blue dazzle of the snow.

"Hullo!" she was crying out in her shrill voice, and waving her hand to them to stop.

William pulled the horse up short, and the woman came plunging through the snow close to his side.

"She's in here," she said, with a knowing smile. The faded fair hair blew over her eyes; she pushed it back with a coquettish gesture; there was a battered prettiness about her thin pink-and-white face, turning blue in the sharp wind.

"When did she get here?" asked Barney.

"This forenoon. She fell down out here, couldn't get no farther. I came out an' got her into the house. Didn't know but she was done to; but I fixed her up some hot drink an' made her lay down. I s'posed you'd be along." She smiled again.

William jumped out of the cutter, and tied the horse to an old fence-post. Then he and Barney followed the woman into the house. Barney looked at the old blue plaid shawl with utter disgust and revulsion. He had always felt a loathing for the woman, and her being a distant relative on his father's side intensified it.

Mrs. Sloane threw open the door, and bade them enter, as if to a festival. "Walk right in," said she.

There was a wild flutter of hens as they entered. Mrs. Sloane drove them before her. "The hen-house roof fell in, an' I have to keep 'em in here," she said, and shooed them and shook her shawl at them, until they alighted all croaking with terror upon the bed in the corner.

Then she looked inquiringly around the room. "Why," she cried, "she's gone; she was settin' here in this rockin'-chair when I went out. She must have run when she see you comin'!"

Mrs. Sloane hustled through a door, the tattered fringes of her shawl flying, and then her voice, shrilly expostulating, was heard in the next room.

The two men waited, standing side by side near the door in a shamed silence. They did not look at each other.

Presently Mrs. Sloane returned without her shawl. Her old cotton gown showed tattered and patched, and there were glimpses of her sharp white elbows at the sleeves. "She won't come out a step," she announced. "I can't make her. She's takin' on terribly."

William made a stride forward. "I'll go in and see her," he said, hoarsely; but Mrs. Jim Sloane stood suddenly in his way, her slender back against the door.

"No, you ain't goin' in," said she, "I told her I wouldn't let you go in."

William looked at her.

"She's dreadful set against either one of you comin' in, an' I told her you shouldn't," she said, firmly. She smoothed her wild locks down tightly over her ears as she spoke. All the coquettish look was gone.

William turned around, and looked helplessly at Barney, and Barney looked back at him. Then Bar-

ney put on his hat, and shrugged himself more closely into his great-coat.

"I'll go and get the minister," he said.

Mrs. Sloane thrust her chin out alertly. "Goin'
to get her married right off?" she asked, with a confidential smile.

Barney ignored her. "I guess it's the best way
to do," he said, sternly, to William; and William
nodded.

"Well, I guess 'tis the best way," Mrs. Sloane
said, with cheerful assent. "I don't b'lieve you
could hire her to come out of that room an' go to
the minister's, nohow. She's terrible upset, poor
thing."

As Barney went out of the door he cast a look
full of involuntary suspicion back at William, and
hesitated a second on the threshold. Mrs. Sloane
intercepted the look. "I'll look out he don't run
away while you're gone," she said; then she laughed.

William's white face flamed up suddenly, but he
made no reply. When Barney had gone he drew a
chair up close to the hearth, and sat there, bent over,
with his elbows on his knees. Mrs. Sloane sat down
on the foot of the bed, close to the door of the other
room, as if she were mounting guard over it. She
kept looking at William, and smiling, and opening
her mouth to speak, then checking herself.

"It's a pretty cold day," she said, finally.

William grunted assent without looking up. Then
he motioned with his shoulder towards the door

of the other room. "Ain't it cold in there?" he half whispered.

"I rolled her all up in my shawl; I guess she won't ketch cold; it's thick," responded the woman, effusively, and William said no more. He sat with his chin in his hands and his eyes fixed absently. The fire was smoking over a low, red glow of coals, the chimney-place yawned black before him, the hearth was all strewn with pots and kettles, and the shelf above it was piled high with a vague household litter. It had leaked around the chimney, and there was a great discolored blotch on the wall above the shelf, and the ceiling. Two or three hens came pecking around the kettles at William's feet.

To this young man, brought up in the extreme thrift and neatness of a typical New England household, this strange untidiness, as he viewed it through his strained mental state, seemed to have a deeper significance, and reveal the very shame and squalor of the soul itself, and its own existence and thoughts, by material images.

He might from his own sensations, as he sat there, have been actually translated into a veritable hell, from the utter strangeness of the atmosphere which his thoughts seemed to gasp in. William had never come fully into the atmosphere of his own sin before, but now he had, and somehow the untidy pots and kettles on the hearth made it more real. He was conscious as he sat there of very little pity for the girl in the other room, of very little love for her, and also of very little love or pity for himself; he felt nothing but a kind of horror. He saw suddenly the alien side of life, and the alien side of his own self, which he would always have kept faced out towards space, away from all eyes, like the other side of the moon, and that was for the time all he could grasp.

Once or twice Mrs. Sloane volunteered a remark, but he scarcely responded, and once he heard absently her voice and Rebecca's in the other room. Otherwise he sat in utter silence, except for the low chuckle of the hens and the taps of their beaks against the iron pots, until Barney came with the minister and the minister's wife.

Barney had taken the minister aside, and asked him, stammeringly, if he thought his wife would come. He could not bear the thought of the Sloane woman's being a witness at his sister's wedding. The minister and his wife were both very young, and had not lived long in Pembroke. They looked much alike: the minister's small, pale, peaked face peered with anxious solicitude between the folds of the great green scarf which he tied over his cap, and his wife looked like him out of her great wadded green silk hood, when they got into the sleigh with Barney.

The minister had had a whispered conference with his wife, and now she never once let her eyes rest on either of the two men as they slid swiftly along over the new snow. Her heart beat loudly in her ears, her little thin hands were cold in her great muff.

She had married very young, out of a godly New England minister's home. She had never known anything like this before, and a sort of general shame of femininity seemed to be upon her.

When she followed her husband into Mrs. Sloane's house she felt herself as burdened with shame—as if she stood in Rebecca's place. Her little face, all blue with the sharp cold, shrank, shocked and sober, into the depths of her great hood. She stood behind her husband, her narrow girlish shoulders bending under her thick mantilla, and never looked at the face of anybody in the room.

She did not see William at all. He stood up before them as they entered; they all nodded gravely. Nobody spoke but Mrs. Sloane, vibrating nervously in the midst of her clamorous hens, and Barney silenced her.

"We'll go right in," he said, in a stern, peremptory tone; then he turned to William. "Are you ready?" he asked.

William nodded, with his eyes cast down. The party made a motion towards the other room, but Mrs. Sloane unexpectedly stood before the door.

"I told her there shouldn't nobody come in," said she, "an' I ain't goin' to have you all bustin' in on her without she knows it. She's terrible upset. You wait a minute."

Mrs. Sloane's blue eyes glared defiantly at the company. The minister's wife bent her hooded head lower. She had heard about Mrs. Sloane, and felt as if she were confronted by a woman from Revelation and there was a flash of scarlet in the room.

"Go in and tell her we are coming," said Barney. And Mrs. Sloane slipped out of the room cautiously, opening the door only a little way. Her voice was heard, and suddenly Rebecca's rang out shrill in response, although they could not distinguish the words. Mrs. Sloane looked out. "She says she won't be married," she whispered.

"You let me see her," said Barney, and he took a stride forward, but Mrs. Sloane held the door against him.

"You can't," she whispered again. "I'll talk to her some more. I can talk her over, if anybody can."

Barney fell back, and again the door was shut and the voices were heard. This time Rebecca's arose into a wail, and they heard her cry out, " I won't, I won't! Go away, and stop talking to me! I won't! Go away !"

William turned around, and hid his face against the corner of the mantel-shelf. Barney went up and clapped him roughly on the shoulder. "Can't you go in there and make her listen to reason?" he said.

But just then Mrs. Sloane opened the door again. "You can walk right in now," she announced, smiling, her thin mouth sending the lines of her whole face into smirking upward curves.

The whole company edged forward solemnly. Mrs. Sloane was following, but Barney stood in her way.

" I guess you'd better not come in," he said, abruptly.

Mrs. Sloane's face flushed a burning red. " I guess," she began, in a loud voice, but Barney shut the door in her face. She ran noisily, stamping her feet like an angry child, to the fireplace, caught up a heavy kettle, and threw it down on the hearth. The hens flew up with a great clamor and whir of wings; Mrs. Sloane's shrill, mocking laugh arose above it. She began talking in a high-pitched voice, flinging out vituperations which would seem to patter against the closed door like bullets. Suddenly she stopped, as if her ire had failed her, and listened intently to a low murmur from the other room. She nodded her head when it ceased.

The door opened soon, and all except Rebecca came out. They stood consulting together in low voices, and Mrs. Sloane listened. They were deciding where to take Rebecca.

All at once Mrs. Sloane spoke. Her voice was still high-pitched with anger.

" If you want to know where to take her to, I can tell you," said she. " I'd keep her here an' welcome, but I s'pose you think I ain't good enough, you're all such mighty particular folks, an' ain't never had no disgrace in your own families. William Berry can't take her to his home to-night, for his mother wouldn't leave a whole skin on either of 'em. Her own mother has turned her out, an' Barney can't take her in. She's got to go somewhere where there's a woman; she's terrible upset. There ain't no other way but for you an' Mis' Barnes to take her home to-night, an' keep her till William gets a place fixed to put her in." Mrs. Sloane turned to the minister and his wife, regarding them with a mixture of defiance, sarcasm, and appeal.

They looked at each other hesitatingly. The minister's wife paled within her hood, and her eyes reddened with tears.

"I shouldn't s'pose you'd need any time to think on it, such good folks as you be," said Mrs. Sloane. "There ain't no other way. She's got to be where there's a woman."

Mrs. Barnes turned her head towards her husband. "She can come, if you think she ought to," she said, in a trembling voice.

The sun was setting when the party started. William led Rebecca out through the kitchen—a muffled, hesitating figure, whose very identity seemed to be lost, for she wore Mrs. Sloane's blue plaid shawl pinned closely over her head and face—and lifted her into his cutter with the minister and his wife. Then he and Barney walked along, plodding through the deep snow behind the cutter. The sun was setting, and it was bitterly cold; the snow creaked and the trees swung with a stiff rattle of bare limbs in the wind.

The two men never spoke to each other. The minister drove slowly, and they could always see Mrs. Jim Sloane's blue plaid shawl ahead.

When they reached the Caleb Thayer house, Barney stopped and William followed on alone after the sleigh.

Barney turned into the yard, and his father was standing in the barn door, looking out.

" Tell mother she's married," Barney sang out, hoarsely. Then he went back to the road, and home to his own house.

CHAPTER XI

BARNEY went to see Rebecca the next day, but the minister's wife came to the door and would not admit him. She puckered her lips painfully, and a blush shot over her face and little thin throat as she stood there before him. "I guess you had better not come in," said she, nervously. "I guess you had better wait until Mrs. Berry gets settled in her house. Mr. Berry is going to hire the old Bennett place. I guess it would be pleasanter."

Barney turned away, blushing also as he stammered an assent. Always keenly alive to the shame of the matter, it seemed as if his sense of it were for the moment intensified. The minister's wife's whole nature seemed turned into a broadside of mirrors towards Rebecca's shame and misery, and it was as if the reflection was multiplied in Barney as he looked at her.

Still, he could not take the shame to his own nature as she could, being a woman. He looked back furtively at the house as he went down the road, thinking he might catch a glimpse of poor Rebecca at the window.

But Rebecca kept herself well hid. After William had hired the old Bennett house and established her there, she lived with curtains down and doors bolted. Never a neighbor saw her face at door or window, although all the women who lived near did their housework with eyes that way. She would not go to the door if anybody knocked. The caller would hear her scurrying away. Nobody could gain admittance if William were not at home.

Barney went to the door once, and her voice sounded unexpectedly loud and piteously shrill in response to his knock.

" You can't come in ! go away !" cried Rebecca.

"I don't want to say anything hard to you," said Barney.

" Go away, go away !" repeated Rebecca, and then he heard her sob.

" Don't cry," pleaded Barney, futilely, through the door. But he heard his sister's retreating steps and her sobs dying away in the distance.

He went away, and did not try to see her again.

Rose went to see Rebecca, stealing out of a back door and scudding across snowy fields lest her mother should espy her and stop her. But Rebecca had not come to the door, although Rose had stood there a long time in a bitter wind.

" She wouldn't let me in," she whispered to her brother in the store, when she returned. She was friendly to him in a shamefaced, evasive sort of way, and she alone of his family. His father and mother scarcely noticed him.

" Much as ever as she'll let me in, poor girl," responded William, looking miserably aside from his sister's eyes and weighing out some meal.

"She wouldn't let mother in if she went there," said Rose. She felt a little piqued at Rebecca's refusing her admittance. It was as if all her pity and generous sympathy had been thrust back upon her, and her pride in it swamped.

"There's no danger of her going there," William returned, bitterly.

And there was not. Hannah Berry would have set herself up in a pillory as soon as she would have visited her son's wife. She scarcely went into a neighbor's lest she should hear some allusion to it.

Rebecca's father often walked past her house with furtive, wistful eyes towards the windows. Once or twice when nobody was looking he knocked timidly, but he never got any response. He always took a circuitous route home, that his wife might not know where he had been. Deborah never spoke of Rebecca; neither Caleb nor Ephraim dared mention her name in her hearing.

Although Deborah never asked a question, and although people were shy of alluding to Rebecca, she yet seemed to know, in some occult and instinctive fashion, all about her.

When a funeral procession passed the Thayer house one afternoon Deborah knew quite well whose little coffin was in the hearse, although she could scarcely have said that anybody had told her.

Caleb came to her after dinner, with a strange, defiant air. "I want a clean dicky, mother; I'm agoin'," said he. And Deborah got out the old man's Sunday clothes for him without a word. She even brushed his hair with hard, careful strokes, and helped him on with his great-coat; but she never said a word about Rebecca and her baby's funeral.

"They had some white posies on it," Caleb volunteered, tremblingly, when he got home.

Deborah made no reply.

"There was quite a lot there," added Caleb.

"Go an' bring me in some kindlin' wood," said Deborah.

Ephraim stood by, staring alternately at his father and mother. He had watched the funeral procession pass with furtive interest.

"It won't hurt you none to make a few lamp-lighters," said his mother. "You set right down here, an' I'll get you some paper."

Ephraim clapped his hand to his side, and rolled his eyes agonizingly towards his mother, but she took no notice. She got some paper out of the cupboard, and Ephraim sat down and began quirling it into long spirals with a wretched sulky air.

Since his sister's marriage Ephraim had had a sterner experience than had ever fallen to his lot before. His mother redoubled her discipline over him. It was as if she had resolved, since all her vigorous training had failed in the case of his sister, that she would intensify it to such purpose that it should not fail with him.

So strait and narrow was the path in which Ephraim was forced to tread those wintry days, so bound and fettered was he by precept and admonition, that it seemed as if his very soul could do no more than shuffle along where his mother pointed.

A scanty and simple diet had Ephraim, and it seemed to him not so much from a solicitude for his health as from a desire to mortify his flesh for the good of his spirit. Ephraim obeyed perforce; he was sincerely afraid of his mother, but he had within him a dogged and growing resentment against those attempts to improve his spirit.

Not a bit of cake was he allowed to taste. When the door of a certain closet in which pound-cake for possible guests was always kept in a jar, and had been ever since Ephraim could remember, was opened, the boy's eyes would fairly glare with desire. "Jest gimme a little scrap, mother," he would whine. He had formerly, on rare occasions, been allowed a small modicum of cake, but now his mother was unyielding. He got not a crumb; he could only sniff hungrily at the rich, spicy, and fruity aroma which came forth from the closet, and swallow at it vainly and unsatisfactorily with straining palate.

Ephraim was not allowed a soft-stoned plum from a piece of mince-pie; the pie had always been tabooed. He was not even allowed to pick over the plums for the pies, unless under the steady watch of his mother's eyes. Once she seemed to see him ap-

proach a plum to his mouth when her back was towards him.

"What are you doing, Ephraim?" she said, and
her voice sounded to the boy like one from the Old
Testament. He put the plum promptly into the
bowl instead of his mouth.

"I ain't doin' nothin', mother," said he; but his
eyes rolled alarmedly after his mother as she went
across the kitchen. That frightened Ephraim. He
was a practical boy and not easily imposed upon, but
it really seemed to him that his mother had seen him,
after some occult and uncanny fashion, from the back
of her head. A vague and preposterous fancy actually passed through his bewildered boyish brain
that the little, tightly twisted knob of hair on the
back of a feminine head might have some strange
visual power of its own.

He never dared taste another plum, even if the
knob of hair directly faced him.

Every day Ephraim had a double task to learn in his
catechism, for Deborah held that no labor, however
arduous, which savored of the Word and the Spirit
could work him bodily ill. If Ephraim had been en-
terprising and daring enough, he would have fairly
cursed the Westminster divines, as he sat hour after
hour, crooking his boyish back painfully over their
consolidated wisdom, driving the letter of their dog-
mas into his boyish brain, while the sense of them
utterly escaped him.

There was one whole day during which Ephraim

toiled, laboriously conning over the majestic sentences in loud whispers, and received thereby only a vague impression and maudlin hope that he himself might be one of the elect of which they treated, because he was so strenuously deprived of plums in this life, and might therefore reasonably expect his share of them in the life to come.

That day poor Ephraim—glancing between whiles at some boys out coasting over in a field, down a fine icy slope, hearing now and then their shouts of glee— had a certain sense of superiority and complacency along with the piteous and wistful longing which always abode in his heart.

"Maybe," thought Ephraim, half unconsciously, not framing the thought in words to his mind— "maybe if I am a good boy, and don't have any plums, nor go out coasting like them, I shall go to heaven, and maybe they won't." Ephraim's poor purple face at the window-pane took on a strange, serious expression as he evolved his childish tenet of theology. His mother came in from another room. "Have you got that learned?" said she, and Ephraim bent over his task again.

Ephraim had not been quite as well as usual this winter, and his mother had been more than usually anxious about him. She called the doctor in finally, and followed him out into the cold entry when he left. "He's worse than he has been, ain't he?" she said, abruptly.

The doctor hesitated. He was an old man with a

moderate manner. He buttoned his old great-coat, redolent of drugs, closer, his breath steamed out in the frosty entry. "I guess you had better be a little careful about getting him excited," he said at last, evasively. "You had better get along as easy as you can with him." The doctor's manner implied more than his words; he had his own opinion of Deborah Thayer's sternness of rule, and he had sympathy with Rebecca.

Deborah seemed to have an intuition of it, for she looked at him, and raised her voice after a manner which would have become the Deborah of the scriptures.

"What would you have me do?" she demanded. "Would you have me let him have his own way if it were for the injury of his soul?" It was curious that Deborah, as she spoke, seemed to look only at the spiritual side of the matter. The idea that her discipline was actually necessary for her son's bodily weal did not occur to her, and she did not urge it as an argument.

"I guess you had better be a little careful and get along as easy as you can," repeated the doctor, opening the door.

"That ain't all that's to be thought of," said Deborah, with stern and tragic emphasis, as the doctor went out.

"What did the doctor say, mother?" Ephraim inquired, when she went into the room again. He looked half scared, half important, as he sat in the great rocking-chair by the fire. He breathed short, and his words were disconnected as he spoke.

His mother, for answer, took the catechism from the shelf, and extended it towards him with a decisive thrust of her arm.

" It is time you studied some more," said she.

Ephraim jerked himself away from the proffered book. " I don't want to study any more now, mother," he whined.

" Take it," said Deborah.

Caleb was paring apples for pies on the other side of the hearth. Ephraim looked across at him desperately. " I want to play holly-gull with father," he said.

" Ephraim !"

" Can't I play holly-gull with father jest a little while ?"

" You take this book and study your lesson," said Deborah, between nearly closed lips.

Ephraim began to weep ; he took the book with a vicious snatch and an angry sob. " Won't never let me do anythin' I want to," he cried, convulsively.

" Not another word," said Deborah. Ephraim bent over his catechism with half-suppressed sobs. He dared not weep aloud. Deborah went into the pantry with the medicine-bottle which the doctor had left ; she wanted a spoon. Caleb caught hold of her dress as she was passing him.

" What is it ?" said she.

"Look here, jest a minute, mother."

"I can't stop, father; Ephraim has got to have his medicine."

"Jest look here a minute, mother."

Deborah bent her head impatiently, and Caleb whispered. "No, he can't; I told him he couldn't," she said aloud, and passed on into the pantry.

Caleb looked over at Ephraim with piteous and helpless sympathy. "Never you mind, sonny," he said, cautiously.

"She—makes—" began Ephraim with a responsive plaint; but his mother came out of the pantry, and he stopped short. Caleb dropped a pared apple noisily into the pan.

"You'll dent that pan, father, if you fling the apples in that way," said Deborah. She had a thick silver spoon, and she measured out a dose of the medicine for Ephraim. She approached him, extending the spoon carefully. "Open your mouth," commanded she.

"Oh, mother, I don't want to take it!"

"Open your mouth!"

"Oh, mother—I don't—want to—ta-ke it!"

"Now, sonny, I wouldn't mind takin' of it. It's real good medicine that the doctor left you, an' father's payin' consid'able for it. The doctor thinks it's goin' to make you well," said Caleb, who was looking on anxiously.

"Open your mouth and *take* it!" said Deborah, sternly. She presented the spoon at Ephraim as if it were a bayonet and there were death at the point.

"Oh, mother," whimpered Ephraim.

"Mebbe mother will let you have a little taste of lasses arter it, if you take it real good," ventured Caleb.

"No, he won't have any lasses after it," said Deborah. "I'm a-tendin' to him, father. Now, Ephraim, you take this medicine this minute, or I shall give you somethin' worse than medicine. Open your mouth!" And Ephraim opened his mouth as if his mother's will were a veritable wedge between his teeth, swallowed the medicine with a miserable gulp, and made a grotesque face of wrath and disgust. Caleb, watching, swallowed and grimaced at the same instant that his son did. There were tears in his old eyes as he took up another apple to pare.

Deborah set the bottle on the shelf and laid the spoon beside it. "You've got to take this every hour for a spell," said she, "an' I ain't goin' to have any such work, if you be sick; you can make up your mind to it."

And make up his mind to this unwelcome dose Ephraim did. Once an hour his mother stood over him with the spoon, and the fierce odor of the medicine came to his nostrils; he screwed his eyes tight, opened his mouth, and swallowed without a word. There were limits to his mother's patience which Ephraim dared not pass. He had only vague ideas of what might happen if he did, but he preferred to be on the safe side. So he took the medicine, and did not lift his voice against it, although he had his thoughts.

It did seem as if the medicine benefited him. He breathed more easily after a while, and his color was more natural. Deborah felt encouraged; she even went down upon her stiff knees after her family were in bed, and thanked the Lord from the depths of her sorely chastened but proud heart. She did not foresee what was to come of it; for that very night Ephraim, induced thereto by the salutary effect of the medicine, which removed somewhat the restriction of his laboring heart upon his boyish spirits, perpetrated the crowning act of revolt and rebellion of his short life.

The moon was bright that night. The snow was frozen hard. The long hills where the boys coasted looked like slopes of silver. Ephraim had to go to bed at eight. He lay, well propped up on pillows, in his little bedroom, and he could hear the shouts of the coasting boys. Now that he could breathe more easily the superiority of his enforced deprivation of such joys no longer comforted him as much as it had done. His curtain was up, and the moonlight lay on his bed. The mystic influence of that strange white orb which moves the soul of the lover to dream of love and yearnings after it, which saddens with sweet wounds the soul who has lost it forever, which increases the terrible freedom of the maniac, and perhaps moves the tides, apparently increased the longing in the heart of one poor boy for all the innocent hilarity of his youth which he had missed.

Ephraim lay there in the moonlight, and longed as he had never longed before to go forth and run and play and halloo, to career down those wonderful shining slants of snow, to be free and equal with those other boys, whose hearts told off their healthy lives after the Creator's plan.

The clock in the kitchen struck nine, then ten. Caleb and Deborah went to bed, and Ephraim could hear his father's snores and his mother's heavy breathing from a distant room. Ephraim could not go to sleep. He lay there and longed for the frosty night air, the sled, and the swift flight down the white hill as never lover longed for his mistress.

At half-past ten o'clock Ephraim rose up. He dressed himself in the moonlight—all except his shoes; those he carried in his hand—and stole out in his stocking-feet to the entryway, where his warm coat and cap, which he so seldom wore, hung. Ephraim pulled the cap over his ears, put on the coat, cautiously unbolted the door, and stepped forth like a captive from prison.

He sat down on the doorstep and put on his shoes, tying them with trembling, fumbling fingers. He expected every minute to hear his mother's voice.

Then he ran down the yard to the woodshed. It was so intensely cold that the snow did not yield to his tread, but gave out quick sibilant sounds. It seemed to him like a whispering multitude called up by his footsteps, and as if his mother must hear.

He knew where Barney's old sled hung in the woodshed, and the woodshed door was unlocked.

Presently a boyish figure fled swiftly out of the Thayer yard with a bobbing sled in his wake. He expected every minute to hear the door or window open; but he cleared the yard and dashed up the road, and nobody arrested him.

Ephraim knew well the way to the coasting-hill, which was considered the best in the village, although he had never coasted there himself, except twice or thrice, surreptitiously, on another boy's sled, and not once this winter. He heard no more shouts; the frosty air was very still. He thought to himself that the other boys had gone home, but he did not care.

However, when he reached the top of the hill there was another boy with his sled. He had been all ready to coast down, but had seen Ephraim coming, and waited.

" Hullo !" he called.

" Hullo !" returned Ephraim, panting.

Then the boy stared. " It ain't you, Ephraim Thayer !" he demanded.

" Why ain't it me ?" returned Ephraim, with a manful air, swaggering back his shoulders at the other boy, who was Ezra Ray.

" Why, I didn't know your mother ever let you out," said Ezra, in a bewildered fashion. In fact, the vision of Ephraim Thayer out with a sled, coasting, at eleven o'clock at night, was startling. Ezra remembered dazedly how he had heard his mother say that very afternoon that Ephraim was worse, that the doctor had been there last Saturday, and she didn't believe he would live long. He looked at Ephraim standing there in the moonlight almost as if he were a spirit.

"She ain't let me for some time; I've been sick," admitted Ephraim, yet with defiance.

"I heard you was awful sick," said Ezra.

"I was; but the doctor give me some medicine that cured me."

Ephraim placed his sled in position and got on stiffly. The other boy still watched. "She know you're out to-night?" he inquired, abruptly.

Ephraim looked up at him. "S'pose you think you'll go an' tell her, if she don't," said he.

"No, I won't, honest."

"Hope to die if you do?"

"Yes."

"Well, then, I run out of the side door."

"Both on 'em asleep?"

Ephraim nodded.

Ezra Ray whistled. "You'll get a whippin' when your mother finds it out."

"No, I sha'n't. Mother can't whip me, because the doctor says it ain't good for me. You goin' down?"

"Can't go down but once. I've got to go home, or mother 'll give it to me."

"A BOYISH FIGURE FLED SWIFTLY OUT OF THE THAYER YARD"

" Does she ever whip you ?"

" Sometimes."

" Mine don't," said Ephraim, and he felt a superiority over Ezra Ray. He thought, too, that his sled was a better one. It was not painted, nor was it as new as Ezra's, but it had a reputation. Barney had won many coasting laurels with it in his boyhood, and his little brother, who had never used it himself, had always looked upon it with unbounded faith and admiration.

He gathered up his sled - rope, spurred himself into a start with his heels, and went swiftly down the long hill, gathering speed as he went. Poor Ephraim had an instinct for steering ; he did not swerve from the track. The frosty wind smote his face, his breath nearly failed him, but half-way down he gave a triumphant whoop. When he reached the foot of the hill he had barely wind enough to get off his sled and drag it to one side, for Ezra Ray was coming down.

Ezra did not slide as far as Ephraim had done. Ephraim watched anxiously lest he should. " That sled of yours ain't no good," he panted, when Ezra had stopped several yards from where he stood.

" Guess it ain't quite so fast as yours," admitted Ezra. " That's your brother's, ain't it ?"

" Yes."

" Well, that sled can't be beat in town. Mine's 'bout as good as any, 'cept that. I've always heard my brother say that your brother's sled was the best one he ever see."

Ephraim stood looking at his brother's old battered but distinguished sled as if it had been a blood-horse. " Guess it can't be beat," he chuckled.

" No sir, it can't," said Ezra. He started off past Ephraim down the road, with his sled trailing at his heels.

" Hullo !" called Ephraim, " ain't you goin' up again ?"

" Can't, got to go home."

" Less try it jest once more, an' see if you can't go further."

" No, I can't, nohow. Mother won't like it as 'tis."

" Whip you ?"

" 'Spect so ; don't mind it if she does." Ezra brought a great show of courage to balance the other's immunity from danger. " Don't mind nothin' 'bout a little whippin'," he added, with a brave and contemptuous air. He whistled as he went on.

Ephraim stood watching him. He had enough brave blood in his veins to feel that this contempt of a whipping was a greater thing than not being whipped. He felt an envious admiration of Ezra Ray, but that did not prevent his calling after him :

" Ezra !"

" What say ?"

" You ain't goin' to tell my mother ?"

" Didn't I say I wasn't ? I don't tell fibs. Hope to die if I do."

Ezra's brave whistle, as cheerfully defiant of his mother's prospective wrath as the note of a bugler advancing to the charge, died away in the distance. For Ephraim now began the one unrestrained hilarity of his whole life. All by himself in the white moonlight and the keen night air he climbed the long hill, and slid down over and over. He ignored his feeble and laboring breath of life. He trod upon, he outspeeded all infirmities of the flesh in his wild triumph of the spirit. He shouted and hallooed as he shot down the hill. His mother could not have recognized his voice had she heard it, for it was the first time that the boy had ever given full cry to the natural voice of youth and his heart. A few stolen races, and sorties up apple-trees, a few stolen slides had poor Ephraim Thayer had; they had been snatched in odd minutes, at the imminent danger of discovery; but now he had the wide night before him; he had broken over all his trammels, and he was free.

Up and down the hill went Ephraim Thayer, having the one playtime of his life, speeding on his brother's famous sled against bondage and deprivation and death. It was after midnight when he went home; all the village lights were out; the white road stretched before him, as still and deserted as a road through solitude itself. Ephraim had never been out-of-doors so late before, he had never been so alone in his life, but he was not afraid. He was not afraid of anything in the lonely night, and he was not afraid of his mother at home. He thought to himself exultantly that Ezra Ray had been no more courageous than he, although, to be sure, he had not a whipping to fear like Ezra. His heart was full of joyful triumph that he was not wholly guilty, since it was the outcome of an innocent desire.

As he walked along he tipped up his face and stared with his stupid boyish eyes at the stars paling in the full moonlight, and the great moon herself overriding the clouds and the stars. It made him think of the catechism and the Commandments, and then a little pang of terror shot through him, but even that did not daunt him. He did not look up at the stars again, but bent his head and trudged on, with the sled-rope pulling at his weak chest.

When he reached his own yard he stepped as carefully as he could; still he was not afraid. He put the sled back in the shed; then he stole into the house. He took off his shoes in the entry, and got safely into his own room. He was in his night-gown and all ready for bed when another daring thought struck him.

Ephraim padded softly on his bare feet out through the kitchen to the pantry. Every third step or so he stopped and listened to the heavy double breathing from the bedroom beyond. So long as that continued he was safe. He listened, and then slid on a pace or two as noiseless as a shadow in the moonlight.

Ephraim knew well where the mince-pies were

kept. There was a long row of them covered with towels on an upper shelf.

Ephraim hoisted himself painfully upon a meal-bucket, and clawed a pie over the edge of the shelf. He could scarcely reach, and there was quite a loud grating noise. He stood trembling on the bucket and listened, but the double breathing continued. Deborah had been unusually tired that night; she had gone to bed earlier, and slept more soundly.

Ephraim broke a great jagged half from the mince-pie; then replaced it with another grating slide. Again he listened, but his mother had not been awakened.

Ephraim crept back to his bedroom. There he sat on the edge of his bed and devoured his pie. The rich spicy compound and the fat plums melted on his tongue, and the savor thereof delighted his very soul. Then Ephraim got into bed and pulled the quilts over him. For the first and only occasion in his life he had had a good time.

The next morning Ephraim felt very ill, but he kept it from his mother. He took his medicine of his own accord several times, and turned his head from her, that she might not notice his laboring breath.

In the middle of the forenoon Deborah went out. She had to drive over to Bolton to get some sugar and tea. She would not buy anything now at Berry's store. Caleb had gone down to the lot to cut a little wood; he had harnessed the horse for her before he went. It was a cold day, and she wrapped herself up well in two shawls and a thick veil over her hood. When she was all ready she gave Ephraim his parting instructions, rearing over him with stern gestures, like a veiled justice.

"Now," said she, "you listen to what I tell you. When your father comes in you tell him I want him to set right down and finish parin' them apples. They are spoilin', an' I'm goin' to make 'em into sauce. You tell him to set right down and go to work on 'em; he can get 'em done by the time I get home, an' I can make the sauce this afternoon. You set here an' take your medicine an' learn your cate-chism. You can study over the Commandments, too; you ain't got 'em any too well. Do you hear?"

"Yes, ma'am," said Ephraim. He looked away from his mother as he spoke, and his panting breath clouded the clear space on the frosty window-pane. He sat beside the window in the rocking-chair.

"Mind you tell your father about them apples," repeated his mother as she went out.

"Yes, ma'am," said Ephraim. He watched his mother drive out of the yard, guiding the horse carefully through the frozen ridges of the drive. Presently he took another spoonful of his medicine. He felt a little easier, but still very ill. His father came a few minutes after his mother had gone. He heard him stamping in through the back door; then his frost-reddened old face looked in on Ephraim.

"Mother gone?" said he.

"She's jest gone," replied Ephraim. His father came in. He looked at the boy with a childish and anxious sweetness. "Don't you feel quite as well as you did?" he inquired.

"Dunno as I do."

"Took your medicine reg'lar?"

Ephraim nodded.

"I guess it's good medicine," said Caleb; "it come real high; I guess the doctor thought consid'ble of it. I'd take it reg'lar if I was you. I thought you looked as if you didn't feel quite so well as common when I come in."

Caleb took off his boots and tended the fire. Ephraim began to feel a little better; his heart did not beat quite so laboriously.

He did not say a word to his father about paring the apples. Caleb went into the pantry and came back eating a slice of mince-pie.

"I found there was a pie cut, and I thought mother wouldn't mind if I took a leetle piece," he remarked, apologetically. He would never have dared take the pie without permission had his wife been at home. "She ain't goin' to be home till arter dinner-time, an' I began to feel kinder gone," added Caleb. He stood by the fire, and munched the pie with a relish slightly lessened by remorse. "Don't you want nothin'?" he asked of Ephraim. "Mebbe a little piece of pie wouldn't hurt you none."

Caleb's ideas of hygienic food were primitive. He believed, as innocently as if he had lived in Eden before the Prohibition, that all food which he liked was good for him, and he applied his theory to all mankind. He had deferred to Deborah's imperious will, but he had never been able to understand why she would not allow Ephraim to eat mince-pie or anything else which his soul loved and craved.

"No, guess I don't," Ephraim replied. He gazed moodily out of the window. "Father," said he, suddenly.

"What say, sonny?"

"I eat some of that pie last night."

"Mother give it to you?"

"No; I clim up on the meal-bucket, an' got it in the night."

"You might have fell, an' then I dunno what mother 'd ha' said to you," said Caleb.

"An' I did somethin' else."

"What else did you do?"

"I went out a-coastin' after you an' her was asleep."

"You didn't, now?"

"Yes, I did."

"An' we didn't neither on us wake up?"

"You was a-snorin' the whole time."

"I don't s'pose you'd oughter have done it, Ephraim," said Caleb, and he tried to make his tone severe.

"I never went a-coastin' in my whole life before," said Ephraim; "it ain't fair."

"I dunno what mother 'd say if she was to find out about it," said Caleb, and he shook his head.

"Ezra Ray was the only one that was out there, an' he said he wouldn't tell."

"Well, mebbe he won't, mebbe he won't. I guess you most hadn't oughter gone unbeknownst to your mother, sonny."

"Barney's sled jest beat Ezra's all holler."

"It did, hey? That allers was a good sled," returned the old man, chuckling.

Caleb went into the pantry again, and returned rattling a handful of corn. "Want a game of holly-gull?" he asked. "I've got a leetle time to spare now while mother's gone."

"Guess so," replied Ephraim. He dragged his chair forward to the hearth; he and his father sat opposite each other and played the old childish game of holly-gull. Ephraim was very fond of the game, and would have played it happily hour after hour had not Deborah esteemed it a sinful waste of time. When Caleb held up his old fist, wherein he had securely stowed a certain number of kernels of corn, and demanded, "Holly-gull, hand full, passel how many?" Ephraim's spirit was thrilled with a fine stimulation, of which he had known little in life. If he guessed the number of kernels right and confiscated the contents of his father's hand, he felt the gratified ambition of a successful financier; if he lost, his heart sank, only to bound higher with new hope for the next chance. A veritable gambling game was holly-gull, but they gambled for innocent Indian-corn instead of the coin of the realm, and nobody suspected it. The lack of value of the stakes made the game quite harmless and unquestioned in public opinion.

The waste of time was all Deborah's objection to the game. Caleb and Ephraim said not a word about it to each other, but both kept an anxious ear towards Deborah's returning sleigh-bells.

At last they both heard the loud, brazen jingle entering the yard, and Caleb gathered all the corn together and stowed it away in his pocket. Then he stood on the hearth, looking like a guilty child. Ephraim went slowly over to the window; he did not feel quite so well again.

Deborah's harsh "Whoa!" sounded before the door; presently she came in, her garments radiating cold air, her arms full of bundles.

"What you standin' there for, father?" she demanded of Caleb. "Why didn't you come out an' take some of these bundles? Why ain't you goin' out an' puttin' the horse up instead of standin' there starin'?"

"I'm goin' right off, mother," Caleb answered, apologetically; and he turned his old back towards her and scuffled out in haste.

"Put on your cap!" Deborah called after him.

She laid off her many wraps, her hood and veil, and mufflers and shawls, folded them carefully, and carried them into her bedroom, to be laid in her bureau drawers. Deborah was very orderly and methodical.

"Did you take your medicine?" she asked Ephraim as she went out of the room.

"Yes, ma'am," said he. He did not feel nearly as well; he kept his face turned from his mother. Ephraim was accustomed to complain freely, but now the coasting and the mince-pie had made him patient. He was quite sure that his bad feelings were due to that, and suppose his mother should suspect and ask him what he had been doing! He was also terrified by the thought of the holly-gull and her unfulfilled order about the apple-paring. He sat very still; his heart shook his whole body, which had grown thin lately. He looked very small, in spite of his sturdy build.

Deborah was gone quite a while; she had left some work unfinished in her bedroom that morning. Caleb returned before she did, and pulled up a chair close to the fire. He was holding his reddened fingers out towards the blaze to warm them when Deborah came in.

She looked at him, then around the room, inquiringly.

"Where did you put the apples?" said she to Caleb.

Caleb stared around at her. "What apples, mother?" he asked, feebly.

"The apples I left for you to pare. I want to put 'em on before I get dinner."

"I ain't heard nothin' about apples, mother."

"Ain't you pared any apples this forenoon?"

" I didn't know as you wanted any pared, mother."
Deborah turned fiercely on Ephraim.

" Ephraim Thayer, look here !" said she. Ephraim
turned his poor blue face slowly ; his breath came
shortly between his parted lips ; he clapped one hand
to his side. " Didn't you tell your father to pare
them apples, the way I told you to ?" she demanded.

Ephraim dropped his chin lower.

" Answer me !"

" No, ma'am."

" What have you been a-doin' of ?"

" Playin'."

" Playin' what ?"

" Holly-gull."

Deborah stood quite still for a moment. Her
mouth tightened ; she grew quite pale. Ephraim
and Caleb watched her. Deborah strode across the
room, out into the shed.

" I guess she won't say much ; don't you be scared,
Ephraim," whispered Caleb.

But Ephraim, curious to say, did not feel scared.
Suddenly his mother seemed to have lost all her
terrifying influence over him. He felt very strange,
and as if he were sinking away from it all through
deep abysses.

His mother came back, and she held a stout stick
in her right hand. Caleb gasped when he saw it.
" Mother, you ain't goin' to whip him ?" he cried out.

" Father, you keep still !" commanded Deborah.
" Ephraim, you come with me !"

She led the way into Ephraim's little bedroom, and he stumbled up and followed her. He saw the stick before him in his mother's hand; he knew she was going to whip him, but he did not feel in the least disturbed or afraid. Ezra Ray could not have faced a whipping any more courageously than Ephraim. But he staggered as he went, and his feet met the floor with strange shocks, since he had prepared his steps for those deep abysses.

He and his mother stood together in his little bedroom. She, when she faced him, saw how ill he looked, but she steeled herself against that. She had seen him look as badly before; she was not to be daunted by that from her high purpose. For it was a high purpose to Deborah Thayer. She did not realize the part which her own human will had in it.

She lifted up her voice and spoke solemnly. Caleb, listening, all trembling, at the kitchen door, heard her.

" Ephraim," said his mother, " I have spared the rod with you all my life because you were sick. Your brother and your sister have both rebelled against the Lord and against me. You are all the child I've got left. You've got to mind me and do right. I ain't goin' to spare you any longer because you ain't well. It is better you should be sick than be well and wicked and disobedient. It is better that your body should suffer than your immortal soul. Stand still."

Deborah raised her stick, and brought it down. She raised it again, but suddenly Ephraim made a strange noise and sunk away before it, down in a heap on the floor.

Caleb heard him fall, and came quickly.

"Oh, mother," he sobbed, "is he dead? What ails him?"

"He's got a bad spell," said Deborah. "Help me lay him on the bed." Her face was ghastly. She spoke with hoarse pulls for breath, but she did not flinch. She and Caleb laid Ephraim on his bed; then she worked over him for a few minutes with mustard and hot-water—all the simple remedies in which she was skilled. She tried to pour a little of the doctor's medicine into his mouth, but he did not swallow, and she wiped it away.

"Go an' get Barney to run for the doctor, quick!" she told Caleb at last. Caleb fled, sobbing aloud like a child, out of the house. Deborah closed the boy's eyes, and straightened him a little in the bed. Then she stood over him there, and began to pray aloud. It was a strange prayer, full of remorse, of awful agony, of self-defense of her own act, and her own position as the vicar of God upon earth for her child. "I couldn't let him go astray too!" she shrieked out. "I couldn't, I couldn't! O Lord, thou knowest that I couldn't! I would—have lain him upon—the altar, as Abraham laid Isaac! Oh, Ephraim, my son, my son, my son!"

Deborah prayed on and on. The doctor and a

throng of pale women came in; the yard was full of shocked and staring people. Deborah heeded nothing; she prayed on.

Some of the women got her into her own room. She stayed there, with a sort of rigid settling into the spot where she was placed and she pleaded with the Lord for upholding and justification until the daylight faded, and all night. The women, Mrs. Ray and the doctor's wife, who watched with poor Ephraim, heard her praying all night long. They sat in grave silence, and their eyes kept meeting with shocked significance as they listened to her. Now and then they wet the cloth on Ephraim's face. About two o'clock Mrs. Ray tiptoed into the pantry, and brought forth a mince-pie. " I found one that had been cut on the top shelf," she whispered. She and the doctor's wife ate the remainder of poor Ephraim's pie.

The two women stayed next day and assisted in preparations for the funeral. Deborah seemed to have no thought for any of her household duties. She stayed in her bedroom most of the time, and her praying voice could be heard at intervals.

Some other women came in, and they went about with silent efficiency, performing their services to the dead and setting the house in order; but they said very little to Deborah. When she came out of her room they eyed her with a certain grim furtiveness, and they never said a word to her about Ephraim.

It was already known all over the village that she had been whipping Ephraim when he died. Poor old Caleb, when the neighbors had come flocking in, had kept repeating with childish sobs, "Mother hadn't ought to have whipped him! mother hadn't ought to have whipped him!"

"Did Mrs. Thayer whip that boy?" the doctor had questioned, sharply, before all the women, and Caleb had sobbed back, hoarsely, "She was jest a-whippin' of him; I told her she hadn't ought to."

That had been enough. "She whipped him," the women repeated to each other in shocked pantomime. They all knew how corporal punishment had been tabooed for Ephraim.

The Thayer house was crowded the afternoon of the funeral. The decent black-clad village people, with reddening eyes and mouths drooping with melancholy, came in throngs into the snowy yard. The men in their Sunday gear tiptoed creaking across the floors; the women, feeling for their pocket-handkerchiefs, padded softly and heavily after them, folded in their black shawls like mourning birds.

Caleb and Deborah and Barney sat in the north parlor, where Ephraim lay. Deborah's hoarse laments, which were not like the ordinary hysterical demonstrations of feminine grief, being rather a stern uprising and clamor of herself against her own heart, filled the house.

The minister had to pray and speak against it; scarcely any one beyond the mourners' room could

"THE THAYER HOUSE WAS CROWDED THE AFTERNOON OF THE FUNERAL"

hear his voice. It was a hard task that the poor young minister had. He was quite aware of the feeling against Deborah, and it required finesse to avoid jarring that, and yet display the proper amount of Christian sympathy for the afflicted. Then there were other difficulties. The minister had prayed in his closet for a small share of the wisdom of Solomon before setting forth.

The people in the other rooms leaned forward and strained their ears. The minister's wife sat beside her husband with bright spots of color in her cheeks, her little figure nervously contracted in her chair. They had had a discussion concerning the advisability of his mentioning the sister and daughter in his prayer, and she had pleaded with him strenuously that he should not.

When the minister prayed for the afflicted " sister and daughter, who was now languishing upon a bed of sickness," his wife's mouth tightened, her feet and hands grew cold. It seemed to her that her own tongue pronounced every word that her husband spoke. And there was, moreover, a little nervous thrill through the audience. Oddly enough, everybody seemed to hear that portion of the minister's prayer quite distinctly. Even one old deaf man in the farthest corner of the kitchen looked meaningly at his neighbor.

The service was a long one. The village hearse and the line of black covered wagons waited in front of the Thayer house over an hour. There had been another fall of snow the night before, and now the north wind blew it over the country. Outside ghostly spirals of snow raised from the new drifts heaped along the road-sides like graves, disappeared over the fields, and moved on the borders of distant woods, while in-doors the minister held forth, and the choir sang funeral hymns with a sweet uneven drone of grief and consolation.

When at last the funeral was over and the people came out, they bent their heads before this wild storm which came from the earth instead of the sky.

The cemetery was a mile out of the village; when the procession came driving rapidly home it was nearly sunset, and the thoughts of the people turned from poor Ephraim to their suppers. It is only for a minute that death can blur life for the living. Still, when the evening smoke hung over the roofs the people talked untiringly of Ephraim and his mother.

As time went on the dark gossip in the village swelled louder. It was said quite openly that Deborah Thayer had killed her son Ephraim. The neighbors did not darken her doors. The minister and his wife called once. The minister offered prayer and spoke formal words of consolation as if he were reading from invisible notes. His wife sat by in stiff, scared silence. Deborah nodded in response; she said very little.

Indeed, Deborah had become very silent. She scarcely spoke to Caleb. For hours after he had gone to bed the poor bewildered old man could hear his wife wrestling in prayer with the terrible angel of the Lord whom she had evoked by the stern magic of grief and remorse. He could hear her harsh, solemn voice in self-justification and agonized appeal. After a while he learned to sleep with it still ringing in his ears, and his heavy breathing kept pace with Deborah's prayer.

Deborah had not the least doubt that she had killed her son Ephraim.

There was some talk of the church's dealing with her, some women declared that they would not go to meeting if she did; but no stringent measures were taken, and she went to church every Sunday all the rest of the winter and during the spring.

It was an afternoon in June when the doctor's wife and Mrs. Ray went into Deborah Thayer's yard. They paused hesitatingly before the door.

"I think you're the one that ought to tell her," said Mrs. Ray.

"I think it's your place to, seeing as 'twas your Ezra that knew about it," returned the doctor's wife. Her voice sounded like the hum of a bee, being full of husky vibrations; her double chin sank into her broad heaving bosom, folded over with white plaided muslin.

"Seems to me it belongs to you, as long as you're the doctor's wife," said Mrs. Ray. She was very small and lean beside the soft bulk of the other woman, but there was a sort of mental uplifting about her which made her unconscious of it. Mrs. Ray had never considered herself a small woman; she seemed always to see the tops of other women's heads.

The doctor's wife looked at her dubiously, panting softly all over her great body. It was a warm afternoon. The low red and white rose-bushes sprayed all around the step-stone, and they were full of roses. The doctor's wife raised the brass knocker. " Well, I'd just as lieves," said she, resignedly. "She'd ought to be told, anyway ; the doctor said so." The knocker fell with a clang of brass.

Deborah opened the door at once. " Good-afternoon," said she.

" We thought we'd come over a few minutes, it's so pleasant this afternoon," said the doctor's wife.

" Walk in," said Deborah. She aided them in through the kitchen to the north parlor. She always entertained guests there on warm afternoons.

The north parlor was very cool and dark ; the curtains were down, and undulated softly like sails. Deborah placed the big haircloth rocking-chair for the doctor's wife, and Mrs. Ray sat down on the sofa.

There was a silence. The doctor's wife flushed red. Mrs. Ray's sharp face was imperturbable. Deborah, sitting erect in one of her best flag-bottomed chairs, looked as if she were alone in the room.

The doctor's wife cleared her throat. " Mis' Thayer," she began.

Deborah looked at her with calm expectation.

"Mis' Thayer," said the doctor's wife, "Mis' Ray and I thought we ought to come over here this afternoon. Mis' Ray heard something last night, an' she came over an' told the doctor, an' he said you ought to know—"

The doctor's wife paused, panting. Then the door opened and Caleb peered in. He bowed stiffly to the two guests; then, with apprehensive glances at his wife, slid into a chair near the door.

"Mis' Ray's Ezra told her last night," proceeded the doctor's wife, "that the night before your son died he run away unbeknown to you, an' went slidin' down hill. The doctor says mebbe that was what killed him. He said you'd ought to know."

Deborah leaned forward; her face worked like the breaking up of an icy river. "Be you sure?" said she.

"Ezra told me last night," interposed Mrs. Ray. "I had a hard time gettin' it out of him; he promised Ephraim he wouldn't tell. But somethin' he said made me suspect, an' I got it out of him. He said Ephraim told him he run away, an' he left him there slidin' when he came home. 'Twas as much as 'leven o'clock then; I remember I give Ezra a whippin' next mornin' for stayin' out so late. But then, of course, whippin' Ezra wa'n't nothin' like whippin' Ephraim."

"The doctor says most likely that was what killed him, after all, an' you'd ought to know," said the doctor's wife.

" Be you sure ?" said Deborah again.

" Ephraim wa'n't to blame. He never had no show; he never went a-slidin' like the other little fellers," said Caleb, suddenly, out of his corner; and he snivelled as he spoke.

Deborah turned on him sharply. " Did you know anything about it ?" said she.

" He told me on 't that mornin'," said Caleb; " he told me how he'd been a-slidin', an' how he eat some mince-pie."

" Eat—some—mince - pie !" gasped Deborah, and there was a great light of hope in her face.

" Well," said the doctor's wife, " if that boy eat mince-pie, an' slid down hill, too, I guess you ain't much call to worry about anything you've done, Mis' Thayer. I know what the doctor has said right along."

The doctor's wife arose with a certain mild impressiveness, as if some mantle of her husband's authority had fallen upon her. She shook out her ample skirts as if they were redolent of rhubarb and mint. " Well, I guess we had better be going," said she, and her inflections were like the doctor's.

Mrs. Ray rose also. " Well, we thought you'd ought to know," said she.

" I'm much obliged to you," said Deborah.

She went through the kitchen with them. When the door was shut behind them she turned to Caleb, who had shuffled along at her heels. " Oh, father, why didn't you tell me if you knew, why didn't you tell me ?" she gasped out.

Caleb stared at her. "Why, mother?" he returned.

"Didn't you know I thought I'd killed him, father? didn't you know I thought I'd killed my son? An' now maybe I haven't! maybe I haven't! O Lord, I thank thee for letting me know before I die! Maybe I haven't killed him, after all!"

"I didn't s'pose it would make any difference," said Caleb, helplessly.

Suddenly, to the old man's great terror, his wife caught hold of him and clung to him. He staggered a little; his arms hung straight at his sides. "Why, what ails you, mother?" he stammered out. "I didn't tell you, 'cause I thought you'd be blamin' him for 't. Mother, don't you take on so; now don't!"

"I—wish—you'd go an' get Rebecca an' Barney, father," said Deborah, faintly. She suddenly wavered so that her old husband wavered with her, and they reeled back and forth like two old trees in a wind.

"Why, what ails you, mother, what ails you?" Caleb gasped out. He caught Deborah's arm, and clutched out at something to save himself. Then they sank to the floor together.

Barney had just come up from the field, and was at his own door when his father came panting into the yard. "What is it? what's the matter?" he cried out.

"Mother's fell!" gasped Caleb.

"Fell! has she hurt her?"

"Dunno—she can't get up; come quick!"

As Barney rushed out of the yard he cast a glance up the hill towards Charlotte's house; in every crisis of his life his mind turned involuntarily to her, as if she were another self, to be made acquainted with all its exigencies. But when he came out on the road he met Charlotte herself face to face; she had been over to her Aunt Sylvia's.

"Something is wrong with mother," Barney said, with a strange appeal. Then he went on, and Charlotte was at his side, running as fast as he. Caleb hurried after them, panting, the tears running down his old cheeks.

"Father says she's fell!" Barney said, as they sped along.

"Maybe she's only fainted," responded Charlotte's steady, faithful voice.

But Deborah Thayer had more than fainted. It might have been that Ephraim had inherited from her the heart-taint that had afflicted and shortened his life, and it might have been that her terrible experiences of the last few months would have strained her heart to its undoing, had its valves been made of steel.

Barney carried his mother into the bedroom, and laid her on the bed. He and Charlotte worked over her, but she never spoke nor moved again. At last Charlotte laid her hand on Barney's arm. "Come out now," said she, and Barney followed her out.

When they were out in the kitchen Barney looked in her face. "It's no use, she's gone!" he said, hoarsely. Charlotte nodded. Suddenly she put her arms up around his neck, and drew his head down to her bosom, and held it there, stroking his cheek.

"Oh, Charlotte," Barney sobbed. Charlotte bent over him, whispering softly, smoothing his hair and cheek with her tender hand.

Caleb had gone for the doctor and Rebecca while they tried to restore Deborah, and had given the alarm on the way. Some women came hurrying in with white faces, staring curiously even then at Barney and Charlotte; but she never heeded them, except to answer in the affirmative when they asked, in shocked voices, if Deborah was dead. She went on soothing Barney, as if he had been her child, with no more shame in it, until he raised his white face from her breast of his own accord.

"Oh, Charlotte, you will stay to-night, won't you?" he pleaded.

"Yes, I'll stay," said Charlotte. Young as Charlotte was, she had watched with the sick and sat up with the dead many a time. So she and the doctor's wife watched with Deborah Thayer that night. Rebecca came, but she was not strong enough to stay. The next day Charlotte assisted in the funeral preparations. It made a great deal of talk in the village. People wondered if Barney would marry her now, and if she would sit with the mourners at the funeral. But she sat with her father and mother in the south room, and time went on after Deborah died, and Barney did not marry her.

CHAPTER XII

A few days after Deborah's funeral Charlotte had an errand at the store after supper. When she went down the hill the sun had quite set, but there was a clear green light. The sky gave it out, and there seemed to be also a green glow from the earth. Charlotte went down the hill with the evening air fresh and damp in her face. Lilacs were in blossom all about, and their fragrance was so vital and intense that it seemed almost like a wide presence in the green twilight.

She reached Barney's house, and passed it; then she came to the Thayer house. Before that lay the garden. The ranks of pease and beans were in white blossom, and there was a pale shimmer as of a cobweb veil over it.

Charlotte had passed the garden when she heard a voice behind her:

"Charlotte!"

She stopped, and Barney came up.

"Good-evening," said he.

"Good-evening," said Charlotte.

"I saw you going by," said Barney. Then he paused again, and Charlotte waited.

"I saw you going by," he repeated, "and—I thought

I'd like to speak to you. I wanted to thank you for what you did—about mother."

"You're very welcome," replied Charlotte.

Barney ground a stone beneath his heel. "I sha'n't ever forget it, and — father won't, either," he said. His voice trembled, and yet there was a certain doggedness in it.

Charlotte stood waiting. Barney turned slowly away. "Good-night," he said.

"Good-night," returned Charlotte, quickly, and she fairly sprang away from him and down the road. Her limbs trembled, but she held her head up proudly. She understood it all perfectly. Barney had meant to inform her that his behavior towards her on the day his mother died had been due to a momentary weakness; that she was to expect nothing further. She went on to the store and did her errand, then went home. As she entered the kitchen her mother came through from the front room. She had been sitting at a window watching for Charlotte to return; she thought Barney might be with her.

"Well, you've got home," said she, and it sounded like a question.

"Yes," said Charlotte. She laid her parcels on the table. "I guess I'll go to bed," she added.

"Why, it's dreadful early to go to bed, ain't it?"

"Well, I'm tired; I guess I'll go."

The candle-light was dim in the room, but Sarah eyed her daughter sharply. She thought she looked pale.

"Did you meet anybody?" she asked.

"I don't know; there wasn't many folks out."

"You didn't see Barney, did you?"

"Yes, I met him."

Charlotte lighted another candle, and opened the door.

"Look here," said her mother.

"Well?" replied Charlotte, with a sort of despairing patience.

"What did he say to you? I want to know."

"He didn't say much of anything. He thanked me for what I did about his mother."

"Didn't he say anything about anything else?"

"No, he didn't." Charlotte went out, shielding her candle.

"You don't mean that he didn't say anything, after the way he acted that day his mother died?"

"I didn't expect him to say anything."

"He's treated you mean, Charlotte," her mother cried out, with a half sob. "He'd ought to be strung up after he acted so, huggin' an' kissin' you right before folk's face and eyes."

"It was more my fault than 'twas his," returned Charlotte; and she shut the door.

"Then I should think you'd be ashamed of yourself," Sarah called after her, but Charlotte did not seem to hear.

"I never see such work, for my part," Sarah wailed out to herself.

"Mother, you come in here a minute," Cephas called

out of the bedroom. He had gone to bed soon after supper.

"Anythin' new about Barney?" he asked, when his wife stood beside him.

"Barney ain't no more notion of comin' back than he had before, in spite of all the talk. I never see such work," replied Sarah, in a voice strained high with tears.

"I call it pretty doin's," assented Cephas. His pale face, with its venerable beard, was closely set about with his white nightcap. He lay staring straight before him with a solemnly reflective air.

"I wish you hadn't brought up 'lection that time, father," ventured Sarah, with a piteous sniff.

"If the Democratic party had only lived different, an' hadn't eat so much meat, there wouldn't have been any trouble," returned Cephas, magisterially. "If you go far enough, you'll always get back to that. A man is what he puts into his mouth. Meat victuals is at the bottom of democracy. If there wa'n't any meat eat there wouldn't be any Democratic party, an' there wouldn't be any wranglin' in the state. There'd be one party, jest as there'd ought to be."

"I wish you hadn't brought it up, father," Sarah lamented again; "it's most killin' me."

"If we hadn't both of us been eatin' so much animal food there wouldn't have been any trouble," repeated Cephas.

"Well, I dunno much about animal food, but I know I'm about discouraged," said Sarah. And she went back to the kitchen, and sat down in the rocking-chair and cried a long time, with her apron over her face. Her heartache was nearly as sore as her daughter's up-stairs.

Charlotte did not speak to Barney again all summer—indeed, she scarcely ever saw him. She had an occasional half-averted glimpse of his figure across the fields, and that was all. Barney had gone back to the old house to live with his father, and remained there through the summer and fall; but Caleb died in November. He had never been the same since Deborah's death; whether, like an old tree whose roots are no longer so firm in the earth that they can withstand every wind of affliction, the shock itself had shaken him to his fall, or the lack of that strange wontedness which takes the place of early love and passion had enfeebled him, no one could tell. He had seemed to simply stare at life from a sunny place on a stone-wall or a door-step all summer.

When the autumn set in he sat in his old chair by the fire. Caleb had always felt cold since Deborah died. When the bell tolled off his years, one morning in November, nobody felt surprised. People had said to each other for some time that Caleb Thayer was failing.

Barney, after his father died, went back to his own forlorn new house to live, and his sister Rebecca and her husband came to live in the old one. Rebecca went to meeting now every Sunday, wearing her mother's black shawl and a black ribbon on her bon-

net, and sitting in her mother's place in the Thayer
pew. She never went anywhere else, her rosy color
had gone, and she looked old and haggard.

Barney went into his sister's now and then of a
Sunday night, and sat with her and William an hour
or so. He and William would sometimes warm into
quite an animated discussion over politics or theology,
while Rebecca sat silently by. Barney went nowhere
else, not even to meeting. Sundays he used to
watch furtively for Charlotte to go past with her
father and mother. Quite often Sylvia Crane used
to appear from her road and join them, and walk
along with Charlotte. Barney used to look at her
moving down the road at Charlotte's side, as at the
merest supernumerary on his own tragic stage. But
every tragedy has its multiplying glass to infinity,
and every actor has his own tragedy. Sylvia Crane
that winter, all secretly and silently, was acting her
own principal rôle in hers. She had quite come to
the end of her small resources, and nobody, except
the selectmen of Pembroke, knew it. They were
three saturnine, phlegmatic, elderly men, old Squire
Payne being the chairman, and they kept her secret
well. Sylvia waylaid them in by-places, she stole
around to the back door of Squire Payne's house by
night, she conducted herself as if it were a guilty
intrigue, and all to keep her poverty hid as long as
may be.

Old Squire Payne was a widower, a grave old
man of few words. He advanced poor Sylvia meagre

moneys on her little lands, and he told nobody. There came a day when he gave her the last dollar upon her New England soil, full of old plough-ridges and dried weeds and stones.

Sylvia went home with it in the pocket of her quilted petticoat under her dress skirt. She kept feeling of it to see if it were safe as she walked along. The snow was quite deep, the road was not well broken out, and she plodded forward with bent head, her black skirt gathering a crusty border of snow.

She had to pass Richard Alger's house, but she never looked up. It was six o'clock, and quite dark; it had been dark when she set out at five. The housewives were preparing supper; there was a smell of burning pine-wood in the air, and now and then a savory scent of frying meat. Sylvia had smelled brewing tea and baking bread in Squire Payne's house, and she had heard old Margaret, the Scotch woman who had lived with the squire's family ever since she could remember, stepping around in another room. Old Margaret was almost the only servant, the only regular and permanent servant, in Pembroke, and she enjoyed a curious sort of menial distinction: she dressed well, wore a handsome cashmere shawl which had come from Scotland, and held her head high in the squire's pew. People saluted her with respect, and her isolation of inequality gave her a reversed dignity.

Sylvia had hoped Margaret would not come in

while she sat with the squire. She was afraid of
her eyes, which flashed keen like a man's under shaggy brows. She did not want her to see the squire
counting out the money from his leather purse, although she knew that Margaret would keep her own
counsel.

She had been glad enough to escape and not see
her appear behind the bulk of the squire in the doorway. Squire Payne was full of laborious courtesy,
and always himself aided Sylvia to the door when
she came for money, and that always alarmed her.
She would drop a meek courtesy on trembling knees
and hurry away.

Sylvia had almost reached the old road leading to
her own house, when she saw a figure advancing
towards her through the dusk. She saw it was a
woman by the wide swing of the skirts, and trembled.
She felt a presentiment as to who it was. She held
her head down and well to one side, she bent over
and tried to hurry past, but the figure stopped.

"Is that you, Sylvy Crane?" said her sister, Hannah Berry.

Sylvia did not stop. "Yes, it's me," she stammered. "Good-evenin', Hannah."

She tried to pass, but Hannah stood in her way.
"What you hurryin' so for?" she asked, sharply;
"where you been?"

"Where *you* been?" returned Sylvia, trembling.

"Up to Sarah's. Charlotte, she's gone down to
Rebecca's. She's terrible thick with Rebecca. Well,

I've been to see Rebecca; an' Rose, she's been, an' I ain't nothin' to say. William has got her for a wife, an' we've got to hold up our heads before folks; an' when it comes right down to it, there's a good many folks can't say much. If Charlotte Barnard wants to be thick with Rebecca, she can. Her mother won't say nothin'. She always was as easy as old Tilly; an' as for Cephas, he's either eatin' grass, or he ain't eatin' grass, an' that's all he cares about, unless he gets stirred up about politics, the way he did with Barney Thayer. I dunno but Charlotte thinks she'll get him back again goin' to see Rebecca. I miss my guess but what she sees him there sometimes. I wouldn't have a daughter of mine chasin' a fellar that had give her the mitten; but Charlotte ain't got no pride, nor her mother, neither. Where did you say you'd been, trapesin' through the snow?"

"Has Rose got her things most done?" asked Sylvia, desperately. Distress was awakening duplicity in her simple, straightforward heart. All Hannah Berry's thoughts slid, as it were, in well-greased grooves; only give one a starting push and it went on indefinitely and left all others behind, and her sister Sylvia knew it.

"Well, she's got 'em pretty near done," replied Hannah Berry. "Her underclothes are all done, an' the quilts; the weddin'-dress ain't bought yet, an' she's got to have a mantilla. Do you know Charlotte ain't never wore that handsome man-

tilla she had when she was expectin' to marry Barney?"

"Ain't she?"

"No, she ain't, nor her silk gown neither. I said
all I darsed to. I thought mebbe she or Sarah would
offer; they both of 'em know how hard it is to get
anything out of Silas; but they didn't, an' I wa'n't
goin' to ask, nohow. I shall get a new silk an' a
mantilla for Rose, an' not be beholden to nobody, if
I have to sell the spoons I had when I was married."

"I don't s'pose they have much to do with," said
Sylvia. She began to gradually edge past her sister.

"Of course they haven't; I know that jest as well
as you do. But if Charlotte ain't goin' to get married
she don't want any weddin'-gown an' mantilla, an'
she won't ever get married. She let Thomas Payne
slip, an' there ain't nobody else I can think of for her.
If she ain't goin' to want weddin'-clothes, I don't see
why she an' her mother would be any poorer for
givin' hers away. 'Twouldn't cost 'em any more
than to let 'em lay in the chest. Well, I've got to go
home; it's supper-time. Where did you say you'd
been, Sylvy?"

Sylvia was well past her sister; she pretended not
to hear. "You ain't been over for quite a spell,"
she called back, faintly.

"I know I ain't," returned Hannah. "I've been
tellin' Rose we'd come over to tea some afternoon
before she was married."

"Do," said Sylvia, but the cordiality in her voice seemed to overweigh it.

"Well, mebbe we'll come over to-morrow," said Hannah. "We've got some pillow-slips to trim, an' we can bring them. You'd better ask Sarah an' Charlotte, if she can stay away from Rebecca Thayer's long enough."

"Yes, I will," said Sylvia, feebly, over her shoulder.

"We'll come early," said Hannah. Then the sisters sped apart through the early winter darkness. Poor Sylvia fairly groaned out loud when her sister was out of hearing and she had turned the corner of the old road.

"What shall I do? what shall I do?" she muttered.

Her sisters to tea meant hot biscuits and plum sauce and pie and pound-cake and tea. Sylvia had yet a little damson sauce at the bottom of a jar, although she had not preserved last year, for lack of sugar; but hot biscuits and pie, the pound-cake and tea would have to be provided.

She felt again of the little money-store in her pocket; that was all that stood between her and the poor-house; every penny was a barrier and had its carefully calculated value. This outlay would reduce terribly her little period of respite and independence; yet she hesitated as little as Fouquet planning the splendid entertainment, which would ruin him, for Louis XIII.

Her sisters and nieces must come to tea; and all the food, which was the village fashion and as absolute in its way as court etiquette, must be provided.

"They'll suspect if I don't," said Sylvia Crane.

She rolled away the stone from the door and entered her solitary house. She lighted her candle and prepared for bed. She did not get any supper. She said to herself with a sudden fierceness, which came over her at times — a mild impulse of rebellion which indicated perhaps some strain from far-off, untempered ancestors, which had survived New England generations—that she did not care if she never ate supper again.

"They're all comin' troopin' in here to-morrow, an' it's goin' to take about all the little I've got left to get victuals for 'em, an' I've got to go without to-night if I starve!" she cried out quite loud and defiantly, as if her hard providence lurked within hearing in some dark recess of the room.

She raked ashes over the coals in the fireplace. "I'll go to bed an' save the fire, too," she said; "it'll take about all the wood I've got left to-morrow. I've got to heat the oven. Might as well go to bed, an' lay there forever, anyway. If I stayed up till doomsday nobody 'd come."

Sylvia set the shovel back with a vicious clatter; then she struck out — like a wilful child who hurts itself because of its rage and impotent helplessness to hurt aught else — her thin, red hand against the bricks of the chimney. She looked at the bruises on it with bitter exultation, as if she saw in them some evidence of her own freedom and power, even to her own hurt.

When she went to bed she stowed away her money under the feather-bed. She could not go to sleep. Some time in the night a shutter in another room up-stairs banged. She got up, lighted the candle, and trod over the icy floors to the room relentlessly with her bare feet. There was a pane of glass broken behind the shutter, and the wind had loosened the fastening. Sylvia forced the shutter back; in a strange rage she heard another pane of glass crack. " I don't care if every pane of glass in the window is broken," she muttered, as she hooked the fastening with angry, trembling fingers.

Her thin body in its cotton night-gown, cramped with long rigors of cold, her delicate face reddened as if before a fire, her jaws felt almost locked as she went through the deadly cold of the lonely house back to bed; but that strange rage in her heart enabled her to defy it, and awakened within her something like blasphemy against life and all the conditions thereof, but never against Richard Alger. She never felt one throb of resentment against him. She even wondered, when she was back in bed, if he had bedclothing enough, if the quilts and bed-puffs that his mother had left were not worn out; her own were very thin.

The next day Sylvia heated her brick oven; she went to the store and bought materials, and made pound-cake and pies. While they were baking she ran over and invited Charlotte and her mother. She did not see Cephas; he had gone to draw some wood.

"I'd like to have him come, too," she said, as she went out; "but I dunno as he'd eat anything I've got for tea."

"Land! he eats anything when he goes out anywhere to tea," replied Mrs. Barnard. "He was over to Hannah's a while ago, an' he eat everything. He eats pie-crust with shortenin' now, anyway. He got so he couldn't stan' it without. I guess he'd like to come. He'll have to draw wood some this afternoon, but he can come in time for tea. I'll lay out his clothes on the bed for him."

"Well, have him come, then," said Sylvia. Sylvia was nearly out of the yard when Charlotte called after her: "Don't you want me to come over and help you, Aunt Sylvia?" she called out. She stood in the door with her apron flying out in the wind like a blue flag.

"No, I guess not," replied Sylvia; "I don't need any help. I ain't got much to do."

"I think Aunt Sylvia looks sick," Charlotte said to her mother when she went in.

"I thought she looked kind of peaked," said Sarah. But neither of them dreamed of the true state of affairs: how poor Sylvia Crane, half-starved and half-frozen in heart and stomach, was on the verge of bankruptcy of all her little worldly possessions.

Sylvia's sisters, practical enough in other respects,

were singularly ignorant and incompetent concerning any property except the few dollars and cents in their own purses.

They had always supposed Sylvia had enough to live on, as long as she lived at all. They had a comfortable sense of generosity and self-sacrifice, since they had let her have all the old homestead after her mother's death without a word, and even against covert remonstrances on the parts of their husbands.

Silas Berry had once said out quite openly to his wife and Sarah Barnard: " That will had ought to be broke, accordin' to my way of thinkin'," and Hannah had returned with spirit: " It won't ever be broke unless it's against my will, Silas Berry. I know it seems considerable for Sylvy to have it all, but she's took care of mother all those years, an' I don't begrutch it to her, an' she's a-goin' to have it. I don't much believe Richard Alger will ever have her now she's got so old, an' she'd ought to have enough to live on the rest of her life an' keep her comfortable."

Therefore Sylvia's sisters had a conviction that she was comfortably provided with worldly gear. Mrs. Berry was even speculating upon the probability of her giving Rose something wherewith to begin housekeeping when her marriage with Tommy Ray took place.

The two sisters, with their daughters, came early that afternoon. Mrs. Berry and Rose sewed knitted lace on pillow-slips; Mrs. Barnard and Charlotte were making new shirts for Cephas; Charlotte sat

by the window and set beautiful stitches in her
father's linen shirt-bosoms, while her aunt Hannah's
tongue pricked her ceaselessly as with small goading
thorns.

"I s'pose this seems kind of natural to you, don't
it, Charlotte, gettin' pillow - slips ready?" said Mrs.
Berry.

"I don't know but it does," answered Charlotte,
never raising her eyes from her work. Her mother
flushed angrily. She opened her mouth as if to
speak, then she shut it again hard.

"Let me see, how many did you make?" asked
Mrs. Berry.

"She made two dozen pair," Charlotte's mother
answered for her.

"An' you've got 'em all laid away, yellowin'?"

"I guess they ain't yellowed much," said Sarah
Barnard.

"I don't see when you're ever goin' to use 'em."

"Mebbe there'd be chances enough to use 'em if
some folks was as crazy to take up with 'em as some
other folks," returned Sarah Barnard.

"I'd like to know what you mean?"

"Oh, nothin'. If folks want chances to make
pillow-slips bad enough there's generally poor tools
enough layin' 'round, that's all."

"I'd like to know what you mean, Sarah Barnard."

"Oh, I don't mean nothin'," answered Sarah Barnard. She glanced at her daughter Charlotte and
smiled slyly, but Charlotte never returned the glance

and smile. She sewed steadily. Rose colored, but she said nothing. She looked very pretty and happy, as she sat there, sewing knitted lace on her wedding-pillows; and she really was happy. Her passionate heart had really satisfied itself with the boyish lover whom she would have despised except for lack of a better. She was and would be happy enough; it was only a question of deterioration of character, and the nobility of applying to the need of love the rules of ordinary hunger and thirst, and eating contentedly the crust when one could not get the pie, of drinking the water when one could not get the wine. Contentment may be sometimes a degradation; but she was happier than she had ever been in her life, although she had a little sense of humiliation when she reflected that Tommy Ray, younger than herself, tending store under her brother, was not exactly a brilliant match for her, and that everybody in the village would think so. So she colored angrily when her aunt Sarah spoke as she did, although she said nothing. But her mother, although she had rebelled in private bitterly against her daughter's choice, was ready enough to take up the cudgels for her in public.

"Well," said Hannah Berry, "two old maids in the family is about enough, accordin' to my way of thinkin'."

"It's better to be an old maid than to marry somebody you don't want, jest for the sake of bein' married," retorted Sarah Barnard, fiercely.

The two sisters clashed like two thorny bushes of one family in a gale the whole afternoon. The two daughters sewed silently, and Sylvia knitted a stocking with scarcely a word until she arose to get tea.

Cephas and Silas both came to tea, which was served in state, with a fine linen table-cloth, and Sylvia's mother's green and white sprigged china. Nobody suspected, as they tasted the damson sauce with the thin silver spoons, as they tilted the green and white teacups to their lips, and ate the rich pound-cake and pie, what a very feast of renunciation and tragedy this was to poor Sylvia Crane. Cephas and Silas, indeed, knew that money had been advanced her by the town upon her estate, but they were far from suspecting, and, indeed, were unwilling to suspect, how nearly it was exhausted and the property lived out. It was only a meagre estimate that the town of Pembroke had made of the Crane ancestral acres. If Silas and Cephas had ever known what it was, they had dismissed it from their minds, they were interested in not knowing. Suppose their wives should want to give her a home and support.

The women knew nothing whatever.

When they went home, an hour after tea, Hannah Berry turned to Sylvia in the doorway. "I suppose you know the weddin' is comin' off pretty soon now," said she.

"Yes, I s'posed 'twas," answered Sylvia, trying to smile.

"Well, I thought I'd jest mention it, so you could

get your present ready," said Hannah. She nudged Rose violently as she spoke.

"I don't care; I meant to give her a hint," she said, chuckling, when they were outside. "She can give you something jest as well as not; she might give you some silver teaspoons, or a table, or sofa. There! she bought that handsome sofa for herself a few years ago, an' she didn't need it more'n nothin' at all. I suppose she thought Richard Alger was comin' steady, but now he's stopped."

Rose was married in a few weeks. The morning of the wedding-day Sylvia went into Berry's store and called William aside.

"If you can, I wish you'd come 'round by-an'-by with your horse an' your wood-sled," said she.

"Yes, guess I can; what is it you want?" asked William, eying her curiously. She was very pale; there were red circles around her eyes, and her mouth trembled.

"Oh, it ain't anything, only a little present I wanted to send to Rose," replied Sylvia.

"Well," said William, "I'll be along by-an'-by." He looked after her in a perplexed way as she went out.

Silas was in the back of the store, and presently he came forward. "What she want you to do?" he inquired of his son.

William told him. The old man chuckled. "Hannah give her a hint 'tother day, an' I guess she took it," he said.

"I thought she looked pretty poorly," said William—"looked as if she'd been crying or something. How do you suppose that property holds out, father? I heard the town was allowing her on it."

"Oh, I guess it 'll last her as long as she lives," replied Silas, gruffly. "Your mother had ought to had her thirds in it."

"I don't know about that," said William. "Aunt Sylvy had a hard time takin' care of grandmother."

"She was paid for 't," returned Silas.

"Richard Alger treated her mean."

"Guess he sat out considerable firewood an' candle-grease," assented the old man.

A customer came in then, and Ezra Ray sprang forward. He was all excited over his brother's wedding, and was tending store in his place that day. His mother was making him a new suit to wear to the wedding, and he felt as if the whole affair hung, as it were, upon the buttons of his new jacket and the straps of his new trousers.

"Guess I might as well go over to Aunt Sylvy's now as any time," said William.

"Don't see what she wanted you to fetch the horse an' sled for," ruminated Silas. "Mother thought most likely she'd give some silver teaspoons if she give anything."

William went out to the barn, put the horse in the sled, and drove down the hill towards Sylvia's. When he returned the old thin silver teaspoons of the Crane family were in his coat-pocket, and Sylvia's dearly beloved and fondly cherished hair-cloth sofa was on the sled behind him.

"What in creation did she send them old teaspoons and that old sofa for?" his mother asked, disgustedly.

"I don't know," replied William, soberly; "but I do know one thing: I hated to take them bad enough. She acted all upset over it. I think she'd better have kept her sofa and teaspoons as long as she lived."

"Course she was upset givin' away anything," scolded his mother. "It was jest like her, givin' away a passel of old truck ruther than spend any money. Well, I s'pose you may as well set that sofa in the parlor. It ain't hurt much, anyway."

Rose and her husband were to live with her parents for the present. She was married that evening. She wore a blue silk dress, and some rose-geranium blossoms and leaves in her hair. Tommy Ray sat by her side on Sylvia's sofa until the company and the minister were all there. Then they stood up and were married.

Sylvia came to the wedding in her best silk gown; she had trembled lest Richard Alger should be there, but he had not been invited. Hannah Berry cherished a deep resentment against him.

"I ain't goin' to have any man that's treated one of my folks as mean as he has set foot in my house to a weddin', not if I know it," she told Rose.

After the marriage-cake and cider were passed around, the old people sat solemnly around the borders of the rooms, and the young people played games. William and his wife were not there. Hannah had not dared to slight them, but William could not prevail upon Rebecca to go.

Barney, also, had not been invited to the wedding. Mrs. Berry had an open grudge against him on her niece's account, and a covert one on her daughter's. Hannah Berry had a species of loyalty in her nature, inasmuch as she would tolerate ill-treatment of her kin from nobody but her own self.

Charlotte Barnard came with her father and mother, and sat quietly with them all the evening. She was beginning insensibly to rather hold herself aloof from the young people, and avoid joining in their games. She felt older. People had wondered if she would not wear the dress she had had made for her own wedding, but she did not. She wore her old purple silk, which had been made over from one of her mother's, and a freshly-starched muslin collar. The air was full of the rich sweetness of cake; there was a loud discord of laughter and high shrill voices, through which yet ran a subtle harmony of mirth. Laughing faces nodded and uplifted like flowers in the merry romping throngs in the middle of the room, while the sober ones against the walls watched with grave, elderly, retrospective eyes.

As soon as she could, Sylvia Crane stole into her sister's bedroom, where the women's outside garments were heaped high on the bed, got her own, opened the side door softly, and went home. The next day she was going to the poor-house, and nobody but the three selectmen of Pembroke knew it. She had begged them, almost on her knees, to tell nobody until she was there.

That night she rolled away the guardian stone from before the door with the feeling that it was for the last time. All that night she worked. She could not go to bed, she could not sleep, and she had gone beyond any frenzy of sorrow and tears. All her blind and helpless rage against life and the obdurately beneficent force, which had been her conception of Providence, was gone. When the battle is over there is no more need for the fury of combat. Sylvia felt her battle was over, and she felt the peace of defeat.

She was to take a few necessaries to the poor-house with her; she had them to pack, and she also had some cleaning to do.

She had a vague idea that the town, which seemed to loom over her like some dreadful shadowy giant of a child's story, would sell the house, and it must be left in neat order for the inspection of seller and buyer. " I ain't goin' to have the town lookin' over the house an' sayin' it ain't kept decent," she said. So she worked hard all night, and her candle lit up first one window, then another, moving all over the house like a will-o'-the-wisp.

The man who had charge of the poor-house came for her the next morning at ten o'clock. Sylvia was all ready. At quarter past ten he drove out of the old road where the Crane house stood and down the village street. The man's name was Jonathan Leavitt. He was quite old but hearty, with a stubbly fringe of white beard around a ruddy face. He had come on a wood-sled for the greater convenience of bringing Sylvia's goods. There were a feather-bed, bolster, and pillows, tied up in an old homespun blanket, on the rear of the sled; there was also a red chest, and a great bundle of bedclothing. Sylvia sat in her best rocking-chair just behind Jonathan Leavitt, who drove standing.

"It's a pleasant day for this time of year," he observed to Sylvia when they started. Sylvia nodded assent.

Jonathan Leavitt had had a fear lest Sylvia might make a disturbance about going. Many a time had it taken hours for him to induce a poor woman to leave her own door-stone; and when at length they had set forth, it was to an accompaniment of shrill, piteous lamentations, so strained and persistent that they seemed scarcely human, and more like the cries of a scared cat being hauled away from her home. Everybody on the road had turned to look after the sled, and Jonathan Leavitt had driven on, looking straight ahead, his face screwed hard, lashing now and then his old horse, with a gruff shout. Now he felt relieved and grateful to Sylvia for going so quietly. He was disposed to be very friendly to her.

"You'd better keep your rockin'-chair kind of stiddy," he said, when they turned the corner into the new road, and the chair oscillated like an uneasy berth at sea.

Sylvia sat up straight in the chair. She had on her best bonnet and shawl, and her worked lace veil over her face. Her poor blue eyes stared out between the black silk leaves and roses. If she had been a dead woman and riding to her grave, and it had been possible for her to see as she was borne along the familiar road, she would have regarded everything in much the same fashion that she did now. She looked at everything—every tree, every house and wall—with a pang of parting forever. She felt as if she should never see them again in their old light.

The poor-house was three miles out of the village; the road lay past Richard Alger's house. When they drew near it Sylvia bent her head low and averted her face; she shut her eyes behind the black roses. She did not want to know when she passed the house. An awful shame that Richard should see her riding past to the poor-house seized upon her.

The wood-sled went grating on, a chain rattled; she calculated that they were nearly past when there was a jerk, and Jonathan Leavitt cried "Hullo!"

"Where you going?" shouted another voice. Sylvia knew it. Her heart pounded. She turned her face farther to one side, and did not open her eyes.

Richard Alger came plunging down out of his

yard. His handsome face was quite pale under a slight grizzle of beard, he was in his shirt-sleeves, he had on no dicky or stock, and his sinewy throat showed.

"Where you goin'?" he gasped out again, as he came up to the sled.

"I'm a takin' Sylvy home. Why?" inquired Jonathan Leavitt, with a dazed look.

"Home? What are you headed this way for? What are all those things on the sled?"

"She's lived out her place, an' the town's jest took it; guess you didn't know, Richard," said Jonathan Leavitt. His eyes upon the other man were half shrewdly inquiring, half bewildered.

Sylvia never turned her head. She sat with her eyes closed behind her veil.

"Just turn that sled 'round," said Richard Alger.

"Turn the sled 'round?"

"Yes, turn it 'round!" Richard himself grasped the bay horse by the bit as he spoke. "Back, back!" he shouted.

"What are you doin' on, Richard?" cried the old man; but he pulled his right rein mechanically, and the sled slewed slowly and safely around.

Richard jumped on and stood just beside Sylvia, holding to a stake. "Where d'ye want to go?" asked the old man.

"Back."

"But the town—"

"I'll take care of.the town."

Jonathan Leavitt drove back. Sylvia opened her eyes a little way, and saw Richard's back. "You'll catch cold without your coat," she half gasped.

"No, I sha'n't," returned Richard, but he did not turn his head.

Sylvia did not say any more. She was trembling so that her very thoughts seemed to waver. They turned the corner of the old road, and drove up to her old house. Richard stepped off the sled, and held out his hands to Sylvia. "Come, get off," said he.

"I dunno about this," said Jonathan Leavitt. "I'm willin' as far as I'm concerned, Richard, but I've had my instructions."

"I tell you I'll take care of it," said Richard Alger. "I'll settle all the damages with the town. Come, Sylvia, get off."

And Sylvia Crane stepped weakly off the wood-sled, and Richard Alger helped her into the house. "Why, you can't hardly walk," said he, and Sylvia had never heard anything like the tenderness in his tone. He bent down and rolled away the stone. Sylvia had rolled it in front of the door herself, when she went out, as she supposed, for the last time. Then he opened the door, and took hold of her slender shawled arm, and half lifted her in.

"Go in an' sit down," said he, "while we get the things in."

Sylvia went mechanically into her clean, fireless parlor; it was the room where she had always re-

"SYLVIA NEVER TURNED HER HEAD"

ceived Richard. She sat down in a flag-bottomed chair and waited.

Richard and Jonathan Leavitt came into the house tugging the feather-bed between them. "We'll put it in the kitchen," she heard Richard say. They brought in the chest and the bundle of bedding. Then Richard came into the parlor carrying the rocking-chair before him. "You want this in here, don't you?" he said.

"It belongs here," said Sylvia, faintly. Jonathan Leavitt gathered up his reins and drove out of the yard.

Richard set down the chair; then he went and stood before Sylvia.

"Look here, Sylvia," said he. Then he stopped and put his hands over his face. His whole frame shook. Sylvia stood up. "Don't, Richard," she said.

"I never had any idea of this," said Richard Alger, with a great groaning sob.

"Don't you feel so bad, Richard," said Sylvia.

Suddenly Richard put his arm around Sylvia, and pulled her close to him. "I'll look out and do better by you the rest of your life, anyhow," he said. He took hold of Sylvia's veil and pulled it back. Her pale face drooped before him.

"You look—half—starved," he groaned. Sylvia looked up and saw tears on his rough cheeks.

"Don't you feel bad, Richard," she said again.

"I'd ought to feel bad," said Richard, fiercely.

"I couldn't help it, that night you come an'

found me gone. It was that night Charlotte had the trouble with Barney. Sarah, she wouldn't let me come home any sooner. I was dreadful upset about it."

"I've been meaner than sin, an' I don't know as it makes it any better, because I couldn't seem to help it," said Richard Alger. "I didn't forget you a single minute, Sylvia, an' I was awful sorry for you, an' there wasn't a Sabbath night that I didn't want to come more than I wanted to go to Heaven! But I couldn't, I couldn't nohow. I've always had to travel in tracks, an' no man livin' knows how deep a track he's in till he gets jolted out of it an' can't get back. But I've got into a track now, an' I'll die before I get out of it. There ain't any use in your lookin' at me, Sylvia, but if you can make up your mind to have me, I'll try my best, an' do all I can to make it all up to you in the time that's left."

"I'm afraid you've had a dreadful hard time, livin' alone so long, an' tryin' to do for yourself," said Sylvia, pitifully.

"I'm glad I have," replied Richard, grimly.

He clasped Sylvia closer; her best bonnet was all crushed against his breast. He looked around over her head, as if searching for something.

"Where's the sofa gone?" he asked.

"I gave it to Rose for a weddin' present. I thought I shouldn't ever need it," Sylvia murmured.

"Well, I've got one, it ain't any matter," said Richard.

He moved towards the rocking-chair, drawing Sylvia gently along with him.

"Sit down, Sylvia," said he, softly.

"No, you sit down in the rocking-chair, Richard," said Sylvia. She reached out and pulled a flag-bottomed chair close and sat down herself. Richard sat in the rocking-chair.

Sylvia untied her bonnet, took it off, and straightened it. Richard watched her. "I want you to have a white bonnet," said he.

"I'm too old, Richard," Sylvia replied, blushing.

"No, you ain't," he said, defiantly; "you've got to have a white bonnet."

Sylvia looked in his face—and indeed hers looked young enough for a white bonnet; it flushed and lit up, like an old flower revived in a new spring.

Richard leaned over towards her, and the two old lovers kissed each other. Richard moved his chair close to hers, and Sylvia felt his arm coming around her waist. She sat still. "Put your head down on my shoulder," whispered Richard.

And Sylvia laid her head on Richard's shoulder. She felt as if she were dreaming of a dream.

CHAPTER XIII

When Richard Alger went home he wore an old brown shawl of Sylvia's over his shoulders. He had demurred a little. "I can't go down the street with your shawl on, Sylvia," he had pleaded, but Sylvia insisted.

"You'll catch your death of cold, goin' home in your shirt-sleeves," she said. "They won't know it's my shawl. Men wear shawls."

"You've worn this ever since I've known you, Sylvia, an' I ain't given to catchin' cold easy," said Richard almost pitifully. But he stood still and let Sylvia pin the shawl around his neck. Sylvia seemed to have suddenly acquired a curious maternal authority over him, and he submitted to it as if it were merely natural that he should.

Richard Alger went meekly down the road, wearing the old brown shawl that had often draped Sylvia Crane's slender feminine shoulders when she walked abroad, since she was a young girl. Sylvia had always worn it corner-wise, but she had folded it square for him as making it more of a masculine garment. Two corners waved out stiffly from his square shoulders. He tried to swing his arms unconcernedly under it; once the fringe hit his hand and he jumped.

He was shame-faced when he struck out into the main road, but he did not dream of taking off the shawl. A very passion of obedience and loyalty to Sylvia had taken possession of him. With every submission after long persistency, there is a strong reverse action, as from the sudden cessation of any motion. Richard now yielded in more marked measure than he had opposed. He had borne with his whimsical will against all his sweetheart's dearest wishes during the better part of her life; now he would wear any insignia of bondage if she bade him.

He had gone a short distance on the main road when he met Hannah Berry. She was hurrying along, her face was quite red, and he could hear her pant as she drew near. She looked at him sharply, she fairly narrowed her eyes over the shawl. "Good-mornin'," said she.

Richard said "Good-morning," gruffly. The shawl blew out against Hannah's shoulder as she passed him. She turned about and stared after him, and he knew it. He went on with dogged chin in the folds of the shawl.

Hannah Berry hurried along to Sylvia Crane's. When she opened the door Sylvia was just coming out of the parlor, and the two sisters met in the entry with a kind of shock.

"Oh, it's you," murmured Sylvia. Sylvia cast down her eyes before her sister. She tried not to smile. Her hair was tumbled and there were red spots on her cheeks.

"Has he been here all this time?" demanded Hannah.

"He's just gone."

"I met him out here. What in creation did you rig him up in your old shawl for, Sylvy Crane?"

"He was in his shirt-sleeves, an' I wasn't goin' to have him catch his death of cold," replied Sylvia with dignity.

"In his shirt-sleeves!"

"Yes, he run out just as he was."

"Land sakes!" said Hannah. The two women looked at each other. Suddenly Hannah threw out her arms from under her shawl, and clasped Sylvia. "Oh, Sylvy," she sobbed out, "to think you was settin' out for the poor-house this mornin', an' we havin' a weddin' last night, an' never knowin' it! Why didn't you say anythin' about it, why didn't you, Sylvy?"

"I knew you couldn't do anything, Hannah."

"Knew I couldn't do anything! Do you suppose me or Sarah would have let all the sister we've got go to the poor-house whilst we had a roof over our heads? We'd took you right in, either one of us."

"I was afraid Silas an' Cephas wouldn't be willin'."

"I guess they'd had to be willin'. I told Silas just now that if Richard Alger didn't come forward like a man, you was comin' to my house, an' have the best we've got as long as you lived. Silas, he said he thought you'd ought to earn your own livin', an' I told him there wa'n't any chance for a woman like you to earn your livin' in Pembroke, that you could earn your livin' enough livin' at your own sister's. Oh, Sylvy, I can't stand it, when I think of your startin' out that way, an' never sayin' a word." Hannah sobbed convulsively on her sister's shoulder. There were tears in Sylvia's eyes, but her face above her sister's head was radiant. "Don't, Hannah," she said. "It's all over now, you know."

"Is he—goin' to have you now—Sylvy?"

"I guess so, maybe," said Sylvia.

"I suppose you'll go to his house, this is so run down."

"He's goin' to fix this one up."

"You think you'd rather live here, then? Well, I s'pose I should. I s'pose he's goin' to buy it. The town hadn't ought to ask much. Sylvy Crane, I can't get it through my head, nohow."

"What?" said Sylvia.

"How you run out this nice place so quick. I thought an' Sarah thought you'd got enough to last you jest as long as you lived, an' have some left to leave then."

Hannah stood back and looked at her sister sharply.

"I've always been as savin' as I knew how," said Sylvia.

"Well, I dunno but you have. You got that sofa, that cost considerable. I shouldn't have thought you'd got that, if you'd known how things were, Sylvy."

" I kinder felt as if I needed it."

" Well, I guess you might have got along without that, anyhow. Richard's got one, ain't he ?"

" Yes, he says he has."

" I thought I remembered his mother's buyin' one just before his father died. Well, you'll have his sofa, then; if I remember right, it's a better one than yours that you give Rose. Now, Sylvy Crane, you jest put on your hood an' shawl, an' come home with me, an' have some dinner. Have you got anything in the house to eat ?"

" I've got a few things," replied Sylvia, evasively.

" What ?"

" Some potatoes an' apples."

" Potatoes an' apples !" Hannah began to sob again. " To think of your comin' to this," she wailed. " My own sister not havin' anything in the house to eat, an' settin' out for the poor-house, an' everybody in town knowin' it."

" Don't feel bad about it, Hannah; it's all over now," said Sylvia.

" Don't feel bad about it ! I guess you'd feel bad about it if you was in my place," returned Hannah. " I s'pose you think now you've got Richard Alger that there's nothin' else makes any odds. I guess I've got some feelin's. Get your hood and shawl, now do; dinner was all ready when I come away."

" I guess I'd better not, Hannah," said Sylvia. It seemed to her that she never would want anything to eat again. She wanted to be alone in her old house, and hug her happiness to her heart, whose starvation had caused her more agony than any other. Now that was appeased she cared for nothing else.

"You come right along," said Hannah. "I've got a nice roast spare-rib an' turnip an' squash, an' you're goin' to come an' have some of it."

When Hannah and Sylvia got out on the main road, they heard Sarah Barnard's voice calling them. She was hurrying down the hill. Cephas had just come home with the news. Jonathan Leavitt had spread it over the village from the nucleus of the store where he had stopped on his way home.

Sarah Barnard sat down on the snowy stone-wall among the last year's blackberry vines, and cried as if her heart would break. Finally Hannah, after joining with her awhile, turned to and comforted her.

"Land sake, don't take on so, Sarah Barnard!" said she ; " it's all over now. Sylvy's goin' to marry Richard Alger, an' there ain't a man in Pembroke any better off, unless it's Squire Payne. She's goin' to have him right off, an' he's goin' to buy the house an' fix it up, an' she's goin' to have all his mother's nice things, an' she's comin' home with me now, an' have some nice roast spare-rib an' turnip. There ain't nothin' to take on about."

Hannah fairly pulled Sarah off the stone-wall. "Sylvy an' me have got to go," said she. "You come down this afternoon, an' we'll all go over to her house, an' talk it over. I s'pose Richard will come to-night. I hope he'll shave first, an' put on his coat. I never see such a lookin' sight as he was when I met him jest now."

"I didn't see as he looked very bad," said Sylvia, with dignity.

"It seems as if it would kill me jest to think of it," sobbed Sarah Barnard, turning tremulously away.

"Don't you feel bad about it any longer, Sarah," Sylvia said, half absently. Her hair blew out wildly from under her hood over her flushed cheeks; she smiled as if at something visible, past her sister, and past everything around her.

"I tell you there ain't nothin' to be killed about!" Hannah called after Sarah; she caught hold of Sylvia's arm. "Sarah always was kind of hystericky," said she. "That spare-rib will be all dried up, an' I wouldn't give a cent for it, if you don't come along."

Richard Alger and Sylvia Crane were married very soon. There was no wedding, and people were disappointed about that. Hannah Berry tried to persuade Sylvia to have one. "I'm willin' to make the cake," said she. "I've jest been through one weddin', but I'll do it. If I'd been goin' with a feller as long as you have with him, I wouldn't get cheated out of a weddin', anyhow. I'd have a weddin' an' I'd have cake, an' I'd ask folks, especially after what's happened. I'd let 'em see I wa'n't quite so far gone, if I had set out for the poor-house once. I'd have a weddin'. Richard's got money enough. I had real good-luck with Rose's cake, an' I ain't afraid to try yours. I guess I should make it a little mite stiffer than I did hers."

But Sylvia was obdurate. She did not say much, but she went her own way. She had gained a certain quiet decision and dignity which bewildered everybody. Her sisters had dimly realized that there was something about her out of plumb, as it were. Her nature had been warped to one side by one concentrated and unsatisfied desire. " Seems to me, sometimes, as if Sylvy was kind of queer," Hannah Berry often said. " I dunno but she's kinder turned on Richard Alger," Sarah would respond. Now she seemed suddenly to have regained her equilibrium, and no longer slanted doubtfully across her sisters' mental horizons.

She and Richard went to the minister's house early one Sabbath morning, and were married. Then they went to meeting, Sylvia on Richard's arm. They sat side by side in the Alger pew; it was on the opposite side of the meeting-house from Sylvia's old pew. It seemed to her as if she would see her old self sitting there alone, as of old, if she looked across. She fixed her eyes straight ahead, and never glanced at Richard by her side. She held her white-bonneted head up like some gentle flower which had sprung back to itself after a hard wind. She had a new white bridal bonnet, as Richard had wished; it was trimmed with white plumes and ribbons, and she wore a long white-worked veil over her face. The wrought net-work, as delicate as frost, softened all the hard lines and fixed tints, and gave to her face an illusion of girlhood. She wore the two curls over her cheeks. Richard had asked her why she didn't curl her hair as she used to do.

All the people saw Sylvia's white bonnet; it seemed to turn their eyes like a brilliant white spot, which reflected all the light in the meeting-house. But there were a few women who eyed more sharply Sylvia's wedding-gown and mantilla, for she wore the very ones which poor Charlotte Barnard had made ready for her own bridal. Sylvia was just about her niece's height; the gown had needed a little taking in to fit her thinner form, and that was all.

Charlotte's mother had brought them over to Sylvia's one night, all nicely folded in white linen towels.

"Charlotte wants you to have 'em; she says she won't ever need 'em, poor child!" she said, in response to Sylvia's remonstrances. Mrs. Barnard's eyes were red, as if she had been crying. It had apparently been harder for her to give up the poor slighted wedding-clothes than for her daughter. Charlotte had not shed a tear when she took them out of the chest and shook off the sprigs of lavender which she had laid over them; but it seemed to her that she could smell that faint elusive breath of lavender across the meeting-house when Sylvia came in, and the rustle of her bridal-gown was as loud in her ears as if she herself wore it.

"Somebody might just as well have them, and have some good of them," she had told her mother, and she spoke as if they were the garments of some one who was dead.

"Seems to me, as much as they cost, you'd ought to wear 'em yourself," said her mother.

"I never shall," Charlotte said, firmly; "and they might just as well do somebody some good." Charlotte's New England thrift and practical sense stretched her sentiment on the rack, and she never made a sound.

Barney, watching out from his window that Sunday, caught a flash of green and purple from Sylvia's silken skirt as she turned the corner of the old road with Richard. "She's got on Charlotte's wedding-dress. She's—given it to her," he said, with a gasp. He had never forgotten it since the day Charlotte had shown it to him. He had pictured her in it, hundreds of times, to his own delight and torment. He had a fierce impulse to rush out and strip his Charlotte's wedding-clothes from this other bride's back.

"She's gone and given it away, and she hasn't got a good silk dress herself; she's wearing her old cloak to meeting," he half sobbed to himself. He wondered piteously, thinking of his savings and of his property since his father's death, if he might not, at least, buy Charlotte a new silk dress and a mantilla. "I don't believe she'd be mad," he said; "but I'm afraid her father wouldn't let her wear it."

The more he thought of it the more it seemed as

if he could not bear it, unless he could buy Charlotte the silk dress. " Her clothes ain't as good as mine," he said, and he thought of his best blue broadcloth suit, and his flowered vest and silk hat. It seemed to him that with all the terrible injury he was doing Charlotte, he also injured her by having better clothes than she, and that that was something which might be set right.

As Barney sat by his window that Sunday afternoon he saw a man coming down the hill. He watched him idly, then his heart leaped and he leaned forward. The man advanced with a careless, stately swing, his head was thrown back, his mulberry-colored coat had a sheen like a leaf in the sun. The man was Thomas Payne. Barney turned white as he watched him. He had not known he was in town, and his jealous heart at once whispered that he had come to see Charlotte. Thomas Payne came opposite the house, then passed out of sight. Barney sat with staring eyes full of miserable questioning upon the road. Had he been to see Charlotte? he speculated. He had come from that direction; but Barney remembered, with a sigh of hope, that Squire Payne had a sister, an old maiden lady, who lived a half-mile beyond Charlotte. Perhaps Thomas Payne had been to see his aunt.

All the rest of the day Barney was in an agony of doubt and unrest over the unsettled question. He had been living lately in a sort of wretched peace of remorse and misery; now it was rudely shaken. He

"THOMAS PAINE ADVANCED WITH A CARELESS, STATELY SWING"

walked the floor; at night he could not sleep. He seemed to be in a very torture-chamber of his own making, and the tortures were worse than any enemies could have devised. Suppose Thomas Payne was sitting up with Charlotte this Sunday night. Once he thought, wildly, of going up the hill to see if there was a light in her parlor, but it seemed to him as if the doubt was more endurable than the certainty might be. Suppose Thomas Payne was sitting up with Charlotte; he called to mind all her sweet ways. Suppose she was looking and speaking to Thomas Payne in this way or that way; his imagination threw out pictures before him upon which he could not close his eyes. He saw Thomas Payne's face all glowing with triumph, he saw Charlotte's with the old look that she had worn for him. Charlotte's caresses had been few and maidenly; they all came into his mind like stings. He knew just how she would put her tender arm around this other man's neck, how she would lift grave, willing lips to his. He wished that they had never been for him, for all they seemed worth to him now was this bitter knowledge. His fancy led him on and on to his own torment. There was a bridal mist around Charlotte. He followed the old courses of his own dreams, after his memories were passed, and they caused him worse agony.

The next morning Barney went to the store. It was absolutely necessary for him to go, but he shunned everybody. He had a horrible fear lest somebody should say, " Hallo, Barney, know Thomas Payne's goin' to marry your old girl ?" He had planned the very words, and the leer of sly exultation that would accompany it.

But he made his purchase and went out, and nobody spoke to him. He had not seen Thomas Payne in the back part of the store behind the stove. Presently Thomas got up and lounged leisurely out through the store, exchanging a word with one and another on his way. When he got out Barney was going down the road quite a way ahead of him. Thomas Payne kept on in his tracks. There was another man coming towards him, and presently he stood aside to let him pass. " Good-day, Royal," said Thomas Payne.

" Good-day, Thomas," returned the other. " When d'ye get home ?"

" Day before yesterday. How are you this winter, Royal ?"

" Well, I'm pretty fair to middlin'." The man's face, sunken in his feeble chest far below the level of Thomas's eyes, looked up at him with a sort of whimsical patience. His back was bent like a bow; he had had curvature of the spine for years, from a fall when a young man.

" Glad to hear that," returned Thomas. The man passed him, walking as if he were vainly trying to straighten himself at every step. He held his knees stiff and threw his elbows back, but his back still curved pitifully, although it seemed as if he were half cheating himself into the belief that he was walking as straight as other men.

Thomas walked on rapidly, lessening the distance between himself and Barney. As he went on he began to have a curious fancy, which he could hardly persuade himself was a fancy. It seemed to him that Barney Thayer was walking like the man whom he had just met, that his back had that same terrible curve.

Thomas Payne stared in strange bewilderment at Barney's back. "It can't be that he has spine disease, that he has got hurt in any way," he thought to himself. The purpose with which he had started out rather paled in his mind. He walked more rapidly. It certainly seemed to him that Barney's back was bent. He got within hailing distance and called out.

"Hallo!" cried Thomas Payne.

Barney turned around, and it seemed as if he turned with the feeble, crooked motion of the other man. He saw Thomas Payne, and his face was ghastly white, but he stood still and waited.

"How are you?" Thomas said, gruffly, as he came up.

"How are you, Thomas?" returned Barney. He looked at Thomas with a dogged expectancy. He thought he was going to tell him that he was to marry Charlotte.

But Thomas was surveying him still in that strange bewilderment. "Look here, Barney," said he, bluntly, "have you been sick? I haven't heard of it."

"No, I haven't," replied Barney, wonderingly.

Thomas's eyes were fixed upon his back. "I didn't know but you had got hurt or something," said he.

Barney shook his head. Thomas thought to himself that his back was certainly curved. "I guess I'll walk along with you a little way," said he; "I've got something I wanted to say. For God's sake, Barney, you are sick!"

"No, I ain't sick."

"You are white as death."

"There's nothing the matter with me," Barney half gasped. He turned and walked on, and his back still bent like a bow to Thomas Payne's eyes.

Thomas went on silently until they had passed a house just beyond. Then he stopped again. "Look here, Barney," said he.

"Well," said Barney. He stopped, but he did not turn or face Thomas. He only presented to him that curved, or semblance of a curved, back.

"I want to speak to you about Charlotte Barnard," said Thomas Payne, abruptly. Barney waited without a word.

"I suppose you'll think it's none of my business, and in one way it isn't," said Thomas, "but I am going to say it for her sake; I have made up my mind to. It seems to me it's time, if anybody cares anything about her. What are you treating Charlotte Barnard so for, Barnabas Thayer? It's time you gave an account to somebody, and you can give it to me."

Barney did not answer.

"Speak, you miserable coward!" shouted Thomas Payne, with a sudden threatening motion of his right arm.

Then Barney turned, and Thomas started back at the sight of his face. "I can't help it," he said.

"Can't help it, you—"

"I can't, before God, Thomas."

"Why not?"

Barney raised his right hand and pointed past Thomas. "You—met—Royal Bennet just—now," he gasped, hoarsely.

Thomas nodded.

"You—saw—his—back?"

"Yes."

"Well, something like that ails me. I—can't help it—before God."

"You don't mean—" Thomas said, and stopped, looking at Barney's back.

"I mean that's why I can't—help it."

"Have you hurt your back?" Thomas asked, in a subdued tone.

"I've hurt my soul," said Barney. "It happened that Sunday night years ago. I—can't get over it. I am bent like his back."

"I should think you'd better get over it, then, if that's all," Thomas Payne said, roughly.

"I—can't, any more than he can."

"Do you mean your back's hurt? For God's sake

talk sense, Barney!" Thomas cried out, in bewilderment.

"It's more than my back; it's me."

Thomas stared at Barney; a horror as of something uncanny and abnormal stole over him. Was the man's back curved, or had he by some subtle vision a perception of some terrible spiritual deformity, only symbolized by a curved spine? In a minute he gave an impatient stamp, and tried to shake himself free from the vague pity and horror which the other had aroused.

"Do you know that you are ruining the life of the best woman that ever lived?" he demanded, fiercely.

Barney looked at him, and suddenly there was a flash as of something noble in his face.

"Look here, Thomas," he said, brokenly, in hoarse gasps. "Last night I—went mad, almost, because —I thought—maybe you'd been to see—her. I— saw you coming down the hill. I thought—I'd die thinking of—you—with her. I can't tell you—what I've been through, what I've suffered, and—what I suffer right along. I know I ain't to be pitied. I know—there ain't any pity—anywhere for anything —like this. I don't pity—myself. But it's awful. If you could get a sight of it, you'd know."

Again to Thomas Payne, looking at the other, it was as if he saw a pale agonized face staring up at him from the midst of a curved mass of deformity. He shuddered.

"I don't know what to make of you, Barney Thayer," he said, looking away.

"There's one thing—I want to say," Barney went on. "I think there's enough of a man left in me—I—think I've got strength enough to say it. She—ought to be happy. I don't want her—wasting her whole life—God knows—I don't—no matter what it does—to me. I—wish— See here, Thomas. I know you—like her. Maybe she'll—turn to you. It seems as if she must. I hope you will— oh, for God's sake, be—good to her, Thomas!"

Thomas Payne's face was as white as Barney's. He turned to go. "There's no use talking this way. You know Charlotte Barnard as well as I do," he said. "You know she's one of the women that never love any man but one. I don't want another man's wife, if she'd have me." Suddenly he faced Barney again. "For God's sake, Barney," he cried out, "be a man and go back to her, and marry her!"

Barney shook his head; with a kind of a sob he turned around and went his way without another word. Thomas Payne said no more; he stared after Barney's retreating figure, and again the look of bewilderment and horror was in his face.

That afternoon he asked his father, with a casual air, if he had heard anything about Barney Thayer getting his back injured in any way.

"Why, no, I can't say as I have," returned the squire.

"I saw him this morning, and I thought his back

looked as if it was growing like Royal Bennet's. I dare say I imagined it," said Thomas. Then he went out of the room whistling.

But, during his few weeks' stay in Pembroke, he put the same question to one and another, with varying results. Some said at once, with a sudden look of vague horror, that it was so. That Barney Thayer was indeed growing deformed; that they had noticed it. Others scouted the idea. "Saw him this morning, and he's as straight as he ever was," they said.

Whether Barney Thayer's back was, indeed, bowed into that terrible spinal curve or not, Thomas Payne could not tell by any agreement of witnesses. If some, gifted with acute spiritual insight, really perceived that dreadful warping of a diseased will, and clothed it with a material image for their own grosser senses; or if Barney, through dwelling upon his own real but hidden infirmity, had actually come unconsciously to give it a physical expression, and walked at times through the village with his back bent like his spirit, although not diseased, Thomas Payne could only speculate. He finally began to adopt the latter belief, as he himself, sometimes on meeting Barney, thought that he walked as erect as he ever had.

Thomas Payne stayed several weeks in Pembroke, and he did not go to see Charlotte. Once he met her in the street, and stopped and shook hands with gay heartiness.

"He's got over caring about me," Charlotte thought to herself with a strange pang, which shocked and shamed her. "Most likely he's got somebody out West, where he is," she said to herself firmly; that she ought to be glad if he had, and that she was; and yet she was not, although she never owned it to herself, and was stanchly loyal to her old love.

Charlotte herself often fancied uneasily that Barney's back was growing like Royal Bennet's. She watched him furtively when she could. Then she would say to herself, another time, that she must have imagined it.

Thomas Payne went away the first of May. That evening Charlotte sat on the door-step in the soft spring twilight. Her mother had just come home from her sister Hannah Berry's. "Thomas Payne went this afternoon," her mother said, standing before her.

"Did he?" said Charlotte.

"You might have had him if you hadn't stuck to a poor stick that ain't fit to tie your shoes up!" Sarah cried out, with sudden bitterness. Her voice sounded like Hannah Berry's. Charlotte knew that was just what her aunt Hannah had said about it.

"I don't ask him to tie my shoes up," returned Charlotte.

"You can stan' up for him all you want to," said her mother. "You know he's a poor tool, an' he's treatin' you mean. You know he can't begin to come up to a young man like Thomas Payne."

"Thomas Payne don't want me, and I don't want him; don't talk any more about it, mother."

"I think somebody ought to talk about it," said her mother, and she pushed roughly past Charlotte into the house.

Charlotte sat on the door-step a long while. "If Thomas Payne has got anybody out West, I guess she'll be glad to see him," she thought. The fancy pained her, and yet she seemed to see Thomas Payne and Barney side by side, the one like a young prince—handsome and stately, full of generous bravery—the other vaguely crouching beneath some awful deformity, pitiful yet despicable in the eyes of men, and her whole soul cleaved to her old lover. "What we've got is ours," she said to herself.

As she sat there a band of children went past, with a shrill, sweet clamor of voices. They were out hanging May-baskets and bunches of anemones. That was the favorite sport of the village children during the month of May. The woods were full of soft, innocent, seeking faces, bending over the delicate bells nodding in the midst of whorls of dark leaves. Every evening, after sundown, there were mysterious bursts of laughter and tiny scamperings around doors, and great balls of bloom swinging from the latchets when they were opened; but no person in sight, only soft gurgles of mirth and delight sounded around a corner of darkness.

After Charlotte went to bed that night she thought she heard somebody at the south door. "It is the children with some may-flowers," she thought. But presently she reflected that it was very late for the children to be out.

After a little while she got up, and stole downstairs to the door, feeling her way through the dark house.

She opened the south door cautiously, and put her hand out. There were no flowers swinging from the latch as she half expected. Her bare feet touched something on the door-step; she stooped, and there was a great package.

Charlotte took it up, and went noiselessly back to her room with it. She lighted a candle, and unfastened the paper wrappings. She gave a little cry. There were yards of beautiful silk shimmering with lilac and silver and rose-color, and there was also a fine lace mantle.

Charlotte looked at them; she was quite pale and trembling. She folded the silk and lace again carefully, and put them in a chest out of sight. Then she went back to bed, and lay there crying wildly.

"Poor Barney! poor Barney!" she sobbed to herself.

The next evening, after Cephas and Sarah had gone to bed, Charlotte crept out of the house with the package under her shawl. It was still early. She ran nearly all the way to Barney Thayer's house; she was afraid of meeting somebody, but she did not.

She knocked softly on Barney's door, and heard him coming to open it at once. When he saw her standing there he gave a great start, and did not say anything. Charlotte thought he did not recognize her in the dusk.

"It's me, Barney," she said.

"I know you," said Barney. She held out the package to him. "I've brought this back," said she.

Barney made no motion to take it from her.

"I can't take it," she said, firmly.

Suddenly Barney threw up his hands over his face. "Can't you take just that much from me, Charlotte? Can't you let me do as much as that for you?" he groaned out.

"No, I can't," said Charlotte. "You must take it back, Barney."

"Oh, Charlotte, can't you—take that much from me?"

"I can take nothing from you as things are," Charlotte replied.

"I wanted you to have a dress. I saw you had given the other away. I didn't think — there was any harm in buying it for you, Charlotte."

"It isn't your place to buy dresses for me as things are," said Charlotte. She extended the package, and he took it, as if by force. She heard him sob.

"You must never try to do anything like this again," she said. "I want you to understand it, Barney."

Then she went away, and left him standing there holding his discarded gift.

CHAPTER XIV

AFTER a while the village people ceased to have the affairs of Barney Thayer and Charlotte Barnard particularly upon their minds. As time went on, and nothing new developed in the case, they no longer dwelt upon it. Circumstances, like people, soon show familiar faces, and are no longer stared after and re-marked. The people all became accustomed to Barney living alone in his half-furnished house season after season, and to Charlotte walking her solitary maiden path. They seldom spoke of it among themselves; sometimes, when a stranger came to town, they pointed out Barney and Charlotte as they would have any point of local interest.

"Do you see that house?" a woman bent on hospitable entertainment said as she drove a matronly cousin from another village down the street; "the one with the front windows boarded up, without any step to the front door? Well, Barney Thayer lives there all alone. He's old Caleb Thayer's son, all the son that's left; the other one died. There was some talk of his mother's whippin' him to death. She died right after, but they said afterwards that she didn't, that he run away one night, an' went slidin' downhill, an' that was what killed him; he'd always had

heart trouble. I dunno; I always thought Deborah
Thayer was a pretty good woman, but she was pretty
set. I guess Barney takes after her. He was goin'
with Charlotte Barnard years ago—I guess 'twas as
much as nine or ten years ago, now — an' they were
goin' to be married. She was all ready—weddin'-dress
an' bonnet an' everything—an' this house was 'most
done an' ready for them to move into; but one
Sunday night Barney he went up to see Charlotte,
an' he got into a dispute with her father about the
'lection, an' the old man he ordered Barney out of
the house, an' Barney he went out, an' he never
went in again — couldn't nobody make him. His
mother she talked; it 'most killed her; an' I guess
Charlotte said all she could, but he wouldn't stir
a peg.

"He went right to livin' in his new house, an' he
lives there now; he ain't married, an' Charlotte ain't.
She's had chances, too. Squire Payne's son, he
wanted her bad."

The visiting cousin's mild, interrogative face peered
out around the black panel of the covered wagon at
Barney's poor house; her spectacles glittered at it
in the sun. "I want to know!" said she, with the
expression of strained, entertained amiability which
she wore through her visit.

When they passed the Barnard house the Pembroke woman partly drew rein again; the old horse
meandered in a zigzag curve, with his head lopping.
"That's where Charlotte Barnard lives," she said.

Suddenly she lowered her voice. "There she is now, out in the yard," she whispered.

Again the visiting cousin peered out. "She's good-lookin', ain't she?" she remarked, cautiously viewing Charlotte's straight figure and fair face as she came towards them out of the yard.

"She ain't so good-lookin' as she used to be," rejoined the other woman. "I guess she's goin' down to her aunt Sylvy's—Sylvy Crane as was. She married Richard Alger a while ago, after she'd been goin' with him over twenty year. He's fixed up the old Crane place. It got dreadful run down, an' Sylvy she actually set out for the poor-house, an' Richard he stopped Jonathan Leavitt, he was carryin' of her over there, an' he brought her home, an' married her right off. That brought him to the point. Sylvy lives on the old road; we can drive round that way when we go home, an' I'll show you the place."

When they presently drove down the green length of the old road, the visiting cousin spied interestedly at Sylvia's house and Sylvia's own delicate profile frilled about with lace, drooping like the raceme of some white flower in one of the windows.

"That's her at the window," whispered the Pembroke woman, "an' there's Richard out there in the bean-poles." Just then Richard peered out at them from the green ranks of the beans at the sound of their wheels, and the Pembroke woman nodded, with a cough.

They drove slowly out of the old road into the

main-travelled one, and presently passed the old Thayer house. A woman's figure fled hurriedly up the yard into the house as they approached. There was a curious shrinking look about her as she fled, her very clothes, her muslin skirts, her light barège shawl, her green bonnet, seemed to slant away before the eyes of the two women who were watching her.

The Pembroke woman leaned close to her cousin's ear, and whispered with a sharp hiss of breath. The cousin started and colored red all over her matronly face and neck. She stared with a furtive shamed air at poor Rebecca hastening into her house. The door closed after her with a quick slam.

It was always to Rebecca, years beyond her transgression, admitted ostensibly to her old standing in the village, as if an odor of disgrace and isolation still clung to her, shaken out from her every motion from the very folds of her garments. It came in her own nostrils wherever she went, like a miserable emanation of her own personality. She always shrank back lest others noticed it, and she always would. She particularly shunned strangers. The sight of a strange woman clothed about with utter respectability and strictest virtue intimidated her beyond her power of self-control, for she always wondered if she had been told about her, and realized that, if she had, her old disgrace had assumed in this new mind a hideous freshness.

After the door had slammed behind Rebecca the two women drove home, and the guest was presently feasted on company-fare for supper, and all these strange tragedies and histories to which she had listened had less of a savor in her memory, than the fine green tea and the sweet cake on her tongue. The hostess, too, did not have them in mind any longer; she pressed the plum-cake and hot biscuits and honey on her cousin, in lieu of gossip, for entertainment. The stories were old to her, except as she found a new listener to them, and they had never had any vital interest for her. They had simply made her imagination twang pleasantly, and now they could hardly stir the old vibrations.

It seemed sometimes as if their hard story must finally grow old, and lose its bitter savor to Charlotte and Barney themselves. Sometimes Charlotte's mother looked at her inquiringly and said to herself, " I don't believe she ever thinks about it now." She told Cephas so, and the old man nodded. " She's a fool if she does," he returned, gruffly.

Cephas had never told anybody how he had gone once to Barney Thayer's door, and there stood long and delivered himself of a strange harangue, wherein the penitence and desire for peace had been thinly veiled by a half-wild and eccentric philosophy; but the gist of which had been the humble craving for pardon of an old man, and his beseeching that his daughter's lover, separated from her by his own fault, should forget it and come back to her.

" I haven't got anything to say about it," Barney had replied, and the old man had seemed to experi-

ence a sudden shock and rebound, as from the unexpected face of a rock in his path.

However, he still hoped that Barney would relent
and come. The next Sunday evening he had himself laid the parlor fire all ready for lighting, and hint-
ed that Charlotte should change her dress. When
nobody came he looked more crestfallen than his
daughter; she suspected, although he never knew it.

Charlotte had never learned any trade, but she had
a reputation for great natural skill with her needle.
Gradually, as she grew older, she settled into the
patient single-woman position as assister at feasts,
instead of participator. When a village girl of a
younger generation than herself was to be married,
she was in great demand for the preparation of the
bridal outfit and the finest needle-work. She would
go day after day to the house of the bride-elect, and
sew from early morning until late night upon the
elaborate quilts, the dainty linen, and the fine new
wedding-gowns.

She bore herself always with a steady cheerfulness;
nobody dreamed that this preparing others for the
happiness which she herself had lost was any trial
to her. Nobody dreamed that every stitch which she
set in wedding-garments took painfully in a piece of
her own heart, and that not from envy. Her faithful needle, as she sewed, seemed to keep her old
wounds open like a harrow, but she never shrank.
She saw the sweet, foolish smiles and blushes of
happy girls whose very wits were half astray under

the dazzle of love; she felt them half tremble under her hands as she fitted the bridal-gowns to their white shoulders, as if under the touch of their lovers.

They walked before her and met her like doppel-gängers, wearing the self-same old joy of her own face, but she looked at them unswervingly. It is harder to look at the likeness of one's joy than at one's old sorrow, for the one was dearer. If Charlotte's task whereby she earned her few shillings had been the consoling and strengthening of poor forsaken, jilted girls, instead of the arraying of brides, it would have been a happier and an easier one.

But she sat sewing fine, even stitches by the light of the evening candle, hearing the soft murmur of voices from the best rooms, where the fond couples sat, smiling like a soldier over her work. She pinned on bridal veils and flowers, and nobody knew that her own face instead of the bride's seemed to smile mockingly at her through the veil.

She was much happier, although she would have sternly denied it to herself, when she was watching with the sick and putting her wonderful needle-work into shrouds, for it was in request for that also.

Except for an increase in staidness and dignity, and a certain decorous change in her garments, Charlotte Barnard did not seem to grow old at all. Her girlish bloom never faded under her sober bonnet, although ten years had gone by since her own marriage had been broken off.

Barney used to watch furtively Charlotte going past. He knew quite well when she was helping such and such a girl get ready to be married. He saw her going home, a swift shadowy figure, after dark, with her few poor shillings in her pocket. That she should go out to work filled him with a fierce resentment. With a childish and masculine disregard for all except bare actualities, he could not see why she need to, why she could not let him help her. He knew that Cephas Barnard's income was very meagre, that Charlotte needed her little earnings for the barest necessaries; but why could she not let him give them to her?

Barney was laying up money. He had made his will, whereby he left everything to Charlotte, and to her children after her if she married. He worked very hard. In summer he tilled his great farm, in winter he cut wood.

The winter of the tenth year after his quarrel with Charlotte was a very severe one — full of snow-storms and fierce winds, and bitterly cold. All winter long the swamps were frozen up, and men could get into them to cut wood. Barney went day after day and cut the wood in a great swamp a mile behind his house. He stood from morning until night hewing down the trees, which had gotten their lusty growth from the graves of their own kind. Their roots were sunken deep among and twined about the very bones of their fathers which helped make up the rich frozen soil of the great swamp. The crusty snow was three feet deep; the tall blackberry vines were hooped with snow, set fast at either end like snares: it was hard work making one's way through them. The snow was over the heads of those dried weeds which did not blow away in the autumn, but stayed on their stalks with that persistency of life that outlives death ; but all the sturdy bushes, which were almost trees, the swamp-pinks and the wild-roses, waxed gigantic, lost their own outlines, and stretched out farther under their loads of snow.

Barney hewed wood in the midst of this white tangle of trees and bushes and vines, which were like a wild, dumb multitude of death-things pressing ever against him, trying to crowd him away. When he hit them as he passed, they swung back in his face with a semblance of life. If a squirrel chattered and leaped between some white boughs, he started as if some dead thing had come to life, for it seemed like the voice and motion of death rather than of life.

Half a mile away at the right other wood-cutters were at work. When the wind was the right way he could now and then hear the strokes of their axes and a shout. Often as he worked alone, swinging his axe steadily with his breath in a white cloud before his face, he amused himself miserably—as one might with a bitter sweetmeat — with his old dreams.

He had no dreams in the present; they all belonged to the past, and he dreamed them over as one sings over old songs. Sometimes it seemed quite possible that they still belonged to his life, and might still come true.

Then he would hear a hoarse shout through the still air from the other side of the swamp, and he would know suddenly that Charlotte would never wait in his home yonder, while he worked, and welcome him home at night.

The other wood-cutters had families. They had to pass his lot on their way out to the open road. Barney would either retreat farther among the snowy thickets, or else work with such fury that he could seem not to see them as they filed past.

Often he did not go home at noon, and ate nothing from morn until night. He cut wood many days that winter when the other men thought the weather too severe and sat huddled over their fires in their homes, shoving their chairs this and that way at their wives' commands, or else formed chewing and gossiping rings within the glowing radius of the red-hot store stove.

"See Barney Thayer goin cross lots with his axe as I come by," one said to another, rolling the tobacco well back into his grizzled cheek.

"Works as if he was possessed," was the reply, in a half-inarticulate, gruff murmur.

"Well, he can if he wants to," said still another. "I ain't goin' to work out-doors in any such weather as this for nobody, not if I know it, an' I've got a wife an' eight children, an' he ain't got nobody."

And the man cast defiant eyes at the great store-windows, dim with thick blue sheaves of frost.

On a day like that Barney seemed to be hewing asunder not only the sturdy fibres of oak and hemlock, but the terrible sinews of frost and winter, and many a tree seemed to rear itself over him threatening stiffly like an old man of death. Only by fierce contest, as it were, could he keep himself alive, but he had a certain delight in working in the swamp during those awful arctic days. The sense that he could still fight and conquer something, were it only the simple destructive force of nature, aroused in him new self-respect.

Through snow-storms Barney plunged forth to the swamp, and worked all day in the thick white slant of the storm, with the snow heaping itself upon his bowed shoulders.

People prophesied that he would kill himself; but he kept on day after day, and had not even a cold until February. Then there came a south rain and a thaw, and Barney went to the swamp and worked two days knee-deep in melting snow. Then there was a morning when he awoke as if on a bed of sharp knives, and lay alone all day and all that night, and all the next day and that night, not being able to stir without making the knives cut into his vitals.

Barney lay there all that time, and his soul became fairly bound into passiveness with awful fetters of fiery bone and muscle; sometimes he groaned, but nobody heard him. The last night he felt as if his whole physical nature was knitting about him and stifling him with awful coils of pain. The tears rolled over his cheeks. He prayed with hoarse gasps, and he could not tell if anybody heard him. A dim light from a window in the Barnard house on the hill lay into the kitchen opposite his bedroom door. He thought of Charlotte, as if he had been a child and she his mother. The maternal and protecting element in her love was all that appealed to him then, and all that he missed or wanted. " Charlotte, Charlotte," he mumbled to himself with his parched, quivering lips.

At noon the next day Cephas Barnard came home from the store ; he had been down to buy some molasses. When he entered his kitchen he set the jug down on the table with a hard clap, then stood still in his wet boots.

Sarah and Charlotte were getting dinner, both standing over the stove. Sarah glanced at Cephas furtively, then at Charlotte ; Cephas never stirred. A pool of water collected around his boots, his brows bent moodily under his cap.

"Why don't you set down, Cephas, an' take off your boots ?" Sarah ventured at length, timidly.

" Folks are fools," grunted Cephas.

" I dunno what you mean, Cephas."

Cephas got the boot-jack out of the corner, sat down, and began jerking off the wet boots with sympathetic screws of his face.

Sarah stood with a wooden spoon uplifted, eying him anxiously. Charlotte went into the pantry.

"There 'ain't anythin' happened, has there, Cephas?" said Sarah, presently.

Cephas pulled off the second boot, and sat holding his blue yarn stocking-feet well up from the wet floor. "There ain't no need of havin' the rheumatiz, accordin' to my way of thinkin'," said he.

"Who's got the rheumatiz, Cephas?"

"If folks lived right they wouldn't have it."

"You 'ain't got it, have you, Cephas?"

"I 'ain't never had a tech of it in my life except once, an' then 'twas due to my not drinkin' enough."

"Not drinkin' enough?"

"Yes, I didn't drink enough water. Folks with rheumatiz had ought to drink all the water they can swaller. They had ought to drink more'n they eat."

"I dunno what you mean, Cephas."

"It stands to reason. I've worked it all out in my mind. Rheumatiz comes on in wet weather, because there's too much water an' damp 'round. Now, if there's too much water outside, you can kind of even it up by takin' more water inside. The reason for any sickness is—the balance ain't right. The weight gets shifted, an' folks begin to topple, then they're sick. If it goes clean over, they die. The balance has got to be kept even if you want to be well. When the swamps are fillin' up with water, an' there's too much moisture in the outside air, an' too much pressure of it on your bones an' joints, if you swallow enough water inside it keeps things even. If Barney Thayer had drunk a gallon of water a day, he might have worked in the wet swamp till doomsday an' he wouldn't have got the rheumatiz."

"Has Barney Thayer got the rheumatiz, Cephas?"
Charlotte's pale face appeared in the pantry door.

"Yes, he has got it bad. 'Ain't stirred out of his bed since night before last; been all alone; nobody knew it till William Berry went in this forenoon. Guess he'd died there if he'd been left much longer."

"Who's with him now?" asked Charlotte, in a quick, strained voice.

"The Ray boy is sittin' with him, whilst William is gone to the North Village to see if he can get somebody to come. There's a widow woman over there that goes out nussin', Silas said, an' they hope they can get her. The doctor says he's got to have somebody."

"Rebecca can't do anything, of course," said Sarah, meditatively; "he 'ain't got any of his own folks to come, poor feller."

Charlotte crossed the kitchen floor with a resolute air.

"What are you goin' to do, Charlotte?" her mother asked in a trembling voice.

Charlotte turned around and faced her father and mother. "I shouldn't think you'd ask me," said she.

"You ain't — goin' — over — ?"

"Of course I am going over there. Do you suppose I am going to let him lie there and suffer all alone, with nobody to take care of him?"

" There's — the woman — comin'."

" She can't come. I know who the woman is. They tried to get her when Squire Payne's sister died last week. Aunt Sylvy told me about it. She was engaged 'way ahead."

" Oh, Charlotte! I'm afraid you hadn't ought to go," her mother said, half crying.

" I've got to go, mother," Charlotte said, quietly. She opened the door.

" You come back here!" Cephas called after her in a great voice.

Charlotte turned around. " I am going, father," said she.

" You ain't goin' a step."

" Yes, I am."

" Oh, Charlotte! I'll go over," sobbed her mother.

" You haven't gone a step out-doors for a month with your own lame knee. I am the one to go, and I am going."

" You ain't goin' a step."

" Oh, Charlotte! I'm afraid you hadn't better," wailed Sarah.

Charlotte stood before them both. " Look here, father and mother," said she. " I've never gone against your wishes in my life, but now I'm going to. It's my duty to. I was going to marry him once."

" You didn't marry him," said Cephas.

" I was willing to marry him, and that amounts to

the same thing for any woman," said Charlotte. "It is just as much my duty to go to him when he's sick; I am going. There's no use talking, I am going."

"You needn't come home again, then," said her father.

"Oh, Cephas!" Sarah cried out. "Charlotte, don't go against your father's wishes! Charlotte!"

But Charlotte shut the door and hurried up-stairs to her room. Her mother followed her, trembling. Cephas sat still, dangling his stocking-feet clear of the floor. He had an ugly look on his face. Presently he heard the two women coming down-stairs, and his wife's sobbing, pleading voice; then he heard the parlor door shut; Charlotte had gone through the house, and out the front door.

Sarah came in, sniffing piteously. "Oh, Cephas! don't you be hard on the poor child; she felt as if she had got to go," she said, chokingly.

Cephas got up, went padding softly and cautiously in his stocking-feet across the floor to the sink, and took a long drink with loud gulps out of the gourd in the water-pail.

"I don't want to have no more talk about it; I've said my say," said he, with a hard breath, wiping his mouth with the back of his hand.

Charlotte, with a little bundle under her arm, hastened down the hill. When she reached Barney's house she went around and knocked at the side door. As she went into the yard she could see dimly a white-capped woman's head in a south window of the Thayer house farther down the road, and she knew that Rebecca's nurse was watching her. Rebecca's second baby was a week old, so she could do nothing for her brother.

Charlotte knocked softly and waited. She heard a loud clamping step across the floor inside, and a whistle. A boy opened the door and stood staring at her, half abashed, half impudently important, his mouth still puckered with the whistle.

"Is there anybody here but you, Ezra?" asked Charlotte.

The boy shook his head.

"I have come to take care of Mr. Thayer now," said Charlotte.

She entered, and Ezra Ray stood aside, rolling his eyes after her as she went through the kitchen. He whistled again half involuntarily, a sudden jocular pipe on the brink of motion, like a bird. Charlotte turned and shook her head at him, and he stopped short. He sat down on a chair near the door, and dangled his feet irresolutely.

Charlotte went into the bedroom where Barney lay, a rigidly twisted, groaning heap under a mass of bed-clothing, which Ezra Ray had kept over him with energy. She bent over him. "I've come to take care of you, Barney," said she. His eyes, half dazed in his burning face, looked up at her with scarcely any surprise.

Charlotte laid back some of the bedclothes whose weight was a torture, and straightened the others.

She worked about the house noiselessly and swiftly.
She was skilful in the care of the sick; she had had
considerable experience. Soon everything was clean
and in order; there was a pleasant smell of steeping
herbs through the house. Charlotte had set an old
remedy of her mother's steeping over the fire—a
harmless old-wives' decoction, with which to supple-
ment the doctor's remedies, and give new courage
to the patient's mind.

Barney came to think that this remedy which
Charlotte prepared was of more efficacy than any
which the doctor mixed in his gallipots. That is,
when he could think at all, and his mind and soul
was able to reassert itself over his body. He had a
hard illness, and after he was out of bed he could
only sit bent miserably over in a quilt-covered rocking-chair beside the fire. He could not straighten
himself up without agonizing pain. People thought
that he never would, and he thought so himself.
His grandfather, his mother's father, had been in a
similar condition for years before his death. People called that to mind, and so did Barney. " He's
goin' to be the way his grandfather Emmons was,"
the men said in the store. Barney could dimly remember that old figure bent over almost on all-fours
like a dog; its wretched, grizzled face turned towards the earth with a brooding sternness of contem-
plation. He wondered miserably where his grandfather's old cane was, when he should be strong
enough in his pain-locked muscles to leave his rock-

"'I'VE COME TO TAKE CARE OF YOU'"

ing-chair and crawl about in the spring sunshine. It used to be in the garret of the old house. He thought that he would ask Rebecca or William to look for it some day. He hesitated to speak about it. He half dreaded to think that the time was coming when he would be strong enough to move about, for then he was afraid Charlotte would leave him and go home. He had been afraid that she would when he left his bed. He had a childishly guilty feeling that he had perhaps stayed there a little longer than was necessary on that account. One Sunday the doctor had said quite decisively to Charlotte, "It won't hurt him any to be got up a little while to-morrow. It will be better for him. You can get William to come in and help." Charlotte had come back from the door and reported to Barney, and he had turned his face away with a quivering sigh.

"Why, what is the matter? Don't you want to be got up?" asked Charlotte.

"Yes," said Barney, miserably.

"What is the matter?" Charlotte said, bending over him. "Don't you feel well enough?"

Barney gave her a pitiful, shamed look like a child. "You'll go, then," he half sobbed.

Charlotte turned away quickly. "I shall not go as long as you need me, Barney," she said, with a patient dignity.

Barney did not dream against what odds Charlotte had stayed with him. Her mother had come repeatedly, and expostulated with her out in the entry when she went away.

"It ain't fit for you to stay here, as if you was married to him, when you ain't, and ain't ever goin' to be, as near as I can make out," she said. "William can get that woman over to the North Village now, or I can come, or your aunt Hannah would come for a while, till Rebecca gets well enough to see to him a little. She was sayin' yesterday that it wa'n't fit for you to stay here."

"I'm here, and I'm going to stay here till he's better than he is now," said Charlotte.

"Folks will talk."

"I can't help it if they do. I'm doing what I think is right."

"It ain't fit for an unmarried woman like you to be takin' care of him," said her mother, and a sudden blush flamed over her old face.

Charlotte did not blush at all. "William comes in every day," she said, simply.

"I think he could get along a while now with what William does an' what we could cook an' bring in," pleaded her mother. "I'd come over every day an' set a while; I'd jest as lieves as not. If you'd only come home, Charlotte. Your father didn't mean anythin' when he said you shouldn't. He asked me jest this mornin' when you was comin'."

"I ain't coming till he's well enough so he don't need me," said Charlotte. "There's no use talking, mother. I must go back now; he'll wonder what we're talking about;" and she shut the door gently upon her mother, still talking.

Her aunt Hannah came, and her aunt Sylvia, quaking with gentle fears. She even had to listen to remonstrances from William Berry, honestly grateful as he was for her care of his brother-in-law.

"I ain't quite sure that it's right for you to stay here, Charlotte," he said, looking away from her uncomfortably. "Rebecca says—'Hadn't you better let me go for that woman again?'"

"I think I had better stay for the present," Charlotte replied.

"Of course—I know you do better for him—than anybody else could, but—"

"How is Rebecca?" asked Charlotte.

"She is getting along pretty well, but it's slow. She's kind of worried about you, you know. She's had considerable herself to bear. It's hard to have folks—" William stopped short, his face burning.

"I am not afraid, if I know I am doing what is right," said Charlotte. "You tell Rebecca I am coming in to see her as soon as I can get a chance."

One contingency had never occurred to Barney in his helpless clinging to Charlotte. He had never once dreamed that people might talk disparagingly about her in consequence. He had, partly from his isolated life, partly from natural bent, a curious innocence and ignorance in his conception of human estimates of conduct. He had not the same vantage-points with many other people, and indeed in many cases seemed to hold the identical ones which he had chosen when a child and first observed anything.

If now and then he overheard a word of expostulation, he never interpreted it rightly. He thought that people considered it wrong for Charlotte to do so much for him, and weary herself, when he had treated her so badly. And he agreed with them.

He thought that he should never stand upright again. He went always before his own mental vision bent over like his grandfather, his face inclined ever downward towards his miserable future.

Still, as he sat after William had gotten him up in the morning, bowed over pitifully in his chair, there was at times a strange look in his eyes as he watched Charlotte moving about, which seemed somehow to give the lie to his bent back. Often Charlotte would start as she met this look, and think involuntarily that he was quite straight; then she would come to her old vision with a shock, and see him sitting there as he was.

At last there came a day when the minister and one of the deacons of the church called and asked to see Charlotte privately. Barney looked at them, startled and quite white. They sat with him quite a long while, when, after many coercive glances between the deacon and the minister, the latter had finally arisen and made the request, in a trembling, embarrassed voice.

Charlotte led them at once into the unfinished

front parlor, with its boarded-up windows. Barney heard her open the front door to give them light and air. He sat still and waited, breathing hard. A terrible dread and curiosity came over him. It seemed as if his soul overreached his body into that other room. Without overhearing a word, suddenly a knowledge quite foreign to his own imagination seemed to come to him.

Presently he heard the front door shut, then Charlotte came in alone. She was very pale, but she had a sweet, exalted look as her eyes met Barney's.

"Have they gone?" he asked, hoarsely.

Charlotte nodded.

"What—did they want?"

"Never mind," said Charlotte.

"I want to know."

"It is nothing for you to worry about."

"I know," said Barney.

"You didn't hear anything?" Charlotte cried out in a startled voice.

"No, I didn't hear, but I know. The church—don't—think you ought to—stay here. They are—going to—take it—up. I never—thought of that, Charlotte. I never thought of that."

"Don't you worry anything about it." Charlotte had never touched him, except to minister to his illness, since she had been there. Now she went close, and smoothed his hair with her tender hands. "Don't you worry," she said again.

Barney looked up in her face. "Charlotte."

"What is it?"

"I—want you—to go—home."

Charlotte started. "I shall not go home as long as you need me," she said. "You need not think I mind what they say."

"I—want you to go home."

"Barney!"

"I mean what—I say. I—want you to go—now."

"Not now?"

"Yes, now."

Charlotte drew back; her lips wore a white line. She went out into the front south room, where she had slept. She did not come back. Barney listened until he heard the front door shut after her. Then he waited fifteen minutes, with his eyes upon the clock. Then he got up out of his chair. He moved his body as if it were some piece of machinery outside himself, as if his will were full of dominant muscles. He got his hat off the peg, where it had hung for weeks; he went out of the house and out of the yard.

His sister Rebecca was moving feebly up the road with her little baby in her arms. She was taking her first walk out in the spring sunshine. The nurse had gone away the week before. Her face was clear and pale. All her sweet color was gone, but her eyes were radiant, and she held up her head in the old way. This new love was lifting her above her old memories.

She stared wonderingly over the baby's little

downy head at her brother. "It can't be Barney," she said out loud to herself. She stood still in the road, staring after him with parted lips. The baby wailed softly, and she hushed it mechanically, her great, happy, startled eyes fixed upon her brother.

Barnabas went on up the hill to Charlotte Barnard's. The spring was advancing. All the trees were full of that green nebula of life which comes before the blossom. Little wings, bearing birds and songs, cut the air. A bluebird shone on a glistening fence-rail, like a jewel on a turned hand. Over across the fields red oxen were moving down plough-ridges, the green grass was springing, the air was full of that strange fragrance which is more than fragrance, since it strikes the thoughts, which comes in the spring alone, being the very odor thrown off by the growing motion of life and the resurrection.

Barney Thayer went slowly up the hill with a curious gait and strange gestures, as if his own angel were wrestling with himself, casting him off with strong motions as of wings.

He fought, as it were, his way step by step. He reached the top of the hill, and went into the yard of the Barnard house. Sarah Barnard saw him coming, and shrieked out, "There's Barney, there's Barney Thayer comin'! He's walkin', he's walkin' straight as anybody!"

When Barney reached the door, they all stood there—Cephas and Sarah and Charlotte. Barney stood before them all with that noble bearing which comes from humility itself when it has fairly triumphed.

Charlotte came forward, and he put his arm around her. Then he looked over her head at her father. "I've come back," said he.

"Come in," said Cephas.

And Barney entered the house with his old sweetheart and his old self.

THE END